上海对外经贸大学外国语言文学一级学科博士点培育项目

孙雪瑛

著

明清小说误译与译者研究

上海三联书店

目　录

第一章 绪论：明清小说的跨文化传播

1.1 明清小说在英语世界的传播

在鲁迅的 28 篇《中国小说史略》中，明清小说史占了一半的篇幅。明代小说是从宋元时期的说话艺术的基础上发展起来，呈现出空前繁荣的局面，"打破了正统诗文的垄断地位，在文学史上，取得了与唐诗、宋词、元曲相提并论的地位"（龚贤，2018）。

其中著名的讲史小说包括《三国志演义》《隋唐志传》和《水浒传》，脱胎于历史演义和英雄传奇，其中既有歌颂个人英雄主义的较有局限性的写史小说，也有揭露了封建统治阶级的罪恶、思想艺术成就较高的历史演义小说；另一类为神魔小说，深受儒、道、释三教合一的宗教大环境的影响和求仙访道思潮的冲击，涉及鬼神魔怪，内容充满奇幻想象，如《西游记》《平妖传》《封神演义》等，其中不乏宣扬宗教迷信，鼓吹神权思想的文字，但一些优秀之作，曲折地反映了现实生活，具有丰富的社会内容；世情小说，鲁迅（2017）称之为"人情小说"，多以社会现实为题材，"大率为离合悲欢及发迹变态之事，间杂因果报应，而不甚言灵怪，又缘描摹世态，见其炎凉"，以《金瓶梅词话》为代表，其他如《平山冷燕》《玉娇梨》《续金瓶梅》《隔帘花影》和《好逑传》等。部分世情小说以写实的手法，描绘了明代城镇生活的广阔画面，反映了社会的黑暗和统治阶级的荒淫腐朽；但大部分小说意图通过世情描写来宣扬因果报应思想，封建糟粕严重，或描绘才子佳人的悲欢离合，思想艺术多平庸低下。

鲁迅在介绍明代小说时，单独开辟了一章节，名为"明之拟宋市人小说"。提及此类，鲁迅（2017：155）解释道："惟至明末，则宋市人小说之流复起，或存旧文，或出新制，顿又广行世间，但旧名湮昧，不复称市人小说也。"此类小说如冯梦龙辑纂的《喻世明言》（一名《古今小说》）、《警世通言》、《醒世恒言》，合称"三言"，收入小说120篇，反映出当时市民阶层的思想、生活和情趣，对后世的白话小说及戏曲都有较大影响。而凌蒙初所编著的《初刻拍案惊奇》《二刻拍案惊奇》，合称"二拍"，实78篇，也较有影响力。此外，明人创作的拟话本小说集还有《石点头》《醉醒石》《西湖二集》等十多种，成就逊于"三言"和"二拍"。这些短篇小说的艺术成就和思想性同样也参差不齐。婚姻爱情题材占重要地位，也有篇目揭露了统治阶级的罪恶和社会的不公正与黑暗面，但粉饰太平，美化统治阶级，宣扬封建礼教和迷信思想等充满封建糟粕的作品不在少数。

余建忠（2007）指出：明代文学以明中叶弘治、正德年间为限，可划分为前后两期。前期文学以长篇小说和戏曲为核心，代表了明代文学的最高成就。四大名著中有三部出自明代，充分证明了明代文学创作的繁荣和章回小说所取得的杰出艺术成就。

继明代小说的伟大成就之后，清代诸多优秀小说在细腻刻画和生动再现封建社会生活百态的同时，批判现实的色彩更加浓郁。清代小说是中国小说史上继明代之后又一个小说创作的高峰时代。曹雪芹的《红楼梦》、蒲松龄的《聊斋志异》、吴敬梓的《儒林外史》和石玉昆的《三侠五义》是其中的杰出代表，代表着中国古代白话小说和文言小说艺术的最高成就。

值得一提的是，《三侠五义》为古典长篇侠义公案小说的经典之作，堪称中国武侠小说的开山鼻祖；同时，作为中国第一部具有真正意义的武侠小说，它掀起了武侠题材文学作品的高潮，对此后的武侠小说的内容取材和叙事走向有着决定性影响。此后武侠公案、短打评书盛极一时，直至现代，武侠名著如金庸的《射雕英雄传》《神雕侠侣》、古龙的《楚留香传奇》、温瑞安的《四大名捕》等武侠小说都受到了他的影响（苗怀明，2003：127）。鲁迅高度赞扬《三侠五义》，其"独于写草野豪杰，辄奕奕有神，间或衬以世态，杂以诙谐，亦每令莽夫分外生色"（鲁迅，2017：167）。

刘绍棠（2003）在《津津乐道》一文中总结：中国小说形成六大门类，耸立六座高峰，有四部是清代小说，即：以《聊斋志异》为高峰的拟古派小说，以《红楼梦》为高峰的人情派小说，以《三侠五义》为高峰的侠义派小说，以《儒林外史》为高峰的讽刺小说。

本文拟选取创作于明代的《水浒传》《金瓶梅词话》，以及清代的两部小说《聊斋志异》《红楼梦》为研究对象。这四部巨著也是英语世界中国古典文学译介与传播的热点领域，产生了众多的作品英译本与研究著述。

1.1.1 《水浒传》在英语世界的传播

《水浒传》是中国小说史上第一部成功的白话长篇小说，开创了长篇英雄传奇的先河（张玉蕾，2018：184），对后世的文学创作有着巨大的影响。

清代著名小说理论家、批评家金圣叹将其与《西游记》《庄子》《离骚》《史记》及杜甫诗合称为"六才子书"。鲁迅把它称为"时代精神所居之大宫阙"，并对小说使用的白描手法高度赞扬，称其好汉之诨名"正如传神的写意画，并不写上名字，不过寥寥几笔，而神情毕肖"（宁宗一，2023：79）。

哥伦比亚大学中国文学名誉教授夏志清认为："与《三国演义》相比，《水浒传》至少在两个主要方面发展了中国的小说艺术，其一，它大量采用了现代读者仍喜闻乐道的白话文体。其二，它在塑造人物、铺陈故事时，能不为史实所囿……《水浒》以真实的日常生活为背景，写了不少江湖豪杰的故事，的确比《三国演义》具有更生动的现实主义特色"。（张文珍，2016：81）

赛珍珠作为诺贝尔文学奖获得者和《水浒传》的译者，称其是"中国生活伟大的社会文献"。

《水浒传》自18世纪中叶开始，陆续译入日本、朝鲜、越南等周边国家，自19世纪起，相继被译成法、英、拉丁、德、俄等文字，在西方广泛传播。其中，英译版本数量最多、影响最大。据周蓉（2023）统计，迄今《水浒传》的英译版本已超22个。

吴永昇等（2017）学者指出，1872—1873年，署名"H. S."的译者在《中国评论》（*The China Review*）第一卷上分4次连载了节译本"*The Adventures of a Chinese Giant*"，由此开启了

《水浒传》的英译历程。

《水浒传》的片段英译包括 1959、1963 年沙博理（Sidney Shapiro）的节译，他翻译了鲁智深和林冲结识、大闹野猪林的章节及智取生辰纲的故事；1965 年美国纽约的格罗夫出版社（Grove）推出的美国汉学家白之编著的《中国文学选集》第一卷中收录的"智取生辰纲"一章节英译；1993 年登特-杨父子合译的 120 回本《水浒传》的第 21 回"虔婆醉打唐牛儿　宋江怒杀阎婆惜"与第 22 回"阎婆大闹郓城县　朱仝义释宋公明"等章节。

据梁佳英（2011）统计，较早的《水浒传》的英文节译本《强盗与士兵》（*Robbers and Soldiers*）由英国汉学家杰弗里·邓洛普（Geoffrey Dunlop）从埃伦施泰因（Albert Ehrenstein）的德文节译本转译而来，于 1929 年由英国的杰拉尔德·豪出版社（Gerald Howe Ltd.）和美国的阿尔福雷德·克诺夫出版社（Alfred A. Knopf）分别出版，被认为是《水浒传》在西方的第一个英文节译本。

美国女作家赛珍珠（Pearl. S. Buck）的 70 回本《水浒传》英译名为《四海之内皆兄弟》（*All Men Are Brothers*）于 1933 年由美国纽约的约翰·戴公司（John Day）与英国伦敦的梅休安公司（Methuen and Co.）出版，此后多家出版社翻印过该译本。

上海商务印书馆于 1937 年出版了杰克逊（J. H. Jackson）翻译的 70 回译本，译名为《发生在水边的故事》（*Water Margin*）。此译本为英语全译本，在英语世界影响力较大，也经其他出版社翻印再出版过数次。

耶鲁大学远东出版社（Yale University Far Eastern Publications）于 1947 年出版了小克伦普（J. I. Crump Jr.）所译的《〈水浒传〉

选译》(*Selections from the Shui-Hu Chuan*),这是一个汉英对照本,其特定的读者群体为中文学习者和爱好者。

1980 年,外文出版社推出了沙博理所译的 "*Outlaws of the Marsh*" 一书,该译本系百回本《水浒传》的第一个英文全译本,被认为是译文质量较高、比较贴近原文的一部。其后该书又多次由外文出版社和外研社再版。

1994—2003 年,香港中文大学出版社先后出版约翰·登特·杨(John Dent-Young)与安莱克斯·登特-杨(Alex Dent-Young)合译的《水浒传》120 回的第一个全译本,译名为《梁山泊的故事》(*The Marshes of Mount Liang*)。

此外,外文出版社和朝华出版社,加拿大、新加坡等国的出版社也推出了若干《水浒传》英文改编本,以连环画本与漫画本为主,目的在于以一种浅显而生动的形式向英语世界的青少年读者推介中文名著。

1.1.2 《金瓶梅》在英语世界的传播

从现在的视角来看,《金瓶梅词话》可以说是一部同人文,是从《水许传》里的《武松斗杀西门庆》一节衍生出来的。然而这一部小说是 100 回的长篇巨著,与《三国志演义》《水浒传》和《西游记》一起,被合称为"四大奇书",曾被郑振铎(2005)称为"中国小说发展的极峰"。但与其他三部小说不同的是,《金瓶梅词话》不是世代累积型作品,而是由文人独立完成,且开"人情小说"之先河,对后来的《红楼梦》等作品产生了深远影响(习斌,2016)。

鲁迅评论《金瓶梅词话》道:"当神魔小说盛行时,记人事者亦突起，其取材犹宋市人小说之'银字儿'，大率为离合悲欢及发迹变态之事，间杂因果报应，而不甚言灵怪，又缘描摹世态，见其炎凉，故或亦谓之'世情书'也。作者之于世情，盖诚极洞达，凡所形容，或条畅，或曲折，或刻露而尽相，或幽伏而含讥，或一时并写两面，使之相形，变幻之情，随在显见"。（鲁迅，2014：145）

在海外，美国大百科全书《金瓶梅》专条评论该书"是中国第一部伟大的现实主义小说"。

《金瓶梅》已被译成英、日、德、俄、法等 10 余种外语，在世界范围内得到广泛传播。其英文译本也早在 20 世纪 20 年代便已开始了海外传播之旅。

已知最早的《金瓶梅》英文译本为 1927 年出版于纽约的节译本 *The Adventures of Hsi Men Ching*（西门庆传奇），译者为朱翠仁（Chu Tsui-Jen）。

1939 年，Bernard Miall 译本 *Chin Ping Mei：The Adventures History of Hsi Men and His Six Wives*（金瓶梅——西门庆和他的六妻妾的故事）在伦敦出版。该版本以德国翻译家 Franz Kuhn 的德语版为第一语言进行翻译，属于节译本。

同年，在老舍的帮助下，Clement Egerton 的全译本 *The Golden Louts*（金莲）由伦敦 Routledge 出版社出版。

1953 年，环球出版发行公司（Universal Publishing and Distributing Corporation）推出了一本名为 *The Harem of Hsi Men*（西门府妻妾成群）的《金瓶梅》英文读本，无署名。

刊载于 1956 年美国阿普尔顿-世纪（Appleton-Century）出版社的《中国文学宝库》一书中由美国 Chai 与 Winbery Chai 翻

译的《金瓶梅》第一回是现存最早的英语片段译文。

1965 年，美国 Brandon House 出版社发布了《金瓶梅》新译本，名为 *The Love Pagoda；the Amorous Adventure of Hsi Men and his Six Wives*（爱欲塔；西门与六妻妾艳史）。该译本未注明译者。

美国芝加哥大学的汉学家芮效卫（David Tod Roy）耗时 20 余年全译了《金瓶梅》，译名为 *The Plum in the Golden Vase or，Chin P'ing Mei*，由普林斯顿大学于 1993 年、2001 年、2006 年、2011 年、2013 年分五卷出版。

除此之外，《金瓶梅》还出现了一些漫画译本，如 1960 年由美国塔托出版公司（Charles E. Tuttle Co.）发行的连环画英译本 *Don Juan of China：an Amour from the "Chin Ping Mei"*（中国的唐璜：《金瓶梅》中的一段孽恋），故事内容涵盖小说原著第十三回到第十九回的内容。

自 1927 年首个节译本在纽约问世，至 2013 年 9 月芮效卫教授翻译完成五卷本《金瓶梅》，《金瓶梅》英译本已有 9 种之多。埃杰顿和芮效卫的两种英文全译本的问世具有重要的里程碑意义，标志着其在英语世界的传播开始向深度和广度展开。

1.1.3　《聊斋志异》在英语世界的传播

《聊斋志异》代表着中国文言短篇小说的最高成就，它不仅吸收了中国历代传奇志怪小说的精华，且糅合了史传文学的独特形式，是一幅 17 世纪中国的广阔画卷。谈及《聊斋志异》对志怪传奇小说的继承和超越以及所取得的成就，鲁迅指出："《聊斋志异》虽亦如当时同类之书，不外记神仙狐鬼精魅故事，然描写委曲，叙次井然，用传奇法，而以志怪，变幻之状，如在目前……《聊斋志异》独于详尽之外，示以平常，使花妖狐魅，多具人情，和易可亲，忘为异类，而又偶见鹘突，知复非人。"（鲁迅，2014：172）

《聊斋志异》创作完成后，其海外传播之旅始于 1784 年，从最初的日文译本，迄今《聊斋志异》共有 20 余个外语语种的译文和译本，其中包括英、法、德、俄、日、韩、越南、意大利、西班牙等语种。其中，以英语译文的数量最多，影响较之于其他译本更大。

王燕（2008）指出，早在 1842 年 4 月的《中国丛报》（*Chinese Repository*）第十一卷第四期上，德国传教士郭实腊（Karl Friedrich August Gutzlaff）就向英语读者介绍了《聊斋志异》，翻译了其中九则故事，译文虽然简单粗略，且经译者大量删改，但却是目前已知的《聊斋志异》在西方的最早译介。

国内有研究者曾认为第一个向英语世界译介《聊斋志异》故事的是美国传教士卫三畏（Samuel Wells Williams）。1848 年，他在个人著述《中国总论》中介绍了《聊斋志异》中的两个故事：《种梨》和《骂鸭》。

其他片段零散的译文包括：

1867 年由英国驻华外交官梅辉立（William Mayers）所翻译的《酒友》前半部分，发表于 *Notes and Queries on China and Japan* 杂志上。此后梅辉立还翻译了《织女》《嫦娥》这两篇聊斋故事，刊载在 *Reader's Manual* 上；

1874—1875 年，英国外交官、汉学家阿连壁（Clement Allen）在 *China View Notes and Queries* 上连续发表了他翻译的

18篇《聊斋志异》中的一系列故事；

1877年，由英国汉学家，驻华领事翟理斯（Herbert Allen Giles）翻译了《罗刹海市》，其英译文 The Lo-cha's Country and Sea Market，发表在 Celestial Empire 上，之后翟理斯断断续续还翻译了其他数个单篇聊斋故事；

英国外交官、汉学家禧在明（Walter C. Hillier）在其1907年出版的《怎样学习中国语》（The Chinese Language and How to Learn It—A Manual for Beginners）中选取了他本人翻译的14篇聊斋故事；

1921年，德国汉学家卫礼贤（Richard Wilhelm）在他所编译的《中国神话故事集》（The Chinese Fairy Book）一书中收录了5个《聊斋》故事的英语译文；

1922年，英国驻中国领事倭讷（Edward Werner）在他的作品《中国神话与传说》（Myths and Legends of China）中，专门设了"狐仙传奇"一章，在翟理斯译文的基础上改写了5篇聊斋故事；

1927年，卜朗特（J. J. Brandt）在《汉文进阶》（Introduction to Literary Chinese）一书中选取了由其翻译的五篇《聊斋志异》中的故事，1936年再版，1944经重新修订后出版，该书本身较有影响力；

1937年，美国摄影师、作家弗朗西斯·卡彭特（Frances Aretta Carpenter）出版了 Tales of a Chinese Grandmother：30 Traditional Tales from China 一书，该书讲述了30个故事，其中有3个故事来自《聊斋志异》；

此外，一些在海外的华裔翻译家也不断从事着译介《聊斋志异》的工作，如潘子延、刘绍铭等人。

在国内，著名翻译家杨宪益和他的英籍夫人戴乃迭（Yang Xianyi and Gladys Yang）在 1956 年及 1962 年合译了共 9 篇《聊斋志异》故事，发表在杨宪益任主编、致力于向海外推荐中国文学和文化的《中国文学》上。

《聊斋志异》现有的十几种译本均为节译、编译和转译本。其中比较有影响力的节译本包括：

1880 年由 T. De la Rue & Company 出版的由剑桥大学教授、汉学家、前英国驻华外交官翟理斯翻译的两卷本《来自一个中国书斋的奇异故事》（*Strange Stories from a Chinese Studio*）被认为是世界上最早的《聊斋志异》英译本。翟理斯选译了 164 篇《聊斋》故事。之后数年经多次再版，并增加了数个篇章。

1913 年，Houghton Mifflin 公司出版了由法国驻华外交官、汉学家乔治·苏利埃·德·莫朗（George Soulie de Moraut）所翻译的 *Strange Stories from the Lodge of Leisures*，共选译了 25 篇《聊斋志异》故事。

1946 年，纽约的 Pantheon Books Inc. 出版了 *Chinese Ghost and Love Stories*，由澳大利亚华裔汉学家邝如丝（Rose Quong）所译，是首部由华人学者创作的《聊斋志异》英译本。其中译者共选择了 40 篇《聊斋志异》故事。

1981 年，以对外译介我国优秀文学作品为宗旨的中国文学出版社通过"熊猫丛书"向国内外推出了《聊斋志异选》（*Selected Tales of Liaozhai*），其中共收录了 17 篇《聊斋志异》的故事，其中绝大多数篇目为我国著名翻译家杨宪益和他的英籍夫人戴乃迭所译。"熊猫丛书"较系统地、大规模地将中国文学中的优秀作品翻译成英文、法文，介绍到国外，在海外享有相当高的知名度。

始于 1982 年、旨在推动中西方文化交流的由商务印书馆启动的《聊斋志异》英译工程，截至 1986 年时已组织专家学者共翻译了 85 篇《聊斋志异》故事，该选译本定名为 *Strange Tales of Liaozhai*，译者为卢允中、陈体芳、杨立义、杨之宏等人，其中卢允中为上海外国语大学英语系教师，《中国比较文学》英文顾问。

1988 年，由莫若强、莫遵中、莫遵均三人合译的 *Selected Translations from Pu Songling's Strange Stories of Liaozhai* 由外语教学与研究出版社出版，译本共选译了 20 篇《聊斋志异》中的故事。

1989 年，两位美国汉学家梅丹理（Denis C. Mair）和梅维恒（Victor H. Mair）翻译的 *Strange Tales from Make-do Studio* 由外文出版社出版，共选译了 51 篇《聊斋志异》故事。此译本也是《聊斋志异》多个英译本中较为重要的版本。

1997 年，人民中国出版社出版了由张庆年、张慈云、杨毅等多名译者共同完成的 *Strange Tales from the Liaozhai Studio*，共三卷本，选译了 194 篇《聊斋》故事。其特色是每篇译文都配有插图。

2006 年，英国企鹅出版集团（Penguin Books）出版了英国汉学家和著名文学翻译家约翰·闵福德（John Minford）所译的 *Strange Tales from a Chinese Studio*，共收录 104 篇《聊斋志异》故事。闵福德因其翻译的中文典籍而闻名，如与霍克斯（David Hawks）合译的《红楼梦》（*The Story of the Stone*）和《孙子兵法》（*The Art of War*）等，他还将金庸的《鹿鼎记》译成了英文版本 *The Deer and the Cauldron*。

2007 年，中国外文出版社的《大中华文库·聊斋志异选》（汉英对照）中收录了 216 篇《聊斋志异》故事，分作四卷本，是迄今为止国内翻译并出版的选译《聊斋志异》篇目最多的英译本，主要选用了黄友义、张庆年、张慈云、杨毅、梅丹理和梅维恒等人的译文，由于译本翻译人员较多，风格较多样化（部分引自孙雪瑛，2016）。

2014 年之前，世界范围内的《聊斋志异》均为节译、选译本，直至 2014 年，美国圣劳伦斯大学英文教授宋贤德（Sidney L. Sondergard）六卷本的《聊斋志异》（*Strange Tales from Liaozhai*）全英译本由 Jain Publishing Company 出版发行，英语世界终于出现了第一部《聊斋志异》全译本。

从上述统计数字来看，20 世纪之前，主要是文化接受国家的译者向本国读者推介"来自异国书斋的神奇故事"，而 20 世纪后半叶开始，中国开始致力于向西方世界输出本国的悠久文化历史，译介经典名著，因此，涌现出较多《聊斋志异》的选译本，这一趋势有利于中国经典名著的进一步国际化，有利于《聊斋志异》在世界范围内的传播。

1.1.4 《红楼梦》在英语世界的传播

《红楼梦》是中国古典文学作品中的瑰宝，是中国古典小说艺术的高峰，被誉为中国古典文学史上思想性和艺术性结合得最好的一部伟大的现实主义小说（朱彤，2022：105）。

《中国大百科全书》评论："《红楼梦》的价值怎么估计都不为过。"《大英全书》："《红楼梦》的价值等于一整个的欧洲。"清朝得舆所著的《京都竹枝词》评论《红楼梦》时有云："开谈不说《红楼梦》，读尽诗书也枉然。"（林木阳、陈移瑜，2018：47）更有学者称其为"一所汉语文学语言的博物馆，汉文文体的档案馆"（梁扬等，2006：1）。

这部古典文学的巅峰之作自 1793 年流传到日本长崎后，据统计，世界各国翻译出版《红楼梦》的语种有 23 种。人民网在 2015 年底的检索结果显示，《红楼梦》在全世界各大图书馆流通的译本有 21 种、166 个版本。

据陈宏薇、江帆（2003：46）考证，在 1830—1987 年的 160 年间，《红楼梦》共出现过 9 种英译本，由此"成为中国文学史上一道独特而灿烂的风景"。另据美国学者葛锐（2012：257—260）调查，从 1812 年的首次摘译起，至 2010 年上海新闻出版发展公司出版《孙温红楼梦绘本》（英文本）止，《红楼梦》英译尝试已达 18 次之多。另据赵朝永（2014）考证，《红楼梦》英译本数量实际应为 12 种。

《红楼梦》英译本传播形式较多，包括摘译本、节译本、缩译本、转译本、全译本及绘画本等。目前可知的 3 个英文全译本分别是英国传教士拉姆维尔·西顿·邦斯尔神父（Reverend Bramwell Seaton Bonsall）英译本手稿、英国汉学家大卫·霍克斯与其女婿约翰·闵福德（David Hawkes and John Minford）全译本以及中国翻译家杨宪益和戴乃迭夫妇的全译本。

1807 年，英国伦敦教会传教士马礼逊（Robert Morrison）到达中国，这是西方第一位进入中国的西方基督教新教传教士。莫里森对中国文学作品很感兴趣，在《中国姓氏族谱》上译介了《红楼梦》。他也是《红楼梦》在英语世界译介的第一人。

但《红楼梦》第一个英文译本是在 1830 年问世的。另外一个较早的将《红楼梦》的故事内容介绍给西方读者的是德国传教士郭实腊，他所撰写的英文版《红楼梦》简介一文，于1842年5月发表在广州出版的《中国丛报》第十一册上。

在1830—1892年，总共出了4个版本的《红楼梦》英文译本。这些译本不仅不准确，而且显得很荒唐，译者翻译的目的是渲染这部书的"异国情调"，满足异国读者的猎奇心理。

1830年，英国皇家学会会员、驻华外交官约翰·弗朗西斯·戴维斯（另译德庇时）（John Francis Davis）摘译了《红楼梦》第三回片段，登载于英国皇家亚洲学会会刊上，他也是英译《红楼梦》诗词的第一人。

1846年，英国驻宁波领事罗伯特·汤姆（Robert Tom）摘译了《红楼梦》第六回片段，登载于杂志《官话汇编》上。

1868—1869年间，英国外交官爱德华·查尔斯·鲍拉（Edward Charles Bowra）英译了《红楼梦》的前八回，并连载于当时的《中国杂志》（*The Chinese Magazine*）上。

19世纪英语世界《红楼梦》篇幅最长、最有影响的译介来自英国驻澳副领事赫利·本克拉夫特·乔利（Henry Bencraft Joly）。乔利完整地翻译了《红楼梦》前56回的内容，且中间无任何删节。该译本分两卷，分别为378页和583页，1892—1893年由Kelly&Walsh Ltd. 出版单行本。较之此前的各种零星的摘译，乔利译本是当时最完整、篇幅最长、最忠实于原著的译本，被学界公认为当时《红楼梦》真正意义上的第一个较为系统的英文节译本。

1927年，纽约大学中国古典文学教师王良志将《红楼梦》翻译成了英文，取英文名为 *Dream of the Red Chamber*。王良志并没按照原书内容全部译出 120 回，而是对原文做了大量的删节，节译成 95 章，约 60 万字，在纽约出版发行。

1929 年、1958 年由纽约道布尔德・杜兰出版公司（Doubleday Doran Co.）和英国乔治・路脱菜西（George Routedge & Sons Ltd.）公司出版发行了哥伦比亚大学中文教授王际真翻译的三卷本《红楼梦》，英文名为 *Dream of the Red Chamber*。此译本第一版共 39 章，第二版 60 章。

1957 年，美国人弗洛伦斯・麦克休（Florence Mchugh）与伊萨贝尔・麦克休（lsabel Mchugh）姐妹的英译本由美国纽约 Pantheon Books Inc. 首次出版，同年，该译本又推出英国伦敦版，由伦敦 Routledge & Kegan Paul 公司出版发行。译本共 50 章，涵盖了全书 120 回内容，共 582 页。

邦斯尔神父翻译《红楼梦》始于 20 世纪 50 年代中期，前后花费 10 年心血才将 120 回内容全部译完，原本计划由纽约亚洲学会出版发行，但当时企鹅出版公司已宣布出版霍克斯译本，因此考虑到市场原因放弃了此译本的出版计划，导致该译本一直没能以纸质形式正式出版发行。邦译本是《红楼梦》首个 120 回英文全译本。其成文之早、体例之全、译文之详，均堪称"红楼英译"历史进程中的一座里程碑（赵朝永，2015：274）。

《红楼梦》的另外两部英文全译本，分别是霍克斯与其女婿约翰・闵福德的全译本 *The Story of the Stone* 和中国翻译家杨宪益与夫人戴乃迭的合译本 *A Dream of Red Mansions*。

英国汉学家、翻译家霍克斯用了 10 年的时间，翻译了《红楼梦》前 80 回，分别在 1973、1977、1980 年出版了英文版《红楼梦》分册，后 40 回由霍克斯的女婿汉学家闵福德完成，在

1982、1986 年由 Penguin Group 出版单行本。书名没有采用以前任何摘译或节译本的英文名称，而是以 *The Story of the Stone*（《石头记》）为名。由此，西方世界第一部全本 120 回的《红楼梦》便诞生了。霍克斯的《红楼梦》英文版，至今在西方世界拥有独一无二的经典地位。霍译的特色是译笔十分流畅优美，译者善于利用西方思维的优势归化原作的语言和文化，译本可读性较强，令英语世界的读者爱不释手，他的译本一版再版，畅销整个英语世界（卢静，2021：196）。

20 世纪 60 年代初，杨宪益和戴乃迭夫妇开始翻译《红楼梦》，其间曾一度中断，最后于 1974 年完成，于 1978—1980 年由外文出版社分三卷出版，译文书名为 "*A Dream of Red Mansions*"。杨宪益夫妇合作翻译的《红楼梦》力求最大程度上忠实于原文、保持原文的语言和文化特色。在译者风格层面，"杨宪益夫妇译文直译是占绝对主导地位的，保持了原文的形象与风貌"（冯庆华，2002：475），且杨译"经常会为读者提供原汁原味的中国文化形式与修辞习惯"（冯庆华，2012：2）。

此外，《红楼梦》英译本包括 1991 年由外研社出版的黄新渠节译的《红楼梦》简易本。该译本共计 30 余万字，整个翻译工程持续 10 年之久，英文名为 "*A Dream in Red Mansions—A Simplified English Version*"，注明为英文简写本。

1.2 明清小说英译研究概述

明清小说在英语世界的译介与传播研究所取得的主要成绩

包括以下几个方面：第一，明清小说英译研究中的作品译本批评研究成为研究的重心。研究者对于作品的一个译本或多个译本进行细致分析或比较研究，权衡得失，探究造成译本差异的各种文本外因素，从而客观评价原作各种译本的文本价值。第二，研究对明清小说在英语世界的传播轨迹进行了较清晰的梳理。明清小说在英语世界的译介综述类研究在一定程度上梳理了明清小说在英语世界的译介与研究成果，历时性视角可以把握明清小说的跨文化传播历程。第三，明清小说英语译本的译者得到了系统的研究。这些译者或来自文化输出国，或来自目的语国家，或为中国学者兼译者，或为驻华外交官和汉学家，或为宗教文化传播者，知识背景构成庞杂，文化身份呈现出多样性。

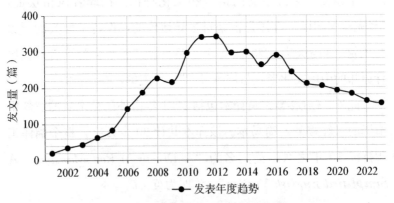

图1.1　《红楼梦》英译研究文献分析图

黄敏等（2006）基于关联理论对《红楼梦》判词英译进行对比评析；陈银春等（2007）以《红楼梦》第一回及其英译的被动句为例探索了汉语主动句英译的语篇功能；肖家燕（2008）基于

《红楼梦》"上—下"空间隐喻的英译策略及差额翻译，研究了优先概念化与隐喻的翻译；周晓寒（2009）基于霍克斯译本，从文化误译角度探索了译者的再创造；李美（2012）从《红楼梦》的误译探讨译者母语在文化传递中的角色；郭挺（2014）基于语境理论对《红楼梦》四个英译本中称谓语误译进行了比较研究；赵朝永（2015）研究了《红楼梦》邦斯尔译本中的误译；王坤（2016）从文化角度研究《红楼梦》中称谓语的误译；蔡魏立（2016）从文化过滤视角对《红楼梦》中的有意误译现象进行了研究；卢晓敏等（2016）对霍克斯《红楼梦》译本的误译原因进行了剖析；宋鹏（2017）从误译现象考证邦斯尔神父英译《红楼梦》之底本；许丹（2018）以霍克斯译本为例研究了认知视域下《红楼梦》中植物隐喻的英译；刘晓天等（2018）分析了《红楼梦》霍克斯译本中习语英译的跨文化阐释；陈功等（2019）探索了《红楼梦》翻译研究的推进过程和研究热点，并为未来研究提供了建议；刘晓天等（2019）对《红楼梦》霍克斯译本中的比喻添加进行了研究；张冰（2020）对《红楼梦》中"小人物"粗鄙语的英译进行了对比研究；蒋亦文等（2020）基于英语世界的读者访谈，研究了英译《红楼梦》副文本推介模式与接受度；王燕（2021）对马礼逊英译《红楼梦》手稿进行了研究；刘佳等（2021）对近10年具有代表性的《红楼梦》英译研究论著予以梳理；李晓静等（2022）研究了生态翻译学视角下《红楼梦》回目中的文化负载词的英译。

表 1.1　《红楼梦》英译研究文献分类表

角度	数量	期刊论文	学位论文	会议论文
译本综述类	248	188	59	1
译文赏析和对比	105	68	35	2
译者研究	155	129	26	0
文化研究	214	168	42	4
语言学视角	174	132	40	2
翻译策略	132	71	61	0
总计	1028	756	263	9

　　作者在中国知网（CNKI）的标准检索中，以 2000—2023 年为时间范围，以"红楼梦"和"英译"为主题词进行检索后进行统计，取得相关文献 1028 篇，其中期刊论文 756 篇，学位论文 263 篇，会议论文 9 篇。研究成果的高峰期在 2011—2012 年间，研究内容集中在译本综述、文化研究、语言学视角、译者研究和翻译策略总结和译文赏析对比等方面。

　　由图 1.3 可见，在所获取的文献中，译本综述类占 24%，文化视角的研究占 21%，语言学视角的研究文献占比为 17%，译者

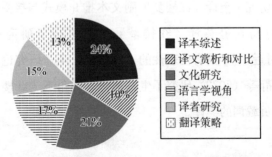

图 1.2　《红楼梦》英译研究文献的研究内容分布图

研究占 15%，翻译策略综述占 13%，译文赏析和对比占 10%。

相比之下，《聊斋志异》的研究从研究论文的数量上就明显落后于《红楼梦》的翻译研究。仅从学术期刊上发表的关于《聊斋志异》英译研究的论文的数量上看，进入 21 世纪前的较长时间内，国内学者对《聊斋志异》英译研究的关注度有限，重视程度不足。21 世纪后，《聊斋志异》英译的专门研究开始发展起来，发表在学术期刊上的相关论文以及有关的学位论文数量都有所增加。

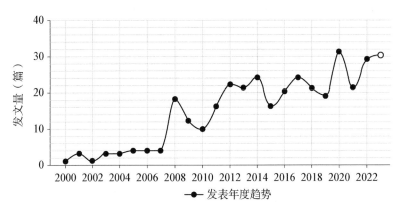

图 1.3　《聊斋志异》英译研究文献分析图

表 1.2　《聊斋志异》英译研究文献分类表

角度	数量	期刊论文	学位论文	会议论文
译文赏析和对比	47	25	21	1
译者研究	14	8	6	0
文化研究	41	24	16	1
语言学视角	28	17	11	0
翻译策略	32	20	11	1
总计	179	111	65	3

由上述分析可见，2000—2023年，《聊斋志异》英译研究相关文献仅有179篇，其中期刊论文111篇，学位论文65篇，会议论文3篇。研究成果的高峰期在2020年。国内《聊斋志异》英译研究主要集中在对《聊斋志异》英译的"总括性介绍、译者研究、翻译策略研究、译文赏析与对比、文化研究、语言学视角研究等方面"（文军、冯丹丹，2011：72—77）。

由图1.4可见，在相关文献中，译文赏析和对比占26%，文化视角的研究占23%，翻译策略综述占18%，语言学视角的研究文献占比为16%，译本综述类占9%，译者研究占8%。

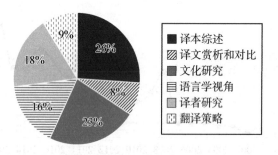

图1.4   《聊斋志异》英译研究文献的研究内容分布图

迟庆立（2008）对《红楼梦》和《聊斋志异》共时和历时性译本进行分析，研究文学作品中文化因素的翻译策略的异同；余欢（2009）从维索尔伦动态顺应三个方面入手比较研究《聊斋志异》翟理斯、杨宪益和梅尔兄弟（另译马尔）译本；朱瑞君（2009）基于乔治·斯坦纳翻译四步骤理论探究翟理斯在《聊斋志异》译本中发挥的译者主体性；卢慧慧（2010）基于伽达默尔阐释学分析《聊斋志异》翟理斯、杨宪益、梅尔兄弟三个译本中文化负载词的翻译；彭劲松等（2010）分析早期

《聊斋志异》译本中无意识和有意识造成的误读现象；任增强（2012）基于钱钟书"媒、讹、化"分析翟理斯译《聊斋志异》的翻译特色；付岩志（2013）探究《聊斋志异》译本海外诠释的三种方式以及文化融合的三个策略；卢静（2013）基于语料库研究《聊斋志异》三个主要英译本的译者风格和翻译特点；陈吉荣等（2014）基于顺应理论分析《聊斋志异》两个英译本中对话翻译语用失误；李海军（2014）探究乔治·苏利埃·德·莫朗《聊斋志异》译本中的伪翻译现象，即译者对故事进行再创作；潘向雪（2014）从符号学出发评析《聊斋志异》大中华文库英译本中官职的英译；王春阳（2014）从语言表述、故事阐释和文化意蕴三方面，对《聊斋志异》翟理斯和闵福德译本进行研究；孙雪瑛（2016）从诠释学视角和语料库翻译学角度研究了《聊斋志异》四个主要译本的风格差异及成因；舒瀚萱（2017）基于互文性理论对翟理斯和闵福德《聊斋志异》译本中的典故翻译进行研究；张强（2018）探究卫三畏英译《聊斋志异》中的叙事重构及其作用；周志莹（2018）基于切斯特曼翻译伦理学从词汇、句法、篇章角度研究《聊斋志异》的重译；钟迪（2019）基于布迪厄社会学理论探究闵福德《聊斋志异》译本翻译特点及背后的影响因素；王文君（2022）通过兰盖克识解理论对闵福德《聊斋志异》译本中的显化现象进行分析；程怡雯（2023）基于副文本研究理论，梳理《聊斋志异》五个译本中注释的内容、特点及其价值；牟晋蕾（2023）基于形象学理论研究闵福德和宋贤德《聊斋志异》译本中的狐妖形象并探究其翻译策略；王树槐（2023）分析翟理斯《聊斋志异》译本中的注释和改译，并表明其对在西方建构客观、真实中国形象作出的贡献。

另外两部明清小说的英译研究就更加不尽如人意，仅从研究论文数量上就可见一斑。

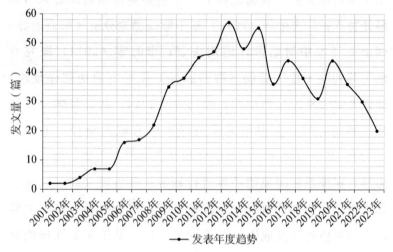

图 1.5 《水浒传》英译研究文献分析图

从 2000—2023 年《水浒传》英译研究相关文献仅有 74 篇，其中期刊论文 39 篇，学位论文 34 篇，会议论文 1 篇。研究成果的高峰期在 2013 年，研究内容集中在译文赏析和对比、语言学视角的英译研究等。

表 1.3 《水浒传》英译研究文献分类表

角度	数量	期刊论文	学位论文	会议论文
译本综述类	7	7	0	0
译文赏析和对比	16	7	8	1
译者研究	7	5	2	0

续　表

角度	数量	期刊论文	学位论文	会议论文
文化研究	10	6	4	0
语言学视角	21	4	17	0
翻译策略	13	10	3	0
总计	74	39	34	1

　　分析可见，2000—2023 年，《水浒传》英译研究相关文献仅有 74 篇，其中期刊论文 39 篇，学位论文 34 篇，会议论文仅有 1 篇。研究成果的高峰期在 2013 年和 2015 年，研究内容较多侧重的是语言学视角的英译研究（28％）、译文赏析和对比（22％）、翻译策略（18％）、文化视角（14％）、译者研究（9％）以及译本综述类（9％），研究内容在深度和广度上与《红楼梦》相比明显落后（图 1.6）。

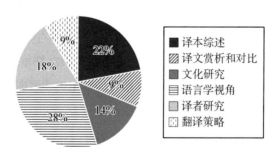

图 1.6　《水浒传》英译研究文献的研究内容分布图

　　成矫林（2002）基于顺应论理论对《水浒传》英译本中具有典型文化空缺习语翻译进行了分析；路东平（2003）从社会、文化、语言、历史及其传统等角度对《水浒传》中的各种称谓的汉英翻译问题进行探讨；陈新月（2004）通过对比分析沙博理《水浒传》译本和赛珍珠《水浒传》译本，探讨了文学翻译中的可译限度问题；卢艳春（2005）本基于沙博理译本，从语用学的角度讨论了《水浒传》中粗俗俚语的语用功能及其翻译方法；袁滔（2006）基于文学文体学理论对《水浒传》的各种文体进行了研究；杨阳（2007）从女性主义翻译理论视角，探讨了赛珍珠是如何运用各种女性主义翻译策略来彰显其译者的主体性；周莉芬（2008）基于埃氏多元系统理论探讨了影响译者翻译策略选择的因素；徐剑平等（2009）从接受理论的视角对译者和读者在翻译中的作用进行了探讨；闫玉涛（2010）研究了沙博理《水浒传》译本中归化和异化的翻译策略；刘婷（2011）在认知语言学的概念隐喻框架中对《水浒传》中动物隐喻的翻译进行了分析；温秀颖（2012）基于登译剖析了译者的语言文化知识及其翻译目的与误译之间的关系；马箐悦（2013）对赛珍珠《水浒传》译本中的创造性叛逆及原因进行了剖析；宋颖（2014）基于《水浒传》沙博理译本分析了译者在熟语翻译中出现的文化意象缺失问题及其原因；潘莹等（2015）对《水浒传》两个英译本中的女性形象进行了分析；刘幼玲（2016）研究了登译《水浒传》中男性服饰的翻译；周梁勋等学者（2017）运用翻译伦理学的观点对《水浒传》的两个英译本进行了对比研究；徐松健（2018）基于《水浒传》三译本从文化概念化视角研究了中国酒形象在翻译中的传播；黄靖雯（2019）从古典诗学视角对《水浒传》中好汉形象及情节异质语境的翻译改写进行了研究；李雅静（2020）从跨文化的角度对比分析了《水浒传》三个英译本中的俗语翻译；赵觅（2021）从认知隐喻视角出发，通过对比《水浒传》四个英译本探究了汉语四字格成语的英译策略。

《金瓶梅》的英译研究总体上与《水浒传》相似，同样存在着投入力量不足，研究文献发表数量不足，研究深度广度欠缺等问题。

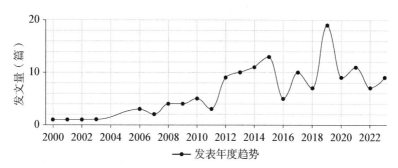

图 1.7　《金瓶梅》英译研究文献分析图

表 1.4　《金瓶梅》英译研究文献分类图

角度	数量	期刊论文	学位论文	会议论文
译本综述类	5	3	1	1
译文赏析和对比	19	11	7	1
译者研究	7	5	2	0
文化研究	9	7	2	0
语言学视角	1	1	0	0
翻译策略	25	12	11	2
总计	66	39	23	4

统计后可见，2000—2023 年，《金瓶梅》英译研究相关文献仅检索到 66 篇，其中期刊论文 39 篇，学位论文 23 篇，会议论文 4 篇。研究成果的高峰期在 2019 年，研究内容较多为翻译策略、译文赏析与对比。

由图 1.8 可见，在相关文献中，翻译策略综述占 37%，译文

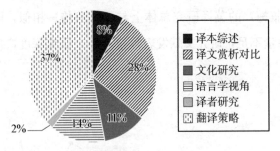

图 1.8   《金瓶梅》英译研究文献的研究内容分布图

赏析和对比占 28％，文化视角的研究占 14％，译者研究占 11％，译本综述类占 8％，语言学视角的研究文献占比仅为 2％。

黄粉保（2009）对《金瓶梅》英译本中的误译现象进行了研究；温秀颖等（2010）基于芮效卫英译《金瓶梅》探索了典籍英译研究；李志华等（2010）基于埃杰顿英译《金瓶梅》探讨了文学翻译中的文化缺失；温秀颖等（2012）对《金瓶梅》两版英译本中的隐喻翻译策略进行了比较研究；聂影影（2012）对《金瓶梅》两英译本中的服饰文化与翻译进行了比较研究；温秀颖等（2013）基于埃杰顿英译《金瓶梅》探讨文学典籍英译中运用陌生化翻译策略保留和再现"他者"的方法及其跨文化传播意义；温秀颖等（2014）基于《金瓶梅》两个节译本和两个全译本探讨了英译的中西文化互动与关联；温秀颖等（2015）基于《金瓶梅》两个英译本从叙事学视角探索了人物话语表达方式的翻译；张玉梅（2015）基于《金瓶梅》两个代表性英译本从语言学视角探讨《金瓶梅》的海外传播和中国文科的"复兴"；张慧琴等（2016）研究了《金瓶梅》两个全译本中的"足衣"译文部分对于中华礼仪文化的传递与体现；金学勤（2017）分析了《金瓶梅》芮效卫英译本为当代中国带来的文化战略启示；张义宏

（2018）对两个英译本中茶饮名称的英译策略进行了探究；唐军等（2018）基于女性主义视域探究了《金瓶梅》芮效卫译本中卜龟章节的女性主义翻译内涵；汤孟孟（2019）从操控理论视角对芮效卫《金瓶梅》译本中有关大运河文化的翻译策略选择进行分析；孙会军（2019）研究了齐林涛于 2018 年出版的第一部《金瓶梅》英译研究专著；房宇华（2019）基于 1980—2018 年中国知网收录的《金瓶梅》翻译研究文献，剖析了其翻译研究的发展脉络和研究现状；齐林涛（2020）基于 20 世纪英美社会的历史文化背景探讨了《金瓶梅》英译过程中的去经典化现象；冯全功等（2020）对《金瓶梅》中的隐喻型性话语以及芮效卫的对应英译进行了研究；胡桑（2020）基于《金瓶梅》两英译本探讨了感官叙事的翻译方法、策略及翻译效果；赵朝永（2020）基于语料库对《金瓶梅》英文全译本进行了语域变异多维分析；潘佳宁（2021）探索了《金瓶梅》芮效卫译本中的"深度翻译"模式；施红梅（2021）以功能对等理论为视角，研究了《金瓶梅》两英译本中双关语的翻译策略；王振平等（2022）基于《金瓶梅》两英译本中文化负载词"天"的翻译探讨了译者的创造性叛逆；李燕等（2022）对《金瓶梅》两英译本中的部分服饰译例进行了翻译策略研究；王振平等（2022）基于《金瓶梅》两英译本中动物隐喻的翻译探讨了译者主体性的发挥；张慧芳（2023）基于《金瓶梅》两英译本从社会翻译学视角对宗教文化英译进行了对比分析。

从上述分析可见明清小说英语译介与对外传播研究存在的问题。

首先，分析可见明清小说英语译介研究成果呈现出不均衡的发展态势。

明代小说中《金瓶梅词话》与《水浒传》虽然已经有研究专著问世，但是无论是研究论文、学位论文、会议论文，成果总量仍有限，需要进一步的挖掘与展开；在清代小说中，多数研究成果主要集中在《红楼梦》的英语译介与传播上，无论是成果数量和成果形式，《红楼梦》稳居首位，而从 1990 年到 1998 年近八年的时间，国内学者对《聊斋志异》英译的研究是空白的，这距最早的 1880 年翟理斯的节译本出版已有逾百年历史，可见国内《聊斋志异》的英译研究起步较晚，关注程度和参与程度明显不够。21 世纪以后，国内对《聊斋志异》的英译研究逐渐重视起来，特别是 2008—2012 年间发表的论文近 51 篇，所占总比例约 73.9%。至于《金瓶梅》和《水浒传》两部作品的英译研究更是远远落后于《红楼梦》，无论研究成果的数量和研究的范畴方面，都亟待加强。

明清小说英语译介研究的内容尚欠多元化，研究力度不够，研究范畴有待突破。

目前，明清小说的研究内容停留在语言对比和翻译策略层面的不在少数。分析可见，当前对于作品的译本研究开展得较为充分，对于作品在英语世界的学术史梳理还很不完善，研究深度广度也因作品的传播效果不同而有较大差异。同时，译者研究还需要进一步加强。张义宏（2016）指出，英语世界的明清小说译介与研究是许多翻译家与汉学家共同努力的结果，因此这方面的研究应该加强。目前来看，尽管对杨宪益与戴乃迭的研究已经取得了一定的成绩，但是有关其他翻译家和汉学家的研究成果还十分有限。从《水浒传》到《红楼梦》，明清小说的译介史上涌现出多位译者，其中既有文化输出国的译者，也有文化输入国的译者；既有英语为母语的译者，也有英语为自身所习得的外语的译者；既有熟悉中国语言和文化的汉学家、翻译家、外交人员、文学家，也有对中国存在一知半解，甚至误解的宗教人士和其他身份复杂的译者，因此，译者身份呈现出多样性，这一研究的重要性也凸显出来。

此外，明清小说英语译介与传播过程中的国别研究还有待加强。虽然已有研究将明清小说置于英语世界的宏观背景下加以审视，但是英语世界是一个较为宽泛的概念，因此还不能准确厘清作品译介方式与传播路径等问题。如果以美国、英国、澳大利亚等国家地域来划分可能会使明清小说英语译介与传播研究的资料梳理更加细致翔实（张义宏，2016）。

1.3　明清小说误译研究概述

针对明清时期文学经典的英译研究取得了一定的成就，但细化到误译视角的研究则还处在起步阶段，研究成果差强人意。

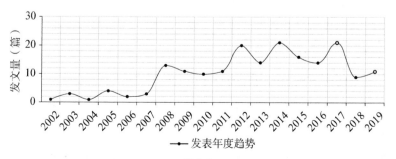

图 1.9

　　对文献主题分布情况进行分析后发现，研究大部分集中在明清小说译本综述、译本对比赏析和翻译策略上，而译者研究、文化研究和交叉学科方面的研究相对较少。经检索，与《红楼梦》误译有关的文献总计 37 条，去除其他语种的研究论文，英译方向的文献仅有 11 篇；《聊斋志异》误译研究共有文献 4 篇，去除俄语和其他语种，仅有一篇文献涉及误译研究。

　　周晓寒（2009）基于霍克斯译本从文化误译角度探索了译者的再创造；李美（2012）从《红楼梦》的误译探讨译者母语在文化传递中的角色；郭挺（2014）基于语境理论对《红楼梦》四个英译本中称谓语误译进行了比较研究；赵朝永（2015）研究了《红楼梦》邦斯尔译本中的误译；王坤（2016）从文化角度研究《红楼梦》中称谓语的误译；蔡魏立（2016）从文化过滤视角对《红楼梦》中的有意误译现象进行了研究；卢晓敏等（2016）对霍克斯《红楼梦》译本的误译原因进行了剖析；宋鹏（2017）从误译现象考证邦斯尔神父英译《红楼梦》之底本。

　　分析结果表明，基于明清小说英译的误译研究在国内尚属鲜见，较少研究将误译与译介效果关联起来进行深入探讨，仅有少量的学位论文涉及。

　　因此，文化研究、利用交叉学科理论和语料库翻译学的研究方法对误译与译介效果进行深入探索，符合当前中国文化走出去战略，符合翻译研究大方向。

　　本研究聚焦于国内有关明清小说英语译介与传播研究的学术著述，旨在对明清小说的英语译介与传播研究做历时性的回顾与梳理，在此基础上探讨英语世界明清小说译介与传播研究中取得的成绩与存在的不足，从而希望为典籍外译与传播研究提供一定的借鉴。

《金瓶梅》是 20 世纪英语世界中国古典文学研究的热点领域之一，是西方翻译家和学者的翻译与研究工作做得较好的典籍之一，不但产生出多样化的译本，而且出现了大量的学术研究成果。但与国内其他典籍英译不同，《金瓶梅》的英译研究尚处于起步阶段，远远落后于《红楼梦》《水浒传》《三国演义》《聊斋志异》等古典小说的英译研究，因此尚存在很大的发展空间。

《红楼梦》作为中国四大名著之首，是举世公认的中国古典小说巅峰之作，而《聊斋志异》作为中国古典小说的杰出代表，标志着我国文言短篇小说创作的最高峰。聊斋红楼，一短一长，一文一白，已形成中国古代小说的双峰，均成为国内外学术界研究的重点，其对外传播和译介研究也取得了不容忽视的成就。

在海外，《红楼梦》和《聊斋志异》两部巨著经历了从译介到研究的渐进式的发展历程。国外学者在研读、翻译这两部作品的基础上，从外国文学、外国文化的整体出发，从民俗学、文化学、心理学、伦理学、比较文学等视角对其分别进行了研究；在国内，近年来新的研究视角如叙事学、接受美学研究也使"红学"和"聊斋学"渐入佳境。

而专门研究明清小说误译的文献则几乎为零，大部分文献对小说英译进行了梳理和述评；对小说的多译本进行译者风格研究；还有少量对四部巨著中文化因素和文化负载词进行研究的期刊论文和学位论文。

统计分析结果表明，基于明清小说英译的误译研究在国内尚属鲜见，较少研究将误译与译介效果关联起来进行深入探讨，由于四部作品产生的时代、基调和风格迥异，体裁上既有文言也有白话，其译文风格也会形成鲜明对照，因此适合置于同一框架下进行对比分析。

本研究拟对明清小说英译本中的误译现象进行分析，同时对误译成因进行研究探索，研究从误读到误译的整个认知过程，探讨译本中的文化过滤、文化误读，以及译者的文化身份等要素，探索如何消除无意误译、合理利用有意的文化误译本身的积极因素，从而将四部经典作品原文中的大量丰富多彩的优秀中华文化有效地传播给目的语读者。本文致力于从明清小说代表作的英译本的误译研究中得出有益于文化传播的翻译策略，研究误译与译介效果的关联，因而研究成果有利于推动中文经典作品向英语世界的译介和传播，从而更加有效地弘扬中华文化，现实意义和应用价值较强。

第二章　误译研究

2.1　从误读到误译

误读是美国当代著名批评家、文学理论家哈罗德·布鲁姆（Harold Bloom）提出的一个较为激进的阅读理论。"'误读'这一现象'被看作是阅读阐释和文学史的构成活动'（姚斯，1987）。布鲁姆否定了一切所谓精确无误的阅读，指出对任何文学作品的解读都可能产生误读的问题。"（孙雪瑛等，2010：147）

哈罗德·布鲁姆在 20 世纪 60 年代通过对英国浪漫派诗人的深入研究，动摇了 T. S. 艾略特的保守形式主义批评在美国学界的支配地位。70 年代前期转向一般文学理论研究，与德·曼、哈特曼和米勒并称耶鲁四大批评家，以诗歌误解和影响的焦虑理论更新了对文学传统的认识，90 年代以后又转向《圣经》和宗教研究。

布鲁姆于 1973 年推出《影响的焦虑》"用一本小书敲了一下所有人的神经"，在美国批评界引起巨大反响。其主要研究领域包括诗歌批评、理论批评和宗教批评三大方面。他以其独特的理论建构和批评实践被誉为"西方传统中最有天赋、最有原创性和最有煽动性的一位文学批评家"。

布鲁姆的诗歌误解和影响的焦虑理论更新了对文学传统的认识，更以其独特的批评实践与理论建构被英国当代著名西方马克思主义文学理论家特里·伊格尔顿誉为"过去十年最大胆、最富有创见的文学理论之一"（洪畅，2021：178）。布鲁姆的理论在英美批评界乃至国际美学界都引起了巨大的反响，也受到了我国学者的广泛重视。

布鲁姆认为：诗歌的影响总是通过对较前一位诗人的误读而发生的，他还把文学影响史归结为对前辈误读、误解和修正的历史。布鲁姆在《误读图示》中进一步完善了他的"影响即误读"的理论，提出："影响不是指较早的诗人到较晚近的诗人的想象和思想的传递承续，影响意味着压根儿不存在文本，而只存在文本之间的关系，这些关系则取决于一种批评行为，即取决于误读或误解——一位诗人对另一位诗人所作的批评、误读和误解。"（布鲁姆，1975：33）

布鲁姆强调这种"影响"过程中的误读、批评、修正、重写就是一种创造与更新，因此，文学史就必然是一部由误读所构成的阐释史。就文学创作而言，布鲁姆认为误读是诗人摆脱前人创作的必要的开拓性的偏离，误读是一种主动的行为，其目的在于摆脱前人影响的巨大阴影，通过对既定解释的有意误读而达到某种创新的境地，即某种程度的"修正式"创新（刘桂兰，2015：82）。

吴冰（2021）认为误读和误译的主要原因可以从文本和诠释者两方面进行分析。首先，从文本方面来说，文本意义的客观确定性在某种程度上与它所依赖的历史文化语境相关。当文本脱离其赖以生存的历史文化语境时，使其中原本客观、确定的东西变得虚无，对读者而言就是意义的空洞。其次，译文的诠释者，即译者在翻译中如果不以"对话者"的姿态，而是以"独白者"的姿态诠释，不倾听文本，不让文本发言，任自己的先入之见掩盖文本中的异质，那就很容易出现误读、误释或误译。

因此，我们必须意识到："翻译是一项高度复杂的双语转换活动，同时也是文化冲突、碰撞和融合的过程。在这一过程中，译者面临的不仅仅是语言文字问题，而且还要受到大量的非语言因素的干扰。虽然译者会尽可能准确忠实地传达原文的信息，但误译仍然不可避免。"（孙雪瑛等，2010：147）

2.2　无意误译和有意误译

方梦之（2004）认为，误译是"对原著错误的翻译，在思想意义上或在文字上背离了原文"，可见误译主要包括对原文的思想的背离和语义上的不对等。误译可分为有意误译和无意误译两类。

无意误译是指"因为译者知识、水平等的欠缺，对原文的语言内涵或文化背景缺少足够的了解与把握，将有的内容译错"（吴家荣，2004：149）。

这一类的无意误译是因译者翻译时的疏忽大意而造成的误译，也就是译者的无心之失造成的。

原文：王子服……十四入泮。（《聊斋志异·婴宁》）

梅译：Wang Zifu……received the baccalaureate at thirteen.

原文中的年龄被译者错误地译为十三岁，虽然与情节无碍，但是明显是译者疏忽导致。这类笔误在各类译作中较为常见。

又如郭实腊的《聊斋志异》的无意误译。

原文："安大业，卢龙人。生而能言，母饮以犬血始止。"（《聊斋志异·云萝公主》）

郭译："A mother bore a child, which from the day it came into the world could speak, and she nourished it with dog's milk."

译文与原文相去甚远。原文为狗血，译文变成"狗的乳汁"。此处的误译也应归类在无意误译中，但更深层次的原因可能在于对中国文化知识的欠缺。

在古代一些巫术仪式中，狗血被用作祭品或净化工具，认为狗血可以用来驱邪或者带来好运，因此在一些祭祀活动中被使用。此外，旧时迷信，传说用狗血淋头，可以使妖人妖法失灵，不能施展其妖法。后多用来指争吵之中，一方被骂得无言可对，平日的本领无法施展，如同妖人被浇了狗血不能施展其伎俩一样。例如《水浒全传》第五十三回：

当日正值府尹马士弘坐衙，厅前立着许多公吏人等，看见半天里落下一个黑大汉来，众皆吃惊。马府尹喝道："你这厮是那里妖人？如何从半天里吊将下来？"李逵吃跌得头破额裂，半晌说不出话来。马知府道："必然是个妖人！"教去取些法物来。牢子、节级将李逵捆翻，驱下厅前草地里。一个虞候掇一盆狗血，劈头一淋。

可见狗血在古代文化中的奇效，可以使妖魔鬼怪现出原形，使其无法施展妖法为害人间，使其无法继续进行变化从而迷惑人心智。在中国古典文学作品中，"犬血"具有其独特的文化内涵，而不仅仅是一种普通的物质文化名词。郭实腊的误译产生的原因是译者没有仔细认真地研读原文，对相关的文化背景知识也缺乏了解，对译文的质量没有足够重视，因此在译文中出现了漏译和误译种种。

《红楼梦》译本中出现的无意误译也不在少数。

原文：薛蟠道："袭人可不是宝贝是什么！你们不信，只问他。"说着，指着宝玉。宝玉没好意思起来。（第二十八回）

杨译："Isn't Xiren a treasure?" demanded Xue Pan. "If you don't believe me, ask him." He pointed at Baoyu. In some embarrassment Baoyu stood up.

原文中的"没好意思起来"是指宝玉开始觉得不好意思了，而译者竟将此理解为了"站起来"，因而将这句话译作："In some embarrassment Baoyu stood up"显然是对原意的曲解，属于无意误译。

在称谓词的翻译上，也出现了一些无意误译。

刘姥姥便拉住一个道："我问哥儿一声，有个周大娘可在家么？"（第六回）

杨译：The old woman caught hold of one of these youngsters and asked, "Can you tell me, brother, if Mrs. Zhou is at home?"

在本回目中，刘姥姥因冬季将至，家中贫困，欲去荣国府"打秋风"，寻沾亲带故的王夫人从而获得些许经济资助，因不认路，找不到可以带她去拜见王夫人的下人，便向旁边玩耍的孩童打听王夫人的陪房周瑞家的在家否。

刘姥姥用"哥儿"一词来称呼陌生的男孩。在《红楼梦》

中，"哥儿"一词被频繁使用，在不同语境下其指称意义也不尽相同，有时是对男性小主人的称呼，有时指称青年男子或对男孩的称呼。在古代，该词语也指对少爷或朋友的儿子的称呼，这是一种对男孩的特定称呼方式。在清代之前，"哥儿"是指官宦人家的子弟，算是一种尊称。但有时家庭中的男子也被其母亲称为"哥儿"，体现了家庭成员之间的亲密关系，例如电视剧《知否》里面的顾廷烨、盛长枫，他们的母亲都称他们为"哥儿"。

因此，杨译为"brother"明显与原文的"哥儿"含义是不对等的，基于杨宪益的文化身份和文化底蕴，且作为文化输出国的母语译者，推断其文化误读导致的文化误译可能性不大，因此推测译者是未能仔细斟酌词义从而造成的误译。

第二种无意误译通常是对原文本的语言和文化产生误读而导致的误译。"文化误读是指由于译者对原语语言与文化知识的欠缺而导致对其文化内涵的误读。这些误解可能源于语言文字误读，但内容往往超越语言文字的范畴，其结果也直接导致文化内涵的曲解与谬译。"（赵朝永，2015）例如：

原文：云儿又道："女儿愁，妈妈打骂何时休！"（第二十八回）

杨译：Yuner went on："The girl's worry：Will the bawd always beat and scold her?"

霍译：She continued："The girl looks glum：Nothing but blows and hard words from her Mum."

原文的"妈妈"称谓在字面上等于英语的"mother"，但云儿作为青楼妓女，用"妈妈"一词来指称鸨母，与亲属关系称谓无关，但是可以在一定程度上体现出封建社会妓院家族管理体制，是中国封建社会中妓女对鸨母的惯常称呼。根据百度百科介绍，老鸨，也叫鸨儿、鸨母，是古代对妓院老板娘的称呼。鸨的最早文献见诸《诗·唐风·鸨羽》："肃肃鸨行，集于苞桑。"相传老鸨是一种已经灭绝的鸟类，古人发现，这种鸟类没有雄性，只有雌性。它们通过与其他种类的鸟进行交配，然后繁殖，很像"人尽可夫"的妓女，所以称呼妓院老板娘为老鸨，其主要职责包括为嫖客推荐妓女、管理并教化妓女，以及协调各方面的关系。

而"妈妈"这个词在宋朝时指鸨母，到清朝转为对年长妇人的称呼，新文化运动以后，才被普遍用于称呼母亲。显然这种用法在英语国家是不存在的。此例中的"妈妈"不同于一般意义上的亲属称谓语，是一种特殊用法。因此杨译为正确翻译，霍译"her Mum"则属文化误译，因未能透彻理解该词的文化内涵而导致的误读。

在文学翻译中，由于文化误读导致的误译也比比皆是。例如庞德所译的中文古诗中存在大量的误译从而引发争议。在《古诗十九首》（其二）中，原文中后四句为：

昔为倡家女，今为荡子妇。

荡子行不归，空床难独守。

庞德的译文：

And she was a courtesan in the old day,

And she has married a sot,

Who now goes drunkenly out,

And leaves her too much alone.

庞德将原诗中的"倡家女"误译成了 courtesan（妓女），误读形成的原因在于庞德本人不仅对中国古代社会的文化了解甚少，对中文更是一窍不通，因此才会造成这样谬以千里的误译。

　　"倡女"在中国古代指"卖艺不卖身的歌女"，词典解释为"以歌舞娱人的妇女"。例如南朝梁何逊《似轻薄篇》诗："倡女掩歌扇，小妇开帘织。"《续资治通鉴·宋理宗绍定五年》中自述："我倡女张凤奴也，许州破，被俘至此。"鲁迅在《南腔北调集·由中国女人的脚推定中国人之非中庸又由此推定孔夫子有胃病》一文中提及："那时太太们固然也未始不舞，但舞的究以倡女为多。"唐代开始"倡家女"确实也为妓女的代名词，但需要根据语境具体区分。如唐代著名诗人崔颢的《渭城少年行》中提到："可怜锦瑟筝琵琶，玉壶清酒就倡家。"因此，此词为多义词，不完全等同于西方人心目中贬义的"妓女"形象，在这首《古诗十九首》中的"倡家"专指从事音乐歌舞的乐人，从唐朝沿用至今，等同于白居易的《琵琶行》中，叙事者"浔阳江头夜送客"时，遇到的琵琶技艺高超的商人妇即是旧日的"倡家女"：

　　自言本是京城女，家在虾蟆陵下住。

　　十三学得琵琶成，名属教坊第一部。

　　曲罢曾教善才服，妆成每被秋娘妒。

　　五陵年少争缠头，一曲红绡不知数。

　　除此文化误译外，庞德还将"荡子"误译为"sot"，意为"醉鬼，酗酒者"，更加是对中国文化中关于离人、思妇这两个意象的误读以及对闺怨诗的误解。

　　"荡子"意指"辞家远出、羁旅忘返的男子"，也指"浪荡子"，即游手好闲，不务正业或败尽家业的人。例如《文选·古诗》："荡子行不归，空床难独守。"杜甫的《冬晚送长孙渐舍人归州》诗："参卿休坐惟，荡子不还乡。"隋代薛道衡的《昔昔盐》："关山别荡子，风月守空闺"。元代本高明的《琵琶记·赵五娘忆夫》："君身岂荡子，妾非荡子妇。"近代严复的《出都留别林纾》诗中也引用了此词："可怜一卷《茶花女》，断尽支那荡子肠。"

经如此理解和翻译后，庞德将春日美景之下，青春美貌的少妇思念远行的丈夫的离愁、闺怨彻底篡改，成了一名从良的妓女嫁给一个酒鬼后独守空房的悲惨故事。难怪台湾诗人余光中指责庞德的《华夏集》是"假李白之名，抒庞德之情"，是"改写""重组""剽窃的创造"。庞德对于古典诗歌的误读和误译是显而易见的。

有意误译指"译者为了某种目的或适应一定的需要，包括读者接受的需要、文化判断与表达的需要等故意对原文的语言内涵、表达方式等作清醒、理智的选择、增删、改换形式等"（吴家荣，2004：149）。有意误译多涉及文化误译。

文化误译源于文化误读，是指"按照自己的文化传统和思维模式，在理解和借鉴异国文化时出现的某些认识上的错位、理解上的偏差、评价上的倾向性，以及视自己需要的文化选择、文化改造和文化接受"（姜智芹，2008）。由于原语文化与目的语文化的差异，中西方在意识形态、宗教信仰、价值观、道德取向、审美等方面存在较大差异，在翻译过程中，译者对文本中的文化内容的翻译存在着主观操控。作为翻译活动主体的译者有目的地采用一些翻译策略，将原文本中难以理解的异域文化进行过滤、改造，从而使其译本得到译语文化读者的认可和接受。

赛珍珠在解读《水浒传》中的姓名文化时，为了使译入语读者意识到在传统中国文化中"姓"和"名"的区别及其重要性，从而更好地了解中国文化，在文中多次强调"姓氏"一词为

"surname"，以及名字为 "name"。

原文：朱全道："小人不敢拜问官人<u>高姓</u>？"柴进答道："小可小旋风便是。"（第五十回）

赛译：Chu T'ung said, "This lowly one does not dare to ask what the <u>high surname</u> of the noble one is." Ch'ai Chin answered, saying, "This lowly one is called The Little Whirlwind."

原文：石秀道："小人不敢拜问二位官人<u>贵姓</u>？"戴宗道："小可<u>姓</u>戴，<u>名</u>宗，兄弟<u>姓</u>杨，<u>名</u>林。"（第四十三回）

赛译：Then Shih Hsiu asked, "This lowly one dares not to ask, but in all reverence what is the <u>noble surname</u> of you two?" And Tai Chung answered, "This lowly one is <u>surnamed</u> Tai and <u>named</u> Chung. My brother is <u>surnamed</u> Yang and <u>named</u> Ling."

可见赛珍珠在翻译《水浒传》时坚持的前见和原则：为使目的语读者更好地了解中国文化，她不厌其烦地反复提及 surname 和 name，等于不断地洗脑读者，最终的目的是使之习惯和接受这一说法，从而提升阅读者的认可和接受度。

涉及原文中的文化负载词的误译的案例较多。例如在《聊斋志异》中，物质文化负载词"鼎"的误译。以下以翟译代指翟理斯译本，梅译指梅丹理梅维恒译本。

原文：曾前匍伏请命，王者阅卷，才数行，即震怒曰："此欺君误国之罪，宜置油<u>鼎</u>！"（《聊斋志异》《续黄粱》）

翟译：Tsêng crawled before him on his hands and knees to receive sentence, and the king, after turning over a few pages of his register, thundered out, "The punishment of a traitor who has brought misfortune on his country: the cauldron of boiling oil!"

梅译：Zeng went forward and prostrated himself to beg for his life. The king read only a few lines from Zeng's file and exploded with anger: "For deceiving your lord betraying your country, you must be thrown into the oil cauldron!"

鼎是我国物质文化中的重要代表，也是宝贵的文化遗产之一。根据徐锴《说文解字系传》："从贞省声。古文以贞为鼎，籀文以鼎为贞。""鼎"的字形模拟的是古代的一种烹饪器具，其形制上面像缸，有圆形也有方形的，有两侧有耳的；下面为足，此字始见于商代甲骨文，其悠久的历史可上溯到四千年前的夏禹时代。

"鼎"的本义是古代的一种炊器。到了奴隶社会，鼎被专用于祭祀和宴飨，因而有"列鼎而食"之说。后又发展成统治阶级的权力象征，是君位和政权的标志，成为传国之重器。再往后，由于礼制之需，又兼做礼器，出现了列鼎，如天子九鼎，诸侯七鼎等，用来别贵贱，分上下。秦汉之后到三国，这种政治功能消失殆尽，也就逐渐成为仿古的陈列品了。鼎有三足，于是比喻三方势力，因此有"三足鼎立"之说。"鼎"的特征是大，因此引申出"盛大"的意思，例如鼎力相助、鼎鼎有名、人声鼎沸等说法（百度百科）。

翟译和梅译中都采用"cauldron"一词代替中国文化中特有的物质名词"鼎"。然而，"cauldron"在英语中是来自法语的外来词，是一种外形较大的敞口型的金属锅，主要用于室外以明火进行烹饪，带有弧形的拎手。

在西方文化中，"cauldron"作为巫术中的一种工具出现于文学作品中，例如莎士比亚在其名剧《麦克白》中就描写了荒野中的三名女巫使用大锅蒸煮蜥蜴、蝙蝠、蜘蛛、毒蛇等食材，熬制成诡异的汤药以施行巫术时使用：

Round about the cauldron go;

In the poison'd entrails throw.

绕釜环行火融融，

毒肝腐脏置其中。（《麦克白》，朱生豪译，2000：99）

可见原文中的"鼎"与译文中的"cauldron"仅在作为烹饪器皿的用途上有共性，但在文化内涵上各不相同。因此翟译和梅译均属误译，其归化的目的是使西方读者对故事中相关情节有所了解，因篇幅所限，两位译者对该器具的文化负载意义没有详加阐述，因而属于有意误译。但在原语读者心目中，鼎的历史典故和重大的象征意义却是不容忽略的。

在电视剧《芈月传》中，秦武王嬴荡带着属下去观赏周天子的九鼎。九鼎并不是一般的国家礼器，相传夏禹曾将天下划为九个州，并命令各州贡献青铜，铸造了九个鼎，象征九州。春秋时期，楚庄王就曾经陈兵洛水，问鼎的大小、高度、重量，给后世留下一个"楚王问鼎"的成语，也成为后世英雄人物图谋天下的代名词。鉴于此，在周人的刺激下，嬴荡亲自上阵举鼎，没想到被九鼎压到口吐鲜血，不治而亡。

这段历史记录的就是举鼎。举鼎在古代是一项具有特殊意义的活动，历史上有记载的举鼎者往往身份不同寻常。而鼎一向被视为国家权力的象征，意义非凡。古人举鼎是为了展示自己有强大的力量和无上的权力（樊登，2023：15）。

与鼎有关的成语包括：人声鼎沸、大名鼎鼎、钟鸣鼎食、革故鼎新、一言九鼎、三足鼎立、鼎鼎大名、鼎折餗覆、尝鼎一脔、尝鼎一商、春秋鼎盛、鼎铛玉石、牛鼎烹鸡、鼎鼎有名、拔山扛鼎、鼎足三分、五鼎万钟、扛鼎抃牛、鼎铛有耳、列鼎而食、刀锯鼎镬、一代鼎臣、鼎鼐调和、鼎镬刀锯、列鼎重裀、金黎鼎盛、三牲五鼎、龙去鼎湖等以及大量与之相关的历史文化典故。因此，"鼎"这一词语是重要的中国文化负载词，内涵非常丰富。

译者在"鼎"的厚重的文化底蕴和目标语读者的理解力和译文的可读性之间选了归化翻译，归根结底是以读者体验为出发点，有目的地采用恰当的翻译策略，将原文本中难以理解的异域文化知识进行改造，因此是典型的有意误译。

诺德（Nord）在谈到翻译错误时曾指出，如果翻译的目的是在目标读者中实现某种特定的功能，那么任何阻碍这种功能实现的翻译都属于翻译错误。因此，当我们重新审视文学翻译批评中的许多"误译"时就会发现，许多误译其实是译者基于某种特定目的有意为之，对于翻译目的的实现有着促进作用（邓婕，2006）。

2.3 误译的诠释学解读

在探讨翻译过程中的误读和误译现象的成因时，首先要研究的是译者的理解和解释的全过程。

翻译是涉及译者、原作者、原文和读者的一种复杂的跨文化交际活动。海德格尔（1987）在《存在与时间》一书中指出，任何解释都依赖于理解者和翻译者的前理解。译者在对原文本的解读过程中，基于自身所处的历史文化语境、固有的意识形态、传统观念、生活习俗和心理结构，接触到原文文本时不可避免地将自己的理解前结构引入到翻译过程中。

伽达默尔秉承了海德格尔的思想，不仅肯定了海德格尔的前理解观念，并将其发展成为"前见"（也译作偏见、成见）概念，为偏见进行了辩护和正名。伽达默尔认为合理的偏见可以帮助理解者和译者去克服历史性带来的种种束缚，译者和理解者如能保持一种开放的心理，易于接受文本的不同之处，从而可以在解释的过程中将自己的前见与文本同化，即可实现新的理解。

海德格尔在《存在与时间》中肯定了存在的时间性和历史性的特征。伽达默尔通过为偏见正名发展了这一概念，将其称为"时间距离"（也译作"时间间距"）。理解者与原文本的时间距离在古典解释学看来会不可避免地导致理解时的障碍，但伽达默尔认为："事实上，具有重要意义的是，在于把时间距离看成是理解的一种积极的创造性的可能性。时间距离不是一个张着大口的鸿沟，而是由习俗和传统的连续性填满，正是由于这种感觉连续性，一切流传物才向我们呈现出来。"（伽达默尔，2004：303）

时间距离是理解者不断产生新的理解的意义的源泉。在理解的过程中，理解者有着自身的出发点，即视看的区域。视域包括理解者从某个立足点出发所看到的一切事物。由于理解的历史性和时间距离的存在，理解者必须将自己置身于历史性的视域之中，才能理解"流传物"（文本）的真正意义。同时，伽达默尔认为，理解者、解释者的视域不是封闭、隔绝的，而是出于不断的运动之中。当理解者的视域与其他视域相遇、交织、碰撞并融合，就形成了新的理解。当前视域与过去视域相结合的状态就是伽达默尔称之为"视域融合"的状态。反映在翻译过程中就是这样一个过程：作为理解和解释的主体的译者从所在的历史文化语境出发，带着理解的历史性产生的偏见，将译者自身的视域与理解的客体——原文本的视域相互碰撞、冲突、交流直至融合，最终构成一个统一整体，达成视域融合（fusion of horizons），形成超越原文作者和译者自身视域的新的视域，达到更高和更新的层次，即完成了翻译，产生了新的译本。

"视界融合是建立在差异基础上的融合。它从理论上印证了翻译中文化过滤现象的历史根源及其存在的无可避免性。"（张德让，2001：23）理解者的偏见和自身的视域影响了理解的过程、解释的方法和解读效果，文化过滤和误译等翻译现象则不可避免。在理解过程中，理解者的视域与原作者和原文的视域不断碰撞、排斥，因此译者不得不对原文进行归化式的解释，对原语文本进行文化过滤。

以《红楼梦》霍克斯译文为例。

原文：然后散了押岁钱并荷包金银锞等物。

霍译：After that the New Year's Eve wish-penny was distributed to servants and children—gold or silver medallions in little embroidered purses.

"押岁钱"也作"压岁钱"或"压祟钱"，在广东叫作"俾利是"，年节习俗之一，其本真来由无考，传说是为了压邪祟。除夕夜吃完年夜饭，长辈要给小辈压岁钱，以祝福晚辈平安度岁。但在有些地区是在大年初一的早上由长辈给晚辈压岁钱，寓意辟邪驱鬼，保佑平安。这笔钱充满了长辈对晚辈的真挚祝愿和关心。中国的传统文化历来重视和谐的家庭氛围和亲情，因此给予和接受"压岁钱"在某种程度上是一种情感纽带的象征。此外，它还反映了中国永恒的社会价值观，即照顾他人和传递爱。这就是原语读者在阅读时会联想到的文化内涵，而目标读者则无法产生这种相关性。霍克斯采取归化译法，将中国的除夕译为 New Year's Eve，压岁钱译为 New Year's Eve wish-penny，形式上体现出了压岁钱的目的和用途，进行了文化过滤后，目的语读者对这一特殊的年节文化现象有所了解，但深层的文化内涵却被省略了。

另一个明显的文化过滤是《好了歌》中的神仙意象和诗歌的主题。

原文标题：好了歌

杨译：All Good Things Must End

霍译文为：The Won-Done Song

原文：世人都晓神仙好

杨译：All men long to be immortals

霍译：Men all know that salvation should be won

杨译把《好了歌》的标题译为"All Good Things Must End"，符合原文中所表达的"可知世上万般，好便是了，了便是好。若不了，便不好；若要好，须是了"的一切皆虚妄的主题思想，即使是鲜花着锦、烈火烹油的繁华景象也不过是"乱烘烘你方唱罢我登场，反认他乡是故乡。甚荒唐，到头来都是为他人作嫁衣裳"的一场虚空的、使人真假难辨的幻境而已。因此杨译将主题理解为出世哲学与入世意欲的矛盾冲突，是基于中国传统哲学思想的理解和阐释。而霍译标题"Won-done Song"和"Men all know that salvation should be won"（世人都晓神仙好）则体现现世的奋斗、成功和享乐与灵魂的最终得救之间的矛盾，侧重基督教中的拯救主题。两种译文中文化背景的差异和过滤都得以体现。

根据伽达默尔的诠释学理论，文本对解释者是保持开放的，文本的意义也是开放的，这一事实决定了对问题的理解和解释都是一个开放的过程，问题也是开放的，会有多种可能的答案，而译者就要从各自的视域出发做出选择，根据各自所持有的前见（偏见）传递原文中丰富的文化信息。由于东西方思维方式的差异，译者文化背景的不同和对文化意象理解的不同，即视域不同，霍、杨的译文存在很大差异。

杨氏作为文化输出国的译者、母语文化的学习者和传播者，深受中国传统文化的影响，在翻译过程中力求将中国传统文化发扬传播。他的前见（偏见）是基于对于求仙悟道的中国古代道家哲学思想，因此对"神仙"的理解与翻译是准确的，即成为"immortals"。而作为文化输入国译者的霍氏的前见则基于其自身的文化背景和特定的读者群体，所以将这一意象归化为"信奉基督教的'信耶稣得永生'的信条，通过信奉基督教、拯救个体的灵魂（salvation）而获得的永生"。因此经霍译解释后的"成为神仙"的愿望就成了"拯救灵魂而获得永生"。可见，译者主观上进行文化过滤的结果是导致了有意识的误译，因为无论哪一位译者，都无可避免地受到各种主客观条件的制约，绝对忠实的译文是不可能的。因此杨译采用异化手段，尽可能保持原语中丰富的文化内涵，而霍译则基于归化原则，为了避免文化冲突而坚持其前见，即伽达默尔所描述的"合理的偏见"，因而导致了对"神仙"这一文化意象的两种截然不同的诠释，对全诗的主题的理解也与杨译大不相同。

在传教士译者郭实腊翻译的《聊斋志异》之《云萝公主》中，译者的文化过滤倾向也比较典型。

原文：一日安独坐，忽闻异香。俄一美婢奔入。曰："公主至。"即以长毡贴地，自门外直至榻前。方骇疑间，一女郎扶婢肩入；服色容光，映照四堵。

郭译：Whilst he was in this fretful mood, there came a splendid cavalcade, and a nymph-like virgin stood forward to inform him, that she was the princess.

郭实腊按照译者个人的理解和译文读者的接受能力，将中国传统文化中腾云驾雾、来去自如、青春永驻、美艳不可方物的仙女意象归化为西方文化中的 nymph。"Nymph"本指希腊、罗马神话中居于山林水泽的仙女，有时被译成精灵和仙女，是多位美貌少女的形象，热爱歌舞，无生老病死之忧。有人认为"nymph"居于山野林水滨、自由自在、窈窕貌美的意象与《楚辞·九歌·山鬼》中所描写的山鬼有相似之处，然而，从原文中的描述来看，云萝公主来无影去无踪，游于四海之外，与这一形象最接近的当属《庄子·逍遥游》中的姑射仙子："藐姑射之山，有神人居焉。肌肤若冰雪，绰约若处子。不食五谷，吸风饮露，乘云气，御飞龙，而游乎四海之外。"这是中国神话传说中的仙子的固有模式，与西方文化中的"nymph"虽有相似之处，但相异之处也颇多。

郭译将云萝公主所代表的中国传统文化中的"仙子"译作古

希腊神话中"nymph"的误译是有意误译，是译者主观性作用于对中国文化意象的解释过程的结果，是译者由于自身偏见而导致的文化过滤。

诠释哲学的理论也同样解释了为何翟理斯在翻译《聊斋志异》时删除了"异史氏曰"评论部分、删除和改写了《聊斋志异》中译者本人认为不能反映中国文学的纯洁性的部分情节。

在翟理斯翻译《聊斋》的时代，英国小说的主流叙事模式基本已经摈弃了18世纪时欧洲小说形成时期故事的叙述者在文本之前、之中和文末进行的插入式点评的模式。19世纪末，美国现实主义作家亨利·詹姆斯（Henry James）提出了"作者隐身"的主张，批判叙述者插入式评论以讨好读者的做法。因此，翟理斯基于这一历史视域，不可能与当时流行的叙事方式相悖，只能考虑到读者的期待视域，从而调整自己的翻译策略，舍弃了"异史氏曰"部分，遵从了英国小说的主流叙事模式，以期将自己的视域与读者的视域融合，从而使译本为更多的读者所接受。

在删除和改写《聊斋志异》中性爱与情色细节描写时，翟理斯同样受其所处的维多利亚时代的道德观的影响，对两性关系持严谨态度，秉持当时英国盛行的清教主义婚恋观，其已有的偏见是：保持中国文学的纯洁，宣扬《聊斋志异》故事中的道德教化作用。因此，译者对不符合这一时代特征、与主流道德取向相悖的故事内容进行了较大幅度的删除和改写。

翟理斯的初衷，即其翻译《聊斋志异》故事的偏见确是有其历史成因的，其翻译策略的选择，对原文内容的或增加或删改都有其存在的合理性。正如伽达默尔（2004）所阐述的，"人类总是身处传统之中，理解过程也被置于传统之中，因此理解者从自身的历史视域出发，将自身的视域带入到文本的视域当中，二者不断融合，从而产生了打上了传统印记的新的文本"。

正如文本的意义是开放的一样，视域也是一个不断形成、发展并与其他视域不断碰撞、交融的动态过程。"理解者和文本固然都有各自的视界，但理解并不是像传统解释学所要求的那样，抛弃自己的视界而置身于异己的视界，这是不可能的。理解一开始，理解者的视界就进入了它要理解的那个视界。"（张德让，2001：24）正因为如此，不仅早期的译者如郭实腊和翟理斯，当代的译者如霍克斯等汉学家在翻译中国古代名著时都采取了删除、改写、归化等策略，同时晚清和近现代诸多中国译者在翻译外国小说时也出现了大量的豪杰译、增删、归化等现象，如林纾、傅东华等人的译作。

以伽达默尔为代表的当代哲学诠释学派认为理解的过程从本质上讲是语言性的，"当我们涉及理解和解释文字性的文本时，语言媒介的解释本身表明理解总是将所说的东西转化为一个人自己的一部分"（伽达默尔，2004：398）。而翻译活动本身就涉及两种语言的转换，同时也是原语文化与译入语文化之间冲突、碰撞和逐渐融合的过程。伽达默尔（2004）认为历史性是人类存在的基本事实。作为历史的存在的人类具有特殊的历史局限性。无论是理解的主体或客体，都内嵌于历史之中。因此以下因素：理解者的历史局限性、由此产生的偏见、解释者最初的视域均有可能导致对原文的误读，伽达默尔将其称之为历史性误读。

2.4　误译的研究价值

英国人类学家爱德华·泰勒（Edward Burnett Tylor）在他所著的《原始文化》一书中，首次提出了文化的定义："文化是一种复杂的整体，其中包括知识、信仰、艺术、道德、法律、习俗以及人们作为社会成员而获得的一切能力和习惯。"（Tylor，2006：45）

中国文学名著中负载了大量的文化信息，这些文化信息借助于语言载体在译文中展现在目的语读者面前，使目的语读者感受到原语文化的独特魅力，从而了解其他国家和民族悠久的文化、历史、社会、风俗、价值观、道德取向、生活方式等诸多方面的信息。例如，西方读者通过阅读《西游记》的译文，感受佛教文化的博大精深和由神仙鬼怪的故事反映出的十六世纪中国的社会现实；通过阅读《水浒传》的译文，了解在异国的草莽英雄的豪气干云，兄弟情深和封建统治者对法外之徒的制裁和制衡以及市井生活全貌；《金瓶梅》的译文使西方读者看到一幅清晰而生动的市井人物与世俗风情画卷；通过阅读《聊斋志异》故事的译文，接触到一个来自神秘东方的书斋里编撰出来的奇幻世界，其中花妖树怪，狐仙鬼侣，情感丰富、情节离奇，人物无一不跃然纸上，使人眼界大开；通过阅读《红楼梦》译文，目的语读者可了解清代中国贵族家庭的兴衰、封建社会的爱情悲剧以及一幅十八世纪中国社会的广阔画卷。

然而，蕴含大量文化信息的中国文学名著也是翻译中的难点。著名翻译理论家苏姗·巴斯奈特（Susan Bassnett）（2004）作为文化翻译学派的领军人物曾说过："如同在做心脏手术时，人们不能忽视心脏以外的身体其他部分一样，我们在翻译时也不能冒险将翻译的言语内容和文化分开处理。"这一论述揭示了语言和文化的不可分。在翻译中，译者不仅要进行语言的转换，同时更要注意文化信息的传递；既要进行符号表层意义的转换，更要仔细研读并诠释每一种语言符号所包含的深刻的文化意蕴。

翻译是一项高度复杂的双语转换活动，同时也是文化冲突、碰撞和融合的过程。"译本对原作的忠实永远只是相对的，而不忠实才是绝对的。"（谢天振，2015）可见，误译是翻译中的客观事实。误读是误译现象的根源，斯坦纳（1975）曾断言：幸运的误读，往往是新的生命的源泉。误读引起的误译分为无意误译和有意误译，对前者研究的目的在于如何在翻译过程中摒除由于"疏忽大意、语言功底浅薄以及缺乏原语国家文化背景知识"（谢天振，2008）而产生的误译，而对有意误译的研究应从更高的视角考量，必须意识到：在忠实原则的指导下，误译虽然有其消极的一面，被看作正确翻译的对立面，但从文化交流的角度来看，对文化的有意误译却有其积极性、独特性和重要性。

纵观我国的翻译史，从中可见翻译家林纾和严复是有意误译的早期代表人物。

当时特定的历史时期的特征是：晚清时期的中国封建社会，由于列强的虎视眈眈和侵略，民族危机日益加深。林纾虽然以翻译爱情小说为开端，一生译著170余种，其中一流作品仅40余种，但林译不仅局限于情爱纠葛，他致力于推荐国外文学名著，更能将文学作品的翻译结合时事。他曾将哈葛德的作品

"Montezuma's Daughter"的标题改译为《英孝子火山报仇录》，突出"孝"字，因其是至圣孔子德育内容的全部精髓，被称为人生八德之首，林纾通过翻译作品来强调儒家的孝道和孝义，来激发国人报国雪耻的壮志。在国家和民族面临生死存亡的危难时刻，林纾大声疾呼，提醒国人要警惕西方列强的侵略本质。因此，他翻译外国小说，尽量选择"名人救世之言"，稍作渲染，以"求合于中国之可行者"（袁荻涌，1994），这是他有意误译的初心。

相比于不懂外语的林纾的"铺纸于几，边听边译"的快速翻译模式，严复在选材和翻译过程上大有不同，他选择了国外十九世纪哲学、社会科学的文本进行精心翻译，把西欧的启蒙思想——自由论、进化史观、文明论、整体论输入中国，把中国带入了"翻译时代"。以《天演论》为例，在翻译过程中他将原文做了改编，又加以发挥，提出了"国家将安所恃而有立与物竞之余?"的深刻问题以引起读者的思考。

在《天演论·译例言》中，严复就首先申明这是"达旨"式的翻译，意在"取便发挥"，而不仅仅在于"字比句次"。因此他"借赫胥黎的书为底本，向中国传播进化论的思想，为了达到翻译目的，他有意对全书加以取舍，改造，撰写大量按语，以补其不足，纠其不当，使一部宣传进化论的普及性书籍，成了当时维新变法的有力武器"（邓婕，2006）。

正是严复的《天演论》使中国人明白"落后就要挨打"的道理，加之当时国家面临危亡的状况，他借此向国人发出了"与天争胜、图强保种"的呐喊。于是随着《天演论》的风行，"物竞天择""优胜劣汰""适者生存"这些概念举国皆知。

林纾的翻译存在选择不精、误译错译漏译较多的缺陷；严复的翻译有目的地进行了选择、增删、加工、改造，例如在《天演论》中加入大量案语（据统计案语占了全书的 1/3 左右）。

二者的有意误译虽然各有差异，但目标却大体相近。林纾翻译的目的，是做"叫旦之鸡"，用西方文学唤醒国人以期开拓眼界；严复翻译的目的，虽有曲抒胸臆之意，但主要是借助西方先进思想来改变中国当时的状况。虽然被批为改译、编译、豪杰译，种种误译遭到诟病，但二人的翻译对后世产生了巨大的影响，翻译风格影响了一代人。

很多译者和读者将误译视为"劣译"，系一生之敌，不仅抨击诟病，且力图克服修正。然而，因疏忽大意和缺乏文化背景知识导致的无意误译固然必须消除，但有意的翻译策略导致的文化误译具有重要的研究价值。

"文化误译在特定的政治、历史、文化语境下，不但可以丰富目标语文化的艺术表现力，启发文学创新意识，使翻译与创作构成一种互动关系；同样也能丰富主体文化，使原文的生命得以延续，从而使译者的再创造成为可能。"（周晓寒，2009）

中西文化因其长期以来的历史传统而产生了种种差异，在文化交流过程中不可避免地会出现碰撞，因此在理解某一部作品时，会产生误读。根据诠释哲学的思想，译者首先是一名读者，在解读原文本的过程中，基于自身所处的历史文化语境、固有的意识形态、传统观念、生活习俗和心理结构，接触到原文文本时不可避免地将自己的理解的前结构引入到解读过程中，从解读到解释再到形成译文，解释了在这一过程中的误读的不可避免。

傅东华是小说 *Gone with the Wind* 翻译的第一人，其后该小说经历了多次重译，但傅译本的经典地位不可撼动。傅译本也是翻译界争议较多的版本。傅译对原著中大量景物和心理描写进行了整段甚至整章节的删除，同时，傅译最显著的特征是归化翻译策略。

原文：Seated with Stuart and Brent Tarleton in the cool shade of the porch of Tara, her father's plantation, that bright April afternoon of 1861, she made a pretty picture.

傅译：一八六一年四月一个晴朗的下午，郝思嘉小姐在陶乐垦植场的住宅，陪着汤家的那一对双胞胎兄弟——一个叫汤司徒，一个叫汤伯伦——坐在一个阴凉的走廊里。这时春意正浓，风景如绣，她也显得特别标致。

小说中的地名和人名均采用了归化的翻译策略，使读者感受到无处不在的中式环境，如陶乐垦植场；姓氏归化为中式，如汤家，郝家，名字也符合中式人名的特点，思嘉，媚兰，司徒和伯伦等等，如下表所示：

	原文	译名
地名	Tara	陶乐
	Georgia	肇嘉州
	Charleston	曹氏屯
	Jonesboro	钟氏坡
	Atlanta	饿狼陀
	Wilmington	卫民屯
	Fayetteville	万叶
	Macon	马岗
	Lovejoy	落迦畦
	Bull Run	雄牛道
	Rough and Ready	癫痫村

	原文	译名
	Maybelle	美白
	Pork	阿宝
	Scarlett O'Hara	郝思嘉
	Melanie Hamilton	韩媚兰
	Rhett Butler	白瑞德
人名	Ashely Wilkes	卫希礼
	Jeems	阿金
	Prissy	百利子
	Stuart Tarleton	汤伯伦
	Frank Kennedy	甘扶澜
	Charles Hamilton	韩察理
	Jonas Wilkerson	魏忠

之所以选择了归化，傅东华在《飘》译序中早有解释："因为译这样的书，与译 Classics 究竟两样，如果一定要字真句确地译，恐怕读起来反要沉闷。即如人名地名，我现在都把它们中国化了，无非要替读者省一点气力。对话方面也力求译得像中国话，有许多幽默的、尖刻的、下流的成语，都用我们自己的成语代替进去，以期阅读时可获如闻其声的效果。还有一些冗长的描写和心理的分析，觉得它跟情节的发展没有多大关系，并且要使读者厌倦的，那我就老实不客气地将它整段删节了……总之，我的目的是在求忠实于全书的趣味精神，不在求忠实于一枝一节。"（转引自罗新璋，1984：442）

为了顺应中国读者的传统文化观和理解接受能力，傅译对原文进行了较大幅度的改写，同时将原著中的人名和地点以及对话进行了归化处理，在翻译过程中从语言、文化、叙事结构等诸方面使译文本土化。傅译的目的很明确，即"以中国文化为归宿，对于妨碍信息交流的异质文化进行改造"（吴笛，2008：110）。傅译这一特点招致了一些翻译批评家们的诟病，有人斥之为"变形的翻译"，有人批评其所做的删改是"无端的删除"，更有甚者称其翻译为"讹译"。

但是傅译有其优势和亮点，在一定的历史时期有其存在的价值和意义。

出版时间	译本名	译者/编者	出版机构
1940	飘	傅东华	上海龙门联合书局
1943	乱世佳人	之江	成都译者书店
1945	风流云散（缩写本）	郑安娜	重庆美学出版社
1945	飘（缩写本）	杜沧白	重庆陪都书店
1979　1980 1985	飘（重印本）	傅东华	浙江人民出版社
1990	乱世佳人	陈良廷	上海译文出版社
1990	飘	戴侃、李野光、庄绎传	人民文学出版社
1991	乱世佳人	黄怀仁、朱攸若	浙江人民出版社
1995	飘	简宗	长春出版社
1995	飘	阿奕、广希	青海人民出版社
1998	飘	李美华	译林出版社
1998	飘	倪海虹	延边人民出版社
1999	飘	张佩玉	大众文艺出版社
2000	飘	马迎春	中国对外翻译出版公司

出版时间	译本名	译者/编者	出版机构
2000	飘	方正	北京燕山出版社
2000	飘	刘微	延边人民出版社
2002	飘	李献民	内蒙古人民出版社
2002	飘（插图本）	范纯海、夏旻	长江文艺出版社
2003	飘	蒋洪新	南方出版社
2003	飘	贾文浩、贾文渊、贾令仪	北京燕山出版社
2005	飘	石蕾	延边人民出版社
2006	飘（全译插图本）	陈辰	中国戏剧出版社
2007	飘	唐建党	广州出版社
2008	飘	张锦	中国国际广播出版社
2009	飘	水木	万卷出版公司
2011	飘	黄健人	中央编译出版社
2012	飘	姜春香	北方文艺出版社
2017	飘	朱攸若	春风文艺出版社
2018	飘	胡元斌	汕头大学出版社
2018	飘	赵永红	煤炭工业出版社
2023	飘	梅静	江苏凤凰文艺出版社

据不完全统计，迄今为止，*Gone with the Wind* 共有 30 种译文，译者（包括合作译者）共 36 人，其中小说译名沿用了傅译的《飘》的译本为 26 种，占全部译本的 86.7%。可见傅译本的影响力之大，从小说篇名的翻译即可见一斑。

Gone with the Wind 傅东华译本虽然长期以来备受争议，但他的开拓之功不可忽视。直至 20 世纪 80 年代末，傅译本始终为

广大读者所拥护并奉为经典。在 20 世纪 30—40 年代，译者为了促进东西方文化交流、推动社会进步，在西学东渐的潮流下，译者为提高译文与读者的期待视域的契合、扩大中国社会的读者群而采取了归化的翻译策略，明显具有文化误译的特征。这也正是伽达默尔所为之辩护和正名的"偏见"观作用于理解和解释过程的体现。傅译之"偏见"之产生，一是受上文所述的当时翻译主流思想的影响，二是考虑到读者的接受能力和理解的历史性的局限，三是译者本人在其再创造过程中深受中国传统小说的写作模式的影响而将重心放在了情节上，因而对原著中景物和心理的大段描写进行了删除。

从傅译《飘》所处的社会历史背景、文化语境、意识形态及其翻译目的出发，许多研究者对傅译进行了辩护。通过对傅译《飘》的重新审视和历史性解读，越来越多的人意识到了有意误译存在的历史客观性和必然性，也认可了文化误译对中西文化交流的促进作用。

陈可培（2011）认为，误译中的文化误译，有助于文化体系之间相互吸收、相互借鉴、不断丰富、不断发展。从译语的文化传统出发进行再创造，使译文在西方文化语境中广泛流传，获得新生。古今中外的翻译史证明，唯有"误译"才能使原作再生，只有从译语文化的角度出发，译者的创造性才能得以发挥。

第三章　明清小说误译研究

　　由于译者各自的宗教信仰、风俗习惯和其所处的自然环境的差异，他们往往会带着各自文化的思维定式在异质文化的交流中与原作者对话，在解读原作的过程中会与原作产生碰撞、冲突、拒斥、交融。因此，误读、误译在翻译实践中时有发生（王松亭等，2011），甚至不可避免。

　　跨文化翻译中存在大量的文化误译，其中一部分是因"译者对原文的语言内涵和文化背景缺乏足够的了解而造成的无意误译"（谢天振，1999：147），表现在翻译质量上，可见译文中译者或死译原文的文化信息，或无意识地呈现一种错误的变形的信息，是译者在翻译中必须注意消除的消极误译。而有意误译是"译者在正确解读原作意图前提下，倾向于目的语主体文化读者群的有意识地对原语文化信息进行加工改造的一种创造性翻译，是一种与原文相等，甚至高于原文的积极误译"（同上）。

　　译者发挥自身的积极性和创造性，对异质文化进行的过滤和改造，其结果就是有意的文化误译。翻译为了达到跨文化交流之目的，要求译者发挥其主体性，努力跨越文化障碍，对源文本中的异质文化进行过滤和改造，这就催生了大量的文化误译。

　　田建鑫（2023）指出：在解读原文的过程中，译者作为一手读者，对原文的意义和文化的传递起着决定性的作用。但是在期待视野的作用下，译者会有意无意地过滤原文的文化。有意文化误译是文化过滤的结果，是译者为了迎合读者的期待视野而采取的翻译手段。有意的文化误译在跨文化交流中的积极作用是毋庸置疑的。

谢天振（2016）认为："有意误译可以鲜明、生动地呈现出不同文化间的碰撞、扭曲与变形，反映出在接受外国文化中产生的误解与误释，所以误译作为翻译的一种特殊存在形式有其独特的研究价值。"

在此基础上，众多翻译研究者从不同视角切入，分析误译现象，并取得了一定的进展。对于造成误译的原因，文化、语言、译者身份和所采取的翻译策略等都是重要的影响因素，其中文化对误译的影响尤其明显。

广义的文化指人类在社会实践过程中所获得的物质、精神的生产能力和创造的物质、精神财富的总和。狭义的文化指精神生产能力和精神产品，包括一切社会意识形态：自然科学、技术科学和社会意识形态。

早在《周易》里，中国古人就有"观乎天文，以察时变；观乎人文，以化成天下"的说法。在英语等外文中，"文化"（Culture）一词来自拉丁文Colere，原意乃指人之能力的培养及训练，使之超乎单纯的自然状态之上。它的原始含义是"耕作"。

英国著名的人类学家泰勒认为："文化或文明，就其广泛的民族学意义来说，乃是包括知识、信仰、艺术、道德、法律、习俗和任何人作为一名社会成员而获得的能力和习惯在内的复杂整体。"人类学家马林诺夫斯基写道："我们发现文化含有两个主要成分——物质的和精神的。"不约而同地，在苏联哲学家罗森塔尔、尤金所编的《哲学小辞典》中，文化也是这样定义的："文化是人类在社会历史实践过程中创造的物质财富和精神财富的总和。"（闵家胤，2023：338）

对于文化的分类体系，按照不同的标准，则有着完全不同的划分方式。美国著名语言学家、翻译理论家尤金·奈达（Eugene A. Nida）（1964）将各类文化因素划分为五大类，包括社会文化（social culture）、物质文化（material culture）、语言文化（linguistic culture）、宗教文化（religious culture）和生态文化（ecological culture）。

王珺（2020）指出："文化负载词"最先在许国璋先生的 *Culturally Loaded Words and English Teaching* 一书中被提及。文化负载词有多种表达方式，如"文化词汇""文化专属词""文化限定词""国俗词语"等。

对于"文化负载词"的界定，不同的学者持有不同观点。

王德春（1990）认为，所谓文化负载词，是与我国的经济、文化、历史等相关的、具有民族文化特色的词语，即国俗语义层面的词语。胡文仲（1999）认为，文化负载词是特定文化范畴的词汇。它是民族文化在语言词汇中直接或间接的反映。包惠南等（2004）认为，文化负载词又可以称为"词汇空缺"，即原语词汇所承载的文化信息在译语中找不到对应词汇。廖七一（2004）认为，文化负载词是标志某种文化中特有事物的词、词组和习语。胡开宝（2006）认为，文化负载词又可以称为"文化限定词""文化局限词"，即受特定国家、特定民族的文化限制，如生活方式、风俗习惯、历史等而形成的词汇。这些词汇的形成与运用都与该特定国家、特定民族的文化有着紧密的关系，其是特定民族文化信息的承载，是特色文化意象的反映（转引自王燕，2020：124）。

　　本文将从奈达划分的五大类别的文化负载词的误译入手，详细分析有意误译现象，探究有意的文化误译在翻译研究中的意义以及有意误译在文化交流中的重要的研究价值，同时对误译成因进行研究探索，研究理解的历史性、因理解中的前见而产生的误读和误译，探讨译本中的文化过滤、文化误读以及译者的文化身份等要素，探索如何消除无意误译、合理利用有意的文化误译本身的积极因素，从而将古典文学名著原文中的大量丰富多彩的优秀中华文化有效地传播给目的语读者。本文致力于从数部明清小说英译本的误译研究中得出有益于文化传播的翻译策略，进而有利于推动中文经典作品向英语世界的译介和传播，从而更加有效地弘扬中华文化。

3.1　社会文化负载词的误译

　　文化负载词是特定文化意义的反映，是从属于某种文化范畴的词汇。文化负载词的翻译从本质上看是词汇文化意义的翻译。

　　王燕（2020）指出，文化负载词具有专有性、陌生性和不对等性等特质。英汉两种语言有着各自的表达习惯与传统，而文化负载词就是对特有国家、民族文化特色的传达，蕴含着深厚的文化底蕴。

　　社会文化负载词是与礼仪、娱乐名称相关的词汇。该类词汇有着独特的民族性，反映的是无形的事物。社会文化负载词中还包含有大量特色词汇，这类词汇本身具有很强的地域性和独特性，其文化意象很难在另一文化中找到对应物。即便找到类似的事物，其文化内涵也很难完全一致（王珺，2020：74）。

明清小说中大量的社会文化负载词的翻译既是传播中国文化过程中的重点，也是进行跨文化翻译的难点所在，此类词语翻译的成败也影响着译文的整体质量。

以下为社会文化负载词的误译案例。

3.1.1　称谓语的误译

《现代汉语词典》分别对称谓语和称呼语做出了解释，认为称谓语是"人们由于亲属和别的方面的相互关系，以及由于身份，职业等等而得来的名称"，而称呼语则是当面打招呼用的称谓语。汉语称谓语除了基本的指示功能之外，还可以表达社会地位的高低，人际关系亲疏，同时通过称谓语展示交际礼仪，具备重要的社会功能。"礼"是中华民族传统道德的基石，也是社会文化中非常重要的组成部分。

下文中，赛珍珠《水浒传》译本简称赛译，沙博理《水浒传》译本简称沙译，芮效卫《金瓶梅》译本简称芮译，杨宪益夫妇《聊斋志异》节译本和《红楼梦》全译本简称杨译，霍克斯《红楼梦》全译本简称为霍译，翟理斯的《聊斋志异》选译本简称翟译，郭实腊译文简称郭译，梅丹理和梅维恒的《聊斋志异》节译本简称梅译。

例1

原文："小人不材，愿献一计"。（《水浒传》第五十六回）

赛译： "This humble one has no skill，but I could try a plan."

对照：

原文：薛霸道："不敢动问大人高姓?"二人道："小人素不识尊官，何与我金子?"（《水浒传》第八回）

沙译："May I have your name，Sir?" queried Xue Ba.

"But we don't know Your Honor. Why should you give us gold?" they asked.

原文中讲话人自称"小人"，是旧时男子对辈分高于己者或官爵高于己之人自称的谦词。例如《左传·隐公元年》："小人有母，皆尝小人之食矣，未尝君之羹。"《三国志·蜀志·霍峻传》："小人头可得，城不可得。"

另有一种情况，系古时老师对学生的称呼。例如《孔子家语·观周》："孔子既读斯文也，顾谓弟子曰：小人识之，此言实而中，情而信。"

此词体现了对话双方的地位高低、特定语境和讲话人的社交礼仪，因此在翻译中需要凸显出其语用功能。《水浒传》原文中称谓语"小人"和"小的"出现频率颇高，据董琇（2009）统计，"小人"在原著中出现了 545 次，赛译中对应的"this humble one"出现了 151 次。其他译者如沙博理等，多数采用了第一人称来翻译谦称"小人"，而赛珍珠的译文却坚持了异化原则，力求突出原文涉及的时代特定的社会关系和人际交往中的礼仪原则。

赛珍珠在自传中提到：据她了解，中国的孩童自七八岁之后就要学习人际关系的准则，学习儒家倡导的"礼"的教义。中国学堂里的老师不仅传授知识，还会培养学生们如何做到举止得当，进退有礼。因此，赛珍珠致力于将中国文化的细节完整地反映在译文中，已达到文化传播的目的。这是赛珍珠翻译《水浒传》过程中的前见，也是其翻译策略的出发点。

因此，在上述译例中，即使人人皆知，"小人"在上下文语境中系谦虚甚至谦卑的自称，抑或只是出于特定历史时期的社交礼仪，当时民众自称为此，赛珍珠为了展示原语文化中的注重礼仪、强调社会地位的高低和尊卑有序，保留了原语特色，选择了异化策略，使得"This humble one"高频率出现，这种翻译策略与沙博理的翻译形成了鲜明对照。沙译对应原文中的讲话人为"二人"，将"小人"意译为"we"，简单明了，与目的语读者的期待视域相符合。

例 2

原文：如海道："天缘凑巧，因贱荆去世……"（《红楼梦》第三回）

杨译："What a lucky coincidence!" exclaimed Ju-hai. "Since my wife's death..."

霍译："It so happens that an opportunity of helping you has just presented itself", said Ru-hai. "Since my poor wife passed on..."

原文中林如海对自己夫人的谦称为"贱荆"，出自明屠隆《彩毫记·泛舟采石》："卑人贱荆，与庐山女道士李腾空有方外之约"。此类称谓还有"拙荆""拙妇""拙妻""荆妇""荆人""荆室""山荆"等。"拙荆"一词源自《列女传》中的记载，涉及"举案齐眉"这一典故。东汉隐士梁鸿的妻子孟光，一向居家简朴，用荆枝做发钗，以粗布做裙子。拙荆中的"拙"指说话者自己，"荆"指荆钗。拙荆即"我这个笨拙的人的妻子"，后来演变成丈夫在别人面前谦称自己的妻子。"拙荆"是一种比较谨慎和自谦的称呼，用来表示对自己和自己的妻子的低调和谨慎，力图在社交中表现出自身的谦逊有礼。黄庭坚有诗云："林中仆姑归，苦遭拙妇骂"，这此处"拙妇"是指说话人对自己妻子的谦称；又如《金瓶梅词话》第五十三回中"荆妇奄逝"，就是西门庆对自己的爱妾李瓶儿的谦称。

虽然这些称谓语的前置修饰词为"拙""贱"，或者中心词为"荆"（意"贫寒"），但在表达上主要是体现自谦和封建社会的礼仪，但有学者认为宋元明清时期，因规范夫妻关系的伦理日益苛严，男女有别、男尊女卑的伦理观念在老百姓的心中也愈发根深蒂固，这一时期，在指称妻子的称谓前加的语素大都是以贬低女性为目的，比"拙"更加谦卑的是"贱"一词，如上文中的"贱荆"和古典文学作品中频繁使用的"贱内"。"贱内"相对于"拙荆"，是一种更加谨慎和自谦的称呼："贱"为谦辞，旧称与自己有关的：贱姓、贱躯等。"贱"指说话者自己，"内"指内人。"贱内"即"我这个卑微之人的妻子"。贱内也有贱荆、拙荆、拙内等变体。

因此，从对妻子的称谓词的历史来看，古代人对妻子的称呼，有着不同的方式，表达不同的情感，也因语境不同而有较大差别。有些称呼是出于尊敬和礼貌，如"夫人"；有些称呼是出于亲切和爱慕，例如"娘子"；有些称呼是出于自谦，如"拙荆"；有些称呼是为了显示谨慎和自责，如"贱内"。这些形形色色的称呼，不仅反映了丰富的文化内涵，也反映了不同历史时期丰富的社会文化和严格的礼仪规范。

原书中林如海正面出场的次数寥寥无几，其中的重头戏便是与其女儿的家庭教师贾雨村商议起复之事。林如海与贾雨村的对话全文为：

"天缘凑巧，因贱荆去世，都中家岳母念及小女无人依傍教育，前已遣了男女船只来接，因小女未曾大痊，故未及行。此刻正思，向蒙训教之恩，未经酬报，遇此机会，岂有不尽心图报之理！但请放心，弟已预为筹划至此，已修下荐书一封，转托内兄务为周全协佐，方可稍尽弟之鄙诚。即有所费用之例，弟于内兄信中已注明白，亦不劳尊兄多虑矣。"

林如海是怎样的一个人呢？要从他的家庭出身说起。原文从贾雨村视角出发，概括其身世和社会地位："至兰台寺大夫，本贯姑苏人氏，今钦点出为巡盐御史，到任方一月有余。原来这林如海之祖，曾袭过列侯，今到如海，业经五世。起初时，只封袭三世，因当今隆恩盛德，远迈前代，额外加恩，至如海之父，又袭了一代；至如海，便从科第出身。虽系钟鼎之家，却亦是书香之族"。结合上文的林如海与贾雨村的谈话，林如海的形象和人品跃然纸上：谦恭厚道，既礼贤下士，又体贴周到，其人品贵重，不愧为钟鸣鼎食之家、书香门第出身的文人。

除了语言中的谦谦有礼，使用了"贱荆""弟""鄙"等谦辞外，整段语言偏书面语，多文言文，字里行间字斟句酌，谦逊有礼，符合其科举出身的官宦身份和较高的社会地位。杨译"贱荆"为"my wife"，直接忽略原词"贱荆"的丰富的历史文化内涵，试图直截了当揭示原文所指。作为母语文化译者的杨宪益考虑到英语读者的理解接受能力而采取了归化策略，省略了对中国称谓语文化的解释，毕竟其内涵较为复杂，对于译者来说，三言两语的注释难以解释清楚，因此杨译进行了简化处理。

而霍译"my poor wife"更贴近原文的谦卑称谓和说话人所展示的社交礼仪。但霍译将"贱"译为"poor"，通过直译与原文对等，通过其创造性的理解，将修饰词转嫁到 wife 一词上，属于文化误译范畴。这种误读和误译是建立在译者自身的情感、意志、审美等文学和创作能力基础之上的（即诠释学所谓的前见），译者在解读原文本的时候，动态地调整自己的期待视野，与原作达成视域融合，"从而使原作的血脉在译本中得到继承，让异域文本在新的文化中获得再生"（周晓寒，2009）。

由此可见，在翻译实践中，由于译者固有的前见导致的文化误译既可以丰富主体文化，另一方面又能又能够发挥译者的再创造，使译文的可读性提升，满足目的语读者的需求。

3.1.2 官职称谓的误译

中国古代的官僚制度历史悠久，可以追溯到商代。不过，真正的官僚制度是从秦朝开始的，它贯穿了中国两千多年的历史。中国古代官僚制度为中国古代的社会治理、文化传承和社会发展奠定了坚实基础，在政治、文化、社会等各个领域都产生了重要影响。

鉴于我国悠久的官僚制度历史，官职文化成为社会文化的重要组成部分。在远古时期，并没有官职的具体设置和称谓，据史料记载，人类社会进入了阶级社会之后才出现官职的设置。"中国的官制有其特殊性，中国的官职称谓也有其特殊性"（卢红梅，2008：22），因此在跨文化翻译中，官职称谓作为社会文化的有机组成部分，其解读和翻译也相当重要。

例 3

原文：人只知道一个兄弟做了<u>都头</u>（《金瓶梅词话》第一回）

芮译：All anybody knows is that you've got a younger brother who's been made a <u>captain</u>.

例 4

原文："西门庆偷娶潘金莲武<u>都头</u>误打李皂隶"（《金瓶梅词话》第九回）

芮译："His-men Ch'ing Conspires To Marry P'an Chin-Lien; <u>Captain</u> Wu Mistakenly Assaults Li Wai-Ch'uan"

两例中涉及"都头"这一官职。都头首先指古代军职名。唐中期为诸军统帅之称，后为一部军队为一都的长官之称。唐僖宗时，当权宦官募神策新军五十四都，各都长官称都将，亦称都头。宋各军指挥使下设此官，属低级军官。五代时，都的编制依然流行。北宋在指挥之下设都的编制，显然也是袭用五代旧制。都一级统兵官，马兵是军使和副兵马使，步兵是都头和副都头，在副兵马使和副都头之下，尚有军头、十将、将虞候、承局和押官。参考《嘉定赤城志》卷十八，台州雄节第六指挥编额五百人，除指挥使和副指挥使各一人外，另设都头三人、副都头五人，十将、将虞候、承局和押官各十人。威果第六十指挥编额四百人，也设十将、将虞候、承局和押官各十人。这两指挥禁兵都不设军头（百度百科）。

然而在《水浒传》小说中，都头显然系旧时衙役、捕快头目的官职名。

例如在下列文学作品中，出现的"都头"均为此类官职：

本县差下这两个都头，每日来勾取。管定了我们，不得转动。（明·施耐庵《水浒传》）

千里神交无一面，若见都头意自倾。（明·沈璟《义侠记·征途》）

这陶三爷是历城县里的都头，在本县红得了不得。（清·刘鹗《老残游记》）

如指军队中的官职，管辖百人的都头算是低微武官。在武松的这个时期，都头其实是一个军事头衔，职位低于指挥使。在县一级里面，负责抓捕工作的衙役，大概有十几人，分两班。而都头其实是人们对于抓捕衙役的统称，也是一种对衙役的敬称。都头如果放在现在的编制里面，应等同于县一级的刑警队队长。这个官职相对于其他的官职来说比较小，是基础官职中的一种，但是实权还是不小的。比他官小的鲁智深，在原著里都可以在大街上横着走，宋江的押司职位也在都头之下。《水浒传》原著中，除了行者武松是阳谷县都头之外，美髯公朱仝是郓城县马兵都头，插翅虎雷横是郓城县步兵都头，青眼虎李云是沂水县都头。

在了解"都头"的历史文化背景知识的基础上，我们就能分析译者对这一社会文化负载词的翻译是准确达意或者是文化误译。芮效卫将此词译为"captain"，很明显采取了归化的策略。根据柯林斯英汉双解大词典，"captain"指（陆军、海军及其他军种）上尉、（体育运动队）队长、船长、机长、警察局副巡官；消防中队长、率队；指挥等。因此译者选择了既指代军队中的官职又指警察局复训官这一职位的 captain 一词，在目的语中找到了原文等效的替代，并没有僵化地全面遵循芮效卫翻译《金瓶梅》的动机"完整再现原书的思想和艺术成就，主要包括创新性修辞手法与互文性叙事特征等复杂信息，以向英语读者全面展示《金瓶梅》的异国风味"（张义宏，2017），并没有将归化与异化切割开来，而是以异化策略为主，将二者相辅相成，互相调和，更好地实现文化的有效传播，为读者所接受。

译者这种有意的文化误译在例 4 的另外一个官职名称的翻译中也有体现。

李皂隶为何在芮译中变成了 "Li Wai-Ch'uan"，译者并没有解释皂隶这一官职的含义呢？

原著是这样提及此人的：

"那武二迳奔到狮子街桥下酒楼前来。且说西门庆正和县中一个皂隶李外传在楼上吃酒。原来那李外传专一在府县前绰揽些公事，往来听气儿赚些钱使。若有两家告状的，他便卖串儿；或是官吏打点，他便两下里打背。因此县中就起了他这个诨名，叫做李外传。"

"皂隶"，古代称之为贱役。古代有"倡优皂卒"四大贱业之说，"倡"就是娼妓，"优"则是戏子，"皂"是皂隶，后专以称旧衙门里的差役。例如《左传·隐公五年》："若夫山林川泽之实，器用之资，皂隶之事，官司之守，非君所及也。"《儒林外史》第八回："皂隶若取那轻的，就知他得了钱了。"

皂隶是替官府衙门跑腿办事的勤杂人员，这些勤杂人员和现在的工勤人员还不一样，手上还是掌握着一点行政权力的。其职责广泛，包括但不限于站堂、缉捕、拘提、催差、征粮、解押等事务。据明制，县署衙役服皂色盘领衫。在京剧中，皂隶着青色布衣、交领、窄袖长袍，下打密褶，腰间系束红布织带。地位更低的，穿青衣外罩一件红布马甲，腰系青丝带。

这种装束不仅是为了识别，也象征着他们在官府中的地位和角色。皂隶的工作性质决定了他们需要执行各种任务，从简单的文书工作到复杂的执法活动，都是皂隶职责的一部分。宋代延续了明制，因此可见《水浒传》中皂隶是低等衙役，没有官方身份，说起来只是官府的奴隶，老百姓尊敬一点称为"公差"。

芮译的一大特点是：译者本人"是《金瓶梅》英译者中汉语水平和汉语文化素养较高的译者，加之对原著的独到认识，使其在翻译过程中表现出对原著的极大尊重，在翻译过程中对原著亦步亦趋，唯恐遗漏任何信息"（张义宏，2017）。因此译者对"皂隶"一词必定经过了研究和考证，不会有意去掉该词选择不译，何况译者还能瞻前顾后，联系到李皂隶的外号进行了翻译。因此可以推断，鉴于此词的文化内涵和悠久历史，译者不仅很难在目的语文化中找到可以对应的词语，甚至解释起来也颇费笔墨，何况李皂隶在全文中完全是一个无足轻重的角色，无非等于一名NPC而已，因此芮效卫舍弃了这一词语的修饰意义，根据上下文的语境，直接译出此人的诨名，即外号，李外传。可见译者在有意误译中的主动性和操控能力，在遇到文化难点时，译者可以根据读者的需求和译者自身的审时度势，发挥主体性，或采取归化，或异化，或直译，或意译，或索性不译。

例 5

原文：六卿来，倒屣而迎；侍郎辈，揖与语……（《聊斋志异·续黄粱》）

翟译：When Privy Councilors came to see him, he would rush out in haste to receive them; when Under-Secretaries of State visited him, he made them a polite bow.

梅译：If one of the <u>six high ministers</u> came, Zeng would rise to greet them that he could barely put his slippers on straight; to <u>vice ministers</u> he bowed with folded hands and made conversation.

《续黄粱》是蒲松龄在唐代传奇《枕中记》的基础上创作的一则传奇故事，其主人公在梦中入仕为官，经历了宦海沉浮，因此篇中涉及较多的官职称谓。其中的"六卿"在中国古代曾指统军执政的官吏，后来演变为吏部、礼部、户部、兵部、刑部、工部尚书的总称。而"侍郎"这一官职名也有着悠久的历史，在秦汉时期指宫廷的近侍，至明清时期辅佐尚书，相当于现代政府各部的副部长。

翟理斯将"六卿"译作"Privy Councilors"，此词在西方国家专用来指君主制国家中为国家大事提供建议的"枢密院委员"或"枢密院顾问"，这一职位在 20 世纪后的许多西方国家已经废止。同时翟译又将"侍郎"译为"Under-Secretaries of State"，即美国的"副国务卿"。美国的国务卿一职始于 1789 年，职位相当于外交部长。这一职位在英国由女王任命，作为内阁成员对首相负责，相当于部长级。而梅氏直接译作现代英美国家常用的 minister 和 vice minister（部长和副部长）两种职位，同样是使用归化手段来处理中国古代文化中的官职名称。

由于翟理斯和梅氏兄弟翻译《聊斋志异》所处的历史时期不同，梅氏比翟理斯晚了一百年，其间官职名称的含义和指向发生了变化，而两种译文则反映了时代的变迁及译者翻译过程中体现出的历史性。梅氏与翟理斯没有采取音译这两种官职并加注解释从而将独特的异国文化传播给本国读者，而是直接选择使用其母语文化中的相近的官职代替，这种有意误译的产生是由译者所代表的文化决定的，译者受到母语文化的影响和制约，带有固定的前见，使其在自身的文化框架下对原文本展开思考和解读，其解释的结果——译本就具有明显的译者的主观选择的特征。

例 6

原文："这李氏亦系金陵名宦之女，父名李守中，曾为<u>国子监祭酒</u>"（《红楼梦》第四回）

杨译：Her father, Li Shouzhong, a notable of Jinling, had served as a <u>Libationer in the Imperial College</u>.

霍译：Li Wan was the daughter of a distinguished Nanking official. Her father, Li Shou-zhong, had been a <u>Director of Education</u>.

其中"国子监祭酒"为官职名称，所涉及的国子监是国立教育机构，宋初承五代后周之制，设国子监，招收七品以上官员子弟为学生。端拱二年（989）改国子监为国子学，淳化五年（994）依旧为监。庆历四年（1044）建太学前，国子监系宋朝最高学府。自设太学和其他各类学校后，国子监成为掌管全国学校的总机构。明初设中都国子学，后改为国子监，掌国学诸生训导的政令。明成祖永乐元年（1403），在北京设国子监，皆置祭酒（校长）从四品、司业（副校长）正六品、监丞正八品、典簿从八品各一员。清代国子监总管全国各类官学（宗学、觉罗学等除外），设管理监事大臣一员；祭酒，满、汉各一员；司业，满、蒙、汉各一员。另设监丞、博士、典簿、典籍等学官。光绪三十三年（1907），并归学部（百度百科）。

国子监祭酒是国子监的最高领导人，官职品级是从三品，有人认为此职位相当于如今的教育部考试中心主任兼高等教育司长（司局级）。也有人考证后认为：国子监就是以前的中央大学，又称"太学""国学"。国子监曾是个清高的学府，国子监祭酒就是主掌大学之法与教学考试的官员。清代翁同龢、陆润庠、王垿等都任过祭酒。

杨译将此词译为"Libationer"并加了限定和解释"in the Imperial College"，字面意思是"国学里的祭酒"，既突出了国子监的文化内涵（皇家大学），也点名了李守忠的地位为"祭酒"。然而"Libationer"的词意在牛津词典中是"one who pours out libations（to a god）"，指在宗教仪式中将酒泼洒在地祭献给所信奉的神的人。这一词意与中文的"祭酒"早期的词意是等同的：祭酒原意指古代飨宴时酹酒祭神的长者，后亦以泛称年长或位尊者。汉代有博士祭酒为博士之首。可见杨译在此处采取了归化和异化相结合的方法，既用归化策略解释了国子监的意义，又通过异化展示了"祭酒"这一官职特定的含义。

与杨译相反，霍译明显采用了归化方法，将"国子监祭酒"一职译为"Director of Education"，在目的语中找到了与原文功能对等的词语，对目的语读者来说，意义直截了当，不需费神去思考猜测，但在传播异域文化的功效上，明显不若异化策略有效。

霍克斯在翻译时，由于中西文化的巨大差异，多采取了归化的翻译策略，这种跨文化的解读方式不可避免地会带来误读和误译，他的译文"尽管在某些方面出现了误译，却也展现了中西文化交流的复杂性和丰富性。这些误译并非全然是负面的，它们在一定程度上反映了译者对原文的深刻理解，以及他在尝试将这部作品融入西方文化语境时所作的努力"（孟天伦，2024：118）。

3.1.3　职业名称的误译

明清时期，随着封建社会经济和文化不断发展，涌现出了各行各业，这些职业反映了当时社会的多样性和复杂性。明清时期的职业种类繁多，涵盖了农业、手工艺、教育、官员、商业、服务业等多个领域。从"三教九流""五行八作"这些成语中可以看到职业种类的繁多和社会地位的高低之分。

例 7

原文：连酒保王鸾，并两个粉头包氏、牛氏都拴了，竟投县衙里来。（《金瓶梅词话》第九回）

芮译：The proprietor of the tavern, Wang Luan, and the two singing girls, whose surnames were Pao and Niu, were also taken into custody, after which they all proceeded to the yamen to appear before the district magistrate.

首先探讨的是"酒保"这一职业。"酒保"旧为酒店里或客栈跑腿人员的称呼，也称"店小二"，主要是负责招呼客人，为客人端茶倒水。《汉书·栾布传》中这样写道："穷困，卖庸（佣）于齐，为酒家保。"颜师古注："谓庸作受顾也。为保，谓保可任使。"

"粉头"是古代对妓女的一种称谓。明清小说中专指妓女；例如在关汉卿的《金线池》第二折中："如今又缠上一个粉头，道强似我的多哩。"又如在《警世通言卷二四：玉堂春落难逢夫》中："他家里还有一个粉头，排行三姐，号玉堂春，有十二分颜色"。因此，此处西门庆和李皂隶饮酒取乐时，如只提及"唱曲儿的"，那么可以是指歌女，卖艺不卖身，但"两个唱的粉头"是指会唱小曲助兴的妓女。

在原著中，酒保和两个唱曲儿的"粉头"亲眼看见武松误打李外传致人死亡，被官府传唤到衙门里作证。这两个特殊的职业名称颇有中国文化内涵。酒保虽然在现代也指类似工作的从业者，可以译为"bar tender, barkeeper"，但是在中国文化中，其地位不高，类似杂役，比店小二多了一些职责，例如为客人奉酒。芮译为"the proprietor of the tavern"，是明显的文化误译，而将"粉头"译为"singing girls"，也属有意误译。

在英语中，"妓女"一词可译为：prostitute, harlot, whore, hooker, street girl, streetwalker, sporting lady 等，采用 lady 和 girls 作为中心词更加委婉，适合在文学作品中做书面语使用。译者没有将二人的妓女职业译出来，只是直译了"唱曲的"，于是译文就成了"singing girls"。那么这二位究竟以何为业，要靠读者自己去领悟了。

因此，在处理文化负载词的时候，译者出于某种目的，选择了某种词意的同时摒弃了另一种词意，既能忠实于原文，又可以赋予译文新的审美价值。

从上例可见，芮译的主要特征是异化策略和直译的方法。他尽可能地以原语文化为中心，最大化地将原语语言和文化信息移植到译入语中，目的在于促进原语文化在目的语国家的传播。芮效卫翻译的初衷和固有的前见就是忠实地传递原著中的文化。正如胡令毅（2014）所总结的："芮氏译本是一种严谨的学者型翻译。芮先生奉行'无字不译'的原则，极注重忠实于原作。为了忠实，即便译文略嫌'拗口'也在所不惜。其译文既通俗可读，又富于文学韵味，且又能在形式上亦步亦趋，尽可能保留原作的风貌。"

例8

原文：那个贾琏，只离了凤姐便要寻事，独寝了两夜，便十分难熬，便暂将小厮们内有清俊的选来出火。（《红楼梦》第二十一回）

杨译：Jia Lian was the sort of man who once away from his wife was bound to get into mischief. Two nights alone were more than he could bear: he vented his ardour on his handsome page boys.

霍译：Jia Lian was the sort of man who will begin getting up to mischief the moment he takes leave of his wife. After only a couple of nights sleeping on his own he began to find abstinence extremely irksome and was reduced to slaking his fires on the more presentable of his pages.

原文：金莲道："我知小厮去接，那院里有你魂儿？罢么，贼负心，你还哄我哩！"（《金瓶梅词话》第十六回）

芮译："The page boy went to fetch you all right," said Chin-lien, "but I doubt if any part of the licensed quarter saw so much as your ghost. So much for that! You lousy two-timer, you still think you can fool me do you?"

在上述两部作品中，"小厮"一词出现频率较高。《金瓶梅词话》中的"小斯"通《红楼梦》里的"小厮"，从明代到清朝，这一词汇的变化可见汉语言的发展史中，汉字的演变过程。

三位译者中，两位将其译为"page boy"（担任侍从的男孩），另一位译者译为"page"（青年侍从），词意差别不大。

　　然而，在中国文化中，"小厮"一词文化内涵异常丰富，涉及中国历史上同性文化的发展史。

　　小厮分很多种，有书童，有伴当，有长随。一般来说年纪小的兼具书童和伴当。如果其男主人是读书人，那么他的小厮就是书童。以《红楼梦》为例，贾宝玉虽然不喜读书，但是必须进家塾就读，因此他的小厮茗烟等人就是书童。贾琏不读书，他的小厮兴儿等人就是伴当。《金瓶梅词话》中的西门庆集地痞、恶霸、淫棍、奸商于一身，与读书无半点关系，也有两个小厮，充当的就是伴当、跑腿以及娈童。书童、清俊的小厮、娈童这几个词体现出明清时代社会的风气，以及男风的蔚然盛行。

　　娈童也称裔宠，意为与男人发生性行为的男童和少年，"娈"字本意形容美好，部首为"女"，即"相貌美丽的女子"。娈字与童搭配，意指被达官贵人玩弄的美少年。娈童之风，远在魏晋南北朝之前就已大盛于世。魏晋到唐朝，娈童之风起起落落。到了宋代，娈童之风再兴。蒙元时虽又衰落，但明清则再度大行于世。尤其清代娈童风大盛，达官贵人豢养男童之风一直延续到民国初年。娈童甚至成为一种文人雅好（百度百科）。

　　因此，根据这一文化背景，贾琏用来发泄性欲的小厮和西门庆家的小厮，其职能绝非只是 page boy（担任侍从的男孩子），其内涵远远大于表面的工作范畴。因此在例 8 中，两位译者均通过准确翻译"出火"这一性文化负载词从而揭示了"小厮"一词丰富的文化内涵。杨译使用了"vent his ardour"，霍译"slake his fires"，比较隐晦地揭示了男主人与地位等同于娈童的小厮之间的性关系。译者对原文、原作者的意图和读者的期待值进行综合研判和考量后，对原语文化负载词进行了解读，并结合了上下文语境给出了正确达意的翻译，完美地解释了"小厮"和"出火"这一组涉及中国古代文化中"男风"的特殊社会现象。

例 9

原文：王婆道："只有一件事最要紧，地方上<u>团头</u>何九叔，他是个精细的人，只怕他看出破绽，不肯殓。"（《水浒传》第二十五回）

赛译：Then the old woman Wang said, "There is only one important thing. There is that one surnamed Ho on this street <u>who attends to the dead</u> and he is a clever man, and it is only to be feared that he will see that there is something amiss with the dead man's look and will not put him into his coffin."

原文中的语境为：潘金莲在王婆的助力下毒杀武大郎后，王担心验尸时被仵作看出破绽，因此提醒西门庆，提前应对后续的仵作验尸一事。此处何九叔的职业名称为"团头"，根据词典释意，宋朝各行业都有市肆，叫作团行。行有行老、团有团头，是各自行业的首领。但是，在成书时间约在 1500—1530 年间的《水浒传》中，潘金莲药鸩武大郎的故事中职业名为"团头"的何九叔到了成书时间约半个世纪后的《金瓶梅》中，却直接变成了"仵作"一词。

例 10

原文：有那多口的说："卖梨的郓哥儿与仵作何九二人，最知详细。"（《金瓶梅词话》第九回）

芮译：A certain busybody also told him, "That Yun-ko who sells pears and Ho the Ninth, <u>the coroner's assistant</u>, are two people who know a good deal about it."

可见何九叔的职业名称团头即是指仵作。他们的职责是负责非正常死亡尸首的检验，类似于现代的法医。芮译采取了归化译法，用 the coroner's assistant 来界定何九叔的职业身份，但芮译强调他是验尸官的助手助理。

百度百科解释：仵作，又称伍作、仵作行人、行人、行首、团头、屠行，首见于五代王仁裕《玉堂闲话》。"伍作"，宋初《疑狱集》最早写定为"仵作行人"。"仵作，验尸之男役"；"仵作——旧时官署检验尸体者，今称检验员；旧时官署中检验死伤的吏役；官署检查刑伤之吏，宋已有之，见《折狱龟鉴》，清改称检验吏；仵作，以检验尸伤、代人殓葬为业的人；旧时官署检验死伤之吏，称仵作，犹今之检验员"；"担任活人与死者的中介者之含意"。"仵字从人从午，故万物至午则中正也；又午位属火，火明破诸幽暗，所以仵作名中人也"。"仵"字本身带有"逆"、违背常理世俗的成分，用其命名的职业其社会评价可见一斑。

原著中的何九叔是一个圆滑通透之人，在社会上想来也是长袖善舞，至少谁也不得罪，明哲保身。为了不惹恶霸西门庆怀疑，他看到武大郎中毒迹象的尸体后假装恶疾突发晕倒在验尸现场；周围闲人散去后，他安慰其妻："你不要烦恼，我自没事。却才去武大家入殓，到得他巷口，迎见县前开药铺的西门庆，请我去吃了一席酒，把十两银子与我，说道：'所殓的尸首，凡事遮盖则个。'我到武大家，见他的老婆是个不良的人，我心里有八九分疑忌。到那里揭起千秋看时，见武大面皮紫黑，七窍内津津出血，唇口上微露齿痕，定是中毒身死。我本待声张起来，却怕他没人做主，恶了西门庆，却不是去撩蜂剔蝎？待要胡卢提入了棺殓了，武大有个兄弟，便是前日景阳冈上打虎的武都头。他是个杀人不眨眼的男子，倘或早晚归来，此事必然要发。"

何九叔在看清事实和审时度势后，既忌惮凶狠狡诈的西门庆，又清醒地预判到，比西门庆更凶猛的打虎英雄武松早晚知道真相，待东窗事发，他必定牵涉其中，恐有性命之忧。然而后续的情节也是世情小说中的精华部分了，因为比何九叔更厉害的角色竟然是他老婆。她的对策绝对是又狠又准又专业。她建议何九叔到火化入殓之日，悄悄捡回两块武大郎的骨头，和西门庆的十两银子一起收好，待武松找上门时作为证据，可保一家老小性命。难怪何九叔大赞"家有贤妻，见得极明"。

"那何九叔将骨头归到家中，把幅纸都写了年月日期，送丧的人名字，和这银子一处包了，做一个布袋儿盛着，放在房里。"正是因为何九叔这位专业法医保存的全面的证据，才有了后来武松杀嫂、斗杀西门庆，发配孟州城，醉打蒋门神，大闹飞云浦，血溅鸳鸯楼等一系列惊世骇俗的复仇故事。

可见，原著中团头/仵作这一角色在推动故事情节中的重要作用。在赛珍珠的译本中，"团头"的翻译采用了解释的方法，译为"who attends to the dead"（照料死者的人，处理尸体的人）。此处令人费解的是，"验尸官"一词在英文中为"coroner"，"法医"为"forensic doctor"或"medical examiner"，为何赛珍珠宁愿用定语从句去模糊地界定并解释这一职业也不愿采用英文中固有的词汇来形成对等的翻译呢？

林语堂对很多评论家诟病的赛珍珠的《水浒传》英译本的评价是：赛译对小说中所包含的宋代的土话、俗语、行话和江湖黑话的翻译比较准确。

赛珍珠没有使用英语中已有的验尸官和法医等目的语的专门术语来解释原文中的"团头/仵作"是符合她本人的翻译动机和目的的。

"每一个翻译行为都有一个既定目的，并且要尽一切可能实现这一目的。"（范祥涛、刘全福，2002：26）赛珍珠翻译《水浒传》的目的和初心在于"实现其汇通中西的文化和合主义理想，其所选择的翻译策略必定为此目的服务"（钟再强，2018：106）。因而在翻译《水浒传》的过程中，赛珍珠在选择翻译策略的时候，一是尽可能把原作的"原汁原味"传递给读者，二是要迎合读者的认知和接受能力。在保持"原汁原味"这一点上，赛译大部分情况下进行了异化和直译，然而，为了符合到她所期望的读者的接受度，赛珍珠也会采用异化归化有机结合、互为补充的翻译策略。

正如赛珍珠在其自传中，谈及选择了《四海之内皆兄弟》为书名时的心态："中文原名（水浒）尽管在汉语中含义非常明显，翻成英文却毫无意义。"因此，无论是原文中的"团头"还是仵作，尽管在汉语中历史悠久，文化内涵丰富，翻译成英文后对西方读者意义不大。何况"团头"一词在目的语中根本无法找到其"原汁原味"的代替。如果采取归化策略翻译此词，代之以"法医""验尸官"等功能对等的名词，必然失去了小说中的特殊朝代的特殊职业名词的悠远之韵味。

在赛珍珠（1948）的译序中，她为自己的直译的翻译方法如是解释："我的兴趣只在于原作这样一部以卓越的方式写就的卓越的故事。我尽可能地直译，因为对我而言，中国句式才是完全契合这个故事的描述方式，我所有的努力都只在于使译作能够尽可能地接近原著风格。因为我想要让那些不了解中国语言的读者至少能有一种阅读原著的感觉。"这也正是有意文化误译的目的和研究价值所在。

3.1.4　风俗习惯文化负载词的误译

中国古代风俗习惯文化是中国传统文化的重要组成部分，涵盖了广泛的生活和节日习俗，体现了中华民族的独特生活方式和价值观。中国古代风俗习惯文化主要包括以下几个方面：节日习俗、婚姻习俗、饮食习俗、礼仪文化等方面。通过这些风俗习惯，我们可以看到中国古代社会的生活方式、价值观念以及文化的传承和发展。

例 11

原文：以书示英，请问"致聘何所"。英辞不受采。又以故居陋，欲使就南第居，若赘焉。马不可，择日行亲迎礼。（《聊斋志异·黄英》）

杨译：He showed this letter to Yellow Flower and asked, "Where shall I send wedding gifts?" But she refused to accept any gifts and because Ma's own house was shabby she urged him to move into hers. This he would not do, however. So they chose an auspicious date and were duly married.

梅译：He asked, "Where should I send the betrothal gift?" Yellow-Bloom would not accept his gift. Due to the rundown condition of his dwelling, she wanted him to live in the south house, as if he were marrying into her family. He refused and chose a suitable day to perform the bride-welcoming ceremony.

　　《聊斋志异》原文中涉及了中国古代的婚嫁习俗，包括下聘、择吉迎娶和入赘等文化负载词语。聘礼多指订婚时男方给女家的财礼，因此作为母语文化译者的杨宪益绝无可能产生误读，将"致聘"译为"send wedding gift"，此举是杨氏夫妇考虑到英语读者的理解接受能力而采取的归化策略的结果，省略了对中国传统婚俗文化的解释，因其程序较为复杂，共需行"六礼"才能完成，其中包括纳采（下聘礼）、问名、纳吉、纳征、请期、迎亲六个环节，对于译者来说，三言两语的注释难以解释清楚明了，因此杨译进行了简化处理。

　　较之于杨译的归化翻译，梅译更为忠实，将"致聘"译为"send betrothal gift"，即"送订婚礼物"，符合中国传统文化中的婚嫁风俗。

　　再看对"入赘"一词的翻译，杨译意译为"urged him to move into hers"（要求男方搬到女方家居住），没有将中国婚嫁文化中特殊的"入赘婚姻"的文化信息传递给西方读者，是一种简化的翻译方法。毕竟"入赘"涉及的不仅仅是男女缔结婚约、婚后男方搬到女家生活的简单形式，而是涉及更深层的文化背景和复杂的家族观念，因为在中国传统文化中，入赘婚姻多是由于女家没有男性继承人，为了传宗接代的目的而招上门女婿的特殊婚俗。为了延续女家的香火，男方到女方家之后要随女家的姓氏，所生子女也要冠以女方的姓氏，因此"入赘"经常被耻笑为"倒插门"，甚至用来讥讽男方"小子无能更姓改名"等等。考虑到这一复杂的文化背景，杨译选择了放弃了对这一文化负载词的深入阐述，没有以解释加注等形式进行译介，是译者基于原文复杂的文化历史背景所构成的视域相对于西方读者对于中国文化的接受视域可能产生较大的文化障碍从而影响对整个文本的理解而进行的选择。梅译采取了折中的译法，将之译为男方"marrying into her family"（男方嫁入女家），但是也没有将中国社会文化中的特殊的"招赘"这一风俗准确传递给西方读者。

例 12

（香菱）竟给薛大傻子作了屋里人，开了脸，越发出挑得标致了。（《红楼梦》第十六回）

杨译：Since he made her his concubine and <u>her face has been slicked</u> she's grown even lovelier. She's too good for that silly foll.

霍译：She's finally been given as "chamber-wife" to that idiot Xue. Now that <u>she has been plucked and painted like a grow-up woman</u> she really does look most attractive.

原文中提及了婚嫁文化习俗中的特殊仪式"开脸"。在中国民间婚俗中，女子在出嫁之前，必须要经历一辈子唯一一次的"开脸"。那么何为"开脸"？

"左弹一线生贵子，右弹一线产娇男，一边三线弹得稳，小姐胎胎产麒麟。眉毛扯得弯月样，状元榜眼探花郎。""开脸"的民俗也称"绞面"。古代女子出嫁之时，会邀请"绞面师"（一位相貌标致且多子女的妇人，有些地方则是由子孙满堂、人缘好、德高寿高的老年妇女）来为新娘绞面，把新娘额前、鬓角的汗毛拔掉，意为让新娘别开生面，祝愿她婚姻幸福美满（网络资料）。

整个开脸的过程，有一系列严格的规矩和作业流程。首先是坐向，"开脸"必须是坐南朝北或坐北朝南，大忌东西坐向，并且要选择在隐秘的闺房。先给新娘脸上扑上一层香粉，再用热毛巾捂一会，然后用红色的双线，变化成有三个头的线阵，两手各拉一个头，线在两手间绷直，另一个线头用嘴咬住、拉开，成"十"字架的形状。只需双手上下动作，双线便有分有合。两线贴近姑娘的脸面，扯开、合拢三下、绞掉脸上的汗毛，脸上所呈现的三根线，因此又叫"弹三线"。就这样反复在脸上绞汗毛，"开脸"结束再将辫子散开，在后脑壳上挽成发髻，并插上簪子及各种饰品。绞净面毛可令颜面光洁，之后重生的汗毛会较细，久而久之，毛囊收缩，能收到长久美容之功效（网络资料）。

这一特殊的婚嫁习俗文化负载词在杨译中为"her face has been slicked"，取"slick"作动词时的词意"使光滑"，从操作后的效果上解释了何为"开脸"，但是这一仪式的文化意蕴没有昭示给目的语读者。杨译的简单化处理，正如田建鑫（2023）指出："文化词语译出会造成与译入语价值观不符或者直接译出会造成译入语读者阅读困难时，这时译者为了提高目标读者的阅读体验感会适当将文化信息简化。"

而霍译的"she has been plucked and painted like a grow-up woman"则进行了增译，既展示"去除脸上的汗毛使其光滑并施粉"的表面现象，又揭示了"如同成年女子一般"的深意，意指"女子已成年"，可以嫁人或成为侍妾。比较之下，杨译简单处理了文化负载词"开脸"，霍译则更细致地增加了文化背景的补充信息。二者都没有将这一文化现象的表象和内涵传递给西方读者，其原因可能是篇幅所限，但考虑到这一特殊文化现象，笔者认为加注译法会更全面地向西方读者展示古老东方的婚庆习俗，有益于文化交流。杨译的简单化和霍译的增补策略在文学翻译过程中，译者为了达到跨文化交流目的，必定要跨越文化障碍，对源文本进行文化过滤和改造，无论是简化还是增补，这里的有意误译都是跨文化翻译的重要手段。

例 13

原文：前儿贵妃省亲回来，我们还亲见他带了几车金银回来，所以家里收拾摆设的水晶宫似的。（《红楼梦》第八十三回）

杨译：That time Her Highness <u>paid a visit home</u>, we saw with our own eyes the cartloads of gold and silver that she brought, which is why the house is fitted out like the crystal palace of the Dragon King.

霍译：That time <u>she went on that grand visitation</u>, we saw it with our own eyes—cartloads of gold and silver she brought along with her, had the old home twinkling away like a fairy palace.

省亲是指女方婚后归家探望父母或其他亲属的礼俗，最早出自《新唐书·卓行传·阳城》。在中国的传统习俗中，已婚女子在春节期间会回家"省亲"，与家人共度佳节。省亲的近义词包括探望、归省，反义词是离亲。

《红楼梦》的"元妃省亲"在小说中有着举足轻重的地位，发生在贾府辉煌的顶峰，是"烈火烹油、鲜花着锦"的"非常喜事"。这是贾府从权势如日中天到逐渐衰败的一个转折点。曹雪芹浓墨重彩式的铺垫和描述，将贾府这段高光时刻详细地展示在读者面前，无论是浩荡的声势，繁琐的礼仪，奢华的景观，人物集中亮相，冗长的对白与交谈，封建制度下的人伦悲剧，都给读者留下了深刻印象。因此，如何正确翻译元春作为贾府背后最大的政治势力的回娘家探亲之"省亲"并非易事。

仅以省亲当日的礼仪为例，作者写道：

　　展眼元宵在迩，自正月初八日，就有太监出来先看方向：何处更衣，何处燕坐，何处受礼，何处开宴，何处退息。又有巡察地方总理关防太监等，带了许多小太监出来，各处关防，挡围幕，指示贾宅人员何处退，何处跪，何处进膳，何处启事，种种仪注不一。外面又有工部官员并五城兵备道打扫街道，撵逐闲人。贾赦等督率匠人扎花灯烟火之类，至十四日，俱已停妥。这一夜，上下通不曾睡。（《红楼梦》第十八回）

　　仅从这一段文字可见元妃省亲的重大意义和封建社会的礼法森严。因此，元春的回娘家探亲不同于普通女性的归省，其内涵深刻，规模宏大，仪式异常繁琐，为译者增加了翻译难度。

　　例 13 中，杨译的主语是"Her Highness"，将"省亲"译为"paid a visit home,"既体现了主语的贵妃身份，又阐明了该传统习俗的本质：回家探亲。霍译为"she went on that grand visitation"通过形容词"grand"加"visitation"更凸显了省亲规模之宏大，仪式之隆重，恰如其分地展示出这一民间习俗背后贾府的政治地位和元春作为贵妃的尊贵身份。因此，无论是杨译有意地在"回家探亲"这一行为之前使用"Her Highness"来凸显元春的身份，还是霍译字斟句酌地选用了"go on that grand visitation"，都已经延伸了"省亲"这一文化负载词的含义，这种有意误译无疑是对传播原语文化有益的。

　　同一文本的两位译者对翻译策略的选择体现了译者在翻译过程中明显的倾向性，即诠释学中的偏见。在翻译复杂的文化意象时，译者究竟是侧重两种语言的转换还是倾向于文化的传播？文本的意义是敞开的，可以满足不同的理解者对意义的期待；不同的解释者带有不同的目的，这决定了译者必然从各自的偏见出发，产生不同的译文。杨译的简化和异化策略和霍克斯归化＋增译策略均有其不同的译介目的，在运用了不同的翻译策略和方法后，也达成了不同的文化传播效果。

一直以来，霍译的归化译法虽然颇有争议，但"误译如同海洋里潜藏的礁石，既可能阻碍航行，也可能成为引领探索的灯塔，霍克斯在翻译《红楼梦》的过程中恰到好处地运用误译，不仅成功地跨越了文化鸿沟，还为这部中国古典文学巨著注入了新的活力"（冯全功，2023：22）。

例14

原文：那妇人道："混沌魍魉！他来调戏我，倒不吃别人笑！你要便自和他道话，我却做不得这样的人！你还了我一纸休书来，你自留他便了！"（《水浒传》第二十四回）

赛译：The woman said,"You stupid fool! He came without shame to insult me and will that not make people laugh at us? If you wish, you may go and live alone with him, then, but I cannot be such a person as that. Give me my paper of divorce and you stay with him and let that be an end to it."

原文的语境是潘金莲勾引小叔子不成，被武松怒斥，之后武松愤怒出走。

原文：武大叫道："二哥那里去？"也不应，一直地只顾去了。武大回到厨下来问老婆道："我叫他又不应，只顾望县前这条路走了去，正是不知怎地了？"那妇人骂道："糊突桶！有甚么难见处！那厮羞了，没脸儿见你，走了出去。我猜他已定叫个人来搬行李，不要在这里宿歇。却不要又留他！"武大道："他搬了去，须吃别人笑话。"

可见潘金莲倒打一耙，颠倒黑白，恼羞成怒后反过来诬陷武松调戏嫂嫂，继而痛骂武大郎糊涂无能，威胁道：若要武松回来住，就一纸休书休了她，要武大在亲兄弟和老婆之间做一个选择。

原文提及的"休书"一词来自古时的不合理的社会法律制度，也称为"退书"，是在中国封建社会男尊女卑的制度下，男女双方解除婚约，由男方出具的一种书面证明。

在封建制度下，当女性被判定犯了七出之条中的任何一条，便可宣布婚姻关系的结束，而女方除了接受别无选择。"七出"又叫作"七去"或"七弃"，是古代休妻的条件、离婚的法律依据。"七出"形成于西周末年，作为礼制中的一部分，到汉唐时编入朝廷的律令。《大戴礼记·本命篇》说："妇有七去：一、不顺父母，去。二、无子，去。三淫，去。四、妒，去。五、有恶疾，去。六、多言，去。七、盗窃，去。"（洪志凡，2019：190）

在这种完全不平等的男女关系的社会里，离婚的权利是仅仅赋予了男人的，更确切地说是男子享有离婚的特权，女人没有离婚的权利，女人在婚姻关系中是被离弃的一方。这种离婚方式是以男子及其父母的意志为转移，不必经诉讼程序，只要作为丈夫一方指出女方犯了七出之条中的任意一条或者多条，或者随意编造借口，即可写一封休书结束一段婚姻。女子此后成了弃妇，不仅会被打上道德品质有亏的标签，还会被父母家人嫌弃，余生在艰难困苦中度过。因此，被丈夫休弃在封建社会是对女子的莫大羞辱，也体现了男尊女卑、女子处于劣势和作为附属品的不平等的封建社会制度。

鉴于此，"休书"不能简单同现在的离婚画上等号，因为原词语体现的是男方独有的权利和女方被动接受别无选择的不平等关系，译为"paper of divorce"是赛珍珠采取的归化策略，无疑是受到西方男女平等的婚恋观的影响，改变了原文中女性卑微屈辱的社会地位，是译者进行了文化过滤导致的有意的文化误译。

"原语文化在进入译入语文化的过程中，为了使其文化顺利被译入语读者接受，媒介者会根据译入语文化的传统习俗、信仰、价值观念等对自身文化做出改变，这样的一个改造、删减和重构的过程就叫作文化过滤。"（田建鑫，2023：103）赛珍珠在这一过程中，将男子单方面宣布离婚并写下文字证明这一特殊的文化现象运用了文化置换的手法，将中国封建社会中休妻的行为用西方的离婚来替代，从而对原文的文化信息进行了过滤和改造，目的是使译入语读者更好地理解原文中的社会文化现象。因此，这种有意的文化误译是可以接受的，是译者发挥自主性、对原文进行了有意误读后做出的选择。

3.1.5 法制文化负载词的误译

法制从古有之，法制史的内容丰富，涵盖了几千年的传统法律文化主要的发展变化过程。中国古书上所说的"命有司，修法制"（《礼记·月令篇》），其中的"法制"是指设范立制，使人们有所遵循的意思。古代法家著作中，也有"法制"一词。《管子·法禁》上写道："法制不议，则民不相私。"《商君书·君臣》上写道："民众而奸邪生，故立法制，为度量以禁之。"韩非也有"明法制，去私恩"的说法。汉代贾谊《新书·制不定》："仁义恩厚，此人主之芒刃也；权势法制，此人主之斤斧也。"清何琇《樵香小记·钧金束矢》："夫圣王之世，法制修明，豪强纵暴，有举其官者矣，安用讼哉？"

　　本文主要探讨中国法制文化中的刑罚制度。夏商时期就已有了具备雏形的刑罚体系，在浩瀚的历史长河中，随着封建王权的不断巩固，国家司法审判和监狱管理体制逐渐成型，量刑原则、管理法规、诉讼制度和司法改革都在不断发展完善，法典编纂水平不断提升。到了明清时期，在文学作品中出现了越来越多的司法案例和执法情节，由于中西方刑罚体系的差异，一些法治文化负载词的翻译颇有难度。

　　例 15

　　原文：一人造反，九族全诛！（《水浒传》第六十一回）

　　赛译：If one man turns rebel against the throne, <u>nine generations</u> must suffer from it.

　　赛珍珠的直译在此非常简单明晰，九族即为九代人"nine generations"。那么赛译是否准确解释了"诛九族"这一中国封建王朝时期严苛残暴的律法条文呢？答案是否定的。

　　据百度百科介绍，九族，泛指亲属，九族一说的出现，与封建社会的刑罚制度有很大关系。但"九族"所指，诸说不同。一说是上自高祖、下至玄孙，即玄孙、曾孙、孙、子、身、父、祖父、曾祖父、高祖父；一说是父族四、母族三、妻族二，父族四是指姑之子（姑姑的子女）、姊妹之子（外甥）、女儿之子（外孙）、己之同族（父母、兄弟、姐妹、儿女）；母族三是指母之父（外祖父）、母之母（外祖母）、从母子（娘舅）；妻族二是指岳父、岳母。

　　封建社会实行残酷的株连法，一人犯法，尤其是犯大法，往往要被灭"九族"，即"株连九族"。随着时代的变迁，今日"九族"之意有了很大变化，其亲属之意已经淡出，变成了对与之有关的一切人的泛称。

然而，三字经对九族的说法是"高曾祖，父而身。身而子，子而孙。自子孙，至玄曾。乃九族，人之伦"。即"高祖、曾祖、祖父、父亲、己身、子、孙、曾孙、玄孙"。从秦代起，"九族"有经学上的今文和古文两种解说，各有其社会、政治背景，分别从不同方面满足统治者的需要（网络资料）。

因此，实际上的九族应该指一切与罪犯相关联的有亲属关系的人等，否则九代人算下来，在罪犯受审定罪的同一时期，其在世的直系亲属最多三到四代人而已，根本无法满足诛杀九代人、几乎灭门以达到严惩罪犯、震慑全社会的刑律之要求。因此，赛译的"九族"仍属于文化误译范畴。

赛珍珠在翻译《水浒传》过程中，坚持直译，力求保持原汁原味地将中国名著推向英语世界，因此，她对"九族"进行了直译，译为"nine generations"。比起"放屁！放屁！"直译为"Pass the wind! Pass the wind!"，九族的译文算是既符合字面意义又比较接近原文本意的翻译了。

据统计，《水浒传》中共出现 17 处诸如"放屁""放狗屁""屁眼""屁滚尿流"等粗俗字眼。这些词和词组虽然粗鄙，却能生动形象地反映出讲话人的性格、出身和地位以及当时的情绪情感。赛珍珠将其中 14 处译成"pass one's wind"或"foul wind"，省译了两处，还有一处"屁滚尿流"译成"so frightened that their waters and wastes burst out"，可谓是极尽忠实，完整复刻了原文的字面意义。然而，赛珍珠的直译有时会让读者觉得译文僵硬，未能领会原文本意和精髓，"丧失原文之韵味，有时甚至成为令人啼笑皆非的误译"（潘群辉、贾德江，2009：106）。学术界批评之声不绝于耳，赛译被冠以"文化陷阱""误读""歪译""死译""胡译""超额翻译""亏损""偏离""失真""语用失误"等繁多罪名。

但是，经考察赛珍珠的教育程度、文学功底和语言修养以及翻译《水浒传》的过程，可得出结论：被定为误译的多数译例系译者的主观操纵和有意识的选择，而非因语言文化知识的欠缺而导致的无意误译。Peter Newmark（1988）强调：评论者应该从译者本人的角度看待译文，了解译者的翻译目的和翻译过程，尽力弄清楚译者为什么要那样译；许多情况下，一些在外人看来明显的"误译"其实是译者有意为之。

赛珍珠的初衷是"把中国名著原原本本地介绍到西方，她希望保留中国古代语言特有的表达方式和行文习惯，要做到这一点，最有效、最便捷的翻译方法就是直译"（马红军，2003：125）。因此，译者本身的偏见导致了作者在选择翻译策略和翻译方法时发挥了自主决策性，从而导致了翻译风格的迥异。

根据哲学诠释学的理论，偏见并非都是错误的和不合理的，偏见各自有其产生的历史性。偏见分为"合法的"和"非法的"两种：一种是正面的"生产性的偏见"；另一种是"阻碍理解并导致误解的成见"。而对进行跨文化翻译的译者来说，所要做的，就是克服不合理的偏见，利用有利于文化传播和交流的积极的偏见，发挥自身文化身份的优势，积极采取措施，发掘有效的翻译手段，从而达成被读者所能接受和认同的翻译效果。赛珍珠的译作在英语世界受众颇多，广受欢迎，时至今日，在互联网上售书公司的推介书目中，仍能频频见到 Pearl S. Buck 的 *All Men Are*

Brothers 的名字，已经足以证明赛珍珠的功底和她的译作的持久的影响力。

例 16

原文：刺史严鞫，竟以酷刑诬服，律拟<u>凌迟处死</u>。（《聊斋志异·续黄粱》）

翟译：Thereupon he was immediately charged by the wife with murder，and on being taken before the authorities was sentenced to die the "<u>lingering death.</u>"（译者脚注：This is the celebrated form of death, reserved for parricide and similar awful crimes, about which so much has been written. Strictly speaking, the malefactor should be literally chopped to pieces in order to prolong his agonies；but the sentence is now rarely, if ever, carried out in its extreme sense. A few gashes are made upon the wretched victim's body, and he is soon put out of his misery by decapitation.)

梅译：The magistrate subjected her to severe interrogation and finally used torture to establish her guilt. The sentence prescribed by law was <u>death by dismemberment.</u>

例 17

原文：唆令男女故失人伦，拟合<u>凌迟处死</u>。（《水浒传》第二十七回）

赛译：Thus by enticing the woman and enticing the man she enticed them to violate a sacred relationship. According to the law, therefore, the old woman ought to <u>die by the slicing of her flesh from her bones, bit by bit.</u>

例 18

原文：便把这婆子推上木驴，四道长钉，三条绑索，东平府尹判了一个字："<u>剐</u>!"（《水浒传》第二十七回）

赛译：Then this old woman was laid across a rack of wood, a beam set upon four posts, and four long nails were pinned through her and three ropes also bound her fast and a sign was written upon her that she was to be <u>sliced to strips</u>.

根据网络资料：凌迟，用于死刑名称，是指处死犯人时将人身上的肉一刀刀割去，是一种肢解的惩罚，包含身体四肢的切割、分离。这是中国封建时代最残酷的一种死刑，俗称剐刑。作为正式刑法始于五代，于清末废除。

中国古代十大酷刑之一的"凌迟"，是一种死刑执行方式，即民间所说的"千刀万剐"。对于"凌迟处死"和"剐"的翻译，在例 16 中，翟译采取了直译加注的方式，对这一严酷刑罚的具体内容、施行步骤做了较详细的解释说明，旨在使西方读者了解中国封建社会刑罚系统中最残酷、最不人道的处罚；而梅译则简单将其描述为"death by dismemberment"，即"肢解"之刑，一语带过。

相对于翟译的忠实和补充注释，梅译为何会对"凌迟"一词产生上述有意误译呢？这要归结于作者的文化身份和再创造中的偏见。梅维恒青年时期研读佛教，后来研究中国敦煌变文，其内容也多为佛经故事及历史传说等，对佛教中的悲悯、仁慈思想领悟颇多，因此对如此残酷的刑罚必然有主观上的反感和厌弃；而热爱惠特曼、华滋华斯等人诗歌的诗人出身的梅丹理对中国文化了解之精深，对中国语言文字运用之流畅，也使其在翻译中以流畅优美的风格对原文进行译介，因此梅译对"凌迟"一词没有详加解释，仅通过意译简介此刑罚的形式，说明译者有意回避原文中过于血腥的、可能引起读者不快的，或者译者自身认为没有必要进行解释和详细注释的文化信息，从而采取了删除不译、转译等方法。在译文的这一特征上，可见译者的偏见在理解和解释的全过程中的导向作用。

作为对照，在例 17、18 中，对原文的"凌迟处死"和"剐"，赛珍珠采取了直译的方法，忠实地翻译出了这种酷刑的实际操作过程，"the slicing of her flesh from her bones, bit by bit"和"sliced to strips"，二者都表明，这种处刑方式是将犯人身体上的肉一点一点切下来，刀刀见骨。绝对忠实，绝对残酷，绝对让读者不寒而栗，其译介效果明显。因此，相对于赛译和翟理斯的加注翻译，《聊斋志异》的梅译本明显是有意误译。

3.1.6 地名文化负载词的误译

地名是代表地理实体的一种语言符号，指特定位置上的地方所赋予的名称。地名往往蕴含着较丰富的社会文化内涵，能够反映原语文化中的历史特征。中国的悠久历史和地大物博的特点可以通过地名文化展现在西方读者面前，因此，地名的翻译因其兼具丰富的文化内涵也不容忽视。然而，在本文研究的四部古典文学名著的译著中，对地名翻译也存在着较多有意的文化误译。

例 19

原文：雨村道："去岁我到金陵地界，因欲游览六朝遗迹，那日进了石头城，从他老宅门前经过。"（《红楼梦》第二回）

杨译："Last year when I was in Jinling," said Yuncun, "on

my to to visit the Six Dynasty ruins I went to the Stone City and passed the gates of their old mansions."

霍译："Last time I was in Jinling," went on Yu-cun, "I passed by their two houses one day on my way to Shi-tou-cheng to visit the ruins."

例 20

原文：（陶曰：）"金陵吾故土，将婚于是。积有薄资，烦寄吾姊。"（《聊斋志异·黄英》）

杨译：Nanjing is my home. I shall marry and settle down here. I have saved a small sum I would like you to take to my sister.

梅译：Nanjing is my home territory, and I'm going to marry here. I've built up some meager funds that I'd like you to take back to my sister.

在例 19 中，对于地名"金陵"一词，杨译和霍译都保留了原词的音译，忠实于原文，使用了"Jinling"。例 20 中，杨译与梅译却没有将"金陵"进行音译从而保持其丰富悠远的文化意蕴，而是根据当代这座城市的名称将之译作"Nanjing"。

作为现今江苏省会的南京在不同历史时期别称众多。金陵是南京的古称，之所以名为金陵要追溯到春秋时期的诸侯争霸，当时楚霸王灭掉越国之后，为了镇守王气，在南京附近的紫金山和幕府山埋藏了大量的黄金，后人因此称南京为金陵（网络资料）。又有资料显示：战国时期楚威王熊商于公元前 333 年在石头城筑金陵邑，金陵之名即源于此。公元 937 年的南唐时期，南京被称为"金陵府"，其历史悠久，是中国四大古都之一，有着"六朝古都"和"十朝都会"等美称。

金陵自古是诗人墨客笔下的宝地，相当于今天的网红打卡地。东晋时期诗人谢朓在《入朝曲》一诗中描述了"江南佳丽地，金陵帝王州，逶迤带绿水，迢递起朱楼"的繁华盛景；唐代诗人李白曾作《金陵三首》，赞金陵"地即帝王宅，山为龙虎盘"；又作《登金陵凤凰台》，既缅怀"吴宫花草埋幽径，晋代衣冠成古丘"，又借此抒发个人的政治抱负和理想无法实现的抑郁之情，叹"总为浮云能蔽日，长安不见使人愁"等等。

据统计，李白作品中有关南京的诗歌近 200 首，仅诗题包含"金陵"一词的就不下 20 首；杜牧在《江南春绝句》中也曾咏叹南京的历史："南朝四百八十寺，多少楼台烟雨中"；刘禹锡在《金陵五题》中借古咏怀，"山围故国周遭在，潮打空城寂寞回"；北宋王安石在《桂枝香·金陵怀古》一词中隐喻现实，给世人留下了千古名句："念往昔、繁华竞逐，叹门外楼头，悲恨相续。千古凭高对此，谩嗟荣辱。六朝旧事随流水，但寒烟衰草凝绿。至今商女，时时犹唱，后庭遗曲。"

纵观文学史，金陵已经成为骚人墨客、豪杰志士怀古的必到之地，根据《历代诗余》中引用《古今词话》的统计，王安石同时代就有三十多人以《桂枝香》一词牌书写金陵怀古词。

金陵是众古都之中最昌盛、灵秀、宏伟之地，就连朱偰先生在点评古都时，都赞叹"金陵、长安、洛阳、燕京四都之中，尤以金陵为最"。

在翻译《红楼梦》时，霍克斯和杨宪益夫妇均使用了音译地名"Jinling"，究其缘由，还是"金陵"一词在原著中的重要地位导致。《红楼梦》原著中"金陵"一词出现了 38 次，"南京"也出现了 13 次。为何曹雪芹时而使用金陵，时而贾母又吵着要回南京？这一谜团据专家解释，首先，原文的世家原籍设定重点在金陵一地，小说中的重要情节例如金陵十二钗，凤姐判词"哭向金陵事更哀"，金陵城起复贾雨村，护官符提及的"阿房宫，三百里，住不下金陵一个史"，"东海缺少白玉床，龙王来请金陵王"，王熙凤历幻返金陵等等的关键词都是金陵。其次，书中设定的原籍名称是为了躲避清朝的文字狱，因此借用了许多明朝的设定，例如书中的金陵，在清朝时人们是不敢也不能称呼为南京，要叫作江宁，只有在明朝时，人们才称它作南京。作者的模糊设定，导致金陵和南京并用，故事的场景忽南忽北，系作者笔法所致。鉴于此，在翻译此词时，二位译者不约而同地使用了音译，旨在与原文中与故事情节息息相关、寓意深刻的世家原籍所在地金陵保持一致。

而杨宪益夫妇与梅氏兄弟在 20 世纪后期重译《聊斋志异》故事的时候，时值中国对内改革、对外开放的重要历史时期，中国古典名著在西方世界的传播对中西方的文化交流意义深远。在这样的时代背景下，两位译者考虑到当代西方读者对中国地名文化的接受能力，主观上放弃了介绍金陵作为六朝古都、历代文化中心的较为复杂的历史背景，而沿用了民国元年（1912 年）孙中山任临时大总统时所定下的名称"南京"，音译为"Nanjing"，有利于西方读者对当代中国城市南京的了解，这种有意的文化误译是译者基于当代文化交流的需求而进行的选择，从诠释学的角度看，也是译者综合考虑了读者的视域和理解的历史性做出的主观选择。

3.1.7　性文化负载词的有意误译

《聊斋志异》和《红楼梦》中有较多或简或繁、或含蓄婉转、或大胆直白的性描写，一些回目和篇目中涉及同性、异性恋等广泛的题材，全文中涉及较多的中国古代性文化的负载词语。《金瓶梅词话》中的性文化负载词和性爱描写俯拾即是，而《水浒传》中也有涉及。对此，不同历史时代的译者带着各自的偏见，对此类内容进行了不同的处理，译文展现出理解的历史性特征。

兰陵笑笑生的《金瓶梅词话》作为明代四大奇书之一，自成书以来，就被历代统治者列为禁书，之所以被列为禁书，主要是在大多数人眼里它是一部淫书。虽然已经被正名，但原著中大量露骨的性描写确实是翻译的难点所在。

例 21

原文：有一个僧人先到，走到妇人窗下水盆里洗手，忽然听见妇人在房里颤声柔气，呻呻吟吟，哼哼唧唧，恰似有人在房里<u>交媾</u>一般。（《金瓶梅词话》第八回）

芮译：One of the monks, who had arrived before the rest, went up to the basin outside the woman's bedroom window to wash his hands. Suddenly he overheard the woman:

In a trembling voice and melting tones.

Sighing and moaning.

Panting and groaning.

Just as though she were engaged in the act of <u>sexual intercourse</u> with someone in her room.

芮译不仅忠实地将"交媾"一词大胆直译为"act of sexual

intercourse"（性交行为），还通过诗体译文"In a trembling voice and melting tones. Sighing and moaning. Panting and groaning"，将潘金莲与西门庆交欢时的"颤声柔气，呻呻吟吟，哼哼唧唧"的声音拟声描摹出来，更加烘托了淫靡放浪的氛围。由此可见，译者对这本奇书的翻译观：严格忠实，尊重原著。其译文中对原著中的性描写和性文化的还原式译介之所以毫无顾忌、大胆写实，还要得益于西方对色情文学审查制度的放宽。

曹雪芹在《红楼梦》中对性爱的描写既有文笔简洁、叙事含蓄型的春秋笔法，如"送宫花贾琏戏熙凤"，"秦鲸卿得趣馒头庵"，也有露骨直白的细致描写。

例 22

原文：贾琏一面大动，一面喘吁吁答道："你就是娘娘，我哪里管什么娘娘！"那媳妇越浪，贾琏越丑态毕露。一时事毕，两个又海誓山盟，难分难舍，此后遂成相契。（《红楼梦》第二十一回）

杨译："You're my goddess," he panted, going all out. "What do I care for any other goddess?" The more wanton the woman, the more debauched Jia Lian revealed himself. At the end of this bout they vowed to be true to each other and could hardly bear to part.

霍译：Jia Lian's movements became more violent. "You are my only goddess!" he said, panting heavily. "I care for no other goddess but you!" At this the Mattress began to grow even more reckless in her incitements and Jia Lian to reveal the more disgusting of his sexual accomplishments. They lay a long time together when it was over, exchanging oaths and promises, unable to break apart. From that day onwards there was a secret understanding between them.

杨译简洁叙事，将贾琏这段欲火难耐的婚内出轨的偷情片段采取了客观的描写，共用英文单词 48 个，将肆意纵欲的贾琏的"大动"译为"going all out"（全力以赴），将"浪"直译为"wanton"（放纵的），"丑态毕露"译为"debauched"（放荡），除了"going all out"隐晦婉转地暗示贾琏在这场偷情行为中如鱼得水，尽情享受性爱过程，其余译文语言均中规中矩，堪称谨慎且保守。

而霍译共用词 76 个，对这段激情片段进行了详细的描绘，为使读者更好地理解浪荡公子贾琏与仆妇的私情，译者还主观地加以场外解说，不厌其烦地描述二者的互动和后续的情感交流。霍克斯将"大动"译为"movements became more violent"（动作激烈），将"浪"译为"more reckless in her incitements"（受引诱后更加不顾一切），"丑态毕露"译为"reveal the more disgusting of his sexual accomplishments"（因其性满足而更加令人作呕），译者可谓是添油加醋式地将这一幕肉欲横流的情色片段进行了细致入微的刻画，做到了字字对译的基础上进行增译，不避讳不遮掩，采取了写实手法。

相对于霍译的大胆直白的译文，杨译在处理性文化词汇的时候，进行了简化和净化。这种有意的误译，要归结于杨氏夫妇翻译《红楼梦》的时代对待性文化的态度。20 世纪 60 年代初，杨宪益和戴乃迭夫妇开始翻译《红楼梦》，其间曾一度中断，最后于 1974 年完成，在保守、闭塞的 60、70 年代，不仅含有性描写的文学作品不能发表面世，即使是有描写爱情、两性亲密关系的文学作品也颇少见。译制片中的恋爱情节也都经过了净化处理，很少见接吻、拥抱等亲密情节，床戏、裸戏更加严格禁止播出，否则将视为"资产阶级自由化"、宣传"资产阶级腐朽思想"，甚至被列为"黄色"作品而遭到查禁。刊登杨宪益翻译的《聊斋志异选》的《中国文学》杂志规定，对涉及爱情或性爱描写的作品不予以录用。美国一位名为瓦乐莉·迈纳的读者在美国报刊《在这个时代》（1983 年 11 月 23 日）上撰写的《中国女作家的生活、工作和希望》一文中就真实地再现了这一段历史：

在同《中国文学》杂志编辑部举行的讨论会中，总编杨宪益告诉我们，只要你不写那些"不健康的东西"，在中国发表作品是很容易的，他没有进一步阐述，但是后来我们听说对性细节的描写一般都是受到查禁的，当西方作品被翻译过来时。性描写的段落往往要被简化或删掉。（转引自林文艺，2011：49）

因此，在杨宪益夫妇翻译的《红楼梦》英译本中，对涉及性爱的描写多采取了净化、淡化、模糊化等手段。可见译本在某一固定历史时期被打上的深深的时代烙印，这种时代性也影响了译者翻译策略的选择。

例 23

原文：女顾室无人，问："君何无家口？"答云："斋耳。"女曰："此所良佳。如怜妾而活之，须秘密勿泄。"生诺之。乃<u>与寝合</u>。使匿密室，过数日而人不知也。（《聊斋志异·画皮》）

翟译：Finding no one there, she asked Wang where his family were; to which he replied that that was only the library. "And a very nice place, too", said she; "but if you are kind enough to wish to save my life, you mustn't let it be known that I am here." Wang promised he would not divulge her secret, and so she remained there for some days without anyone knowing anything about it.

《聊斋志异》中诸多篇章涉及人鬼、人狐恋情，因此关于性爱的描写俯拾皆是。据笔者统计，蒲松龄在《聊斋志异》中有较多的涉及性爱的情节，如《巧娘》中傅生的性无能，《周克昌》中的性压抑，《伏狐》中人狐相交的性暴力，《书痴》中的性无知，《封十三娘》中的女同性恋，《黄九郎》中的男同性恋，《犬奸》中的人兽交合，《五通》中的五通神强奸民妇，《韦公子》中的乱伦，《陈云栖》中的群交淫乱，《人妖》中的双性恋和人妖等等，其涉及范围之广、大胆与开放程度令读者震惊。然而，这些细节在译者翟理斯的笔下，或被修改情节，或直接删除，男女情事几乎无迹可寻（孙雪瑛，2016：150）。

如例 23 中《画皮》，王生路遇陌生美貌女子将其带回自己的书房藏匿并与之发生关系，类似金屋藏娇包养的情节在翟理斯的译文中只剩下"so she remained there"（她留在这里），而涉及男女性事的王生与女鬼"乃与寝合"被译者隐去，但是其他情节仍一字不漏地译出。

据笔者考证，翟理斯在其所翻译的《聊斋志异》的 164 个故事中，凡是涉及男女情事、"颠倒衣裳"、"色授魂与"的性爱情节，均采取了删除和改写的方式。

译者为何要对原文中涉及男女性爱的情节进行净化和主观操纵从而导致了译文中明显的有意误译呢？

译者翻译策略的选择离不开他所处的特定的历史文化语境，

离不开翟理斯所处的清教主义盛行的维多利亚时代。

起源于 16 世纪的清教崇尚克制与禁欲，对两性之间行为规范的标准严格。基于此，翟译对原文中的性文化负载词和相关情节都进行了文化过滤，"根据自身的文化背景和时代精神的要求，对外来因素进行重新改写、解读和利用"（尹建民，2011：337）。翟译不仅将异质文化进行了过滤，将大量中国文化特有的意象进行了归化处理，更多的是根据自身的理解的历史性、所处时代的道德观而对原文中的涉及性爱的所谓"不纯洁"的内容进行净化和改造。

文化过滤在诠释哲学中，意味着译者的视域和原作的视域在碰撞、交融的过程中，译者用译语文化对原文中的文化因素进行过滤，从而在冲突中逐渐达成两者的融合。因此，"视界融合的过程也是视界碰撞的过程，这一过程不是用一种视界代替另一种视界，而是必定同时包括两者的差异和交互作用。视界融合是建立在差异基础上的融合。它从理论上印证了翻译中文化过滤现象的历史根源及其存在的无可避免性"（张德让，2001：24）。

3.1.8　科举制度文化负载词的有意误译

作为中国历代封建王朝选拔官员的一种制度，科举制度因采取分科取士的方法而被称作科举制。此制度从隋朝开始一直沿用至清朝光绪年间，共有约一千三百年的悠久历史，已经成为中国文化的一部分，同时也成为现代选拔任用官员、晋升、各级各类考试、技能评定的最大参照体系，成为世界文化的一部分。

明清小说中涉及科举文化的小说比比皆是：《聊斋志异》《儒林外史》《红楼梦》《西游记》无不谈及科举，《水浒传》则从侧面反映了科举文化背景下的等级意识观念、进阶之难、文人道德品质低劣等弊端。而《儿女英雄传》《十二楼》等才子佳人小说中的男主更是离不开科举考试这一特殊设定。科举文化负载词由于其自身体系的复杂、历史背景的悠久和文化内涵之丰富，其解读和翻译对译者来说是跨文化翻译过程中的一大难点。

例 24

原文：王子服……十四入泮。（《聊斋志异·婴宁》）

翟译：Wang Tzǔ-fu……took his bachelor's degree at the age of fourteen.

杨译：Wang Zifu …… passed the district examination at fourteen.

梅译：Wang Zifu……received the baccalaureate at thirteen.

古代学宫之前有泮水，因此学堂成为"泮宫"，"入泮"就代指古代学生入学接受正规的学堂教育。科举时代后，学童入学后成为生员即为"入泮"。在我国清朝，"入泮"专指通过乡试考中秀才。因此，三种译文中杨译最接近原文，译作"passed the district examination"（通过乡试）；而翟译和梅译均将此文化负载词进行归化处理，使用了"took his bachelor's degree"（获得学士学位）和"received the baccalaureate"（取得学士学位）。此外，梅译中出现了对年龄的无意误译，误将 14 岁译成了 13 岁。可见在三位译者中，母语译者对科举文化负载词的翻译最准确，目的语国家的译者为避免文化差异造成理解上的偏差，有意识地采取了归化翻译策略。

例 25

原文：这林如海姓林名海，表字如海，乃是前科的探花，今

已升至兰台寺大夫，本贯姑苏人氏，今钦点出为巡盐御史，到任方一月有余。（《红楼梦》第二回）

杨译：……where he learned that the Salt Commissioner that year was Lin Hai his courtesy name was Lin Ruhai-who had <u>come third in a previous Imperial examination</u> and recently been promoted to the Censorate. A native of Gusu, he had now been selected by the Emperor as a Commissioner of the Salt Inspectorate. He had been little more than a month in this present post.

霍译：This Lin Ru-hai had <u>passed out Florilege, or third in the whole list of successful candidates</u>, in a previous Triennial, and had lately been promoted to the Censorate. He was a Soochow man and had not long taken up his duties in Yangchow following his nomination by the emperor as Visiting Inspector in that area.

所谓"探花"，是指科举制度中殿试第三名，殿试又称"御试""廷试""廷对"等，是唐、宋、元、明、清时期科举考试之一。会试中选者才有资格进阶到更高一级考试。殿试的目的是对会试合格进行区别、选拔官员等。殿试为科举考试中的最高一段。历史记载最早的殿试由武则天创制于神都紫微宫洛城殿。

明清时期的殿试分为三甲：一甲三名赐进士及第，通称状元、榜眼、探花；二甲赐进士出身，第一名通称传胪；三甲赐同进士出身。

杨译对"探花"这一科举文化负载词没有进行直译，而是进行了释义，将殿试第三名的探花解释为"come third in a previous

Imperial examination"，符合明清殿试需在紫禁城内的保和殿等大殿举行的事实，因此译者将殿试解释为"皇家的考试"，虽然有意识地避开了对"探花"一词的直观解释，但译文易于目的语读者理解。

霍克斯将"探花"译为"passed out Florilege"，并做了补充说明，"or third in the whole list of successful candidates, in a previous Triennial"（三年一次的殿试中获第三名），对"探花"的理解准确，同时对古代殿试的文化背景的解读也是正确的。殿试的频率通常为三年一次。殿试是科举考试的终极阶段，在会试之后举行，目的是对会试合格的考生进行进一步的选拔，因此霍译使用了"successful candidates"，指代"会试合格的考生"。

在考察几部明清小说对科举文化负载词的翻译时，笔者发现一个有趣的现象，《聊斋志异》的译者梅氏兄弟和翟理斯，《红楼梦》的汉学家译者霍克斯均将科举制度中相对复杂的文化因素进行了归化处理，形成了有意误译。他们将中国的科举制度的逐级晋升的体系与大学中的学位制度联系起来。从童生起步的中国知识分子通过乡试、会试成为举人之后再参加殿试，金榜题名后则获得进士资格。这几位译者在翻译过程中，将秀才与学士学位获得者等同起来，会试中举后等同于获得硕士学位，高中进士后等于获取博士学位。

从这一对照可以看出，几位西方译者以目的语读者的接受视域审视原文，对原文中的科举文化负载词进行了分析和解读，考虑到了原文与读者之间的时间距离和空间距离可能产生的理解的障碍，译者均进行了有意的误译，将科举制度文化移植到西方的学位制度当中，从而使对于西方读者而言的"陌生的、遥远的、时空中分离出来的东西变成熟悉的、现刻的、跨越时空的东西"
（章启群，1998：129），克服了理解的历史性所造成的误读和误
解，进行了积极的、建设性的阐释，因此，其归化策略在诠释学
视域下的合理性就在此显现出来。

3.2　物质文化负载词的误译

物质文化负载词，即与衣食住行等物质文化相关的词汇。某
一特定历史时期、地理环境之下的具有特殊文化含义的日常生活
中的器具、用品等名称都可归为物质文化负载词一类。本文探讨
的几部小说创作的时间距今最长可达 500 年之久，因此许多物质
名词的所指发生了改变，物质文化负载词的翻译也成为明清小说
对外译介中的难点所在。

例 26

原文：婆子暗暗地欢喜，道："来了！这刷子当败！"（《水浒
传》第二十三回）

赛译：The old woman, secretly pleased, said to herself, "It
is coming! This brush ought to suffer. "

辞典对刷子的定义是：刷子是一种用于刷除污垢或涂抹用的
工具。它通常由毛、棕、塑料丝、金属丝等材料制成，可以是长
型或椭圆形，有些带有柄。例如《水浒传》第二十一回："这边
放着个洗手盆、一个刷子，一张金漆桌子上，放一个锡灯台"；
《儒林外史》第十九回："他每日在店里，手里拿着一个刷子刷头
巾"。因此，赛珍珠的译文就直译作了"this brush"。

然而，宋元至明清时期的文学作品中出现的刷子却另有寓意。

元代无名氏《冤家债主》第二折："不养蚕来不种田，全凭说谎度流年。为甚阎王不勾我，世间刷子少我钱。"又有《金瓶梅词话》第二回："这刷子尫得紧，你看我着些甜糖，抹在这厮鼻子上，交他抵不着。"明末凌濛初编著拟话本小说集《二刻拍案惊奇》中也提及此词："看来我是个刷子，他也是个痴人。"

可见，"刷子"的比喻意义是傻瓜，也指浪子、好色之徒。在上文三个例句中，词义都脱离了物质名词"刷子"的原本所指，取其喻意。

赛珍珠曾说："我的作品风格来源于我关心的人物。如果人物是美国人，我会自然地使用简短的句子、犀利的短语和快速的对话。如果人物是中国人，我就会首先用中文思维，在我脑海中形成的故事，纯用中文来组织，然后将汉语逐句翻译为英文，而自己并没有意识到这点。但是当我再改写这些英文时，就发觉人物都不对劲了，仿佛我将他们拽入一间陌生的房屋，他们一下变得无所适从了。"（董琇，2010：50）可见，赛珍珠始终坚持将原汁原味的中国文化通过直译传递给英语读者，先进行的是中文思维，然后再考虑目的语读者。译者并没有采取意译从而将"刷子"一词的比喻意义：傻瓜、浪子展示给读者。为了凸显明代民间语言的生动活泼的特色，赛译有意保留了"刷子"的物质名词属性，在译文中避开了其比喻意义，直接使用英语中对等的物质名词"brush"进行直译，这一有意误译体现了译者的特殊文化身份导致的翻译观。

赛珍珠在翻译过程中，为了保留《水浒传》中明代特有的语言表达方式，甚至采取词对词、句对句的翻译方式，力求忠实，以期传达出"中国英语"的味道。这和她的文化身份是不可分的。译者的文化身份对其采取的翻译策略和文化取向都具有定向作用。赛珍珠对《水浒传》这一名著的文学价值的高度欣赏和她的文化交融观使其进行了翻译对象和翻译策略的选择。赛珍珠曾说自己很欣赏《水浒传》的章回体特色、口语化文字，若将这部优秀的中国文学作品译介到西方，可以让西方了解中国的文化和文学。因此，为了保留原著中的语言特色和文化特质，赛译的异化策略和直译的翻译方法几乎贯穿全文。

例 27

原文：且说武大，终日挑担子出去，街上卖<u>炊饼</u>度日。（《金瓶梅词话》第一回）

芮译：To resume our story, Wu the Elder made his living by shouldering his carrying pole and peddling <u>steamed wheat cakes</u> on the street all day.

此处芮效卫将"炊饼"译成"steamed wheat cakes"（蒸制小麦蛋糕），这种归化翻译明显是有意误译。

据张义宏（2017）考证，《金瓶梅》中的糕点类食品种类繁多，"其中以'饼'字命名的最多，如炊饼、果馅椒盐金饼、烙饼、荷花饼、卷饼、梅桂菊花饼儿、果馅饼、玫瑰元宵饼、果馅团圆饼、菊花饼、松花饼、顶皮饼、白面蒸饼、玉米面鹅油蒸饼、酥油松饼、玫瑰饼、蒸酥果馅饼儿等"。

一个有趣的现象是，将上文使用 ChatGPT 进行翻译，译文如下："there are many types of pastries in *Jin Ping Mei*, with the most common being those named with the character "饼"

(bǐng, meaning "cake" or "pancake"). These include chuibing (steamed cake), guoxianjiaoyan jinbing (fruit-filled spiced golden cake), laobing (griddled cake), hehuabing (lotus cake), juanbing (rolled cake), meiguijvhuabing (plum, osmanthus, and chrysanthemum cake), guoxianbing (fruit-filled cake), meiguiyuanxiaobing (rose dumpling cake), guoxian tuanyuanbing (fruit-filled reunion cake), jvhuabing (chrysanthemum cake), songhuabing (pine flower cake), dingpibing (top-layer cake), baimian zhengbing (white-flour steamed cake), yumian eyou zhengbing (cornmeal and goose oil steamed cake), suyou songbing (butter puff pastry), meiguibing (rose cake), and zhengsu guoxianbing (steamed flaky fruit-filled cake). "

也就是说，AI 翻译时，先进行了音译，然后使用旁注再进行解释，主要是阐明糕点的内容和制备方式，但是绝大部分饼类都被翻译成"cake"，归化的翻译策略是显而易见的，因此，文学和跨文化翻译仍然离不开译者的主导作用，若归化翻译一枝独大，不利于文化交流。

宋代各种美味的面食中，最为读者熟知的莫过于武大郎售卖的炊饼。网络资料显示：炊饼是一种面食，主要原料是面粉，配料包括果肉、蔬菜，调料有食用盐、食用油、白砂糖等。炊饼是通过笼屉蒸制而成的，类似于现代的馒头，但可能形状略有差异。炊饼的历史可以追溯到古代，其制作方法和名称在不同历史时期有所变化。

在宋朝，由于避讳宋仁宗赵祯的名字"祯"与"蒸"同音，蒸饼被改称为炊饼。这种叫法很快在市井中普及开来，成为一种大众食品。当时的炊饼大多是实心无馅的，用笼屉蒸熟，因此也被称为笼饼或馒头。炊饼在北宋京城汴梁非常普遍，是市民的主食之一，每天中午，汴梁的街巷里叫卖的有粥、炊饼、辣菜饼和春饼。清明节出游时，汴梁人都会带上枣粥、炊饼和鸭蛋。炊饼不仅是一种食物，还承载着丰富的历史文化内涵。它在不同的历史时期有着不同的名称和做法，但始终是人们日常生活中不可或缺的一部分。通过了解炊饼的历史和文化，我们可以更好地理解中国传统饮食文化的多样性和丰富性（网络资料）。

宋人黄朝英所作《缃素杂记》中记载："凡以面为食具者，皆为之饼；故火烧而食者，呼为烧饼；水瀹而食者，呼为汤饼；蒸笼而食者，呼为蒸饼。"由于《水浒传》故事发生的年代设定为宋代，因此武大售卖的炊饼就是使用蒸笼蒸出来的蒸饼，并非读者误以为的烧饼、烤饼之类，更不是外国人眼中的蛋糕。芮效卫将其译成"steamed wheat cakes"，用一种类似解释的意译，但是本质上是归化翻译。

在翻译《金瓶梅》中的各式糕点时，"芮译本以追求译文的完整忠实性为前提，使用了 cake，pastries，dumpling，junket，roll，bun，crisp，wonton 等多样化的英语词汇加以区分，对于糕点原料制作部分几乎不做任何省略。总体而言，其异化翻译策略与直译方法在一定程度上有助于英语读者对于《金瓶梅》原文中糕点文化的了解"（张义宏，2017：124）。

译者在访谈录中曾经提及：原著在某种程度上就像一部百科全书，涉及了方方面面的中国传统文化。为了更好地翻译此书，将中国文化完整而忠实地展现在西方读者面前，芮效卫预先研读中国传统算命技艺、烹饪饮食等方面的书籍，因此推断，译者不可能会对"炊饼"产生误读。其归化的译法，与译者大多时间采取的异化翻译策略糅合在一起，起着调和作用。此处"炊饼"的有意误译体现出茵效卫在饮食文化英译中存在误解。因此，在翻译饮食文化负载词时，应多用直译和音译来保留原文的饮食文化特色，力求最大程度上保持了中国饮食文化的独特之处和魅力，从而有效传播原语文化。

例 28

原文：将道人肩上的褡裢抢了过来背着……（《红楼梦》第一回）

杨译：He transferred the sack from the Taoist's shoulder to his own.

霍译：But Shi-yin merely snatched the satchel that hung from the other's shoulder and slung it from his own.

Sack 通常是一个大袋子，以结实的布或皮革制成，用于储存或运输面粉、煤炭、蔬菜、谷物等。而 satchel 通常是用结实的布或皮革制成的小包，用带挎在肩上。

从上述词语解释中可以看出，"sack"和"satchel"都是由同样的材料制成的，用于储存物品，但它们在大小上略有不同。此外，霍克斯关注的是"扛在肩上"的用法，而杨强调的是尺寸大小。但是这两个英语词汇都无法展示"褡裢"一词丰富的文化内涵和中国古代民众外出时置物容器的悠久历史和变迁。

根据网络资料，褡裢亦作"褡连"和"褡联"，是古代和近代我国民间使用的一种布口袋，通常用很厚、很结实的家织粗棉布制成，少数也有用皮革或绸缎制作的。褡裢的形状为长方形，中间开口，两端各成一个袋子。大的褡裢盛装衣物、被褥，可搭在马背上；小的褡裢装置银两、铜钱和小件物品，挂在腰间。最常用的是中号的褡裢，两端各一尺左右，可搭在肩上。农家赶集会带上褡裢，商人、读书人和账房先生外出时，里面放着纸、笔、墨盒、信封信笺、印章印泥、地契文书、证件账簿……且总是将它搭在肩上，空出两手行动方便。

杨宪益夫妇和霍克斯对原文中独特的物质文化负载词"褡裢"进行了文化过滤，从英语词汇中选取了外形上比较接近、用途相似的"sack"和"satchel"对其进行了文化置换，归化的结果出现了有意误译。"经过文化过滤的译文迎合了读者的期待视野，满足了译语文化的价值取向和审美习惯，提高了文本在译语中的可接受性。要想文学被异质文化接受，文化过滤在翻译活动中必不可少，而有意误译是接受主体基于文化的内在要求而主动选择的结果。"（田建鑫，2023：105）

例 28

原文：陋室空堂，当年笏满床。（《红楼梦》第一回）

杨译：Mean huts and empty halls

Where emblems of nobility once hung.

霍译：Mean hovels and abandoned halls

Where courtiers once paid daily calls.

"笏"作为中国古代高官显贵的象征，被赋予了特殊的文化内涵。杨译采取了增译的方法，最大程度地传递了这一文化信息，而霍克斯的意译却未能将这种特殊的物质文化负载词直接转移到目的语中，但是这种有意的文化误译并非失败或者错误的翻译。

"笏"原指古代大臣上朝拿着的手板，用玉、象牙或竹片制成，上面可以记事，称为朝笏。《说文解字》写道：笏，竹部，公及士所搢也。从竹勿声。案：籀文作，象形。义云佩也。古笏佩之。此字後人所加。呼骨切。

《广韵》中解释道：笏，一名手版，品官所执。《舆服杂事》有记载：五代以来，惟八座尚书执笏，以笔缀手版头，紫囊裹之。其馀王公、卿、士但执手版，主于敬。不执笔，示非记事官也。《正字通》写道：明制，笏，四品以上用象牙，五品以下用木，以粉饰之。又据《明史·舆服三》记载：文武官一品至五品，笏由象牙所制成。六品至九品，原材料为槐木。

可见，笏不是普通的物质名词，而是中国古代官场上官员手中所执记事或所执之板状物，同时也是权力的象征，在文学作品中常见。《红楼梦》第一回的"笏满床"则来源于典故"满床笏"，出自《旧唐书·崔义玄传》："开元中，神庆子琳等皆至大官，群从数十人，趋奏省闼。每岁时家宴，组佩辉映，以一榻置笏，重叠于其上"。后来俗传误为郭子仪事，讲述了唐朝名将汾阳王郭子仪六十大寿时，七子八婿前来祝寿，由于他们都是朝廷里的高官，皆手持笏板，拜寿时将各自的笏放满床头（一说放满象牙床）。后来这个故事通过绘画、戏剧和小说等形式在民间广泛流传。至明清两代，《满床笏》几乎无人不知，这一典故被用来借喻家门兴盛，满门高官，贵不可言。

《红楼梦》原文中三次出现"满床笏"，恰如其分地印证了《满床笏》典故的广为流传和寓意。《好了歌》解中出现"当年笏满床"，与"陋室空堂"和"蛛丝儿结满雕梁"的凄凉败落形成了鲜明对照，所谓的鲜花着锦、烈火烹油的鼎盛时期转眼成了过眼烟云。

在第二十九回"享福人福深还祷福，多情女情重愈斟情"中，曹雪芹描述了贾府众人前往清虚观打醮的全过程：

贾母在正面楼上坐了，凤姐等占了东楼，众丫头等在西楼，轮流伺候。贾珍一时来回："神前拈了戏，头一本《白蛇记》。"贾母问："《白蛇记》是什么故事？"贾珍道："是汉高祖斩蛇方起首的故事。第二本是《满床笏》。"贾母笑道："这倒是第二本上？也罢了。神佛要这样，也只得罢了。"又问第三本。贾珍道："第三本是《南柯梦》。"贾母听了，便不言语。

这三本剧的寓意很明显，从创业史到发家史，所有的荣华富贵最终不过是南柯一梦，醒来一场空，也难怪贾母听了立刻无语。

"满床笏"第三次出现是在原著第七十一回中，恰逢贾母八十大寿，亲朋好友和宫中都送来大量礼物：

贾母因问道："前儿这些人家送礼来的，共有几家有围屏？"凤姐儿道："共有十六家有围屏，十二架大的，四架小的炕屏。内中只有江南甄家一架大屏十二扇，大红缎子缂丝'满床笏'，一面是泥金'百寿图'的，是头等的。"

这一情节中，《满床笏》富贵寿考的故事迎合了贾母的心思，也非常应景，且这一典故是富贵吉祥之兆，同时，也是作者的暗示：虽然此际繁华满眼，豪礼如山，高门大户贵客如云，却是"忽喇喇似大厦将倾，昏惨惨似灯将尽"的末世狂欢。

因此，"笏"和"满床笏"不仅是物质文化负载词，同时也承载了社会文化中官场文化和民俗文化的更多内涵。回看杨译的"emblems of nobility"（贵族的象征符号、象征物）和霍克斯的"courtiers once paid daily calls"（侍臣们每天来拜见），二者的意译方法均属有意误译，是在复杂文化负载词无法通过直译为目的语读者清晰完整展示原文的文化内涵时的一种折中之举。

当原语中的富含文化信息的词语译出会造成与译入语价值观不一致或者直接译出会造成目的语读者理解困难甚至误解时，译者可以通过意译的翻译方法，或将原语中的文化信息进行简化，或将该文化负载词进行解释性翻译，从而提高目标读者的阅读体验，消除阅读困难带来的对异域文化的误解、疏远甚至排斥感。

在文化负载词量丰富、文化信息复杂的文学翻译中，译者虽然尽全力突破文化障碍，运用了多种翻译策略和翻译技巧来阐释文化现象，为目的语读者提供流畅易懂的译文，从而对某一部文学作品、某一个遥远的、充满未知华彩的异域文化产生浓厚的兴趣。然而在原著、译者、翻译策略、目标语读者等多种因素的影响下，译者难以对每一处文化负载词都能够进行尽善尽美的翻译，难以在忠实于原文的同时也可满足译文读者的期待视域，这就导致了在跨文化翻译中，译者对大量的文化负载词采取了直译的方式，没能传递词语背后的历史文化。

例 29

原文：这西门庆头戴缠棕大帽，一撒钩绦，<u>粉底皂靴</u>，进门见婆子，拜四拜。（《金瓶梅词话》第七回）

芮译：Hsi-men Ching was wearing a large palmetto hat, a long gown fastened at the waist with a sash, and <u>white-soled black boots</u>.

原著中，西门庆受媒婆蛊惑，为娶人美钱多的孟玉楼为妻，特意高调打扮，足蹬粉底皂靴去拜见孟玉楼的亲属杨姑娘。粉底皂靴的打扮，在某种程度上既体现了对他人高度尊重的礼节，同时也在彰显西门庆的经济实力和一定的社会地位。然而，西门庆穿着靴子却是严重违法行为，如在特定时期，可能会面临严厉的刑罚。

据叶丽娅（2011）在《中国历代鞋饰》一书中记载，"明洪武二十五年，朝廷又进一步下令：严禁庶民、商贾、技艺、步军、余丁及杂役等穿靴，只能穿皮札（革翁），唯独天寒地冻的北方地区，允许用牛皮直缝靴，违者处以极刑。""文武百官朝服配皂靴。皂靴面料采用皮、缎、毡等，大多染成黑色，多用于男子。"且"头顶缠棕大帽，脚踏粉底乌靴"，是形容明代官员之冠靴的。

在原著第七回中，西门庆只是一位开生药铺的商人，到了第三十回，才有了理刑副千户的官职，所以其在当时的穿着明显是僭越和违规行为。然而，明朝中后期，随着经济的不断发展，社会阶级结构发生了变化，商人的地位在逐步提升中，因此，这种服饰上僭越和违禁的现象也逐渐增多。因此，有学者认为："基于原文中暗含的西门庆僭越服饰礼仪，显示其体面和地位，不妨在皂靴的后面补注'only court officials and people from upper class are allowed to wear the white soled black boots while normal folks don't have this right'（皂靴只有朝廷官员以及社会上层人士可以穿着，普通民众禁穿），也可以在 white soled black boots 前面补加形容词'ceremonial'（仪式或典礼所用的）作为定语，加深读者对皂靴所承载的礼仪文化的理解和认识"（张慧琴 武俊敏，2016：55）。

可见，在古典文学作品英译过程中，针对特定历史文化背景下的文化负载词，或含有寓意的文化信息，译者进行了有意误译或者有意避开不译的情形不在少数，体现出中国文化负载词语翻译的复杂性和难度。

例 30

原文：有尚书某购以<u>百金</u>，邢曰："虽万金不易也。"（《聊斋志异·石清虚》）

翟译：A high official next offered Hsing <u>one hundred ounces of silver</u> for it; but he refused to sell it even for ten thousand.

杨译：A certain minister offered <u>one hundred ounces of silver</u> to buy it, to which Mr Xing replied, "I won't sell it even for ten thousand ounces!"

梅译：A certain board minister offered to buy the stone for <u>one hundred pieces of gold</u>, but Xing said, "I wouldn't give it up, ever for ten thousand pieces."

《聊斋志异》原文中提到的主要货币为白银，也作"白镪"。因《聊斋志异》使用的语言为文言文，因此货币单位与文白相兼的《红楼梦》中的货币单位有明显差距。《红楼梦》中直接使用银子、白银等物质名词，使用"两"作为金衡单位。例如：

例 31

原文："这是二十<u>两</u>银子，暂且给这孩子做件冬衣罢"。（《红楼梦》第六回）

杨译："Here's twenty <u>taels</u> to make the child some winter clothes."

霍译："Here is the twenty <u>taels</u> of silver," said Xi-feng. "Take this for the time being to make some winter clothes for the children with."

　　对比可见《红楼梦》原著中通用货币为白银和黄金，银两出现的词频更高，例 31 中两位译者都采取了直译的方法，找到了"两"这一词的对等"tael"，与原文中的词意保持一致。

　　而《聊斋志异》中出现较多的文言文的货币为"金"。所谓"百金"并非百两黄金，在先秦两汉时期，"百金"指百斤铜，宋代以后，白银为流通货币，"百金"即指百两银。而英语国家的货币单位中的盎司可分为金衡盎司和常衡盎司。1 金衡盎司＝31.1035 g，1 常衡盎司＝28.3495 g。一盎司约相当于中国旧度量衡（16 两为一斤）的一两。

　　从货币的等值换算角度看来，例 30 中，翟译和杨译是正确的，将一两银等同于英国度量衡单位中的一盎司。从历史文化的角度衡量，二者均采取了归化策略，用译语文化中的金衡单位代替了原语文化中的单位，以使读者在阅读中易于理解和接受中文中的度量衡单位，因此，二者的翻译均为有意误译。而梅译则对"金"的理解和解释出现了概念性的错误，将其理解为"gold"（黄金），是对历史文化知识的欠缺而导致的文化误读，属于无意误译。梅译在其所翻译的其他篇章中对"金"这一货币的解释都为"gold（黄金）"，如在《连城》篇中，原文"以千金列几上"被译成"spreading one thousand taels of gold out on the table"。

　　由此可见，在翻译中，尤其是在跨文化翻译中，译者必然要面对原文本中存在于语篇之外的具有鲜明的文化特征的负载词语的解读和翻译的重任。在本文研究的这几部古典文学名著中，物质文化负载词数量巨大，承载了大量历史文化信息和隐喻，因此译者应综合考虑读者的接受能力和理解视域，考虑译语文化的特征，从而选择各自的解读方式和翻译方法，或删除不译、或改写、或直译意译结合、或采取文内直译、文外加注等手段，填补由于文化差异所造成的读者认知上的空缺，达到文化交流和传播的目的。

3.3　宗教文化负载词的误译

宗教是人类社会发展进程中的特殊的文化现象，是"人类文化发展过程中衍生出的一种特殊形式，从人类学和文化学的角度来讲，它伴随着人类文化的产生和发展。因此，不同的宗教反映了不同的文化，宗教文化在人类文化发展过程中起着重要的作用"（陈竞春，马佳瑛，2023：132）。

从广义上讲，宗教本身是一种以信仰为核心的文化，也是整个社会文化的一部分。狭义而言，在语言与翻译领域，宗教文化作为文化的一个分支，与社会文化、物质文化、生态文化、语言文化并列。宗教文化与人类文明共同发展，不断丰富传统历史文化宝库。在古典文学著作中，宗教文化不仅涉及中国道教，佛教的渗透力也随处可见。宗教信仰存在于每一种文化，不同的宗教也导致信奉者遵循各自的习俗和传统。宗教文化负载词即指这些宗教色彩浓重的词汇。

例 32

原文：宋江道："我今番走了死路，望神明庇佑则个！神明庇佑！神明庇佑！"（《水浒传》第四十一回）

赛译：Then trembling, Sung Chiang said to himself, "This time I have gone into a blind alley and I pray the god to protect me. O God, protect me! O God, protect me!"

《水浒传》原著中涉及的宗教主要是中国传统道教和佛教。宋江在梁山泊站稳脚跟之后,"恐老父存亡不保。宋江想念,欲往家中搬取老父上山,以绝挂念",然而晁盖却认为"寨中人马未定,再停两日,点起山寨人马,一径去取了来",方保无虞。宋江一意孤行,打算"和兄弟宋清搬取老父连夜上山来,那时乡中神不知,鬼不觉"。晁盖仍旧担忧其"路中倘有疏失,无人可救"。然而宋江道:"若为父亲,死而无怨。"当日苦留不住,宋江执意前去,结果在还道村遭遇追兵,几乎束手就擒,命悬一线之际,他祈祷"神明保佑",这里的"神明"首先泛指一般的神灵,然而仔细考察原著,会发现小说中的神话背景主要源自中国古代道教神话。

道教神系是道教中对于神灵的分类和体系化构建,包括以三清和玉皇大帝为首的最高神、辅佐神、文化之神、战神、财富之神、吉祥之神、幽冥鬼神等多个部分。这些神灵在道教信徒中地位尊崇,是他们信仰和崇拜的对象。因此,赛珍珠在此处采取的归化译法,是明显的有意的文化误译,以基督教中的上帝代替了道教神话中的诸神,与原著中的神话和文化意象相去甚远。

第四十一回的回目名称"还道村受三卷天书,宋公明遇九天玄女""九天玄女"被赛珍珠译为"The Goddess Of The Ninth Heaven",还有一处"玄女"译为"The Dark Goddess"。

九天玄女,简称玄女,俗称玄牝氏、九天娘娘、九天玄女娘娘、九天玄母天尊、九天玄阳元女圣母大帝玄牝氏,中国古代神话中的传授过兵法的女神,后经道教奉为高阶女仙与术数神。她在民俗信仰中的地位崇高显赫,乃是一位深谙军事韬略,法术神通的正义之神，形象经常出现于中国各类古典小说之中，成为扶助英雄铲恶除暴的应命女仙，故而她在道教神仙信仰中的地位重要，其信仰发源可追溯至先秦以前（网络资料）。在《水浒传》原著中，九天玄女一词共出现 7 次，在第四十二回和第八十八回"颜统军阵列混天象阵，宋公明梦授玄女法"中，都有详细情节讲述宋江得到九天玄女的帮助。可见，道教中的神仙形象"九天玄女"在整部小说中的重要意义。

赛珍珠在翻译这一文化负载词时采取了异化策略，有意地将异质文化中的特殊宗教文化意象展示给目的语读者，虽然未能以注释或解释的补充方法对"九天玄女"的文化背景进行进一步阐明，但对于文化信息量巨大的一部文学名著来说，简单直译可以使译入语读者大致了解中西方宗教文化的差异以及由此而产生的不同的神祇体系。

例 33

原文：长老心忙，打鼓错拿徒弟手；沙弥情荡，磬槌敲破老僧头。从前苦行一时休，万个金刚降不住。（《金瓶梅词话》）

芮译：

The abbot is so flustered;

He grabs the hand of an acolyte

instead of his drumstick.

The novice is so carried away;

He hammers on the pate of an old monk

Instead of the bronze chime.

All the merit of their former austerities

comes to nothing in a moment;

Even a myriad guardian deities

could not reduce them to order.

原著中这一情节出自第八回"盼情郎佳人占鬼卦，烧夫灵和尚听淫声"。毒杀武大之后，因担心武松出差归来追究，西门庆、王婆和潘金莲密谋，约定"八月初六日，是武大百日，请僧烧灵。初八日晚，娶妇人家去"，这样潘金莲"幼嫁由亲，后嫁由身。古来叔嫂不通门户"，即使武松回来也不能干涉嫂子另嫁他人。到了烧灵当日，原文细致描写了潘金莲出场后众和尚的丑态百出：

原文：且说潘金莲怎肯斋戒，陪伴西门庆睡到日头半天，还不起来。和尚请斋主拈香金字，证盟礼佛，妇人方才起来梳洗，乔素打扮，来到佛前参拜。众和尚见了武大这老婆，一个个都迷了佛性禅心，关不住心猿意马，七颠八倒，酥成一块。但见：班首轻狂，念佛号不知颠倒；维摩昏乱，诵经言岂顾高低。烧香行者，推倒花瓶；秉烛头陀，误拿香盒。宣盟表白，大宋国错称做大唐国；忏罪阇黎，武大郎几念武大娘。长老心忙，打鼓借拿徒弟手；沙弥情荡，磬槌敲破老僧头。从前苦行一时休，万个金刚降不住。

译文中，芮效卫以"abbot"（男修道院长，寺院男住持）对应"长老"，以"novice"（见习修士）代替"沙弥"，以"guardian deities（守护神）"代替"金刚"。其总体的翻译策略是归化翻译。

网络资料中，对"长老"一词的定义，除了指老年人外，是佛教对释迦上首弟子的尊称。如：长老舍利弗；长老须菩提，或是住持僧的尊称，见宋善卿《祖庭事苑·释名谶辨·长老》："今禅宗住持之者，必呼长老。"又如《水浒传》第四回："寺里有五七百僧人，为头智真长老，是我弟兄。"此外，"长老"为僧人的尊称，通常用于称呼那些德高望重、修行有成的僧人。因此，芮效卫选择了"abbot"来替代"长老"这一宗教文化词语，是经由译者发挥自身对译文的操纵性之下进行了文化过滤，属于文化替换。

"沙弥"常见于佛教，是梵语译音，指的是初落发为僧，已受十戒但尚未受具足戒的男性僧徒，年龄范围一般在七至二十岁之间。沙弥作为佛教徒，需要遵守佛教戒律，修行佛法。他们的职责可能包括参与寺院的日常活动、学习佛法、协助其他僧人等。沙弥在佛教寺院中通常处于较低的地位，但随着修行的深入和经验的积累，他们有机会晋升为更高级别的僧人，如比丘等。芮效卫同样进行了归化，使用"novice"代替"沙弥"，等于基督教中的见习修士，其地位可以等同于沙弥。

至于金刚，在我国多指在佛教的（主要是西藏密宗）护法神，经常手持金刚杵，象征能够摧伏外道、守护佛法、击败邪魔的力量。这些护法神被称为执金刚神，金刚力士或密迹金刚，简称为金刚，也做"金刚手菩萨"，被认为具有摧毁一切障碍、保护修行者的力量。民间流传的"四大金刚"是传统文化中的护法神，被尊崇为四大金刚，包括东方持国天王、南方增长天王、西方广目天王和北方多闻天王。他们各自守护着须弥山的四峰，身穿不同颜色的盔甲，手持不同的法宝，代表着不同的意义。他们的形象和故事在中国文化中非常受欢迎，被尊崇为不同的神祇。

因此，"金刚"即是守护之神，护法之神，直译为"guardian deities"中规中矩，但却并非佛教中原汁原味的四位怒目圆睁、手持法器的佛教护法的原始形象。因此，芮译在这一案例中的归化译法，虽然在译入语中找到了可以对等的形象来指代原文中的宗教文化负载词，却失去了原文中异域文化中的风味。译者有意地进行文化过滤，采取了归化的翻译策略，是因为"任何翻译活动的开展都是以'交流'为目的，但是只有异域文化不再如天书般地难懂，并且能在本土形式里得到很好的阐释时，其交流的目的才能真正实现。所以，翻译的进程中归化是不可避免的。其间，异域文本被烙上使本土特定群体易于理解的文字和文化价值的烙印"（许宝强，袁伟，2001：38）。

然而，没有任何一部译作，全文仅仅采用一种单一的归化或者异化翻译策略。更多的情形是两种策略并用共存，或者交替使用，以达到文化交流和传播的目的。同样是芮效卫的译本中，以下译例则是采取了异化和归化策略并存：

例 34

原文：听法闻经怕无常，红莲舌上放豪光。（《金瓶梅词话》第三十九回）

芮译：Hearing the Dharma and heeding the scriptures,
　　　she is afraid of death；
　　　The red lotus-blossom tongue of the preacher emits
　　　rays of light.

译者对"法"的解释为"Dharma"，意为"达摩的佛法"，"经"译为"scriptures"（圣经的经文）也就是说，前半部分采取了异化策略，后半部分的宗教文化负载词则运用了归化手段。此外，译者将"无常"意译为"death"，取其婉转喻"死亡"之意。

马海燕（2022）认为："归化和异化是文学翻译中的文化策略问题，而直译与意译则是语言策略问题。极端的归化或过度的异化都不可取。极端的归化会使原语文化的异国色彩消失殆尽，最终难以达到不同文化的交流和融合。而过度的异化则会导致译文晦涩难懂，给文化交流带来困难。"

归化和异化翻译并不是两种互相矛盾和排他存在的，而是相辅相成的关系。"不论是归化还是异化，也不论是直译还是意译，都可以看作是为了适应翻译生态环境所做出的一种翻译策略选择。"（胡庚申，2004：125）

《红楼梦》是中国文化集大成者，是一部文化与社会的百科全书，具有鲜明的民族性，书中宗教文化负载词数量较大，因此在文化典籍英译中，需要尽最大可能还原中国宗教文化。

例 35

原文：（宝玉）满面泪痕泣道："家里姐姐妹妹都没有，单我有，我说没趣；如今来了这么一个神仙似的妹妹也没有，可知这不是个好东西。"（《红楼梦》第三回）

杨译：His face stained with tears, Bao-yu sobbed, "None of the girls here has one, only me. What's the fun of that? Even this newly arrived cousin who's lovely as a fairy hasn't got one either. That shows it's no good".

霍译："None of the girls has got one," said Bao-yu, his face streaming with tears and sobbing hysterically: "Only I have got one, it always upsets me. And now this new cousin comes here who is as beautiful as an angel and she hasn't got one either, so I know it can't be any good."

上文中宝黛初见，贾宝玉发现如此美貌的林妹妹居然没有玉，不禁闹了起来。他将林黛玉比作"神仙"，是指中国神话中的神仙意象。这类女性神仙，也称仙女，特点是"品德高尚，智慧非凡，纤尘不染，高雅脱俗，且具有非凡能力、长生不死"，在神仙体系中地位较高，例如嫦娥仙子；也有一些地位略低，主要特点是美貌绝伦，超凡脱俗，例如王母娘娘的七仙女等。因此，在文学语境中多用来形容容颜姣好，端庄秀丽，清新脱俗的女子。

两种译文中，杨译采取异化策略，译为"fairy"，符合原著中的文化意象，相比之下，霍克斯的有意误译明显。他采取了归化策略，将"神仙"一词用基督教中的 angel（天使）一词来代替。

《水浒传》开篇就是洪太尉不听劝阻开启封印，放走了伏魔殿镇压的妖魔。梁山一百单八将为"三十六天罡星、七十二地煞星"妖魔转世，这也是全书涉及的最重要的神话设定之一。

例 36

原文：读千卷之书，每闻古今之事，未见神仙有如此徒弟！既系妖人！牢子，与我加力打那厮！（《水浒传》第五十二回）

赛译：I have read a thousand books and I hear always of things both now and past, and never did I see a holy man have such an acolyte as this! He is naught but a witch-man. Gaolers, beat him for me with all your strength!

上文中的"神仙"一词，赛珍珠的译法是将其归化为"holy man"（圣人）。原著中的罗真人被称作"现世的活神仙"，连牢头狱卒都道："这蓟州罗真人是天下有名的得道活神仙"。所以原文中的宗教文化负载词明显是指道教神话的"神仙"，因此赛译是有意的文化误译。

至于《聊斋志异》这部奇书，除少数现实主义情节外，大部分篇幅充满了志怪和神话色彩。作者构建了独特的狐仙鬼魅等形象，多姿多彩，其中宗教文化负载词汇丰富。

例 37

原文：少慕道，闻劳山多仙人，负笈往游。（《聊斋志异·崂山道士》）

翟译：This gentleman had a penchant for the Taoist religion; and hearing that at Lao-shan there were plenty of Immortals*, shouldered his knapsack and went off for a tour thither.

（*译者注：The "angles" of Taoism-immortality in a happy land being the reward held out for life on earth in accordance with the doctrine of Tao. ）

杨译：…… who had admired Taoism from childhood. Hearing that there were many immortals on Mount Laoshan, he packed his bags and set off to make a trip there.

梅译：From youth onward he was attracted to Taoist arts. Hearing that immortals abounded on Lao Mountain, he packed his books on his back and set out there on adventure.

《崂山道士》是《聊斋志异》中的名篇，因其情节玄奇幻且寓意深刻，在我国是家喻户晓、老少皆知的一个奇幻故事。上海美术电影制片厂在 1981 年制作的同名木偶动画片上映后，《崂山道士》被更多的少年儿童观众所了解。

三种译文都将"仙人"译为"immortals"，可见三位译者对中国道教文化中的"神仙"一词均有深入的了解，然而比较之下，只有翟理斯的译文采取了文内直译、文外加注的方法。翟译直接将"神仙"的形象译作"长生不死者"，但在其注释中，却仍然保持了翟译的一贯翻译策略：归化翻译，解释了中国道教信仰中的"神仙"即等同于基督教中的天使，因其在人世间的种种善行而得到奖赏，得以在乐园之中获得永生。

然而，中国传统文化中的"神仙"这一意象内涵丰富，历史源远流长。我国的神系可分为儒教和道教两个体系，后者的流传度更广泛。道教所信仰的神仙大致可分为两大类，即"神"和"仙"。"神"是指神祇，即天神、地祇、物灵、地府神灵、人体之神、人鬼之神等；其中天神、地祇、阴府神灵、人体之神一类的"神"，是先天存在的真圣。仙是古代中国神话中称有特殊能力、可以长生不死的人，仙不同于神有先天的存在，仙只能通过后天的修炼而成。

"神仙"这一特殊的文化意象，在中国传统文化中指神话传说中具有特殊能力、能够长生不老的人；而在道教文化中则专指通过修炼得道从而获得超自然的能力而变得无所不知、无所不能、可以随意变幻形态、生活于凡人无法抵达的境界之中的群体。

早在《山海经》中就已经出现对长生不死的人物之描述，至战国时代，上至王侯、下至平民中都流传着长生不死的信仰。中国历史上第一位统一六国的帝王秦始皇，听信术士的蛊惑，耗巨资派人到东海蓬莱一带去寻求长生不死的仙药，不可谓不痴迷。大概秦始皇坚信，人类若可得仙药，便可如嫦娥一般，得道升仙，不死不朽，其霸业就可千秋万载、生生世世不易主了。

提及神仙，首先是外貌之美，其次是具有仙法。庄子就曾在

《逍遥游》中描述了他心目中的神人形象："藐姑射之山,有神人居焉,肌肤若冰雪,淖约若处子,不食五谷,吸风饮露,乘云气,御飞龙,而游乎四海之外。其神凝,使物不疵疬而年谷熟"。

古代诗词中多见神仙和仙子二字。在白居易的《长恨歌》中描述了世外桃源般的仙境和风姿绰约的仙子："忽闻海上有仙山,山在虚无缥缈间。楼阁玲珑五云起,其中绰约多仙子";李白的《江上吟》:"仙人有待乘黄鹤,海客无心随白鸥";杜甫的《望岳》:"安得仙人九节杖,拄到玉女洗头盆";朱庆馀《赠道者》:"独住神仙境,门当瀑布开";卢纶的《送王尊师》:"梦别一仙人,霞衣满鹤身";陆游的《一落索·识破浮生虚妄》:"俯仰人间今古,神仙何处";欧阳修的《采桑子·春深雨过西湖好》:"兰桡画舸悠悠去,疑是神仙";唐寅的《桃花庵歌》:"桃花仙人种桃树,又摘桃花换酒钱"等等,不胜枚举。

古典文学作品中对神仙书写最多的自然非《西游记》莫属。且不说以玉皇大帝为首的天庭众神,散落在人间的地仙鬼仙和散仙就穿插在全书各处。

在第二十四回中,"说这座山名唤万寿山,山中有一座观,名唤五庄观,观里有一尊仙,道号镇元子,混名与世同君","又见那二门上有一对春联:长生不老神仙府,与天同寿道人家",可见大仙镇元子在仙界的资历匪浅,就连他观里的人参果,作者都不厌其烦地描述:"那观里出一般异宝,乃是混沌初分,鸿蒙始判,天地未开之际,产成这颗灵根。盖天下四大部洲,惟西牛贺洲五庄观出此,唤名草还丹,又名人参果。三千年一开花,三千年一结果,再三千年才得熟,短头一万年方得吃。似这万年,只结得三十个果子。果子的模样,就如三朝未满的小孩相似,四肢俱全，五官咸备。人若有缘得那果子闻了一闻，就活三百六十岁；吃一个，就活四万七千年。"人参果的与天地同寿和神奇功效也侧面烘托着神仙镇元大仙的地位。而在孙悟空推倒果树闯祸后，四处寻找帮手，找到福禄寿三星求解，三星惊道："你这猴儿，全不识人。那镇元子乃地仙之祖，我等乃神仙之宗；你虽得了天仙，还是太乙散数，未入真流，你怎么脱得他手?"神仙系统的复杂性和等级森严可见一斑。

在《红楼梦》第六十三回"寿怡红群芳开夜宴　死金丹独艳理亲丧"中，贾敬长期在道观中与诸道士炼丹以求成为长生不死的神仙，最终因服食丹药而殒命。事发后，众道士慌忙辩称："原是老爷秘法新制的丹砂吃坏事，小道们也曾劝说'功行未到，且服不得'，不承望老爷于今夜守庚申时，悄悄地服了下去，便升仙了。这恐是虔心得道，已出苦海，脱去皮囊，自了去也。"可见修炼成仙的渊源之深，直至清代仍盛行此道。

在例 37 的三种译文中，翟理斯的有意误译显而易见是受自身的偏见所左右，从而将原语文化中的意象进行了跨文化的操控，从自身的文化观、宗教观出发，将原文中的文化意象归化为目的语读者耳熟能详、广泛认同的意象。正如勒菲维尔 (Lefevere，1992) 在《翻译、改写以及对文学名声的制控》一书中就曾指出的：翻译从本质上而言是译者对原著的改写。成功的译者实际上操控原著在目的语中的接受和传播。翟译的有意操纵多次体现在对宗教文化负载词的有意误译之中。

例 38

原文：江西孟龙谭，与朱孝廉客都中。偶涉一兰若，殿宇禅舍，俱不甚弘敞，唯一老僧挂搭其中。见客入，肃衣出迓，导与

随喜。(《聊斋志异·画壁》)

翟译:A KIANG-SI gentleman, named Mêng Lung-T'an, was lodging at the capital with a Mr. Chu,M. A. , when one day chance led them to a certain <u>monastery</u>, within which they found no spacious halls or meditation chambers, but only an old priest in déshabillé. On observing the visitors, he arranged his dress and went forward to meet them, <u>leading them round and showing whatever there was to be seen.</u>

梅译:While staying in the capital, Meng Longtan of Jiangxi and Master of Letters Zhu happened upon a <u>monastery</u>. Neither the shrine-hall nor the meditation room was very spacious, and only one old monk was found putting up within. Seeing the guests enter, the monk straightened up his clothes, went to greet them and <u>showed them around the place.</u>

原文中的"兰若"与"随喜"都是佛教用语。

"兰若"是梵文"阿兰若"的音译,本意指茂密、人迹罕至的森林,引申为寂静之处、远离喧嚣处等,后来泛指一般的佛寺。

在蕴含丰富的佛教文化的名著《西游记》中,全文中没有"兰若"一词,而蒲松龄在《尸变》《画壁》《长清僧》《聂小倩》《促织》《辛十四娘》《封三娘》《西湖主》《豢蛇》《僧术》《钟生》《李生》共十二篇故事中均使用了"兰若"一词指代佛教寺庙。

翟译与梅译都使用了"monastery"一词代替佛教的寺院,而杨宪益夫妇在《促织》的一文中,使用了"temple"一词来翻译原文中的"兰若"。

"Monastery"源于希腊语，有"独居"之意，同时拉丁语中的后缀"ium"用来表示"……之地"的概念，例如英语中的水族馆 aquarium（盛水的容器）、体育馆 gymnasium（练习之地）等，而这一拉丁语后缀衍生出的"arium、orium、erium"等后缀形式在英语中拼写形式为"ary、ory、ery"，意为"聚集……的场所"，例如英语中的工厂 factory（工作的场所）、天文台 observatory（观测天象之场所）等等。

因此，monastery 一词在英语中多指修道院，是修道士、僧侣或修女等或集体或独自修行之所。而杨译所用的 temple 一词表述也不够完整，因其也指神殿、圣堂、教堂等古希腊的宗教场所和基督教中的教堂及教士的居所。鉴于此，翟译与梅译选择了西方宗教中常用的词语来代替佛教专有名词，是基于目的语读者的理解和接受能力而选择的归化手段。但鉴于原文鲜明的佛教文化特征，在进行文学翻译和跨文化传播时，Buddhist temple 才是对佛教寺院一词忠实而准确的翻译，而两位目的语国家的译者的翻译均属有意的文化误译。

随喜是佛家语，本意为见人行善事，随之而生欢喜心之意。一般用作布施的代语，后借指游谒寺院。例如南朝梁沉约的《忏悔文》："弱性蒙心，随喜赞悦"；明代吴承恩的《西游记》第十二回："若敬重三宝，见善随喜，皈依我佛，承受得起，我将袈裟、锡杖，情愿送他"；清代孔尚任《桃花扇·闲话》："募建水陆道场，修斋追荐，并脱度一切冤魂，二位也肯随喜么？"

两位译者都比较准确地译出了"随喜"一词的本质："show someone around the place"。然而，在赛珍珠的《水浒传》译文里，"随喜"却变了味道。

例 39

原文：和尚道："敝寺新造水陆堂了，要来请贤妹随喜，只恐节级见怪。"（《水浒传》第四十四回）

赛译：The priest said，"We have now built our Hall of Land and Water and I have long desired to come hither and invite you，my Good Sister，to go there and take your pleasure as you please. I did but fear your lord might be displeased."

然而，赛珍珠的直译 "to go there and take your pleasure as you please" 表达的却是 "去那里玩得开心，只要你开心就好"。实际上，简单翻译为 "go there" 虽然损失了宗教文化特色，但至少表达出了 "随喜" 的实质，然而赛译画蛇添足地直译了 "随喜"，就完全扭曲了原文的宗教文化。这种文化误译必定让目的语读者对宗教文化产生误解，既不了解新造的水陆堂是何物，也不理解为何去了水陆堂就可以开心愉悦。

赛译对原语文化的直译和异化翻译策略离不开译者翻译的初心。在译著的序言中，她说："对于中国最著名小说之一《水浒传》的翻译，我并非想要做出一些学术上的建树，阐述解释和史实考据上并非完完全全一丝不苟。事实上，在翻译这部小说的时候我一点学术上的兴趣都没有，我的兴趣只在于原作这样一部以卓越的方式写就的卓越的故事。我尽可能地直译，因为对我而言，中国句式才是完全契合这个故事的描述方式，而我所有的努力都只在于使译作能够尽可能地接近原著风格。"

赛珍珠对 "随喜" 的误译虽然如其他直译一样因其简单粗暴和字字对译会遭到批评，但译者的主体性得到了充分地发挥，更加凸显原语语言和文化特色。正如韦努蒂（1992）所指出的:"提倡异化翻译法的核心就是要开创一种抵制目的语主流文化价值观的翻译理论与实践,从而彰显外语文本的语言和文化差异。"

例 40

原文:看你赵<u>檀越</u>面皮,与你这封书,投一个去处安身。我这里决然安你不得了。(《水浒传》第三回)

赛译:But I have considered the honor of your <u>guarantor</u> Chao and I give you this letter to a place where you can be at rest. Here surely we cannot tolerate you.

例 41

原文:"朱<u>檀越</u>! 何久游不归?"(《聊斋志异·画壁》)

翟译:"Friend Chu! what makes you stay away so long?"

梅译:"Why do you tarry so long, my good <u>patron</u>?"

由于某些原语词汇很难在目的语中找到完全对等的表达方式,尤其针对复杂的宗教文化负载词语的翻译,译者多会进行有意误译。

在例 40 中,赛珍珠的译文选取了"guarantor"一词代替佛教术语"檀越",但该英文词的意思为"担保人",因此已经脱离佛教这一宗教文化语境。

例 41 的两组译文对佛教术语"檀越"一词的翻译完全不同,翟译改用普通问候语的"Friend"+姓氏的称呼形式来表达,选择了对佛教文化负载词"檀越"采取改译的方法。而梅译将"檀越"一词译作"patron",是归化翻译策略,但在词义上,并不能与原文语义完全等同,即并未达到功能对等。

根据资料显示,"檀越"是梵文,有将其音译为"陀那钵底"

"陀那婆"的。梵汉并举的称呼是：檀越施主、檀越主、檀那主、檀主等，指施与僧众衣食或出资举行法会的信众。大乘佛教中观派重要论著《大智度论》上说："问曰：云何名檀？答曰：檀名布施，心相应善思，是名为檀。有人言：'从善思起身、口业，亦名为檀。'有人言：'有信、有福田、有财物，三事和合时，心生舍法，能破悭贪，是名为檀。'"也就是说，"檀"本是布施之意。佛教传入我国后，又加入"越"字，意为通过布施善行可以越过生死苦海。

《水浒传》第三回"赵员外重修文殊院，鲁智深大闹五台山"中，鲁智深在五台山文殊院落发为僧后，仍然百无禁忌，从不遵守佛寺的清规戒律，屡屡犯戒，因此寺中侍者对长老抱怨："智深好生无礼！全没些个出家人礼面！丛林中如何安着得此等之人！"然而长老听后却喝止道："胡说！且看檀越之面，后来必改。"此处的"檀越"就是出资舍钱在寺里的鲁智深的引荐人、施主赵员外，并非赛珍珠认为的担保人。

虽然在《西游记》全文中出现频率最高的是"施主"一词，共计出现 41 次，而"檀越"一词在《西游记》中仅出现一次，但词义仍同《水浒传》中的词义，专指为佛教寺院及僧众捐款捐物的资助人。

在《水浒传》中，"施主"一词出现 15 次，"檀越"共出现 8 次，可见以佛教为主的宗教文化在中国古典文学名著中的重要地位。

而英语中的"patron"一词的词源是拉丁语中的"patronus"，意思是"庇主，恩主，保护人"，但从中世纪后期到文艺复兴时代，此词多指"赞助人、主顾、庇护人"，是当时出资供养艺术家的有权势者，或指通过订购手工艺者的产品而赞助其生活和生产的主顾。偶见"守护神"的词义。见以下例句：

In 1755 British writer Samuel Johnson published an acerbic letter to Lord Chesterfield rebuffing his <u>patron</u> for neglecting and declining support. 1755 年，英国作家塞缪尔·约翰逊发表了一封致切斯特菲尔德勋爵的讽刺信，斥责其赞助人忽视并且拒绝支持他。

Uruk, for instance, had two patron gods—Anu, the god of the sky and sovereign of all other gods, and Inanna, a goddess of love and war—and there were others, <u>patrons</u> of different cities. 例如，乌鲁克有两个守护神——阿努，天空之神，是所有其他神的主宰；伊娜娜，是爱与战争女神；还有其他不同城市的守护神。

可见"patron"与"檀越"在文化层面和语言层面的差别。二者源于不同的文化历史背景，但是在对客体的援助形式上是相同的，即"通过物资或资金支持进行赞助"，因此梅译选择了"patron"一词代替原文中有佛教文化背景的专有名词"檀越"，在时间距离中将自身的理解视域与读者的理解视域相融合，在两种文化中架起了一道桥梁，因而其有意的误译是译者的正确选择，是在文化交流过程中遇到障碍时的译者的主体性的体现。

从翟理斯到赛珍珠，再到梅氏兄弟翻译《聊斋志异》，从 19 世纪到 20 世纪后半叶，经历的时间跨度较大，译者的翻译目的、翻译策略和翻译风格差距较大。海德格尔在其《存在与时间》(1987) 中肯定存在的时间性和历史性，认为时间距离导致现代读者理解经典文学作品时存在障碍。然而伽达默尔 (2004) 却否定了这一观点，认为时间距离是具有积极意义的，它可以成为新的理解的源泉。

伽达默尔（2004）认为，每一位译者都从自己的所处的历史时代出发，努力克服时间距离产生的隔阂，突破种种障碍，将自己的视域与历史上的原作者的视域结合起来，在不间断的理解过程中运动着，融合着，以期产生能为读者所理解的新文本，达到与读者的视域相融合。因此，译者的主体性在翻译过程中凸显，不仅能够对原文进行改写增删，还可以根据翻译目的、读者期待来适时调整翻译策略。这就导致了有些译者偏爱归化翻译，有些专注于异化策略；有的执着于直译，致力于将原语文化原封不动、原汁原味地呈现给译入语读者，有些译者则从目的语读者视角出发，力求改善其阅读体验，使异域文化融入本民族文化，从而更容易被接受。

正如孙致礼所总结的："翻译基本上是一种语言转换活动，但又不是一项纯粹的语言转换活动，它还牵涉到各种非语言因素，特别是牵涉到种种文化因素，因为语言作为文化的载体，往往带有一定的文化色彩。所以，我们翻译外国文学作品时，不仅要考虑语言的差异，还要密切注视文化的差异，力求最大限度地保存原文所蕴涵的异域文化特色。"（孙致礼，2002：43）

3.4　语言文化负载词的误译

语言文化负载词源于特定的语言文化，是指反映某一语言社会中语音和文字特征的词语。此类词语负载了文化内涵，具有一定民族特色，例如汉语中的成语、歇后语、诗词、对仗词、典故等。

语言是文化的载体。同一词汇在不同语言中含义不同，而相同的表达方式在不同的交际场合也具有各不相同的功能。中文中大量的成语、典故、歇后语等以其形式上的特征和语义上的特殊性，负载了大量的历史传统、风俗习惯等文化内容，这些简洁有力、生动优美、富于修辞色彩的语言文化负载词成为文学作品中亮丽的风景。然而，此类文化负载词因其含义不能从字面意义推断，译者需要尽最大可能地传递原著语言上的魅力和文化特质。通过"尽量传达原作的异域文化特色，尽量传达原作的异语语言形式"，从而使读者"欣赏文学作品特有的韵味，领略外国文学别具一格的情调"（孙致礼，2002）。

例 42

原文：宋清答道："我只闻江湖上人传说沧州横海郡柴大官人名字……"（《水浒传》第二十一回）

赛译：Sung Ching answered, "I asked those people on rivers and lakes and they said, 'We have always heard of the good name of the great Chai Chin near Chang Chou.' ..."

"江湖"一词在《水浒传》原著中共计出现 87 次，是小说中一个颇为重要的词汇。此词在中国文化中有多重引申含义。江湖的本义是指广阔的江河、湖泊，后衍生出"天下"的意思，与河流、湖泊关联甚微。后来也泛指古时不接受朝廷控制指挥和法律约束而适性所为的社会环境。因此，江湖一词逐渐演变成较为多面或特定的用语。《庄子·大宗师》里的江湖与明清小说中的江湖差异较大："泉涸，鱼相与处于陆，相呴以湿，相濡以沫，不如相忘于江湖。"《水浒传》则明确地把江湖看成是英雄豪杰、法外之徒杀人放火和争夺利益之处,在原著中多出现在"江湖好汉""江湖上人称""名闻江湖""走江湖""逃在江湖上""江湖上来往""飘荡江湖""流落江湖"等语境中。深谙中国古典文学的赛珍珠,当然知道"江湖"在《水浒传》中真正内涵,但是她在译文中却显示明显的有意误译特征。

据统计,赛珍珠译文中总计出现直译"rivers and lakes"十次,可见其执着地将原语文化特色原封不动地展示给目的语读者的翻译风格。

例 43

原文:西门庆道:"不敢动问娘子,<u>青春多少</u>?"(《水浒传》第二十三回)

赛译:… and Hsi Men Ch'ing said, "I do not dare to ask how many <u>springs and autumns</u> the good wife has passed."

例 44

原文:妇人又问道:"叔叔,<u>青春多少</u>?"(《水浒传》第二十三回)

赛译:The woman asked again, "Brother-in-law, how many <u>green springtimes</u> have you passed?"

例 45

原文:太师大喜,便问:"将军<u>青春多少</u>?"(《水浒传》第六十二回)

赛译:The prime minister was greatly pleased and he asked him, saying, "How many <u>green springs</u> have you passed?"

"青春"一词的主要释义为:一指春天,春季草木茂盛,其色青绿；二指青年时期，年纪轻；三指年岁；四指美好的时光，珍贵的年华。该词语最早出现在《楚辞·大招》中："青春受谢，白日昭只。"其他如唐代杜甫《闻官军收河南河北》诗："白日放歌须纵酒，青春作伴好还乡"；唐司空曙《送曹同椅》诗："青春三十馀，众艺尽无如"；清代李渔《意中缘·拒妁》："你如今的青春也不小了，早些相中一个才郎。"

在以上三例中，赛珍珠对"青春"一词进行了不同处理。例43 中，赛珍珠将<u>青春多少</u>转译为"春秋几何"，译文为"how many springs and autumns the good wife has passed"，与原文意思相去不大。

"春秋"一词，常用来表示一年四季。中国古代先民极其重视春、秋两季的祭祀，由此"春秋"衍生出更多的语言含义，常常用来表示：年，一年，四季，四时，光阴，年龄等。例如《战国策·楚策四》："今楚王之春秋高矣，而君之封地，不可不早定也。"北魏杨炫之《洛阳伽蓝记·永宁寺》："皇帝晏驾，春秋十九。"赛译选择了"springs and autumns"代替"青春"，是对译者的中文功底和对中华文化的谙熟的一种佐证，对那些激烈批评赛译扭曲、荒谬以及译者完全不了解中国文化的负面声音来说也是一种有力反击。

译者在使用"spring"和"autumn"两个词后，使语言意蕴悠长，为平凡的日常对话平添了历史文化赋予语言的强烈美感。但在接下来两例中，赛译使用直译且是字字对应，将"青春"译为"green springtimes"和"green springs"，这与赛译的主要翻译原则一样，凸显了"原汁原味"，这种文化误译对于推介异域文化是颇多裨益的。

例 46

原文：好半日，两个云雨方罢。（《水浒传》第四十四回）

赛译：After a long time only were they finished with each other.

"云雨"除了指自然界两种现象外，其比喻意义在文学作品中更为常见。最初"巫山云雨"的含义中并无男女情爱这一内涵，其原义是指巫山上的神女能够兴云降雨。天降雨露，促进了庄稼成长，使天下百姓过上富足安乐的日子。而"云雨"指男女欢会之情事源于宋玉《高唐赋》："妾在巫山之阳，高丘之阻，旦为朝云，暮为行雨。朝朝暮暮，阳台之下。"后世则广泛借用了其比喻意义，如唐朝诗人李白在《清平调》中写道："一枝红艳露凝香，云雨巫山枉断肠"；唐代刘禹锡《巫山神女庙》诗："星河好夜闻清佩，云雨归时带异香"；宋代晏几道《河满子》："眼底关山无奈，梦中云雨空休。"

然而，对于原著中明显的男女性爱的描写，赛珍珠却没有遵循她对大部分原语文化负载词语的异化处理方式和直译的方法，而是采取了意译，译为"they were finished"，这是赛译打破常规方法的一个典型案例。董琇（2009）指出：赛珍珠对于"性"的态度是：她"呼吁一种坦率和健康的视角，她说在中国，人体的功能，包括性，都是用直率的方式展现，她认为男女关系往往被一些委婉（euphemism）和遁词（evasion）所破坏，因此在遇到中文中有关性的委婉语时，她没有选择将该表达移植到英语中"。可见翻译方法的选择映射着译者的意识形态和价值取向。

例 47

原文：（水溶）一面又向贾政道："令郎真乃龙驹凤雏……."
（《红楼梦》第十五回）

杨译：(The prince) turned to observe to Jia Zheng, "Your son is truly <u>a dragon's colt</u> or <u>young phoenix</u> . . . ."

霍译：. . . the prince observed to Jia Zheng that "the <u>young phoenix</u> was worthy of his sire . . ."

"龙驹凤雏"这一成语最早出自唐代房玄龄《晋书·陆云传》："云字士龙，六岁能属文，性清正，有才理。少与兄机齐名，虽文章不及机，而持论过之，号曰二陆。幼时吴尚书广陵闵鸿见而奇之，曰：'此儿若非龙驹，当是凤雏。'"后世据此典故引申出成语"龙驹凤雏"，用来比喻英俊聪颖的少年，可用作恭维语，例如宋代范纯仁《祭谢秘丞文》："识君之初，君方幼龄。龙驹凤雏，神骨天成"；元朝梁寅《送贡士颜子中》诗："北庭贵胄多才华，历历科名映前后。吾观子中何俊拔，龙驹凤雏世稀有"；明代罗大纮《祭万亲母龙孺人》："兰苗玉立，凤雏龙驹。易书和熊，一体不殊。"

对比这两个版本的译文，可以发现两位译者在翻译"龙驹凤雏"这一成语上存在一定差异。在中国文化中，龙是古代传说中的一种神异动物，能兴云布雨，善于变化，并掌管天下的水系。后来龙被作为帝王的象征，封建时代有关帝王的事物也用龙作修饰语。

龙是华夏民族的图腾，也是华夏民族的象征，华夏民族自称是龙的传人。龙在中华文化中有着重要的地位，代表着吉祥、活力、勇敢和权力。龙在封建时代被作为皇帝的象征。杨译以传播中国传统文化为目的，采取了异化手段，直译为"a dragon's colt or young phoenix"，完整地将原文中的文化意象移植到了目的语文化中，带给读者一种独特的文化体验。

霍译则考虑到目的语读者对龙这一形象的负面理解，有意不译"龙驹"，而是选择了"凤雏"，将其译为"the young phoenix"，原因在于凤凰在西方的文化中，是在火中重生的一种神奇鸟类，形象偏于正面，因此被译者采纳。但是在西方国家，龙通常被视为邪恶的象征，这一观念深受宗教、神话传说和文学作品的影响。在基督教文化中，龙常常与撒旦联系在一起，象征着邪恶和破坏。例如，在《圣经·启示录》中，龙被描绘为撒旦的化身，代表着诱惑和罪恶。在文学作品中，龙的形象也经历了演变。早期的龙通常被描述为拥有强大的力量和魔法，能够喷火或毒气。随着时间的推移，龙的形象变得更加复杂。在影视作品中，有些龙是为害人间的毒龙，为勇士所斩杀；有的则在凶猛恐怖的外表之下，随着剧情发展显露出善良纯真的一面，例如《怪物史莱克》里的守卫高塔里落难公主的火龙和俄罗斯电影《他是龙》中被女主唤醒人性的恶龙。

例 48

原文：薛文龙悔娶河东狮 贾迎春误嫁中山狼（《红楼梦》第七十九回）

杨译：Xue pan marries a fierce lioness and repents too late

Yingchun is wrongly wedded to an ungrateful wolf

霍译：Xue Pan finds to his sorrow that he is married to a termagant

And Ying-shun's parents betroth her to a Zhong-shan wolf

《红楼梦》第七十九回的回目可谓文化内涵极为丰富，十六字中包含两个著名典故："河东狮"和"中山狼"。前者也称为

"河东狮吼"，出自苏轼的《寄吴德仁兼简陈季常》："龙丘居士亦可怜，谈空说有夜不眠。忽闻河东狮子吼，拄杖落手心茫然"，用来比喻悍妒的妻子对丈夫大吵大闹，借以讥讽惧内的人。后者出自明代马中锡《东田文集》中的《中山狼传》，该词原指东郭先生在中山误救一只狼，结果脱困后的恶狼却要吃掉东郭先生。后人根据这则故事提炼出"中山狼"这一成语，用于比喻忘恩负义、恩将仇报的人。文字见于明末清初钱澄之的《报恩行》："君不见中山狼，猎人追奔窜道傍。老儒救其死，反眼睢盱爪牙张，攫取老儒充饥肠"和明末清初宋琬的《义虎行》："楚国谷于菟，书传非荒唐。作诗表厥异，愧彼中山狼。"

杨译使用了"a fierce lioness"诠释河东狮吼的所指，即：凶悍的母狮子；将"中山狼"直译和意译结合，译为"an ungrateful wolf"，意为"忘恩负义的狼"。译文如实地将母狮子和狼两种特殊的中国文化意象译介到目的语文化中，保留了原文的喻体，但是仍然没有能传译出原有的文化典故。霍译本以归化的策略将这个词译为"termagant"（泼妇、悍妇），这个词曾指英国早期戏剧中虚构的狂暴之神，虽然具有了古典韵味，但却省略了对"河东狮"这一典故的释义和注解，意译后的译文削弱了原文中的文化意象，不利于传递原语文化。

对于翻译中的文化典故的可译与不可译，黄东琳认为："可译与不可译的程度不是一成不变的，翻译工作者的任务就是要努力使不可译转化为可译，提高可译度"（黄东琳，2001：102）。因此，杨译和霍译的翻译策略各有优势，但若考虑将原语文化中的意象和历史典故准确传递到目的语中，归化、异化，直译和意译仍需全面考量，甚至可以结合起来，从而实现跨文化传播，提高读者的阅读体验。

例49

原文："在下敢不铭心刻骨，同哥一答里来家。"《金瓶梅词话》第十三回）

芮译："How could your wish that I should accompany your husband home be anything but：Imprinted in my heart and engraved on my bones?"

"刻骨铭心"这一成语寓意是铭刻在心灵深处，形容记忆深刻，难以忘却，出自《上安州李长史书》，也作"铭心刻骨"和"镌心铭骨"。

在小说原文中，西门庆向李瓶儿表态，既然把李瓶儿的丈夫花子虚带出去宴饮游乐，就要完好无损带回来，对此他牢记于心，定会不负嘱托，绝对不能有任何疏忽。因此，此处"铭心刻骨"表达的意思是"牢记于心，不敢忘记"。从原语读者的视角看，此处译为"牢牢记住，不辱使命，不负嘱托"更为恰当。但芮效卫的直译一字不漏，用了"imprint"和"engrave"两个表示"印刻""深深镌刻"的词语，从语义上来看，属于过度翻译，若作回译，其翻译效果反而不如意译，因此，芮译有意为之，重点是要突出西门庆面对觊觎对象李瓶儿时，其号称将使命和责任深深铭记于胸的信誓旦旦和花言巧语。

正因如此，芮译的有意误译效果令人耳目一新，可以使目的语读者感受到原语中语言文化特色。且芮效卫对书中的方言语气谙熟，翻译中使用了设问句，充分还原了"敢不"一词的含义，其译文不仅语义对等，形式上也做到了对等。

奈达（1964）在《翻译理论与实践》一书中指出："动态对

等是指用接受语言复制出与原语信息最切近的自然对等，首先是意义对等，其次是文体对等。"由此可见，芮译是创造性的翻译，力图将原语中的语言文化原封不动移植到译文中，因此达成了功能对等，这样的译文是符合读者期待的。

例 50

原文：温秀才道："<u>貂不足，狗尾续</u>。学生匪才，焉能在班门中弄大斧，不过乎塞责而已。"（《金瓶梅词话》第六十六回）

芮译：Licentiate Wen replied：

"<u>When sable-tailed cap ornaments run out，They can only be supplanted by dog tails.</u>

Your pupil is lading in talent. How could I：

Show off my skill with an axe before the gate of Lu Pan, the master carpenter?

All I can do is endeavor to fulfill my responsibilities."

貂为一种皮毛珍贵的动物有着独特的价值。我国古代时，皇帝的侍从用貂尾作帽子的装饰。据《晋书·赵王伦传》记载，当时由于任官太滥，貂尾不足，就用狗尾代替，是为"貂不足，狗尾续"，后来演化为"狗尾续貂"。芮译"When sable-tailed cap ornaments run out，They can only be supplanted by dog tails"，通过直译，表明了狗尾续貂的现象即"当貂尾巴做的帽子装饰用完的时候，只能用狗的尾巴代替"。然而，芮译在此处提供的背景文化信息有限，目的语读者在阅读时会产生一定的理解和联想困难，无法将"貂尾原料耗尽，用狗尾来替代"与上下文关联起来，容易形成理解断层。然而，芮效卫为了使英语读者对该谚语中的特殊的文化意象有所了解，有意地选择了直译，保存了原语文化的特色。

例 51

原文：赵员外道："要是留提辖在此，恐怕会有些<u>山高水低</u>，他日教提辖怨恨……"（《水浒传》第四回）

赛译：But Chao said，"If I let the captain stay here it will be <u>as dangerous as mountain too high and waters too deep</u>. Then if trouble comes，you will hate me … "

原著中出现的"山高水低"这一成语多用来比喻意外的灾祸或不幸的事情，多指人的死亡。同义词为"三长两短"。资料显示，这一用法多出现在明代以后的文学作品中，例如《水浒传》第四回和第三十二回都出现了该成语；明代冯梦龙《醒世恒言》卷八："万一有些山高水低，有甚把臂，那原聘还了一半，也算是他们忠厚了"；《初刻拍案惊奇》卷二十三："夫人知道了，恐怕自身有甚山高水低，所以悲哭了一早起了"；清代吴敬梓的《儒林外史》第二十回："居士，你但放心，说凶得吉。你若果有些山高水低，这事都在我老僧身上。"

鲁达因一时义愤填膺，拳打镇关西后不得不走上逃亡之路，途中遇到被救女子的父亲，后者将其介绍给女子的官人赵员外，此人不仅家财丰厚，且有一颗侠义之心，便收留了鲁提辖。然而赵员外担心时间久了，人多口杂，万一走漏消息，鲁提辖恐有灾祸，若有"山高水低"，难免负了恩人，招惹怨恨，因此赵员外想出了万全之策：送鲁达到五台山落发出家，可免牢狱之灾，保一生平安。

赛译仍然采取了直译的方法，但为了使译文中独特的语言文化负载词能够为读者所理解和接受，在"山高"和"水低"之前增加了"as dangerous as",作为"mountain too high and waters too deep"的释义,因此,译者积极采取了应对措施,即使异化手段看起来突兀难解,但经解释性补充后,"遇到危险"的词意被明示,"山高水低"这一成语的喻义并没有被曲解或者误译,而是有意地将原文中独特的文化特色保留了下来。

例 52

原文:那西门庆正和这婆娘在楼上取乐,听见武松叫这一声,惊得<u>屁滚尿流</u>。(《水浒传》第二十六回)

赛译:Now that Hsi Men Ching was at that very moment upstairs with the woman seeking happiness and when he heard this shout from Wu Sung, he was so frightened that <u>his wind burst from him and his water came out of him</u>.

"屁滚尿流"常用来形容一个人惊慌失措的状态。此处赛译和以往的翻译方法几乎相同,均采取了直译手法,意图展现当时的场景:当西门庆听到武松的声音后,吓得惊慌失措,胆战心惊,甚至达到了"屁滚尿流"的境地。那么,西门庆到底是真的被吓得屎尿齐下还是仅仅是一种夸张的表达方式呢?赛珍珠选择了直译,目的就是希望通过保留中国古代语言特有的表达方式和行文习惯,从而将中国名著原原本本地介绍到西方,所以她认为直译是最佳选择。于是乎,在赛译《水浒传》中,出现大量的直译,其真实还原程度甚至令众多翻译评论家将之斥为"误译",例如"吃酒"被译为"eat wine","江湖好汉"译作"a gaol fellow of the rivers and lakes","不足挂齿"译为"need not hang upon the teeth"等等。

对于赛珍珠的误译,一种看法是:翻译中个别字句的疏漏在所难免，毕竟赛珍珠非地道的中国人，即使是来自本国的资深译者，也不能完全保证汉译英时不存在任何疏忽。因此，赛译确实存在大量误译。而另一种看法却是：赛珍珠这种极端的直译"完全是有意为之，作为一个精通中美语言的文学家和翻译家，她的语言功底毋庸置疑。她舍弃地道、简洁的英语，而按照原文结构翻译，增加译文的汉语特征，再现了汉语的思维方式和语言特色，使译文处处显出中国英语的痕迹，从而借助翻译实现了向西方传播中国文化的意图"（张静，2011：52）。

例 53

原文：晚斋灭烛，冀旧梦可以复寻，而<u>邯郸路渺</u>，悔叹而已。（《聊斋志异》《莲花公主》）

翟译：In the evening he put out his candle, hoping to continue his dream; but, alas! the <u>thread was broken</u>, and all he could do was to pour forth his repentance in sighs.

梅译：Later that night he blew out the candles in his studio, hoping to find his way back to the same dream, but <u>the road was lost in haze</u>. All he could do was heave a sigh of regret.

原文中的窦生梦中被某国王召见，后来与美貌的公主结为夫妇，醒来发觉梦中的王国竟然是蜜蜂的栖息之地，公主不过是嘤嘤鸣叫于耳畔的蜂子而已。故事中的"邯郸路渺"出自中国明代著名戏剧家汤显祖的"临川四梦"（又称玉茗堂四梦）之一的《邯郸记》。故事取材于唐代沈既济的传奇《枕中记》，讲述了穷困书生卢生在邯郸的一间小客栈偶遇仙人吕洞宾后，借其瓷枕入睡后所经历的宦海沉浮、一世浮华，醒来却是美梦一场、厨中黄粱未熟的传奇故事。

临川四梦中,《牡丹亭》和《紫钗记》描写男女之间的悲欢离合,是儿女风情戏;而《南柯记》与《邯郸记》则写梦幻人生,醒来皆空,为社会风情剧。蒲松龄不仅在《聊斋志异》中创作了与《邯郸记》如出一辙的《续黄粱》,在《莲花公主》中,也能看到《南柯记》中淳于棼梦入槐安国(即蚂蚁国)被招为驸马、繁华过后,万象皆空、人生若梦的影子。《邯郸记》和《南柯记》是中国文学作品中以梦境喻人生的经典之作,问世后广为流传,并在语言中以成语和典故的形式流传至今,如"黄粱一梦""南柯一梦"等。对于这一经典的文化意象,翟译为"thread was broken",梅译为"the road(to the dream land)was lost in haze",均为意译,都没有深入介绍"邯郸记"这一文学典故,由此可见,含有人名、地名的大量的历史典故在翻译中都是棘手的难题,其不可译性显而易见。译者面临的困难是:要么直译加注释,介绍该典故来龙去脉,但是篇幅大大增加,不够言简意赅;要么采取意译方法,方便读者阅读和了解,然而文化背景和文化特色则有所损失。

例 54

原文:乃升堂而跪,曰:"为桃故,杀吾子矣!如怜小人而助之葬,当结草以图报耳。"(《聊斋志异》《偷桃》)

翟译:He then approached the dais and said, "Your peach, gentlemen, was obtained at the cost of my boy's life; help me now to pay his funeral expenses, and I will be ever grateful to you."

梅译:He paused to walk up to the hall, where he knelt and pleaded:"My son lost his life because of that peach. If you take pity on me and help with the burial，I swear that I will <u>repay you even after death</u>."

"结草以报"与"结草衔环"都是汉语成语，同时也是历史典故，比喻受人恩惠后希望尽自己所能来报答对方。据网络资料介绍，"结草"之典故来自《左传·宣公十五年》：

秋七月，秦桓公伐晋，次于辅氏。壬午，晋侯治兵于稷以略狄土，立黎侯而还。及洛，魏颗败秦师于辅氏。获杜回，秦之力人也。初，魏武子有嬖妾，无子。武子疾，命颗曰："必嫁是。"疾病，则曰："必以为殉。"及卒，颗嫁之，曰："疾病则乱，吾从其治也。"及辅氏之役，颗见老人结草以亢杜回，杜回踬而颠，故获之。夜梦之曰："余，而所嫁妇人之父也。尔用先人之治命，余是以报。"

由此可见，"结草"一说历史悠久，其中蕴含着丰富的语言文化信息。

翟译对历史典故选择了意译，将其解释为"I will be ever grateful to you"（我会永远感激你）；梅译也同样选择了意译，但在译文中体现了"即使现在无法报答，死后也要报恩"（repay you even after death）的强烈的感激之情和执意回报的决心。可见，在翻译过程中，究竟采取直译还是意译的方法，要视具体语境而定，有时取决于译者的翻译目的和读者的期待视野和翻译的效果，即译者的视域与读者的视域的融合程度与最终达到的效果。

在将一种语言形式转换为另外一种语言形式的过程中，涉及复杂的文化信息的传递时，译者可以选择不再局限于原文的形式上的对等，而是注重译语的流畅性和可读性，侧重原语和译语之间意义上的对等。因此，两种译文虽然没有译出"结草以报"的典故而选择了意译，从而造成了有意的误译，但在语言形式无法达到对等的情况下，译者选择将原文中的主要信息和思想内容用地道流畅的译语表达出来，能够为目的语读者所理解和接受，也不失为一种正确的选择。

3.5　生态文化负载词的误译

生态文化负载词多为反映某一语言社会中的自然环境和地理环境特征的词语，即由于某一国家或民族独特的自然现象、地理环境、气候条件等特征的影响而产生的词汇，例如有区域和地域特征的动植物、地形、地貌等均属于此类。

语言于人类所生存的自然环境之中产生和发展演变，自然环境不仅影响人类的生活生产方式和行为习惯，也对特定的语言社会中的人们的思维方式和语言的使用产生了不容忽视的影响。

生态文化负载词意蕴深厚，除了表面的浅层含义之外，多有比喻寓意，本身便具有一定的模糊性，因此这类文化负载词在跨文化翻译中也为译者提出了挑战。

例 55

原文：每日三瓦两舍，风花雪月。（《水浒传》第一回）

赛译：Every day they wasted money in small towns and in houses of ill repute such as men call "Wind, Flowers, Snow, Moonlight."

此处的"风花雪月"原指旧时诗文里经常描写的自然景物，包含四种自然界的意象，意为"四时之景"。后比喻堆砌词藻、内容贫乏空洞的诗文，也指男女情爱之事，或花天酒地的荒淫生活。

该词语出自宋代邵雍《伊川击壤集序》："虽死生荣辱，转战于前，曾未入于胸中，则何异四时风花雪月一过乎眼也。"邵雍才学出众，虽不曾出仕，却是出名的大家名士，从年少时的壮志满怀到逐渐看淡人生的起落，他受到了儒学和易学之影响，因而写下"虽死生荣辱，转战于前，曾未入于胸中，则何异四时风花雪月一过乎眼也"的名句，感叹人生不过是四时之景，繁华终究成为过眼烟云。

宋代以来，"风花雪月"经常在文学作品中出现。例如：宋·曹彦约《偶成》诗："雪月风花总不知，雕奇镂巧学支离。"元·乔吉《金钱记》三折："本是些风花雪月，都做了笞杖徒流。"明·凌濛初《二刻拍案惊奇》卷二十二："当初风花雪月之时，虽也曾劝谏几次，如水投石，落得反目。"清·吴敬梓《儒林外史》十三回："小弟每常见前辈批语，有些风花雪月的字样，被那些后生们看见，便要想到诗词歌赋那条路上去，便要坏了心术。"

因此，该成语绝非字面意义上的自然景观，春有百花，夏日清风，冬来飘雪，秋月当空的四时景象虽然浪漫美好，但在小说原文中，上下文为：高俅陪着一位员外之子吃喝玩乐，挥霍其家财，"每日三瓦两舍，风花雪月"，这里是指二人在勾栏妓院这样的场所寻欢作乐，荒淫无度，因此，赛译的"Wind, Flowers, Snow, Moonlight"明显为有意误译。译者这样的选择，导致译文看似僵化难懂，但这与赛珍珠的翻译动机是一致的，"我力图保留原文的意义与风格，甚至连枯燥乏味之处都是原汁原味的"，而对于生态文化负载词的翻译，赛珍珠同样坚持直译，要将原文中的意象逐字对译出来，其翻译方法的选择，明显体现了译者的主体性和最初的偏见。赛珍珠的偏见在于其翻译的目的：她力图将原文中的意义和风格都保留下来，如实传递给目的语读者，因此，在其译文中，直译和异化翻译占了大多数。

偏见也称"前见"，是文本的理解者对文本持有的固有态度，也是理解的基础和出发点。译者和理解者在解释的过程中将自己的前见与文本同化，即可实现新的理解。这种新的理解就是译文，无论其采取了直译还是意译，归化抑或异化策略，都反映了译者原有的偏见对翻译过程的操控。

例 56

原文：那时西岳华山，有个陈传处士，是个道高有德之人，能辨风云气色。（《水浒传》楔子）

赛译：Now at the great Western Mountain Hua there was a certain Ch'en T'uan, who was a Taoist hermit. He was a man of deep religion and of great virtue and he could divine the winds and the clouds.

"风云气色"是一个天文术语，文献资料显示，"唐朝是中国古代天文观测学发展的一个重要阶段。这一时期，中国的天文观测取得了重要的成就。也就是在这一时期，中国的观星占星术也达到了一个高峰。这时的'天文学'具有了浓厚的人文内涵，成为儒教正统之学之一，为统治者教化天下提供了规范，出现了'观乎天文，以察时变'的现象。唐朝的天文机构主要由太史局、

浑天监和司天台等部门组成。其中的太史局和司天台分别是唐朝前期和后期最重要的观星机构。"（百度百科）

史料记载：唐代太史局有太史令二人，太史丞二人，书令史四人，其职能为："掌观察天文、稽定历数，观日月星辰之变，风云气色之异，并率其属而占候。"这里"风云气色"和"日月星辰"相对应，指四种天文现象，是观测的重点。对此，赛译仍进行了直译，但对这四种现象进行了缩译，仅译出了"风云"二词，即"the winds and the clouds"。

例 57

原文：太公连忙道："客人休拜。你们是行路的人，辛苦风霜，且坐一坐。"（《水浒传》第二回）

赛译：The old lord said quickly, "Let the honorable guest not make such an obeisance. You are travelers and you have suffered much from wind and frost. Pray seat yourselves."

中文的"风霜"意为岁月变迁，也常用来指艰难困苦。例如元代马致远《黄梁梦》第四折："一梦中十八年，见了酒色财气，人我是非，贪嗔痴爱，风霜雨雪。"明·张缙彦《袁石寓（袁可立子）饷边》："昨日射雕犹住马，谁将长铗净风霜。"清·蒲松龄《聊斋志异·王成》："王生平未历风霜，委顿不堪。"

因此，赛珍珠直译后，"风霜"即是"wind and frost"，至于读者如何理解，译者为其留下了开放的解读空间。读者要么理解为"一路走来历经风霜天气"，要么领悟到中文的比喻意义的魅力，明白"风霜"指代艰难困苦，因此，赛译的有意误译并不难被读者所接受，相反，在传递原语的独特魅力方面，可谓颇有效果。

例 58

原文：先生不知是那里人，来我家里投宿，言说善晓阴阳，能识风水。（《水浒传》第三十一回）

赛译：But I do not know from whence this priest came except he came to my home to pass the night and he told everyone，"I am skilled in geomancy and I know the meaning of winds and waters."

"风水"即"堪舆"。堪，天道；舆，地道。中国传统文化之一。"风水"多指住宅基地、坟地等的形势，如地脉、山水的方向等。赛珍珠将"风水"这一中国特有的文化负载词直译为"winds and waters"，保留了中国文化的原汁原味，时至今日，"风水"一词在多种文本的翻译中，都采用这种直译的方式，用来向英语读者展示中国独特的堪舆文化。

例 59

原文：正是花木瓜，空好看！（《金瓶梅词话》第一回）

芮译：He's a real quince：Good to look at，but not fit to eat.

花木瓜，果实名，即木瓜，比喻外表好看，其实无用。常用来比喻人中看不中用，徒有其表。原著中潘金莲勾引武松被拒，武松搬离武大郎的家，潘金莲不仅反咬一口诬陷武松勾引她，还在一旁咒骂不休。

原文：那妇人在里面喃喃呐呐骂道：却也好！只道是亲难转债，人只知道一个兄弟做了都头怎的养活了哥嫂，却不知反来嚼咬人！正是花木瓜，空好看。搬了去，倒谢天地，且得冤家离眼前。武大见老婆这般言语，不知怎的了，心中只是放它不下。

此处潘金莲要表达的意思是：武松看起来是个人物，外表堂堂，其实没什么用处，甚至都不能养活哥嫂，因此虚有其表。

"花木瓜"一词，芮效卫译为"Quince"，词意为：温柏；柑橘；榅桲，木梨；榅桲果实；蔷薇科，意思是外表好看的柑橘，这里对 quince 一词的选用系有意误译，将木瓜这种多汁的水果意象替换成了柑橘类，虽与原文相去甚远，但译者进行了补充："Good to look at，but not fit to eat"，完整表达了虚有其表，里外不一，废物点心的比喻意义。这种意象替换式的意译，加之补充翻译"not fit to eat"（不适合食用），可以在一定程度上弥补直译带来的不同文化的陌生感，更易为读者接受和理解。

例 60

原文：（潘金莲）说道："我的哥哥，这一家都谁是疼你的？都是露水夫妻。"（《金瓶梅词话》第十二回）

芮译："Darling，" she said，"who is there in the whole household who really loves you? Out of all these cases of Cohabitation amid the dewdrops."

"露水夫妻"是指暂时结合的非正式夫妻，通常也指不正当的男女关系。这个词语的字面意思是像露水一样短暂和不稳定的关系，因为露水通常在夜间形成，早晨就会消失，象征着这种关系的短暂易逝。这一词语来源不可考，但据网络资料显示，《金瓶梅词话》是最早使用此词的有记录的文学作品，其他例如清代李渔的《意中缘·诳姻》："非是我蹉跎好事，冷落鸳帏，念不比那露水夫妻，到处便成佳会。"

小说中潘金莲为了获得西门庆的宠爱，声称其他妻妾与西门庆并非真爱，都是短暂且不稳定的男女关系，无非是一夜欢情的性关系而已，唯有她自己才是愿意与其共度一生一世、真心相付的女子。

芮译将其译作 cohabitation amid the dewdrops（露水中的同居），保留了"露水"的比喻修辞，同时使用 cohabitation（同居关系）来翻译"夫妻"，重点强调"同居关系"而非长久的正式夫妻，因此译文可视作直译法与意译法的整合使用，文体形式上包含了比喻，内容上也突出了非正式夫妻关系，因此，达成了与原文在形式和意义上的对等。

可见，在芮译本中译者最大限度地保留了原著的文体和风格，正如他在接受中国学者访谈时所说："我的《金瓶梅》翻译不但是语言上的，更是文体、修辞和文化上的翻译。"

例 61

原文：张四道："我见此人有些行止欠端，在外眠花卧柳，又里虚外实，少人家债负。只怕坑陷了你。"（《金瓶梅词话》第七回）

芮译："This is the sort of man whose：Conduct is lacking in rectitude. He's always away from home：Sleeping among the flowers and lolling beneath the willows. Moreover，he's：Solid without，but hollow within，and is up to his neck in debt. I'm only afraid he'll be the ruination of you."

"眠花卧柳"亦作眠花藉柳、眠花醉柳，意思是狎妓，最早出现在《金瓶梅词话》中。花草树木之类属于生态文化负载词，然而，在文中明显用于比喻意义，花柳的词典释义为：1.鲜花杨柳；2. 指繁华游乐之地；3. 指妓院或娼妓、妓女。旧时代的花柳病就是性传播疫病，古人认为这是寻"花"问"柳"之病。

芮译本直译作"Sleeping among the flowers and lolling

beneath the willows"（睡在百花丛中，躺在柳树下）。若非对照了原文，查看出处，笔者甚至以为所读的文本是赛珍珠所译的《水浒传》。二者对文化负载词的直译，在此处如出一辙。虽然译者保留了原文的比喻，但是其喻义不详，容易给读者造成理解困难甚至误解。以芮效卫对中国文化的谙熟程度，当然不会曲解"眠花卧柳"一词的比喻意义，但他选择了直译，根本原因依然离不开他翻译中国文学作品的初衷，其目的是让英语世界的读者领略异国风情，理解外国文化的独特之处，所以在翻译熟语如俚语和谚语的过程中，"芮效卫大多采用直译的方式，并在全书后加注释以帮助读者理解，而没有一味地从方便读者阅读的角度出发而采取意译或省译的方式"（朱振武，2023：62）。

例 62

原文：对立东风里，主人应解怜。（《红楼梦》第十八回）

杨译：Facing each other in the soft east wind!
They surely bring their mistress peace of mind!

霍译：Their mistress, standing in the soft summer breeze
Finds quite content in everything she sees.

这首诗名为《怡红快绿》，是十一首《大观园题咏》中的一首，是元妃省亲时游赏大观园时的"颂圣应酬"之作，其实是由林黛玉代贾宝玉所作。这两句的意思是：芭蕉与海棠如此含情脉脉地在春风里相对站立，院中主人应懂得如何把它们来爱怜。诗中的"东风"，杨译为"soft east wind"，直译的基础上增加了修饰词，突出温暖轻柔的春风拂面，万物欣欣向荣；而霍译为"soft summer breeze"，则涉及了有意误译。

《红楼梦》原著中出现"东风"共十四次，去除重复语境，共十三次，如下图所示：

第五回	清明涕送江边望，千里东风一梦遥
第十八回	对立东风里，主人应解怜
第二十二回	游丝一断浑无力，莫向东风怨别离
第五十回	桃未芳菲杏未红，冲寒先已笑东风
第六十三回	莫怨东风当自嗟
第七十回	桃花帘外东风软，桃花帘内晨妆懒
第七十回	东风有意揭帘栊，花欲窥人帘不卷
第七十回	凭栏人向东风泣，茜裙偷傍桃花立
第七十回	嫁与东风春不管，凭尔去，忍淹留
第七十回	三春事业付东风，明月梅花一梦
第七十回	白玉堂前春解舞，东风卷得均匀
第八十二回	但凡家庭之事，不是东风压了西风，就是西风压了东风

由此可见，原著中"东风"一词，在前八十回全部出自诗词，而后八十回只出现两次，且是在同一句日常对白中。因此，考量"对立东风里，主人应解怜"诗句中"东风"一词的翻译，既要了解中国特有的诗词文化，也要考虑到地理位置的差异而导致的生态文化的迥异。

我国地处欧亚大陆的东南，春天从海洋吹来的东风温暖宜人，因而"东风"在汉语里的文化含义是温暖宜人的风，尤指春风，例如唐朝韩翃的"春城无处不飞花，寒食东风御柳斜"；宋代王令的"东风来几日，穷巷不见春。不知得花由，只见插花人。东风能几时，听尔多欢欣。徒恐春风归，汝我同悲辛"；朱熹的"等闲识得东风面，万紫千红总是春"；明代兰茂的"东风破早梅，向暖一枝开"；清高鼎的"草长莺飞二月天，拂堤杨柳醉春烟。儿童散学归来早，忙趁东风放纸鸢"；因此可以确定《红楼梦》诗词中的东风指春天里的温暖和煦的微风。

因此，杨译旨在传递中国文化中特有的生态文化，选择了直译，虽然在目的语国家，位于欧亚大陆西北的英国，东风是从欧洲大陆北部吹来的，寒冷刺骨，但是杨宪益夫妇坚持将中国文化中独特的地理现象真实地呈现给外国读者，因此选择直译，但充分考虑到了地域差异导致的东风西风的性质和季节特点差异，杨译在"东风"前增加了描述形容词"soft"，完美地诠释了中国的"东风"的内涵，考虑到目的语读者的接受，杨译也可算作一种有意误译，明知此东风非彼东风，仍有意而为之，增词翻译更是体现了译者的再创造。

译者再创造是指"译者在尊重原作品意义的基础上，通过语言、文化、情境等方面的再创造使译文更贴近目标语言读者的语境，以达到更好的传达效果。通常情况下，误译在翻译中能够起到再创造的作用"（孟天伦，2024：116）。对"东风"一词的增译，表明杨译对生态文化负载词的翻译进行了再创造，有意误译的效果显而易见。

再看霍译对"东风"一词的解读，他也采取了增词翻译，用"soft"作为修饰词，而"东"这一方向方位词被隐去，直接用"summer breeze"代替，笔者认为霍克斯对季节的理解可能是无意误译，由于对诗词背景、原语文化背景和生态文化的理解不够准确，才将诗词中的春季误读，理解为夏季；而将东风译为"温和的微风"，有意地避免了直译"东风"带来理解上的误区和偏差，总体而言是一种有意误译。这种误译体现了霍克斯的主观性解读和阐释。误译在一定程度上"反映了译者对原文的深刻理解，以及他在尝试将这部作品融入西方文化语境时所作的努力"（孟天伦，2024：118）。

例 63

原文：怅望<u>西风</u>抱闷思，蓼红苇白断肠时。（《红楼梦》第三十八回）

杨译：I gaze around in the <u>west wind</u>, sick at heart；

A sad season of the red smartweed and white reeds.

霍译：The <u>autumn wind</u> that through the knotgrass blows，

Blurs the sad gazer's eyes with unshed teas.

《红楼梦》中涉及的"西风"一词共有八处，前八十回均出自诗词曲赋，八十回后出现在日常对话中，诗词中的"西风"均指秋风。秋风起，伤别离，也预示着万物开始凋零，气温降低，凛冬将至，景致变得萧条清冷。

第十一回	西风乍紧，初罢莺啼；暖日当暄，又添蛩语
第三十七回	娇羞默默同谁诉，倦倚西风夜已昏
第三十八回	怅望西风抱闷思，蓼红苇白断肠时
第五十一回	团圆莫忆春香到，一别西风又一年
第七十八回	尔乃西风古寺，淹滞青磷；落日荒丘，零星白骨。
第七十八回	汝南泪血，斑斑洒向西风；梓泽馀衷，默默诉凭冷月
第八十二回	但凡家庭之事，不是东风压了西风，就是西风压了东风

英国位于欧亚大陆的西北，西风是从大西洋吹来的温暖而潮湿的风，给英国大地带来勃勃生机。除了人尽皆知的英国浪漫主

义诗人雪莱（Percy Bysshe Shelley）的诗歌《西风颂》（Ode to the west wind），英国桂冠诗人约翰·梅斯菲尔德（John Masefield）的诗《西风》（The West Wind）中，读者很容易发现英国的西风等同于中国古代诗词中的东风。

It's a warm wind, the west wind, full of birds' cries;

I never hear the west wind but tears are in my eyes,

For it comes from the west lands, the old brown hills,

And April's in the west wind, and daffodils.

温暖的西风中百鸟歌唱

听闻西风起我热烈盈眶

它来自西边褐色的山峦

四月的春风吹绽了水仙

再看两组译文：杨译依旧直译了"西风"一词，而霍译则为"the autumn wind"（秋风），避开了可能产生误解的方向性词汇，采用了意译方法，直接将季节作为修饰限定词，这种有意的误译最大程度避免了读者的误解。

例 64

原文：但凡家庭之事，不是东风压了西风，就是西风压了东风。（《红楼梦》第八十二回）

杨译：In every family, if the east wind doesn't prevail over the west wind, then the west wind is bound to prevail over the east wind.

霍译：In every family affair, one side or the other has to win. If it's not the East Wind it's the West.

前两例涉及真实的地理特征的生态文化词汇，但是在此例中，东风和西风比喻家庭中两方势力，原文语境中涉及中国古代一夫多妻制的文化。东方和西风代表正房和妾两种势力。

中国古代妻妾制度是中国古代社会结构中的重要组成部分，主要体现在"一夫多妻制"的基础上，允许男性拥有多个妻子和妾室。在法律上，正妻和妾的地位有明确的区别。例如《唐律疏议》和《宋刑统》等法律文献均规定了妻妾的不同地位和权利。正妻是家庭的正式成员，而妾则更多被视为男性的财产，可以买卖和处置。

这种法律上的不平等导致了社会中对女性的不公平待遇，尤其是在家庭内部的权力斗争中，正妻往往占据主导地位，而妾室则处于弱势，经常遭受欺凌和虐待，甚至被虐杀、出卖和转让。但也有特例，当男性偏宠妾室时，会导致妾拥有一定的权利，不仅可以与正妻抗衡，还有可能在资源调配、家庭话语权等方面碾压正房，甚至还有男子宠妾灭妻、抬妾为妻的案例，例如宫斗类文学作品和影视作品如《甄嬛传》《宫心计》等，宅斗剧如《知否知否应是绿肥红瘦》《大宅门》等。然而自古以来，无论宅斗还是宫斗，归根结底是一夫多妻制导致的权利和地位的斗争，只不过是规模上和场景上有差异。

在《红楼梦》第八十二回中，贾宝玉再次去家塾读书后，袭人闲来无事不禁担忧自己的将来："忽又想到自己终身本不是宝玉的正配，原是偏房。宝玉的为人，却还拿得住，只怕娶了一个利害的，自己便是尤二姐香菱的后身。素来看着贾母王夫人光景及凤姐儿往往露出话来，自然是黛玉无疑了。那黛玉就是个多心人。想到此际，脸红心热，拿着针不知戳到那里去了，便把活计放下，走到黛玉处去探探他的口气。"在林黛玉面前，袭人提起薛蟠的老婆夏金桂虐待小妾香菱，又联想到王熙凤和尤二姐的纠葛，想借机探听林黛玉的口风，这才有了黛玉所说的"不是东风压了西风，就是西风压了东风"一说。

对于这一比喻意义，杨氏夫妇仍然采取直译，东风和西风就是"east wind，west wind"，而霍克斯则直译意译结合，东风和西风既译为"one side or the other"用来指代家中妻妾两股势力，又在后半句补充了非此即彼："If it's not the East Wind it's the West"（要么东风获胜，要么西风获胜），将原文的比喻意象完整保留的同时，也考虑到读者的接受能力，因此通过意译补充了"one side of the other"，将东风和西方指代的宅斗的双方清晰地展示给目的语读者。

因此霍克斯的组合译法系有意而为之，目的是既保留原语的文化特色，又可以使目的语读者一目了然文中涉及的争斗双方，因而有意误译的结果是好的，是有利于提升读者的阅读体验的，在多数情况下，"在翻译中，文化误译作为接受主体即译者对他者文化的选择、吸收与扬弃，体现了译者的主动性与创造性"（周晓寒，2009：130）。

例 65

原文："癫蛤蟆想吃天鹅肉，没人伦的混帐东西……"（《红楼梦》第十一回）

杨译："A toad hankering for a taste of swan，" scoffed Pinger. "The beast hasn't a shred of common decency."

霍译："What a nasty，disgusting man!" said Patience. "A case of 'the toad on the ground wanting to eat the goose in the sky'."

"癞蛤蟆想吃天鹅肉"是汉语俗语,比喻人不自量力,缺少自知之明,一心想谋取不可能到手的东西。资料显示该俗语最早出现在施耐庵的《水浒传》第一百零一回:"我直恁这般呆!癞蛤蟆怎想吃天鹅肉!"

癞蛤蟆和天鹅作为两种生活习惯和活动范围迥异的两种生物,在俗语中凸显出差异之巨大,对比之鲜明。一个在天上展翅翱翔,优雅高贵,为人类所景仰;一个在地上,丑陋不堪,只能爬行于淤泥之中,遭人厌恶,避之不及。英语中 toad 有"令人讨厌的人"之意,"toad in the hole"有时也用来形容某人或某事在某个环境中显得格格不入或不合时宜。在英语中,天鹅象征着优雅,如 as elegant as a swan。此外,在希腊神话中,天鹅据说是阿波罗的神鸟,与音乐和歌曲有着密切联系,因此常用天鹅来比喻文艺。传说天鹅平素不唱歌,而在它死前,必引颈长鸣,高歌一曲,以这种方式勇敢地面对死亡和新生的到来。因此,swan song 指"艺术家或作家的最后一个作品、最后一次表演"。

杨译本中保留了原语的文化因素,将癞蛤蟆和天鹅进行了直译,而霍译本仅保留"癞蛤蟆"的意象,采取了直译手法,却用"鹅"(goose)的形象代替了"天鹅"。这种文化替换是基于鹅和天鹅所隐含的象征意义的不同。英语中的鹅在活着的时候是一种普通的家禽,死后常以烤鹅的形式出现在传统的圣诞节晚宴上。在西方,鹅有时被视为呆和蠢的象征,但在儿童文学作品中,是很受喜爱的主题,带有较为可爱和轻松的情感色彩。霍克斯将鹅和癞蛤蟆放在一起,主要突出鹅作为美味食物的一种,遭到癞蛤蟆的垂涎,但在天空中的烤鹅又无法得到,因此符合原文的比喻意义,讽刺垂涎凤姐美貌的贾瑞不自量力,缺乏自知之明,也突出了王熙凤的高高在上，遥不可及。如果忠实于原文，译为"天鹅"，会造成西方读者的误解，毕竟在西方文化中，无论是典故还是传说，没有将天鹅作为食物饕餮一餐的比喻，因此，这样的特殊文化意象不适合移植到目的语当中。霍克斯有意误译的目的是顺应目的语读者的文化习惯，也体现了中西方生态文化的差异。

孟天伦（2024）指出："每种文化都有其独特的价值观、信仰体系、行为准则和思维模式。这些文化要素在很大程度上塑造了个体的世界观和认知框架。当人们接触到与自己文化不同的文本时，很容易将自己的文化预设带入对文本的解读中，从而产生误读"。

为了避免读者错误的理解和解读，霍克斯从源头上消除了可能产生误读的因素，将癞蛤蟆所垂涎的天鹅换成了普通的鹅，动词为"想吃"（want to eat），上下文喻义清晰，加上补充地点状语后，the toad on the ground 和 the goose in the sky 形成了天壤之别，在二者之间架设了无法逾越的障碍，避免了读者的误读，因此是文化误译的一个典型的正面案例。

例 66

原文：女曰："仙尘路隔，不能相依。妾亦不忍以鱼水之爱，夺膝下之欢。容徐谋之。"（《聊斋志异》《罗刹海市》）

翟译：His wife replied, "The way of immortals is not that of men. I am unable to do what you ask, but I cannot allow the feelings of husband and wife to break the tie of parent and child. Let us devise some plan."

梅译："Faerie and earth have separate roads," she said,

"They cannot remain together. I cannot bear, for the sake of our <u>marital love</u>, to deny you the happiness of being at hour parents' side. Give me time to think of a way."

杨译："An immortal must not live like a mortal," she replied. "I cannot go with you, but neither would I let <u>the love of husband and wife</u> stand in the way of your love for your parents. Let us consider this again later."

"鱼水之爱"通"鱼水之欢",该成语取鱼与水的亲密之意,喻男女亲密和谐的情感或性生活。其近义词有鱼水相欢、胶漆相投,出自元王实甫《西厢记》第二本第三折:"小生到得卧房内,和姐姐解带脱衣,颠鸾倒凤,同谐鱼水之欢,共效于飞之愿。"因此,该成语主要指男女和谐亲密的感情生活和性生活。

翟理斯将"鱼水之爱"译为"the feelings of husband and wife",看不出丝毫夫妻和谐的性关系字样,这是基于他所处的时代的主流诗学观和道德倾向而产生的有意误译。译者选择净化原文中的涉及性文化的词语,有意以"feelings"代替男女之间鱼水之欢,性爱和谐,其文化误译的原因在于翟理斯所处时代为清教主义盛行的维多利亚时代。起源于 16 世纪的清教崇尚克制与禁欲,对两性之间行为规范的标准严格。"这种清教行为准则在那个时期的文学中留下很深的烙印。只要涉及性的话题,维多利亚作家总是想尽办法回避"(余苏凌,2011:468)。

因此,翟理斯由于理解的历史性的制约,从自己的时代出发,从创作之初就带着一种强调道德教化的偏见,对《聊斋志异》中的性爱描写进行了或彻底的删除,或含蓄地改写,以期达到净化文本之目的。

梅氏兄弟将此词译为"marital love"（夫妻之爱），含蓄而概括，简洁明了，但对原文中的生态文化意象：鱼和水以及各自代表的文化内涵却选择了忽略，或多或少反映了文化的不可译性，也造成了译语中原语丰富的语言文化上的损失。

杨译本译为"the love of husband and wife"更加抽象且概括，也避开了涉及性爱的"鱼水之欢"的原本意义。杨氏夫妇翻译《聊斋志异选》的时代在保守、闭塞的 80 年代初，出版物中绝对不可涉及不健康的东西，性细节的描写一般都是受到查禁的。在杨宪益夫妇翻译的与《聊斋志异选》同时期问世的《红楼梦》译本中，杨译也采取了净化、淡化、模糊化等手段处理性爱描写。可见译本在某一固定历史时期被打上的深深的时代烙印。

例 67

原文：房中植此一种，则合欢、忘忧，并无颜色矣。若解语花，正嫌其作态耳。（《聊斋志异》《婴宁》）

杨译：A plant of this sort in your home would beat all other flowers supposed to delight men, surpassing even the Flower of Wit* which has always struck me as rather overrated.

*译者注：Emperor Minghuang of the Tang Dynasty used to compare the lotus flower to his favourite Lady Yang and called her the Flower of Wit.

梅译：If some of these were planted in a room, then herbs like Forget-Your-Sorrow and Joy of Union would not make much of an impression, while "the flower that understands speech"* would seem to be putting on air.

*译者注：First used by the Tang emperor Xuanzong in

reference to his beloved concubine Yang Yuhuan.

对原文中生态文化负载词的理解和翻译，杨译与梅译既有相同点，也有相异之处。在对"解语花"这一典故的处理方式上，杨译采取了意译加注，梅译则选择使用直译加注，既可以使读者了解这一生态文化负载词语的比喻意义，同时也向读者介绍了典故之由来，有利于传播原语文化。

合欢是常见的观赏类植物，又名绒花树、夜合花，英文名称为"Silktree Albizziae Flower"，可简写作"silktree flower"。合欢的寓意为"百年好合"，树形美观优雅，花色鲜艳，可以净化空气，是一种保护生态的植物，还具有一定的药用价值。合欢这种植物在中国文化中常用来象征恩爱忠贞，夫妻好合。

忘忧草，学名萱草，即金针菜、黄花菜，英文名称为"Hemerocallis fulva"，也作"Tiger lily"。

"萱草作为中国传统的庭院花卉，在古代社会长期的历史发展中，积淀了丰富的象征意蕴，而萱草文化也逐渐融入到了人们的日常生活中。萱草的文化价值主要有三：一为忘忧，二为宜男，三则代指母亲"（百度百科）。据《诗经》中描述，古代游子远行前，会在北堂种下萱草，以期减轻母亲对游子的思念，忘忧消愁，因此有："北堂幽暗，可以种萱"的诗句；三国时期魏著名思想家、文学家嵇康在《养生论》中提及"合欢蠲忿，萱草忘忧"，故萱草也被称作忘忧草。

杨译将合欢花、忘忧草笼统译为"flowers supposed to delight men"（使人开心的花朵），简洁概括，直接取其喻意；而梅译则将忘忧草直译为"Forget-Your-Sorrow"，将合欢花译为"Joy of Union"，意在将中国文化中合欢和忘忧草两种植物的比喻意义和文化内涵介绍给目的语读者，因此采取了异化的手段，可见译者是有意不使用这两种植物在英语中的固有的名称。梅译的偏见在于：使用异化手段可以促进文化交流，使目的语读者感受原语文化中的异国风情和独特韵味，了解原语文化中的精妙的内涵；同时有意地创作出两个新的植物名称，这样有意误译产生的陌生化效应也能满足读者对译文的审美期待。

例 68

原文：适有瓜葛丁姓造谒，翁款之。(《聊斋志异》《梦狼》）

翟译：One day a distant connection, named Ting, called at the house; and Mr. Pai, not having seen this gentleman for a long time, treated him with much cordiality.

杨 译：One day a distant relative named Ding, long a stranger to the house, visited Mr Bai and was given a very warm reception.

梅译：One day a relative named Ding came to call, and the squire enterntained him.

在《聊斋志异》原著中，"瓜葛"一词共出现 10 次，其中 9 处意为"亲属关系"，一处意为"关联"。

例如在《聊斋志异·小谢》篇中："部院勘三郎，素非瓜葛，无端代控，将杖之，扑地遂灭"；《宫梦弼》篇：刘媪急进曰："此老身瓜葛，王嫂卖花者，幸勿罪责"；《续黄粱》篇："或有厮养之儿，瓜葛之亲，出则乘传，风行雷动"；《颠道人》篇："章丘有周生者，以寒贱起家，出必驾肩而行。亦与司农有瓜葛之旧"；《小梅》："忽门外有舆马来，逆女归宁。向十余年，并无瓜葛，共议之，而女若不闻"；《王桂庵》："此翁与有瓜葛，是祖母嫡孙，何不早言？"

　　而对"瓜葛"这一生态文化负载词，例 69 中三种译文都采取了意译的方法，揭示了"relative"（亲戚）关系，但是杨译和翟译进行了增词翻译，突出了远亲"distant"，梅译则选择了简洁概括为"a relative"（一位亲属）。

　　例 69

　　原文：生曰："我所谓爱，非<u>瓜葛</u>之爱，乃夫妻之爱。"（《聊斋志异》《婴宁》）

　　翟译："1 was not talking about <u>ordinary relations</u>," said Wang, "but about husbands and wives."

　　杨译："It is not <u>relatives</u> that I am referring to, but love between husband and wife."

　　梅译："What I mean by love is not <u>between gourds on the same vine</u>, but love between husband and wife."

　　同样表示"远亲"之意的"瓜葛"，三位译者中，翟译和杨译均准确诠释了原文，删除了瓜与葛这两种植物的原来的植物意象，直接意译为"ordinary relations"和"relatives"。而梅译则对特有的生态文化负载词进行了有意的误译，保留了瓜葛的植物名称，采取了直译手法，将王子服与婴宁之间这种亲戚之情译作"love between gourds on the same vine"（同一条藤上结出来的葫芦一般的情感），比较形象生动地借用了自然界的植物意象来比喻亲戚关系。葫芦为草质藤本攀援植物，其果实结于爬藤上，未摘取之前，果实与藤条连在一起。因此，梅译虽然有意隐去了瓜和葛所比喻的"亲戚之情"的文化内涵，并将瓜葛的意象用葫芦和藤的意象来替换，能够将中文中的生动的生态文化意象在目的语中形象地表达出来，这一有意误译通过保留原语文化中的意象，将异域文化中的特质更加形象生动地介绍给目的语读者，有利于中国文化在西方世界的有效传播。

3.6　小结

习近平总书记多在讲话中强调：必须坚定文化自信。文化是一个国家、一个民族的灵魂。如何在中国文学作品对外译介过程中充分展示中华文化的魅力，使更多的目标读者更好地理解原语文化中的精髓所在，是跨文化翻译的重要任务之一。

富含大量的文化内容的承载体即文化负载词语是众多中国古典文学名著在语言方面的共同特质之一。廖七一认为，文化负载词标志着某文化中特有的事物，不仅有词和词组，还包括习语、成语和典故，在漫长的历史进程中逐渐积累的文化负载词反映了该民族独特的生活方式。简单来说，文化负载词就是包含特定文化的词（胡玥，2023：68）。

文化负载词是最能体现语言中浓郁的民族色彩和鲜明的文化特色。文化负载词为译者提出了更高的翻译标准。译者必须作为一名双文化人，对原语文化中的信仰、习俗、审美、价值观等精神层面的知识有深入了解和一定的知识储备，这样才能够尽量忠实地传达原语文化的精髓。在文学翻译中，译者必须准确地理解、诠释原著中的社会文化、宗教信仰、语言特色、生态和物质文化负载词所传递的丰富的内涵。这一点既是跨文化翻译的重点，也是难点所在。

　　笔者研读分析了四部古典文学名著的英译本后，重点研究了对于文化负载词进行的有意的文化误译。作为翻译活动主体的译者有目的地采取一种或多种翻译策略，将原文本中所涉及的异域文化内容进行删减、改造，这种对文本中的文化内容的翻译过程的主观操控属于有意误译。译者或大量使用异化策略，或倾向于归化手段，或将二者结合起来，从而形成了不同的翻译风格，文化信息的传递效果因而各有不同。有些译者，如赛珍珠在翻译《水浒传》时，为了保留和移植原文的文化形象及色彩，大量使用了异化策略和直译方法，在语言文化负载词方面尤为突出；翟理斯在翻译《聊斋志异》时，受自身的前见、道德观和所处历史时期的主流诗学影响，对性文化负载词和与此相关的情节采取意译、删除和改写的策略，力图保持文学的纯洁性；芮效卫在翻译文化负载词时，侧重异化策略和直译的方法，最大化地将原语语言和文化信息移植到译入语中，目的在于促进原语文化在目的语国家的传播；杨宪益夫妇在翻译《红楼梦》和《聊斋志异选》时，主要采取异化策略从而保留原语中的文化特色，以期更好地向海外读者传播中国文化；霍克斯的文化误译则体现在其归化策略上，其出发点是读者接受为中心的翻译观和作品总体的可欣赏性。

　　从前文的大量误译译例可见，简单意译会剥夺了目的语读者对原文内容的知情权，使渴望了解中国文化的目的语读者在阅读中难以获取充满异域魅力的异国文化，无法满足其期待视野和审美需求；全部采取异化策略虽然一定程度上可抵御目的语文化价值观，弱化其在译文中的主导地位，从而充分体现出文化差异并将异质文化引入到译入语文化中来，但由于理解的历史性和时间距离的作用，大量的原语文化无法为目的语读者一一理解和接受；而一概的归化虽然以流畅的译入语形式掩盖了原语文化与目的语文化之间的差异，译者以目的语中的主流文化价值观取代了原语文化价值观，原文的陌生感被淡化，导致译作失去了原文中的异域风情和独特韵味，成为文化交流和原语文化有效传播过程中的障碍。

王珺指出："文化负载词的翻译依赖其本身所存在的语言文化环境，文化环境所包含的诸多因素，如自然环境、历史文化、风俗民情、宗教信仰、审美取向、价值观念、思维方式等都直接影响翻译的准确性和文化性。"《译学词典》认为应当"以文化交流为出发点，客观估计读者的文化接受力，采取灵活的翻译手段，尽可能做到译语既保留原文的文化信息和文化色彩，又具有可读性"（王珺，2020：76）。

从一定数量的误译译例分析结果看，即使译者努力整合各种翻译方法，尽可能灵活变通地处理原文中的文化内容，从而使译文更好地发挥传递原文中的文化信息的作用，误译仍是跨文化翻译中不可避免的，尤其是文化误译。

不同译者对文化负载词语所采取的不同翻译策略也体现了诠释哲学领域中的视域融合的概念。对异质文化究竟是采取归化策略还是异化策略，体现了译者的视域和原作者的视域在达成理解的过程中的碰撞和交融过程。

视域融合的过程是二者视域相碰撞和冲突的过程，但"这一过程不是用一种视界代替另一种视界，而是必定同时包括两者的差异和交互作用。视界融合是建立在差异基础上的融合。它从理论上印证了翻译中文化过滤现象的历史根源及其存在的无可避免性"（张德让，2001：25）。这一论述也解释了文化误读和有意误译现象的不可避免性。在一部译作中，译者的视域完全取代原作者的视域是不可能实现的，而原文和译文从语言形式到信息的完全对等，以及译者的完全隐身无法实现。因此译者应尽力使自身的视域与原作者的视域达成差异基础上的融合，而非消灭文化差异，从而使译文符合读者的理解视域和期待视域，达成了视域融合即意味着翻译的成功。

第四章 明清小说误译之译者研究

4.1 基于语料库的译者风格差异

探讨翻译作品的特色时，必定会涉及译者风格。Baker（2000）将语言和非语言因素考虑在内，认为译者风格是"译者留在目的语文本中的一系列语言和非语言的特征，即译者的痕迹"。黄立波（2021）对译者风格的定义是"指译者的规律性语言产出行为所反映出的译者个性化特征及其所产生的效果"。从语言运用的层面看，方梦之（2004）认为译者风格是"译者的人格倾向、选题倾向、文笔色彩以及译者所遵循的翻译标准、使用的翻译方法和译文语言运用技巧等特点的综合"。

20 世纪 90 年代，西方翻译界开始关注译者风格这一研究方向。Mona Baker 提出借助语料库开展译者风格研究，借此来关注不同译者的译文表现出的整体翻译风格差异，如在词汇多样性、句子复杂程度、叙事方式等方面的不同（黄立波，2021：100）。王克非（2012）在论述基于语料库的翻译文体学的研究框架时认为，研究者可以"利用语料库通过计算机软件对各类文本（包括从文体类型、语言变体和文本类型角度分类的文本）的文体特征进行语言学的量化描写，在充分描写和分析的基础上从语言内、外加以解释"。胡开宝（2011）指出，在基于语料库进行译者风格研究时，"可以将该领域的研究建立在语料分析和数据统计的基础上，从而避免译者风格研究的主观性和随意性。"

因此本文对四部古典文学名著所展开的译者研究也遵循这一研究路线，基于语料库翻译研究所常用的软件对各译者的译作语言层面所涉及的词汇、句子特征和篇章进行量化分析和比较（同一原文的不同译本），从而体现译者风格上的差异与特色。

4.1.1　基于语料库的《水浒传》赛珍珠英译本译者风格

赛珍珠耗时近五年完成的《水浒传》英译本，被认为是这部中国古典文学名著的第一部英文全译本，在英语世界一经推出就进入热销榜，时至今日仍然具有相当大的影响力。然而赛译《水浒传》也因其大量的异化和直译导致了颇多的负面评价，尤其语言风格方面争议较大。通过语料库分析软件，可以从更客观的角度评价其翻译风格和特色。

类符（type）是指语料库中的不同词汇，或每个第一次单独出现的词形。形符（token）是指语料库中出现的所有词形。类符/形符比（type/token ratio）指文本中类符与形符的比率。

在语言学中，类符常用于衡量文本的词汇丰富度。类符对句子的复杂度和文本的多样性有重要影响。类符的使用可以帮助分析文本的语言特征，例如在自然语言处理中，类符的使用频率和分布可以帮助识别文本的主题和风格。类符/形符比在一定程度上反映了语料的用词变化，比值越大，表明该文本使用的不同词汇数量越大，反之则越少。

赛珍珠译《水浒传》的基本数据图

Lines	4314
Words (types)	Now: 11018　When loaded: 11018
Words (tokens)	Now: 576981　When loaded: 576981
Type-token ratio	Now: 52.3671　When loaded: 52.3671
Characters	2264567
Sentences	26425
Words/sentence	21.8347

由统计可见，赛译作为《水浒传》的全译本，总形符数（tokens）为576981，类符数为11018，类符形符比52.3671，平均句长为21.8个词语。

沙博理译《水浒传》的基本数据图

Lines	18921
Words (types)	Now: 14180　When loaded: 14180
Words (tokens)	Now: 385075　When loaded: 385075
Type-token ratio	Now: 27.1562　When loaded: 27.1562
Characters	1636901
Sentences	34626
Words/sentence	11.1210

笔者也对另外一位译者沙博理翻译的《水浒传》英译本进行了统计，其总形符数（tokens）为385075，低于赛译的576981；类符数为14180，高于赛译的11018；类符形符比27.1562，而赛译类符形符比52.3671；平均句长为11.1个词语，而赛译为21.8个词语。

由此可见，赛译词汇量较之于沙译更大，词汇也更加丰富，句长几乎达到沙译的一倍。

利用 Concordance 320 统计译本的词长总体分布情况（word length distribution），结果如下：

赛珍珠译《水浒传》词长分布图

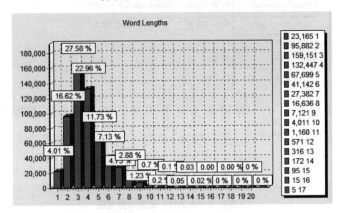

沙博理译《水浒传》词长分布图

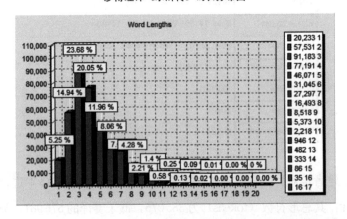

Wimmer（1994）强调词长为"维持语言自组织性能的多种控制循环的重要成分"。作为计量语言学研究的主要内容的词长分布特征应用于翻译研究后，通过数据分析和对比能够体现出译

本的文体特征和译者风格。从上图可见，赛珍珠在译本中偏好使用三字母词汇和四字母词汇，其中三字母词汇为最频繁使用类型，占 27.58％，4 字母词汇在词汇长度分布中所占比例为 22.96％。沙博理译本中也偏重于三字母词汇和四字母词汇，其中三字母词汇占 23.68％，四字母词汇在词汇长度分布中所占比例为 20.05％，略低于赛译。

赛珍珠译《水浒传》高频词前六十位

高频词 1—30		高频词 31—60	
Headword	No.	WILL	2881
AND	35050	HAD	2859
THE	32883	OUT	2852
TO	15726	WERE	2467
HE	12776	AS	2427
OF	11708	COME	2414
A	8822	WENT	2283
"	7298	ONE	2265
IN	6735	WE	2239
HIS	6647	DO	2224
I	6622	GO	2213
YOU	6435	THEM	2212
IT	5537	WHEN	2201
THEY	5323	TWO	2130
WAS	5226	ME	2127
THEN	5083	MY	2127
NOT	4864	CHIANG	2118
IS	4661	AT	1990
THIS	4589	FROM	1985
THAT	4539	NOW	1933
SAID	4506	WHO	1932
HIM	3829	SO	1907
THERE	3733	WU	1867
FOR	3524	MEN	1864
BUT	3400	ARE	1787
HAVE	3296	MAN	1737
WITH	3204	CAME	1734
ALL	3186	INTO	1691
SUNG	3167	GREAT	1552
BE	3001	YOUR	1441
ON	2947		

高频词是在某一文本里使用频率高于其他词的词语。"用一个词语在整个文本中所占的百分比或者该词语在整个词频中所处的前后位置来决定该词语是否为高频词"（冯庆华，2012：5）。通过高频词的统计数据可以比较直观地看出不同译者对部分词汇使用的偏好，可以体现出译者的语言风格。赛译高频词第一位为 and，可以假设赛珍珠偏好是使用较长句式，通过研究高频词在正文中的例句来判定译者是否有此倾向，从而也能推断其平均句长形成的原因。

沙译《水浒传》高频词前六十位

高频词 1—30		高频词 31—60	
THE	22926	HAVE	1451
AND	13267	AS	1356
TO	10551	BUT	1346
"	9174	WU	1295
A	7982	MY	1278
OF	6930	OUT	1220
HE	5909	LI	1217
IN	4917	TWO	1214
YOU	4705	YOUR	1195
HIS	4638	WE	1191
WAS	3550	THIS	1130
WITH	3037	UP	1124
I	2899	THEIR	1118
HIM	2756	ALL	1085
ON	2670	BY	1021
THEY	2421	IF	986
SONG	2399	WHEN	951
THAT	2222	ONE	897
IT	2189	INTO	895
FOR	2121	THEN	895
SAID	1986	MAN	888
ME	1709	NO	874
IS	1681	AN	871
BE	1665	ARE	859
HAD	1621	GO	856
FROM	1568	MEN	840
AT	1547	HERE	821
WERE	1530	BROTHER	790
JIANG	1496	THREE	790
THEM	1473	NOT	789

TEC 与 BNC 中排名前三十位的高频词

	TEC	BNC
Rank	Word	Word
1	the	the
2	and	of
3	to	and
4	of	to
5	a	a
6	in	in
7	I	that
8	he	is
9	was	it
10	that	was
11	her	for
12	it	's
13	his	on
14	with	be
15	she	with
16	had	I
17	on	he
18	for	as
19	as	by
20	you	you
21	is	at
22	at	are
23	my	this
24	not	not
25	but	have
26	from	had
27	me	his
28	they	from
29	him	but
30	be	they

　　与英国曼彻斯特大学的 Mona Baker 等研究人员所创建的世界上首个翻译英语语料库 TEC（Translational English Corpus）以及英国国家语料库 BNC（British National Corpus）的词频表对照后发现，发现赛译中排名前三十位的高频词与这两个语料库的前三十位高频词重合率较高。

赛珍珠译《水浒传》主要高频词 and 搭配使用情况索引

t day did they all mingle blood with wine and drink it	and	when they had drunk themselves to mighty drunkenness, they
lay!" On that day did they all mingle blood with wine	and	drink it and when they had drunk themselves to mighty drunk
ad thus vowed, all the host together shouted assent	and	they said, "We would but meet again, life after life, generatio
ch have his clear reward for good or evil; let Heaven	and	all the gods together search our hearts!" When Sung Chiang
ds ill, then let the Spirit Of Heaven search among us	and	the Demons Of Earth encompass us, for surely this one will d
ay, or if among these is such an one who begins well	and	ends ill, then let the Spirit Of Heaven search among us and
in it. If there be one among us who will not endure	and	who cuts asunder this high purpose, or answers yea only wit
of Earth despise us. In this day we unite our purpose,	and	until we die we will not be divided in it. If there
ne other, yet each face noble in its way; one hundred	and	eight of us, each with his separate heart, yet each heart pure
eaven and Earth as father and mother. One hundred	and	eight of us, each face differing from the other, yet each face
ne stars, and we point to Heaven and Earth as father	and	mother. One hundred and eight of us, each face differing fron
hren according to the stars, and we point to Heaven	and	Earth as father and mother. One hundred and eight of us, eac
ther in this one hall, brethren according to the stars,	and	we point to Heaven and Earth as father and mother. One hun
e do ponder on this, that once we were scattered far	and	wide, but now are we gathered together in this one hall, bret
g, Wang Ting Lu, Ju Pao Ss邢, Pei Sheng, Shih Ch'ien	and	Tuan Ching Chu, these with all their true hearts here togethe
nd year of the Emperor Hsuen Ho in the fourth moon	and	on the twenty-third day the righteous heroes of Liang Shan P
ung Chiang knelt in front of them to make their vow,	and	he said, "In this second year of the Emperor Hsuen Ho in
ch had burned incense they all knelt there in the hall	and	Sung Chiang knelt in front of them to make their vow, and
l their voices together and they answered, "So be it!"	And	when each had burned incense they all knelt there in the hal
th great joy and they all joined their voices together	and	they answered, "So be it!" And when each had burned incens
n." Then were all who heard this filled with great joy	and	they all joined their voices together and they answered, "So t
hen all aid me, your chief, that we may lift our heads	and	make reply to Heaven." Then were all who heard this filled
e heart and trust each other, whether living or dead,	and	we must all aid each other in any woe. Do you then
venant with Heaven, and we must all have one heart	and	trust each other, whether living or dead, and we must all aid
gether then must we make a covenant with Heaven,	and	we must all have one heart and trust each other, whether livi
a few words to say. If we be the stars of Heaven	and	of Earth gathered here together then must we make a coven
ame into the hall and there burned an urn of incense	and	again he said to them, "Today we are no longer as we
hieftains together and so they all came into the hall	and	there burned an urn of incense and again he said to them
e drums to be beaten to call the chieftains together	and	so they all came into the hall and there burned an urn
haped houses and there they waited for their orders	and	when these commands were given each obeyed. On the next
and these all went to the gooseflight-shaped houses	and	there they waited for their orders and when these commands
vere some who were not appointed to a special task,	and	these all went to the gooseflight-shaped houses and there th
shed feasting everyone was in a mighty drunkenness	and	so each went to his own house. Among these there were son
place, each took his own despatch and his own seal	and	when they had finished feasting everyone was in a mighty dr
hieftain to his own place, each took his own despatch	and	his own seal and when they had finished feasting everyone w
obbers' lair, Sung Chiang, had finished his commands	and	when he had appointed every chieftain to his own place, each
nd year of the Emperor Hsuen Ho in the fourth moon	and	on the twenty-second day, at the great gathering in the lair,

沙博理译《水浒传》主要高频词 and 搭配使用情况索引

左语境	and
a Plague Marshal Hong Releases Demons by Mistake After Five Dynasties' turmoil	and
s Demons by Mistake After Five Dynasties' turmoil and strife, The clouds dispers…	and
spersed and revealed the sky, Refreshing rain brought old trees new life, Culture	and
wers, Under the heavens all was serene, Men dozed off at noon midst gay birds	and
lar named Shao Yaofu, also known as Master Kang Jie. From the end of the Tang	and
er. How true was the verse: Zhu, Li, Shi, Liu, Guo founded Liang, Tang, Jin, Han	and
in, Han and Zhou. Fifteen emperors fifty years in a row, Bringing hardship, tumult	and
tue, was born. A red glow suffused the sky when this sage came into the world,	and
following morning. He was in fact the God of Thunder descended to earth. Brave	and
ed. With a staff as tall as himself he smote so hard that four hundred prefectures	and
prefectures and districts acknowledged his sovereignty. He swept the land cle…	and
established his court at Bianliang. Tai Zu was the first of eighteen Song emperors	and
d years. That is why Master Shao Yaofu said in his praise: The clouds dispersed	and
rone to Marshal Zhao in the Eastern Capital." Chen clapped his hands to his brow	and
on. For this is in accord with the will of Heaven above, the laws of Earth below,	and
v, and the hearts of men between." Marshal Zhao accepted the abdication in 960	and
d the abdication in 960 and established his regime. He ruled for seventeen years,	and
ong was actually a re-incarnation of the Barefoot Immortal. When he came down	and
the Barefoot Immortal. When he came down and was born on earth he cried day	and
ion, inviting any man who could cure him to come forward. Heaven was touched	and
ut even revealing his name. What were the eight words? They were these: "Civil	and
e the future emperor. The civil affairs star became Bao Zheng, prefect of Kaifeng	and
The imperial court was snowed under with petitions for relief from every district	and
petitions for relief from every district and prefecture. More than half the soldiers	and
ef from every district and prefecture. More than half the soldiers and residents in	and
liers and residents in and around the Eastern Capital died. Bao Zheng, counsellor	and
Bao Zheng, counsellor and prefect of Kaifeng, published the officially approved…	and
empt to save the people. But to no avail. The plague grew worse. All the high civil	and
il and military officials conferred. They gathered in the Hall of the Water Clock	and
n come forward. If there are none, this court will adjourn." Zhao Zhe, the Premier,	and
court will adjourn." Zhao Zhe, the Premier, and Wen Yanbo, his deputy, advanced	and
nd said: "The plague is raging unabated in the capital. Victims among the soldiers	and
mong the soldiers and the people are many. We hope Your Majesty, in a forgiving	and
e Your Majesty, in a forgiving and benevolent spirit, will reduce prison sentences	and
; in a forgiving and benevolent spirit, will reduce prison sentences and cut taxes,	and

左语境	and
strife, The clouds dispersed and revealed the sky, Refreshing rain brought old trees	and
revealed the sky, Refreshing rain brought old trees new life, Culture and learning on	and
learning once again were high. Ordinary folk in the lanes wore silk, Music drifted fr	and
towers, Under the heavens all was serene, Men dozed off at noon midst gay birds	and
flowers. This eight-lined poem was written during the reign of Emperor Shen Zong	and
all through the Five Dynasties, times had been troubled. One short-lived dynasty ha	and
Zhou. Fifteen emperors fifty years in a row, Bringing hardship, tumult and woe. In t	and
woe. In time, the way of Heaven took a new turn. At Jiamaying, Tai Zu, the Emperor	and
fragrance still filled the air the following morning. He was in fact the God of Thunde	and
magnanimous, he was superior to any emperor who had ever lived. With a staff as	and
districts acknowledged his sovereignty. He swept the land clean and pacified the C	and
pacified the Central Plains. Naming his empire the Great Song, he established his co	and
founder of a dynasty lasting four hundred years. That is why Master Shao Yaofu s	and
revealed the sky. For the people it was indeed like seeing the sun again. At that time	and
laughed so delightedly that he fell off his donkey. Asked the reason for his joy, he s	and
the hearts of men between." Marshal Zhao accepted the abdication in 960 and esta	and
established his regime. He ruled for seventeen years, and there was peace throug	and
there was peace throughout the land. He was succeeded by his younger brother, T	and
was born on earth he cried day and night without cease. The imperial court posted	and
night without cease. The imperial court posted a proclamation, inviting any man who	and
sent the Great Star of White Gold in the guise of an old man. Announcing he could	and
whispered eight words into his ear. At once the prince stopped crying. The old man	and
military affairs, both have their stars." The fact was that the Jade Emperor of Heave	and
a senior member of the Dragon Diagram Academy. The military affairs star became	and
prefecture. More than half the soldiers and residents in and around the Eastern Cap	and
residents in and around the Eastern Capital died. Bao Zheng, counsellor and prefec	and
around the Eastern Capital died. Bao Zheng, counsellor and prefect of Kaifeng, pub	and
prefect of Kaifeng, published the officially approved prescriptions and spent his ow	and
spent his own money on medicines in an attempt to save the people. But to no avail	and
military officials conferred. The they gathered in the Hall of the Water Clock and wa	and
waited for daybreak, when court would be held, so that they could appeal to the en	and
Wen Yanbo, his deputy, advanced and said: "The plague is raging unabated in the c	and
said: "The plague is raging unabated in the capital. Victims among the soldiers and	and
the people are many. We hope Your Majesty, in a forgiving and benevolent spirit, wi	and
benevolent spirit, will reduce prison sentences and cut taxes, and pray to Heaven t	and
cut taxes, and pray to Heaven that the people be relived of this affliction." The empe	and
pray to Heaven that the people be relived of this affliction." The emperor at once or	and

赛珍珠译《水浒传》主要高频词 but 搭配使用情况索引

	but	
st together shouted assent and they said, "We would	but	meet again, life after life, generation after genera
r this high purpose, or answers yea only with his lips	but	in his heart says nay, or if among these is such an
be one, in sorrow one; our hour of birth was not one,	but	we will die together. Our names are writ upon the
er on this, that once we were scattered far and wide,	but	now are we gathered together in this one hall, br
ed from the other and they went down the mountain.	But	let it not be told now of all those Taoists who ret
ght, then will we be grateful truly for so great a favor.	but	if there is any rebuke from Heaven I pray that it b
, shaped like tadpoles, and such as no man can read.	But	among the Taoists there was one surnamed Ho a
all pass onward upon the happy way. This would I do,	but	I do not know what my brothers think of it." Then
Ch'ao Kai returned to Heaven we have done naught	but	go down the mountain and forth to battle, and be
old, Pei Yo. He had been formerly a man of Yu Chou,	but	because his eyes were green and his beard yellow
he dashed forward with all his strength to do battle.	But	Sung Chiang parted them and he called to Lu Chi
y would fain have dished forward to kill Chang Ch'ing.	But	Sung Chiang, seeing him there, himself went to m
hang Ch'ing would now fain have escaped from them	but	he could not and he was laid hold upon by the thr
ves were darkened and he would have fain retreated,	but	there was no way to go either forward or backwar
turned to look at each other face could not see face.	But	this was magic that Kung Sun Sheng had made. C
fain have gone and seized the grain upon the boats	but	the magistrate said, "General, do you watch your
in heart, nor did he go in pursuit of Lu Chi Shen.	But	he guarded the carts and brought them into the c
led he had not. He did but walk on with great strides.	But	he forgot to be heedful of the stones. Even as he
een the enemy, but he pretended he had not. He did	but	walk on with great strides. But he forgot to be hee
carrying his staff and by now he had seen the enemy,	but	he pretended he had not. He did but walk on with
nd the light of the stars filled the sky. They had gone	but	a little more than three miles when they saw a cr
answered, "This plan is excellent, indeed, and do you	but	watch well your chance," and he commanded the
and poured forth wine to congratulate Chang Ch'ing,	but	first he commanded that a long rack be placed up
ve him he could not withstand so many and he could	but	take Liu T'ang and return to the city of Tung Ch'a
kless of his life he withstood L邦 Fang and Kao Shen.	But	he was not prepared against Yien Ch'ing, who sav
s full of fear and impatience. He threw his flying dart,	but	he did not strike Hua Yung or Ling Ch'ung and sin
and he let it fly to So Ch'ao. So Ch'ao dodged swiftly,	but	it was too late and it struck upon his face and the
uld not leave him and he plunged after Chang Ch'ing	but	he forgot to guard himsdf against the stones. Cha
was evil, left Tung P'ing and galloped into his ranks.	But	Tung P'ing would not leave him and he plunged a
hold on Tung P'ing's weapon and all to pull him over,	but	he could not pull him over, and the two wrestled.
ung P'ing thrust his weapon toward the other's back.	But	Chang Ch'ing leaned over to the earth and Tung F
t risen and already the stone had struck for its mark.	But	Tung P'ing's eyes were clear and his hand was qu
en bag and brought forth a stone. His right hand had	but	just risen and already the stone had struck for its
P'ing said, "Others may be wounded by your stones,	but	how can you make me afraid?" Chang Ch'ing, hold
e this and he meditated secretly in his heart, "I have	but	come after Sung Chiang, and if I do not show forth
it, and it struck full on the sword and sparks flew out.	But	Kuan Sheng had not the heart to do battle with hi

赛珍珠译《水浒传》主要高频词 be 搭配使用情况索引

Context...	N...	...Context
until we die we will not be divided in it. If there	be	one among us who will not endure and who cuts as
unite our purpose, and until we die we will not	be	divided in it. If there be one among us who will not
rt, yet each heart pure as a star; in joy we shall	be	one, in sorrow one; our hour of birth was not one, bi
their voices together and they answered, "So	be	it!" And when each had burned incense they all kne
we have been. I have a few words to say. If we	be	the stars of Heaven and of Earth gathered here tog
ext day Sung Chiang commanded the drums to	be	beaten to call the chieftains together and so they a
who shall bear the chief banner in battle shall	be	Ju Pao Ss邢. "This is in the second year of the Empe
u. He in charge of the walls about the lair shall	be	The Nine Tailed Turtle T'ao Chung Wang. He who s
He who shall be in charge of the feasting shall	be	one who is The Smiling Faced Tiger Chu Fu. He in cl
shall be The Iron Fan Sung Ch'ing. He who shall	be	in charge of the feasting shall be one who is The Sr
who shall govern the spreading of feasts shall	be	The Iron Fan Sung Ch'ing. He who shall be in charge
sheep and cows and all such beasts there shall	be	one who is The Dagger Devil Ch'ao Cheng. He who
govern the building or repairing of houses shall	be	one, who is The Blue Eyed Tiger Li Y邦n. For the bui
olosives, fireballs and rockets and the like, shall	be	Thunder That Shakes The Heavens Ling Chen. He w
hall govern the making of all metal things shall	be	The Gold Spotted Leopard T'ang Lung. He who mak
internal and external, shall be one and he shall	be	The Magic Physician An Tao Ch'uan. He who shall c
sician for men, both internal and external, shall	be	one and he shall be The Magic Physician An Tao Ch
e Purple Bearded Huang Fu Tuan. He who shall	be	physician for men, both internal and external, shall
l the ills of the beasts shall be one and he shall	be	The Purple Bearded Huang Fu Tuan. He who shall b
physicians who heal the ills of the beasts shall	be	one and he shall be The Purple Bearded Huang Fu 1
king of banners and garments and the like shall	be	The Strong Armed Gorilla Hou Chien. He who shall
s and proofs of surety shall be one and he shall	be	The Jade Armed Warrior Ching Ta Chien. He who sl
shall carve the seals and proofs of surety shall	be	one and he shall be The Jade Armed Warrior Ching
both great and small, shall be one and he shall	be	The Jade Banner Pole Meng K'an. He who shall car
king of boats of war, both great and small, shall	be	one and he shall be The Jade Banner Pole Meng K'a
and paying out, there shall be one, and he shall	be	The God Of Accounting Chiang Ching. He who shall
grain, both receiving and paying out, there shall	be	one, and he shall be The God Of Accounting Chiang
ents and rewards there shall be one and it shall	be	The Iron Faced P'ei Hs邦an. To count the treasure a
judge of punishments and rewards there shall	be	one and it shall be The Iron Faced P'ei Hs邦an. To c
t forth and despatches and the like and it shall	be	The Magic Scribe Siao Jang. To judge of punishmen
lies shall be sixteen in number. One there shall	be	in charge of all commands sent forth and despatche
vife Hu. Those who shall seek out supplies shall	be	sixteen in number. One there shall be in charge of a
Is'ai Ch'ing. Two horsemen warriors there shall	be	who shall govern the spies among all the companie
and The Lone Fire K'ung Liang. Two there shall	be	to govern executions, and these are The Iron Armed
Like Jen Kuei Of Old Kao Shen, and there shall	be	two also from among the fighting men on foot, The
guard among the central army, and these shall	be	The Lesser Duke L邦 Fang and He Who Is Like Jen F

赛珍珠译《水浒传》主要高频词 when 搭配使用情况索引

	when	
did they all mingle blood with wine and drink it and	when	they had drunk themselves to mighty drunkenness, t
eaven and all the gods together search our hearts!"	When	Sung Chiang had thus vowed, all the host together s
voices together and they answered, "So be it!" And	when	each had burned incense they all knelt there in the
l houses and there they waited for their orders and	when	these commands were given each obeyed. On the ne
e, each took his own despatch and his own seal and	when	they had finished feasting everyone was in a mighty
' lair, Sung Chiang, had finished his commands and	when	he had appointed every chieftain to his own place, e
man was appointed to his own place." On that day	when	the great chieftain of the robbers' lair, Sung Chiang,
wentysecond day, at the great gathering in the lair,	when	each man was appointed to his own place." On that
red tablet and Siao Jang was told to write it down.	When	he had finished writing and they all had read it, they
at spirit paper be burned and that they all scatter.	When	dawn was newly come he caused a vegetable meal
es and open up the earth and search for the flame.	When	they had dug not yet three feet into that earth they
and it struck the earth at the full south of the altar.	When	they looked again The Eye Of Heaven was closed. Al
ilk and it came from the northwest gate of heaven.	When	they all looked there was as it were a great plate of
d this thrice. On the seventh day at the third watch,	when	Kung Sun Sheng was upon the highest terrace of the
men. Outside the hall there were warrior gods and	when	all were placed and nothing lacking the Taoists cam
ot heard of from ancient times even until now. "Yet	when	in the past our fighting men went forth they killed m
im. Then was Sung Chiang filled with pleasure and	when	he had comforted the people he sent forth a comma
e and his children and go with us up the mountain."	When	Sung Chiang heard these words he was filled with p
f them heard this, and who dared say a word more?	When	Sung Chiang had made the vow thus everybody beg
could he stay the falling city and withstand them?	When	he heard the sounds of bursting fireballs on all four
vered the sky and the dark mists were over all and	when	the horsemen and the soldiers turned to look at eac
y. They had gone but a little more than three miles	when	they saw a crowd of carts and upon the banners ove
l 邦 Fang and Kao Shen seized Ting T? Sheng.	When	Chang Ch'ing came to save him he could not withsta
es. They had thus fought some five or seven rounds	when	Chang Ch'ing turned his horse and went away. Then
and if I do not show forth my skill in war then	when	I go up the mountain surely will I have no great hon
had but just brought them back to their own ranks	when	again Chang Ch'ing let fly a stone. Kuan Sheng rais
ground. Chu T'ung made haste to go and save him	when	again there was a stone and it flew upon the back o
his heart and he would have recalled his company,	when	someone was heard to cry out in a mighty voice from
t the two had brought their horses face to face	when	Chang Ch'ing had already a stone hidden in his han
arbed club he dashed forward in front of the ranks.	When	Sung Chiang looked he saw it was that warrior victo
eet Chang Ch'ing and they fought but a few rounds	when	Yien Shun could not withstand the enemy and he tu
hen from behind his horse a warrior flew forth, and	when	he looked to see who this was, it was that Five I-Iue
the battle?" Sung Chiang's words were not finished	when	from behind his horse a warrior flew forth, and wher
ted together. They had fought less than five rounds	when	Chang Ch'ing retreated, and Ch'邦 Ling pursued hin
arbed spear and he came to the front of the ranks.	When	Sung Chiang looked at him it was he who bore the c
y followed Sung Chiang beneath the gate banners.	When	the drums had been thrice beaten Chang Ch'ing upo
at the enemy and they had fought but a few rounds	when	Chang Ch'ing went away. Hao Ss 邗 Wen pursued hi

赛珍珠译《水浒传》主要高频词 who 搭配使用情况索引

	Who	
od Victor In A Hundred Battles Warrior Of Fire Warrior	Who	Wars Against Tigers White Faced Goodman White Spo
le Armed Warrior Jade Banner Pole Kirlq Of The Devils	Who	Roll Earth Lesser Duke Lsser One Whom No Obstacle
Guardian Star God He Who Is Like Jen Kuei Of Old He	Who	Rules Three Mountains Heaven Flying God Iron Armed
er Guardian God In The Clouds Guardian Star God He	Who	Is Like Jen Kuei Of Old He Who Rules Three Mountain
nd Water Beast Dwarf Tiger Eagle In The Clouds Eagle	Who	Flutters Eight Against The Sky Armed Lo Chao Eye Of I
ger Single Flower Iron Armed Yellow Haired Doq Eagle	Who	Flutters Against The Sky Devil Faced Oyster That Turn
I Lone Fire Curly Haired Spotted Necked Tiger Warrior	Who	Wars Against Tigers Heaven Flying God Pursuing God
led He Who Rules Three Mountains Vanguard God He	Who	Is Like Jen Kuei Of Old Lone Fire Curly Haired Spotted
ed Lo Chao Ugly Warrior Sick Tiger Purple Bearded He	Who	Rules Three Mountains Vanguard God He Who Is Like
Dry Land Water Beast Wily Warrior King Of The Devils	Who	Roll Earth Ten Foot Green Snake Female Tiger Female
He Whom No Obstacle Can Stay Nine Dragoned One	Who	Heeds Not His Life Swift Vanguard Opportune Rain M
Tiger Dragon Who Roils Rivers Black Whirlwind Eagle	Who	Smites The Heavens Leopard Headed Redheaded Dev
eat Sword Dragon In The Clouds Winged Tiger Dragon	Who	Roils Rivers Black Whirlwind Eagle Who Smites The H
his heart says nay, or if among these is such an one	who	begins well and ends ill, then let the Spirit Of Heaven
it. If there be one among us who will not endure and	who	cuts asunder this high purpose, or answers yea only w
will not be divided in it. If there be one among us	who	will not endure and who cuts asunder this high purpos
t our heads and make reply to Heaven." Then were all	who	heard this filled with great joy and they all joined thei
went to his own house. Among these there were some	who	were not appointed to a special task, and these all we
shall be The Nine Tailed Turtle T'ao Chung Wang. He	who	shall bear the chief banner in battle shall be Ju Pao S
He who shall be in charge of the feasting shall be one	who	is The Smiling Faced Tiger Chu Fu. In charge of the
eading of feasts shall be The Iron Fan Sung Ch'ing. He	who	shall be in charge of the feasting shall be one who is
hall be one who is The Dagger Devil Ch'ao Cheng. He	who	shall govern the spreading of feasts shall be The Iron
heep and cows and all such beasts there shall be one	who	is The Dagger Devil Ch'ao Cheng. He who shall govern
overn the building or repairing of houses shall be one,	who	is The Blue Eyed Tiger Li Y邦. For the butchering of p
ll be Thunder That Shakes The Heavens Ling Chen. He	who	shall govern the building or repairing of houses shall b
nqs shall be The Gold Spotted Leopard T'ang Lung. He	who	makes all explosives, fireballs and rockets and the like
nd he shall be The Magic Physician An Tao Ch'uan. He	who	shall govern the making of all metal things shall be Th
nd he shall be The Purple Bearded Huang Fu Tuan. He	who	shall be physician for men, both internal and external,
orilla Hou Chien. He who shall govern those physicians	who	heal the ills of the beasts shall be one and he shall
like shall be The Strong Armed Gorilla Hou Chien. He	who	shall govern those physicians who heal the ills of the I
e shall be The Jade Armed Warrior Ching Ta Chien. He	who	shall govern the making of banners and garments and
e and he shall be The Jade Banner Pole Meng K'an. He	who	shall carve the seals and proofs of surety shall be one
d he shall be The God Of Accounting Chiang Ching. He	who	shall govern the making of boats of war, both great an
nd The Ten Foot Green Snake The Goodwife Hu. Those	who	shall seek out supplies shall be sixteen in number. On
er Ts'ai Ch'ing. Two horsemen warriors there shall be	who	shall govern the spies among all the companies, and t
, and these shall be The Lesser Duke L邦 Fang and He	Who	Is Like Jen Kuei Of Old Kao Shen, and there shall be

　　由以上高频词搭配可见作者的语言风格。在赛译本中，高频词第一位是 and，频次 35 050 次，而作为对照的沙译中，and 是排在第二位的高频词，频次为 13 267，远低于赛译。

　　由上图可见，and 在上下文连接中的关键作用，同时也使得译本的平均句长居于高位。"赛译本中的连词 and 与其它三个译本存在显著性差异，再以赛氏原创作品《大地三步曲》为参照语料库，考察发现该作品的词表首位词也同样是定冠词 and，从而可断定赛氏的有关中国题材的无论是译文还是作品呈一致的特征。此外，and 的过量使用，是句子变长的主要因素之一"（刘克强，2013）。

赛译平均句长为 21.8 个词语，相比之下，沙博理《水浒传》译本平均句长仅为 11.1。在句子结构上，赛译高频率使用了 who、when 来连接主从句，使句子语义完整且连贯，文体整洁有序；使用了 but 转折连词，将主从句紧密连接起来，介乎口语和书面语之间，更偏于口语化特征。至于高频词 be，考察搭配后可见，赛译使用了较多的主语＋shall be 结构，用来表示即将发生的动作，也颇符合原著中白话文叙事风格。鉴于《水浒传》是中国历史上第一部用白话文写成的章回体小说，赛珍珠的翻译侧重原汁原味译出其文体风格，因此原语的口语化特征在译文中得以充分体现出来。

4.1.2　基于语料库的《金瓶梅》芮效卫英译本译者风格

芮效卫的《金瓶梅词话》英译本翻译历时三十余年，几乎耗去了他半生的精力，2013 年 11 月 19 日《纽约时报》艺文版以半版篇幅专访芮效卫，盛赞其译本"不但是文学翻译，而且为了解中国文化打开了一扇窗"。芮译本高度尊重原著，雅俗共赏，对原文的语言风格和蕴含的中国文化充分还原，为海外中国文学研究提供了不可多得的宝贵素材。

芮效卫译《金瓶梅》的基本数据图

Lines	43645
Words (types)	Now: 24043　When loaded: 24043
Words (tokens)	Now: 972524　When loaded: 972524
Type-token ratio	Now: 40.4494　When loaded: 40.4494
Characters	4259562
Sentences	46382
Words/sentence	20.9677

由统计可见，芮译作为《金瓶梅》的全译本，总形符数（tokens）为 972 524，类符数为 24 043，类符形符比 40.449 4，平均句长为 20.97 个词语。其总形符数巨大，远远超过了赛珍珠译《水浒传》的总形符数 576 981，也高于杨宪益夫妇的《红楼梦》全译本的总形符数 641 611，略高于霍译《红楼梦》的总形符数 847 594，由此基本数据可见芮译本容量巨大，其英译本 5 卷的总页数是 2 500 多页，其中注释多达 4 400 多条。

利用 Concordance 320 统计译本的词长总体分布情况，结果如下：

芮效卫译《金瓶梅》词长分布图

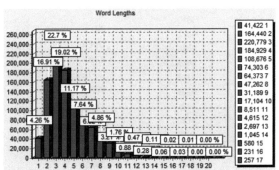

从上图可见，芮效卫在译本中偏好使用二字母词汇、三字母词汇和四字母词汇，其中二字母词汇占比为 16.91%，三字母词汇为最频繁使用类型，占 22.7%，四字母词汇在词汇长度分布中所占比例为 19.02%。

芮效卫译《金瓶梅》高频词前 60 位

高频词 1—30　　　　　　　　　　　　　　高频词 31—60

Headword	No.		
THE	53587	WHEN	4173
TO	36824	OUT	4159
AND	28213	YOUR	3947
OF	26113	NOT	3932
A	18891	THEY	3856
"	14838	THEM	3787
IN	14424	BUT	3695
YOU	11440	UP	3641
THAT	10818	ME	3455
HER	9661	MY	3343
HE	8935	SO	3221
WITH	8828	ARE	3162
IT	8656	BY	3136
FOR	8531	WERE	2990
HIS	8134	FROM	2979
ON	7435	ALL	2900
WAS	7413	WHO	2869
IS	6711	TWO	2837
AS	6659	THEIR	2806
SHE	6613	IF	2797
I	6022	BEEN	2707
SAID	5888	THEN	2545
HAD	5665	ONE	2517
HSI-MEN	5413	AFTER	2452
HIM	5229	NO	2372
CHING	5191	WILL	2372
BE	4720	THERE	2369
THIS	4555	AN	2314
HAVE	4528	HAS	2291
AT	4223	INTO	2252

芮效卫译《金瓶梅》主要高频词 the 搭配使用情况索引

Sung fights a tiger on ching-yang ridge; Pan Chin-lien disdains her mate and plays the
ridge; Pan Chin-lien disdains her mate and plays the coquette. There is a lyric to the
te and plays the coquette. There is a lyric to the tune "Pleasing Eyes" that goes: The
had only to meet with Yu-chi and Lady Chi, For all their valor to come to naught. The
and Lady Chi, For all their valor to come to naught. The subject of this lyric is
related to each other as substance is to function. Thus, when beauty bedazzles the
bstance is to function. Thus, when beauty bedazzles the eye, passion is born in the
zzles the eye, passion is born in the heart Passion and beauty evoke each; the heart
, passion is born in the heart Passion and beauty evoke each other; the heart and
heart and the eye are interdependent. This is a fact that, from ancient times until
present day, gentlemen of moral cultivation ought never to forget. As two men of
people just like ourselves who are most affected by passion"; and "Beauty is like
d by passion"; and "Beauty is like the lode stone which exerts its unseen pull on
when obstacles intervene. If this be true even for nonsentient objects, how much
the more must it be so for man, who must spend his days striving to survive in
of passion and beauty?" "The hero grips his 'Hook of Wu.'" Hook of Wu is
es such as Kan-chiang, Mo-yeh, Tai-o, Hook of Wu, Fish Gut, and Death's-head.
ath's-head. The lyric speaks of heroes with temperaments of iron and stone and
mperaments of iron and stone and the sort of heroic prowess that vaults across
prowess that vaults across the heavens like a rainbow, who yet did not escape
ste of allowing their ambitions to be blunted by women. It then goes on to refer to
mon-King of Western Chu, whose name was Hsiang Chi, or Hsiang Yu. Because
Chu, whose name was Hsiang Chi, or Hsiang Yu. Because the First Emperor of
he First Emperor of the Chin dynasty was so lacking in virtue that he: Garrisoned
the Chin dynasty was so lacking in virtue that he: Garrisoned the Five Ranges to
y was so lacking in virtue that he: Garrisoned the Five Ranges to the south, Built
in virtue that he: Garrisoned the Five Ranges to the south, Built the Great Wall
arrisoned the Five Ranges to the south, Built the Great Wall to the north, Filled
Five Ranges to the south, Built the Great Wall to the north, Filled in the sea to the
south, Built the Great Wall to the north, Filled in the sea to the east, Constructed
Wall to the north, Filled in the sea to the east, Constructed the O-pang Palace in
the sea to the east, Constructed the O-pang Palace in the west, Swallowed up the
onstructed the O-pang Palace in the west, Swallowed up the Six States, Buried
n the west, Swallowed up the Six States, Buried the scholars alive, and
Burned the books, Hsiang Yu rose up in rebellion against him and was joined by
of Han, whose name was Liu Chi, or Liu Pang. Liu Pang rolled up like a mat
was Liu Chi, or Liu Pang. Liu Pang rolled up like a mat the territory in which

coquette. There is a lyric to the tune "Pleasing Eyes" that goes: The hero grips
tune "Pleasing Eyes" that goes: The hero grips his "Hook of Wu,"Eager to cut of
hero grips his "Hook of Wu,"Eager to cut off ten thousand heads. How is it that
subject of this lyric is the words passion and beauty, two concepts that are rel
words passion and beauty, two concepts that are related to each other as sub
eye, passion is born in the heart Passion and beauty evoke each other; the hea
heart Passion and beauty evoke each other; the heart and the eye are interdepe
heart and the eye are interdependent. This is a fact that, from ancient times unt
eye are interdependent. This is a fact that, from ancient times until the present
present day, gentlemen of moral cultivation ought never to forget. As two men o
Chin dynasty once said, "It is people just like ourselves who are most affected t
lode stone which exerts its unseen pull on the needle even when obstacles inte
needle even when obstacles intervene. If this be true even for nonsentient obj
more must it be so for man, who must spend his days striving to survive in the
realm of passion and beauty?" "The hero grips his 'Hook of Wu.'" Hook of Wu
name of an ancient sword. In those days there were swords with names such
lyric speaks of heroes with temperaments of iron and stone and the sort of her
sort of heroic prowess that vaults across the heavens like a rainbow, who yet
heavens like a rainbow, who yet did not escape the fate of allowing their ambiti
fate of allowing their ambitions to be blunted by women. It then goes on to refe
Hegemon-King of Western Chu, whose name was Hsiang Chi, or Hsiang Yu. B
First Emperor of the Chin dynasty was so lacking in virtue that he: Garrisoned
Chin dynasty was so lacking in virtue that he: Garrisoned the Five Ranges to th
Five Ranges to the south, Built the Great Wall to the north, Filled in the sea to
south, Built the Great Wall to the north, Filled in the sea to the east, Constructe
Great Wall to the north, Filled in the sea to the east, Constructed the O-pang Pr
north, Filled in the sea to the east, Constructed the O-pang Palace in the west,
sea to the east, Constructed the O-pang Palace in the west, Swallowed up the
east, Constructed the O-pang Palace in the west, Swallowed up the Six States
O-pang Palace in the west, Swallowed up the Six States, Buried the scholars
west, Swallowed up the Six States, Buried the scholars alive, and Burned the
Six States, Buried the scholars alive, and Burned the books, Hsiang Yu rose u
scholars alive, and Burned the books, Hsiang Yu rose up in rebellion against hi
books, Hsiang Yu rose up in rebellion against him and was joined by the King o
King of Han, whose name was Liu Chi, or Liu Pang. Liu Pang rolled up like a
territory in which the capital of the First Emperor had been located and thus put
capital of the First Emperor had been located and thus put an end to the Chin dy

芮效卫译《金瓶梅》主要高频词 and 搭配使用情况索引

1 Wu Sung fights a tiger on ching-yang ridge; Pan Chin-lien disdains her mate
"Eager to cut off ten thousand heads. How is it that a heart forged out of iron
iron and stone, Can yet be melted by a flower? Just take a look at Hsiang Yu
Pang: Both cases are equally distressing. They had only to meet with Yu-chi
all their valor to come to naught. The subject of this lyric is the words passion
. Thus, when beauty bedazzles the eye, passion is born in the heart Passion
e, passion is born in the heart Passion and beauty evoke each other; the heart
once said, "It is people just like ourselves who are most affected by passion";
for man, who must spend his days striving to survive in the realm of passion
words with names such as Kan-chiang, Mo-yeh, Tai-o, Hook of Wu, Fish Gut
Gut, and Death's-head. The lyric speaks of heroes with temperaments of iron
eath's-head. The lyric speaks of heroes with temperaments of iron and stone
g Palace in the west, Swallowed up the Six States, Buried the scholars alive,
holars alive, and Burned the books, Hsiang Yu rose up in rebellion against him
e a mat the territory in which the capital of the First Emperor had been located
t Emperor had been located and thus put an end to the Chin dynasty. Later he
ng Yu agreed to make the Hung Canal a boundary line between their territories
oms, that he took her with him on his campaigns so they could be together day
esult of this was that he was finally defeated by Liu Pang's general, Han Hsin
of his homeland, the region of Chu, he realized that his situation was hopeless
can uproot mountains,My valor knows no peer; But the times are against me,
Moreover, you're such a beauty that Liu Pang, who is a ruler addicted to wine
ly life," Yu-chi wept. Then, asking Hsiang Yu for his sword, she slit her throat
impment beneath the liquescent sky; How could he bear to turn back his head
in Sau-shui. Yet, with his three-foot sword in hand, he slew the white snake
rose in righteous revolt in the mountainous area between the districts of Mang
districts of Mang and Tang. Three years later he destroyed the Chin dynasty,
lth year of his reign destroyed the Chu, thereby winning the empire for himself
whose title was Prince Ju-i of Chao. Because Empress Lu was jealous of her
ood, Lady Chi was extremely uneasy. One day when Emperor Kao-tsu was ill
ying, "After you have fulfilled your ten thousand years, on whom shall my son
," the emperor said. "When I hold court tomorrow I'll depose the heir apparent
set up your son in his stead. How would that be? Lady Chi dried her tears
at the Four Gray beards of Mount Shang be induced to come out of retirement
rent. When Emperor Kao-tsu saw these four men with their snow-white hair
Emperor Kao-tsu saw these four men with their snow-white hair and beards
saw these four men with their snow-white hair and beards and imposing ca

plays the coquette. There is a lyric to the tune "Pleasing Eyes" that goes: Th
stone, Can yet be melted by a flower? Just take a look at Hsiang Yu and Liu
Liu Pang: Both cases are equally distressing. They had only to meet with Yu
Lady Chi, For all their valor to come to naught. The subject of this lyric is the
beauty, two concepts that are related to each other as to functi
beauty evoke each other; the heart and the eye are interdependent. This is a
the eye are interdependent. This is a fact that, from ancient times until the pr
"Beauty is like the lode stone which exerts its unseen pull on the needle even
beauty?" "The hero grips his 'Hook of Wu.'" Hook of Wu is the name of
Death's-head. The lyric speaks of heroes with temperaments of iron and sto
stone and the sort of heroic prowess that vaults across the heavens like a ra
the sort of heroic prowess that vaults across the heavens like a rainbow, wl
Burned the books, Hsiang Yu rose up in rebellion against him and was joined
was joined by the King of Han, whose name was Liu Chi, or Liu Pang. Liu Pa
thus put an end to the Chin dynasty. Later he and Hsiang Yu agreed to make
Hsiang Yu agreed to make the Hung Canal a boundary line between their terr
divided the empire between them. Now, in the course of their conflict, Hsiang
night. The result of this was that he was finally defeated by Liu Pang's gene
had to flee by night as far as Yin-ling, where the enemy troops caught up wi
expressed his sorrow in song: My strength can uproot mountains,My valor k
my steed will run no more. My steed will run no more,So what can I do
women, is sure to take you for himself if he should see you." "I would rather
died. The Hegemon-King was so moved by her act that, when the time came
bid Yu-chi farewell?" Now the King of Han, Liu Pang, was originally no more f
rose in righteous revolt in the mountainous area between the districts of Man
Tang. Three years later he destroyed the Chin dynasty, and in the fifth year
in the fifth year of his reign destroyed the empire fo
establishing the Han dynasty. But he became infatuated with a woman whos
wished her no good, Lady Chi was extremely uneasy. One day when Emper
lay with his head in her lap, Lady Chi began to weep, saying, "After you hav
I be able to rely?" "That shouldn't be a problem," the emperor said. "When I
set up your son in his stead. How would that be?" Lady Chi dried her tears
thanked him for his favor. When Empress Lu heard about this she summoned
lend their support to the heir apparent. One day the Four Gray beards appea
beards and imposing caps and gowns, he asked them who they were. They
imposing caps and gowns, he asked them who they were. They identified th
gowns, he asked them who they were. They identified themselves as Maste

芮效卫译《金瓶梅》主要高频词 that 搭配使用情况索引

ien disdains her mate and plays the coquette. There is a lyric to the tune "Pleasing Eyes"	that	goes: The hero grips his "Hook of Wu,"Eager to cut off ten thousand heads. How is
The hero grips his "Hook of Wu,"Eager to cut off ten thousand heads. How is it	that	a heart forged out of iron and stone, Can yet be melted by a flower? Just take
come to naught. The subject of this lyric is the words passion and beauty, two concepts	that	are related to each other as substance is to function. Thus, when beauty bedazzles
on and beauty evoke each other; the heart and the eye are interdependent. This is a fact	that	, from ancient times until the present day, gentlemen of moral cultivation ought never t
c speaks of heroes with temperaments of iron and stone and the sort of heroic prowess	that	vaults across the heavens like a rainbow, who yet did not escape the fate of allowin
hi, or Hsiang Yu. Because the First Emperor of the Chin dynasty was so lacking in virtue	that	he: Garrisoned the Five Ranges to the south, Built the Great Wall to the north, Filled
s. But he was so infatuated with his favorite, Yu-chi, who possessed the kind of beauty	that	can topple kingdoms, that he took her with him on his campaigns so they could be tog
ed with his favorite, Yu-chi, who possessed the kind of beauty that can topple kingdoms,	that	he took her with him on his campaigns so they could be together day and night. The
him on his campaigns so they could be together day and night. The result of this was	that	he was finally defeated by Liu Pang's general, Han Hsin, and had to flee by night as
east of the Yangtze River, but he could not bear to part with Yu-chi. Hearing the armies	that	surrounded him on all sides singing the songs of his homeland, the region of Chu, he
ounded him on all sides singing the songs of his homeland, the region of Chu, he realized	that	his situation was hopeless and expressed his sorrow in song: My strength can upr
tions on my account," Yu-chi said to him. "Not really," the Hegemon-King replied. "It's just	that	we can't bear to give each other up. Moreover, you're such a beauty that Liu Pang,
plied. "It's just that we can't bear to give each other up. Moreover, you're such a beauty	that	Liu Pang, who is a ruler addicted to wine and women, is sure to take you for
for his sword, she slit her throat and died. The Hegemon-King was so moved by her act	that	, when the time came, he followed suit by cutting his own throat. A historian has com
t. A historian has composed a poem to commemorate this event: Gone was the strength	that	could uproot mountains,the dream of hegemony destroyed; Laying aside his sword,
ot mountains,the dream of hegemony destroyed; Laying aside his sword, he merely sa...	that	his steed would run no more. As bright moonlight flooded the encampment beneath t
court tomorrow I'll depose the heir apparent and set up your son in his stead. How would	that	be?" Lady Chi dried her tears and thanked him for his favor. When Empress Lu hear
d her husband's chief adviser, Chang Liang, for a secret consultation. Chang Liang rec...	that	the Four Gray beards of Mount Shang be induced to come out of retirement and lend
ve liked to replace the heir apparent, but these four men have lent him their support. Now	that	his wings are full-grown his position will prove difficult to shake." Lady Chi wept inc
e Four Seas, So what can we do? Of what avail are stringed arrows, Against a target	that	lies beyond their reach? The emperor finished his song and, in the end, did not make
oig." Poets have remarked, on reaching this point in their evaluations of these two rulers,	that	Liu Pang and Hsiang Yu were certainly heroes of their day and yet did not escape th
ambitions to be blunted by these two women. Although the position of wife is superior to	that	of concubine, the calamity that befell Lady Chi was even crueler than that which be
e two women. Although the position of wife is superior to that of concubine, the calamity	that	befell Lady Chi was even crueler than that which be fell Yu-chi. Thus it is that the
e is superior to that of concubine, the calamity that befell Lady Chi was even crueler than	that	which be fell Yu-chi. Thus it is that the way of a wife or concubine who wishes
calamity that befell Lady Chi was even crueler than that which be fell Yu-chi. Thus it is	that	the way of a wife or concubine who wishes to serve her husband faithfully and yet
intact within her own windows is hard. With regard to these two rulers, is it not true	that	: They had only to meet with Yu-chi and Lady Chi, For all their valor to come to
with Yu-chi and Lady Chi, For all their valor to come to naught? There is a poem	that	testifies to this: The favorites of Liu Pang and Hsiang Yu are much to be pitied; Thes
kew;its revelation is sufficient to make the Yellow River flow backward. The story goes	that	during the years of the Cheng-ho reign period of Emperor Hui-tsung of the Sung dyna
four wicked ministers, Kao Chiu, Yang Chien, Tung Kuan, and Tsai Ching, with the result	that	the empire was thrown into great disorder. The people were unable to pursue their
ficials, corrupt functionaries, Evil magnates, and delinquent commoners in the empire. At	that	time, in Yang-ku district of Shantung Province, there was a man named Wu Chih who
els with anyone. Because of the hardship created by a famine in the locality, he decided	that	he would have to let his younger brother fend for himself, sold the house they had in
herited from their forebears, and moved to the district town of Ching-ho. Now at the time	that	this occurred Wu Sung, because he had beaten up the military affairs commissioner,
lows of the world and was so: Chivalrous by nature and open-handed with his wealth,	that	people called him Little Lord Meng-chang. In fact, Master Chai was a direct descend
Sung was, he offered him a place to stay on his manor. But who could have anticipated	that	Wu Sung would come down with a case of malaria that required him to recuperate o
But who could have anticipated that Wu Sung would come down with a case of malaria	that	required him to recuperate on the premises for more than a year pon his recovery he
on the road, Wu Sung arrived on the border between Yang-ku and Ching-ho districts. At	that	time there was a ridge of hills on the border of Shantung Province called Ching-yang
these hills there was a bulging-eyed, white-browed tiger who had eaten so many people	that	travelers along that route were few. The authorities had ordered the licensed hunter

芮效卫译《金瓶梅》主要高频词 with 搭配使用情况索引

Just take a look at Hsianq Yu and Liu Panq: Both cases are equally distressinq. They had only to meet	with	Yu-chi and Lady Chi.
'Hook of Wu.'" Hook of Wu is the name of an ancient sword. In those days there were swords	with	names such as Kan-chiang,
swords with names such as Kan-chianq, Mo-yeh, Tai-o, Hook of Wu, Fish Gut, and Death's-head. The ...	with	temperaments of iron and stone and the sort of heroic prowes
between their territories and divided the empire between them. Now, in the course of their conflict, ...	with	the help of plans provided by Fan Tsenq,
plans provided by Fan Tsenq, to defeat the Kinq of Han in seventy-two military engagements. But he ...	with	his favorite,
so infatuated with his favorite, Yu-chi, who possessed the kind of beauty that can topple kingdoms, th...	with	him on his campaigns so they could be toqether day and night
Panq's qeneral, Han Hsin, and had to flee by night as far as Yin-linq, where the enemy troops caught ...	with	him.
he might have sought help from the area east of the Yanqtze River, but he could not bear to part	with	Yu-chi.
what can I do? Oh, Yu-chi, Yu-chi,What is to be done? When he finished singinq his face was streake...	with	tears.
Yu-chi farewell? Now the Kinq of Han, Liu Panq, was originally no more than a neiqhborhood head in ...	with	his three-foot sword in hand,
his reiqn destroyed the Chu, thereby winninq the empire for himself and establishinq the Han dynast...	with	a woman whose maiden name was Chi.
her and wished her no qood, Lady Chi was extremely uneasy. One day when Emperor Kao-tsu was ill ...	with	his head in her lap,
out of retirement and lend their support to the heir apparent. One day the Four Gray beards appear...	with	the heir apparent.
One day the Four Gray beards appeared in court with the heir apparent. When Emperor Kao-tsu saw...	with	their snow-white hair and beards and imposinq caps and gowr
death of Emperor Kao-tsu, to rid herself of her apprehensions, Empress Lu had Prince Ju-i of Chao put...	with	poisoned wine and so mutilated Lady Chi as to turn her into a
wishes to serve her husband faithfully and yet keep her head and neck intact within her own window...	With	reqard to these two rulers,
own windows is hard. With reqard to these two rulers, is it not true that: They had only to meet	with	Yu-chi and Lady Chi,
She was less fortunate than Yu-chi, who has a tomb. Now why do you suppose your narrator is so pr...	with	explicatinq the two words passion and beauty.
who is embodied in a tiqer and enqenders a tale of the passions. In it a licentious woman commits a...	with	a decadent man-about-town:
emperor bestowed his trust and favor upon the four wicked ministers, Kao Chiu, Yanq Chien, Tunq Ku...	with	the result that the empire was thrown into qreat disorder.
six feet in stature, and Broad-shouldered as they come. From his youth he had cultivated his strength...	with	the spear and quarter staff.
and muddle headed to a ridiculous deqree. He was disposed to mind his own business and did not pi...	with	anyone.
Chai Chin enjoyed patronizinq the heroes and stout fellows of the world and was so: Chivalrous by n...	with	his wealth,
offered him a place to stay on his manor. But who could have anticipated that Wu Sunq would come ...	with	a case of malaria that required him to recuperate on the prem
at an inn by the side of the road for a few bowls of wine to bolster his couraqe. Then,	with	his quarter staff at the ready,
ridqe in larqe strides. Before he had qone so far as half a li he saw another public notice, stamped	with	an official seal,
to cross even durinq dayliqht hours. Be it known that anyone who disreqards these instructions proc...	With	a loud voice Wu Sunq proclaimed,
As this qust of wind passed by, the yellow leaves from the clump of tanqled trees fell to the qround	with	a rustlinq noise and,
passed by, the yellow leaves from the clump of tanqled trees fell to the qround with a rustlinq noise ...	with	a sudden roar,
a rustlinq noise and, with a sudden roar, out jumped a ferocious striped tiqer, as biq as a water buffal...	with	bulqinq eyes and a white forehead.
haste to put the rock between himself and his assailant. The tiqer was both hunqry and thirsty. Pawi...	with	its front claws,
and thirsty. Pawinq the qround with its front claws, it stretched itself and qave first one lash and then...	with	its tail.
behind itself. Plantinq its front paws on the qround, it stretched its trunk and made a swipe at Wu Su...	with	its hindquarters.
it by dodqinq to one side. It so happens that when tiqers attack people, if they fail to overcome them	with	a pounce,
half exhausted. When Wu Sunq saw that the tiqer's strength was failinq, he turned around, swunq hi...	with	both hands,

芮效卫译《金瓶梅》主要高频词 when 搭配使用情况索引

	when	
two concepts that are related to each other as substance is to function. Thus,	when	beauty bedazzles the eye, passion is born in the heart Passion and beauty evoke
and "Beauty is like the lode stone which exerts its unseen pull on the needle even	when	obstacles intervene. If this be true even for nonsentient objects, how much the mo
will run no more, So what can I do? Oh, Yu-chi, Yu-chi, What is to be done?	when	the finished singing his face was streaked with tears. "Your highness must be sac
, she slit her throat and died. The Hegemon-King was so moved by her act that,	when	the time came, he followed suit by cutting his own throat. A historian has compose
sious of her and wished her no good, Lady Chi was extremely uneasy. One day	when	Emperor Kao-tsu was so moved by her act that, Lady Chi began to weep
ad. How would that be?' Lady Chi dried her tears and thanked him for his favor.	When	Empress Lu heard about this she summoned her husband's chief adviser, Chang L
parent. One day the Four Gray beards appeared in court with her apparent.	When	Emperor Kao-tsu saw these four men with their snow-white hair and beards and I
·Lu-li. Greatly astonished, the emperor asked, "Why did you not choose to come	When	We offered you employment in the past, only to appear today in the company of ou
direct descendant of Chai Jung, Emperor Shih-tsung of the Later Chou dynasty.	When	Chai Chin saw what a fine fellow Wu Sung was, he offered him a place to stay
M. and 3:00 P.M., and prohibiting them from crossing the ridge at any other time.	When	Wu Sung heard about this he laughed out loud and stopped at an inn by the side
n official seal, posted on the gate of a temple to the tutelary god of the mountain.	When	Wu Sung looked at this notice he saw that the message read as follows: There is
aw that the sun was slowly setting behind the mountains. It was the tenth month	when	the days were short and the nights long, so it got dark early. Wu Sung continued
the nights long, so it got dark early. Wu Sung continued on his way for a while	when	he began to feel the effects of the wine. Looking into the distance he saw a tangl
e effects of the wine. Looking into the distance he saw a tangled clump of trees	when	he had made his way, at a fast clip, through this clump of trees he came upon
striped tiger, as big as a water buffalo, with bulging eyes and a white forehead.	When	Wu Sung saw this he cried out, "Ai-ya!" rolled off the black rock, grabbed his quart
e in his stomach into cold sweat. What happened was quick	When	Wu Sung saw the tiger pounce at him he dodged to one side so that the tiger
swipe at Wu Sung his hindquarters. Wu Sung managed to jump to one side.	When	the tiger saw that it had failed to sideswipe Wu Sung it gave a roar that shook
e. But Wu Sung once again evaded it by dodging to one side. It so happened	when	tigers attack people, if they fail to overcome them with a pounce, a sideswipe, or a
th a pounce, a sideswipe, or a lash of the tail, their powers are half exhausted.	when	Wu Sung saw that the tiger's strength was failing, he turned around, swung his ar
this stroke of luck and drag the tiger down to the foot of the ridge." But	when	he approached the pool of blood in which it was lying and tugged at the tiger with
I'm done for!" Before his very eyes, these two tigers stood up in front of him.	When	Wu Sung gave a closer look he saw that there were two men, clothed in tiger skins
ng replied: "I neither alter my given name whenabroad, Nor change my surname		at home. I am a man of Yang-ku district, Wu Sung by name, and the second sibling
mal welcome, all came out to see the show. The entire district was in an uproar.	When	Wu Sung arrived at the courtroom he put down the tiger and the tiger was
le the thirty taels of reward money to the licensed hunters, who went their way.	When	the magistrate saw that Wu Sung was a man of virtue and integrity, and a stout fel
he had moved to Ching-ho district where he rented a house on Amethyst Street.	When	people observed his meek disposition and unsightly appearance they gave him the
erests and often patronized his steamed wheat cates and sat around in his shop	when	they had nothing better to do. the Wu Elder was always so obliging that everyone
After the death of her father her	When	Chin-lien was only eight years old, she sold her into the household of Imperial Com
e, but fear of his wife's temper had prevented him from making a move. One day	when	the mistress of the household was out of the way on a visit to a neighbor, Mr
entioning. In broad daylight he dozed off, and At night he couldn't stop sneezing.	When	the mistress of the household got wind of what was going on behind her back she
l evenings succeeded one another, and this situation had prevailed for some time	When	Mr. Chang suddenly came down with a venereal chill and: Alas and alack, died. W
Mr. Chang suddenly came down with a venereal chill and: Alas and alack, died.	When	the mistress of the household discovered what had been going on, without more a
The only thing he can be counted on to do every day is to guzzle his wine.	When	you get right down to it, you could jab him with an awl without arousing him. What
ys been true that: Women of beauty and men of talent are seldom matched; Just	When	you're in the market for gold you can never find a seller. Every day Wu the Elder
dissolute young scamps in the neighborhood who were seldom up to any good.	When	they saw the way that Wu the Elder's wife was: Dolling herself up so slickly, Emp
e is a poem that testifies to this: Chin-lien's beauty is certainly worthy of remark;	When	she laughs her eyebrows rise up like spring peaks. If she ever encounters a dash
ue to live on that part of Amethyst Street and wanted to move somewhere else.	When	he raised this issue with his wife he said, "You lousy muddle-headed ignoramus!
p the sum. What's so difficult about that? They can always be replaced later on	when	we're better off than we are now." Wu the Elder allowed himself to be persuaded

通过对芮译《金瓶梅》中的前六十位高频词的分析可见，芮译本的语言特色为雅俗如一，尊重原著，其平均句长 20.97，其句式的特点离不开 and，when，that 等连接词和介词 with。虽然芮译本第一位高频词 the 使用了 53 587 频次，但考虑到文本容量，该词语的大量使用并不具有明显个性化特征，但芮译本使用 and 共计 28 213 频次，使用 that 共计 10 818 次，when 共计 4 173 次。作为并列连词的 and 在文中既表示句子前后两部分的并列、承接和先后关系，也体现出动作上的伴随关系和意义上的增补，在实际使用中明显增加了句长。而引导时间状语的连接词 when 和引导主从复合句的 that 也起了同样作用。介词 with 共计出现 8 828 次，除了表示"和某人一起"的例句之外，译者大量使用 with＋无生命名词和 with＋身体动作状态类词语（如 with a roar，with tears 等）伴随状语，也是芮译在用词上的一个明显特色。

正如芮效卫在接受访谈时所说，"我在英语译本中建立这种文体特征就是引起英语读者注意汉语中这种文体风格变化的大致界限。例如，用更加正式的英语来翻译习语、上疏和宗教仪式文本等。与此相反，用非常白话的文体风格来翻译俚语、俗语等，但是早期的译作没有做到这一点。我尽量使得英语读者理解与掌握原文中的这种修辞复杂性。总之，我的《金瓶梅》翻译不但是语言上的，更是文体、修辞和文化上的翻译。"

4.1.3　基于语料库的《聊斋志异》三个英译本译者风格

《聊斋志异》节译本、零散译文较多，笔者仅选取了篇幅较长、文笔优美的翟理斯译本、致力于将中国文学推向世界的杨宪益夫妇的译本和 20 世纪 80 年代两位美国汉学家梅丹理、梅维恒的选译本。

翟理斯译《聊斋志异》的基本数据图

Lines	1425
Words (types)	Now: 9887　When loaded: 9887
Words (tokens)	Now: 171410　When loaded: 171410
Type-token ratio	Now: 17.3369　When loaded: 17.3369
Characters	723064
Sentences	7451
Words/sentence	23.0050

梅译《聊斋志异》的基本数据图

Lines	1642
Words (types)	Now: 10669　When loaded: 10669
Words (tokens)	Now: 115689　When loaded: 115689
Type-token ratio	Now: 10.8435　When loaded: 10.8435
Characters	496049
Sentences	7733
Words/sentence	14.9604

杨宪益译《聊斋志异》的基本数据图

Lines	1409
Words (types)	Now: 4783　When loaded: 4783
Words (tokens)	Now: 36112　When loaded: 36112
Type-token ratio	Now: 7.5501　When loaded: 7.5501
Characters	152549
Sentences	2301
Words/sentence	15.6940

　　如图所示，通过比较这三个译本的基本数据，可以发现由于选译的篇目数量上的差异，三个译本的总形符数（tokens）由高到低分别为：翟译 171 410，梅译 115 689，杨译 36 112。总类符数（types）由高到低为：梅译 10 669，翟译 9 887，杨译 4 783，表明杨译由于篇幅相对较短而显示出类符数偏低的特征。翟译与梅译容量相差较大，但是类符数却是梅译略高于翟译。考察类符形符比后发现，翟译类符形符比最高，为 17.336 9，梅译和杨译相近，表明翟译词语变化性大，词汇量最为丰富。考察每句平均包含的词汇数量后，发现平均句长以翟译为首，为 23 个词汇，

同一时代的杨译和梅译平均句长相近，杨译为 15.69，梅译为
14.96。因此，在文体风格上，翟译描写性更强，叙事详尽，杨
译和梅译偏于简洁。

利用 Concordance 320 统计三个译本的词长总体分布情况，
结果如下：

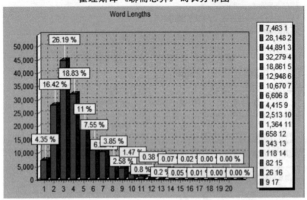

翟理斯译《聊斋志异》词长分布图

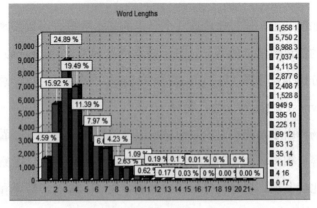

杨宪益译《聊斋志异》词长分布图

梅译《聊斋志异》词长分布图

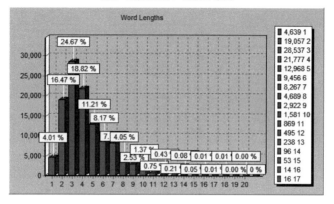

从上图可见，翟译较之于杨译、梅译问世的时间相差约百年，但三个译本在词长上的共同特征是偏好使用二字母词汇、三字母词汇和四字母词汇，其中三字母词汇为最频繁使用类型。

对比三字母词汇在词汇长度分布中所占比率，得出的结果为：翟译占 26.19%，杨译占 24.89，梅译占 24.67。

再统计二字母、三字母和四字母词汇在词汇长度分布中所占比例之和后，发现三种译本数值相近，翟译 61.44%，杨译 60.3%，梅译为 59.96%。

由此可见，通过词汇层面的词长分布来探索三位译者的风格可以发现，三位译者的用词风格都倾向于频繁使用二字母、三字母和四字母词汇。

统计三个译本的前三十位高频词的结果如下：

翟译高频词前三十位　　　　杨译高频词前三十位　　　　梅译高频词前三十位

Rank	Freq	Word	Rank	Freq	Word	Rank	Freq	Word
1	8568	the	1	1676	the	1	5790	the
2	7342	and	2	1163	to	2	3422	to
3	5192	to	3	1125	and	3	3215	and
4	4249	a	4	923	he	4	3045	a
5	4039	of	5	620	his	5	2638	of
6	3416	he	6	581	of	6	1679	in
7	3062	was	7	558	in	7	1614	he
8	2835	his	8	514	was	8	1608	was
9	2461	in	9	505	with	9	1587	his
10	1877	that	10	357	that	10	1263	The
11	1832	him	11	342	him	11	1175	her
12	1541	had	12	331	it	12	1011	with
13	1350	her	13	304	you	13	971	that
14	1329	at	14	292	for	14	934	for
15	1326	with	15	285	her	15	925	I
16	1155	it	16	285	I	16	902	him
17	1119	I	17	285	s	17	889	you
18	1112	for	18	281	had	18	861	it
19	1098	as	19	270	but	19	784	s
20	1071	on	20	213	The	20	760	had
21	1025	you	21	212	she	21	736	on
22	1016	but	22	210	on	22	684	not
23	959	she	23	203	as	23	656	she
24	955	s	24	202	not	24	623	He
25	928	not	25	190	man	25	583	but
26	924	by	26	180	this	26	563	is
27	895	which	27	174	at	27	562	out
28	822	they	28	161	they	28	554	as
29	806	when	29	155	be	29	523	at
30	800	then	30	146		30	505	be

三十个高频词中，三个译本重合的高频词为：the，and，to，of，a，he，his，it，I，was，in，him，that，on，she，had，her，with，as，but，which，for，be，not。上述高频词主要集中在介词、冠词、连词、代词等虚词上。

与百年前翟理斯译本不同的是，杨译本与梅译本居于前三十位的高频词中，出现了 be 动词和否定词 not。而翟译的高频词中的 which 在杨译和梅译中并没有出现在前三十位高频词表中。

which 一词在 BNC 各类子库中的出现频率

SECTION	ALL	SPOKEN	FICTION	MAGAZINE	NEWSPAPER	NON-ACAD	ACADEMIC	MISC
FREQ	361373	22657	25860	23493	30936	76522	91205	89700
PER MIL	3,754.00	2,273.96	1,688.32	3,235.06	2,955.34	4,639.05	5,946.80	4,305.22
SEE ALL SUB-SECTIONS AT ONCE								

　　从上图可见，which 在各个子库中的数据均显示出这一连词应用的普遍性，由于在从句中的连接作用以及表意的完整和严谨性，使其更多地为学术类作品所使用。

翟理斯译《聊斋志异》高频词 which 搭配使用情况索引

the well might not be that of her p.　husband, to which the woman replied that she felt sure it was; and a
say." The uncle at first refused to do this; upon which the magistrate was obliged to threaten him, until
er if she could say who was the real murderer; to which she replied that Hu Ch'êng had done the deed. "No
gs, and darkness came over the face of the earth, which the astonished spectators now perceived to be caus
ld goose, was followed to his home by the gander, which flew round and round him in great distress, and on
e frightened herd p.　chose　out a fat elephant, which he seemed as though about to devour. The others re
arrow from his quiver and shot the lion dead, at which all the elephants below made him a grateful obeisa
jumped down and collected them in a bundle, after which the elephant conveyed him to a spot whence he easi
plaints of the kind, besides innumerable cases in which the missing man's relatives lived at a distance an
he east of the province, not far from the pass by which traders from the north connect their line of trade
k.　Such was the horrible story, the discovery of which brought throngs to the Viceroy's door to serenade
　Shortly afterwards, Hou's case was called; upon which he went forward and　knelt down, as did also a ho
ent forward and　knelt down, as did also a horse which was prosecuting him. The judge now informed Hou th
prosecutor was attacked by the cattle-plague, for which I treated him accordingly; and he actually recover
destiny had doomed it to death on the very day on which it had died; whereupon the judge cried out, "Your
ourhood, and was suffering very much from thirst, which you relieved for me by a few spoonfuls of gruel. I
days in preparing for death, at the expiration of which I will come and fetch you. I have purchased a smal
small appointment for you in the realms below, by which you will be more comfortable." So Hou went home
he bade his lictors prepare stones and knives, at which they were much exercised in their minds, the sever
e case is a simple one; for although I cannot say which of you two women is the guilty one, there is no do
would have no share in the bribery and corruption which was extensively carried on, and at which the highe
rruption which was extensively carried on, and at which the higher authorities connived, and in the procee
gher authorities connived, and in the proceeds of which they actually shared. The Prefect tried to bully h
so far as to abuse him in violent language, upon which Mr. Wu fired up and exclaimed, "Though I am but a
n this Prefecture." "One," replied the medium; at which the company laughed heartily, until the medium con

be 一词在 BNC 各类子库中的出现频率

SECTION	ALL	SPOKEN	FICTION	MAGAZINE	NEWSPAPER	NON-ACAD	ACADEMIC	MISC
FREQ	643638	39726	79009	41059	62392	107922	135444	158086
PER MIL	6,686.22	5,994.38	4,966.21	5,653.96	5,961.16	6,542.64	8,834.26	7,587.46
SEE ALL SUB-SECTIONS AT ONCE								

　　Be 动词因其复杂的语法功能成为语言学和二语习得研究的重点，其理论价值和应用价值不容忽视。在语法中的重要地位也通过 BNC 各类子库中的出现频率凸显出来，该词当之无愧是句子结构中的脊柱，在各个子库中的使用频率均在高位。

梅译《聊斋志异》高频词 be 的搭配使用情况索引

```
nt: "I've already exceeded the time limit. I will be going back to face execution. What can I use to co
 convoy official is innocent: no punishment shall be meted out to him. Not long ago we removed your con
f the place is ever fixed. I am afraid there will be an unending stream of people going there to air th
eek and unresourcerul. Zhuqing often urged him to be bold, but he was never able to follow her advice.
rvant went looking for him, but he was nowhere to be seen. The boatmen wanted to leave, but the knots i
o, you have your own wife back home. What would I be to you then?" It would be better to leave me here
back home. What would I be to you then?" It would be better to leave me here to make a home away from h
 that the distance was long and that he would not be able to come often, but Zhuqing brought out a suit
n embroidered pouch which, when opened, proved to be filled to the mouth with gold coins. At this he se
m ready to go into confinement any day." "Will it be an oviparous or viviparous birth?" Yu joked. "Now
h and bones are more substantial. This one should be different than the ones I had before." After sever
 his father, on the understanding that they would be back in three months. After their arrival, his wif
d little clouds. From a distance they appeared to be stuffed with floss. Then a certain local despot ca
allotted lifetime. That way you and the stone can be together until the end. Is that your wish?" "It is
 are as many openings in this stone as there will be years in your life." With that he took his leave a
ished Xing not to grieve at his loss: "I'll only be parting with you for a little more than a year. Ne
he eighth month come to Haidaimen at dawn. You'll be able to buy my freedom for two strings of coppers.
nt to call on it. Though his efforts continued to be ineffective, the fox spirit did not disturb parts
illment of my prayers and invocations. What could be the harm in granting me a look at your brilliant c
dred newly minted coppers for your use. I may not be well off, but I am no miser. If you are in a predi
eing taken. One day a cooked chicken which was to be served to guests disappeared. That night the schol
e gotten there? Then it dawned on him: "This must be the fox spirit's doing." Whereupon he recounted al
ntil the wound healed so that the character could be incised again according to the stroke order and fo
```

从以上两个主要高频词 which 和 be 分别在翟译和梅译中的搭配情况可见，翟理斯偏爱使用以 which 引导的定语从句，因其可以使句子语法结构更加严谨，句式更加丰富，从而使语言显得庄重、正式又不失灵活，同时传递更多完整的信息，有利于故事叙事。也可以看到，翟译倾向于使用介词＋which 引导定语从句的格式，例如 in which，by which，after which，from which，upon which 等。此外，翟译在定语从句使用中更多地使用了非限定性定语从句，在高频词 which 搭配使用情况索引表的 25 个例句中，64％的句子都使用了 which 引导的非限定性定语从句。

梅译使用的高频词 be 在搭配使用情况索引表所列举的 23 个例句中，1 个用于祈使句，11 个用于表即将发生的动作，11 个表示有意识的行动或愿望以及虚拟语气。在 11 个表达意愿、对行为的推测的句子中，大部分的语气词用于小说人物的对话中，以直接引语的形式出现，would be，could be，should be，can be，must be，may be 等搭配用来表达小说中人物彬彬有礼、间接委婉的表达方式。因此从上述高频词的搭配特点可见，通过对人物语言的精雕细琢来刻画人物形象、渲染故事情节也是梅译语言风格的特色之一。

本文也研究了三个译本的独特词情况。独特词是指"在一个文本中词频达到一定水准而在另一个类似文本或其它多个类似文本中词频为零的词语"（冯庆华，2008：269）。通过考察译本的独特词，可以从词汇层面比较直观地反映译者的风格。本文选取了翟理斯译本中的独特词 alas，杨宪益译本中的 recorder 一词和梅译中的 chronicler 和 underworld 作为典型译例进行分析。

alas 一词在翟译中的使用情况索引

alas 一词在 BNC 各类子库中的出现频率

SECTION	ALL	SPOKEN	FICTION	MAGAZINE	NEWSPAPER	NON-ACAD	ACADEMIC	MISC
FREQ	617	12	175	97	61	86	38	148
PER MIL	6.41	1.20	11.00	13.36	5.83	5.21	2.48	7.10
SEE ALL SUB-SECTIONS AT ONCE								

翟译使用了这样一个在英法等语言中较常用的感叹词，体现了其翻译过程中明显的归化特征。通过与 BNC 各类子库中该词使用频率对照可见，该词出现频率最高值 175 次是在小说子库中。因此，翟译在文学翻译中使用 alas 一词符合文学作品的语言

特征，该词的使用有助于表达丰富的情感，在文学作品中更为适用。

　　杨译的独特词中出现了 recorder 一词，此词在《聊斋志异》故事中的词意并非"书记员，记录器，录音师或录音机"，而是"记录人，笔录者"，是对"异史氏"的翻译。其具体使用情况如下：

recorder 一词在杨译中的使用情况索引

ursed the old priest for being so heartless.	The recorder of these marvels comments: "Hearing this, who can
city, everyone knew he was the son of a fox.	The recorder of these marvels comments, "Personally, I don't ad
e following day at dawn she had disappeared.	The recorder of these marvels comments: Wealth springs from ind
would laugh at anyone just like his mother.	The recorder of these marvels comments: Foolish laughter seems
t, imagining her to be only in her twenties.	The recorder of these marvels comments: Because the son was vir
ith a clap of thunder the princess vanished.	The recorder of these marvels comments: Men must put on false,
over eighty, showed him his father's grave.	The recorder of these marvels comments: Only those who will not
carriage were more splendid than a noble's.	The recorder of these marvels comments: The emperor may do a th
ds, disposing of them all within a few days.	The recorder of these marvels comments: How true it is that thi
rial Censor. Thus the whole dream came true.	The recorder of these marvels comments: Many officials in this
uld have nothing more to do with each other.	The recorder of these marvels comments: That the fox was a thor
ny further happenings of a marvelous nature.	The recorder of these marvels comments: The world may lament wh
and placed them in his father's tomb again.	The recorder of these marvels comments: The most precious or be

　　由上图可见，recorder 搭配的都是 of these marvels，意思是"奇闻异事的记录者"，也即原著中蒲松龄所说的"异史氏"。作为文化输出国的优秀译者，杨宪益夫妇不仅在内容上忠实于原著，在形式上也与原文一致，对"异史氏曰"部分与原文中其他情节同样予以重视，没有对这一部分进行删减和明显的改译。反观其他译者，删除不译"异史氏曰"这部分评论的译者较多。因此在杨译中，"异史氏"被直译为"the recorder of these marvels"，"异史氏曰"译作"the recorder of these marvels comments"。可见杨译综合使用直译和意译等方法，该异化的地方异化，该归化的地方也不拘泥于原文，灵活地再现了原著的风貌，准确地传递着丰富多彩的中华文化。而针对"异史氏曰"这一特殊词语的翻译，梅译中出现的独特词恰恰就有 chronicler 一词：

chronicler 一词在梅译中的使用情况索引

t the old Taoist was nothing but a reprobate.	The Chronicler of the Tales comments: "No one who hears of this i
ut the city knew he was a fox spirit's child.	The Chronicler of the Tales comments: "I envy Scholar Kong not be
ed him over to the authorities for execution.	The Chronicler of the Tales comments: "I have ob?served that payi
ly a coin-sized scab. Even this soon healed.	The Chronicler of the Tales comments: "How foolish are the people
commissioner-general with a high reputation.	The Chronicler of the Tales comments: "To chop short the crane'
one he saw, much in the manner of his mother.	The Chronicler of the Tales comments: "Judging from her persisten
o the end of her years, or so the story goes.	The Chronicler of the Tales comments: "In order to keep a pleasur
estowed presents of even greater munificence.	The Chronicler of the Tales comments: " 'Foolishness' or fixati
o's name was Nian and his soubriquet, Danian.	The Chronicler of the Tales comments: "Some may call it foolish
of thunder shook the room, and she was gone.	The Chronicler of the Tales comments: "The ways of the world are
nave been equalled by an aristocratic family.	The Chronicler of the Tales comments: "The emperor may use someth
ase and have the charges against him dropped.	The Chronicler of the Tales comments: "The old burial grounds of
ntains, and no one knows what became of him.	The Chronicler of the Tales comments: "Blessings are given to the
ght to prison, where he soon died of illness.	The Chronicler of the Tales comments: "A man who finds a hibiscus
iding in a carriage under an official canopy.	The Chronicler of the Tales comments: "For parents to receive pos
with the scholar just as the Hao family did.	The Chronicler of the Tales comments: "To find one matchless bea

chronicler 一词在 BNC 各类子库中的出现频率

SECTION	ALL	SPOKEN	FICTION	MAGAZINE	NEWSPAPER	NON-ACAD	ACADEMIC	MISC
FREQ	190	0	0	5	6	45	60	34
PER MIL.	1.68	0.00	0.00	0.69	0.57	2.73	3.91	1.83
SEE ALL SUB-SECTIONS AT ONCE								

从例句中可见，梅译忠实地翻译了"异史氏曰"部分，将其完整准确地译作"the chronicler of the Tales comments"，其中 chronicler 一词意为"编年史家，年代史编者；记录者"，因此这一词语经常出现在传记、学术题材的作品中，从 chronicler 一词在 BNC 各类子库中的出现频率的图表中也得到了数据的支持，因 chronicler 一词在 BNC 学术作品中出现频率最高。

梅译对"异史氏曰"的处理得当，使译文与原文不仅在形式上与蒲松龄引入《史记》的"太史公曰"的评论体例最为接近，语义上也有较高的契合度。

通过统计还发现，梅译使用较多的是独特名词。其中多用来表达原作中涉及的宗教文化的词语如 hermitage（偏僻的寺院），monk（僧人），acolyte（道观中的徒弟，侍僧），underworld（冥界）。涉及社会文化、科举制度的独特词包括：baccalaureate（学士，对应原文中的"入泮"）和 studio（书房，书斋）等。

underworld 一词在梅译中的使用情况索引

give back his life. Am I Yama, king of the **underworld**? In a fit of anger he struck Chen with his
rly well. What we read in the court of the **underworld** is pretty much the same as what you have in
e defied." "What do you do in the court of the **underworld**?" "Judge Lu recommended me for a position overse
This is the constant grief she bears there in the **underworld**. If you don't grudge the trouble and expense of ea
ck to life. "I was called before the king of the **underworld**," he told them. "Because of my lifelong honesty,
r spirit in the governor's yamen and taken to the **underworld** court. The king of the underworld sent him to be r
nd taken to the **underworld** court. The king of the **underworld** sent him to be reborn into a rich family in consid
ou died over a year ago," he said. "This is the **underworld**, isn't it?" "No, it isn't. This is the grotto
e. I carried my regret over this with me into the **underworld**. When you so kindly visited us, I had a chance lis
ey built a gigantic spirit guard and guide to the **underworld** out of papier mache, and outfitted them with black
ing. The paper mansion that was to be sent to the **underworld** had the grandeur of a palace. It was a complex of
The notice boards have already been posted in the **underworld**. Fifth-Brother Yu was not selected!" Hearing this
on and Yu replied, "The Marquis of Huan inspects **underworld** functionaries once every thirty years and tours th
f Huan arrived the night before last and tore the **underworld** ranking notice board to pieces. Only one third of
ead, he told her that they were now united in the **underworld**. "You are wrong," she said. "I am too disobedie

underworld 一词在 BNC 各类子库中的出现频率

SECTION	ALL	SPOKEN	FICTION	MAGAZINE	NEWSPAPER	NON-ACAD	ACADEMIC	MISC
FREQ	209	1	49	27	23	46	23	38
PER MIL	2.17	0.10	3.08	3.73	2.20	2.91	1.50	1.83

Underworld 一词在词源词典中意思是"下层社会",也指希腊神话中冥王哈得斯的地府,还用于指代地球。该词在 1900 年之后也指"黑社会"。在 BNC 各类子库中,此词属于常用词,使用频率较高的子库仍是小说类,与《聊斋志异》原文文本类型一致。《聊斋志异》原文中含有大量与阴曹地府、冥界、阎王等有关的中国文化特色的词汇,例如在《席方平》《陆判》《考城隍》《某公》等篇目中都频繁出现了冥府、阎王等词汇。梅译将此词译为"underworld",与目的语读者对冥界的认知相符合,可以使读者联想起希腊神话中黑暗无边的由冥王哈得斯统治的冥界,传说是所有死者唯一的归宿,这也是梅译使用归化翻译策略的体现。

4.1.4 基于语料库的《红楼梦》两个英译本译者风格

由统计可见,杨译本作为《红楼梦》的全译本,总形符数(tokens)为 641611,类符数为 20045,类符形符比 32.0085,平

杨译《红楼梦》的基本数据图

Lines	21174
Words (types)	Now: 20045　When loaded: 20045
Words (tokens)	Now: 641611　When loaded: 641611
Type-token ratio	Now: 32.0085　When loaded: 32.0085
Characters	2713795
Sentences	46909
Words/sentence	13.6778

霍译《红楼梦》基本数据图

Lines	27752
Words (types)	Now: 28050　When loaded: 28050
Words (tokens)	Now: 847594　When loaded: 847594
Type-token ratio	Now: 30.2173　When loaded: 30.2173
Characters	3627004
Sentences	54811
Words/sentence	15.4639

均句长为 13.68 个词语。霍译作为《红楼梦》的另一个全译本，总形符数（tokens）为 847 594，类符数为 28 050，类符形符比 30.217 3，平均句长为 15.463 9 个词语。从类符形符比可见，杨译的词汇较之于霍译则更加丰富。译本的类符形符比越大，"说明译文的词汇变化性越大，文本的信息量越高，理解难度也相对越大；反之，比值越小，说明词汇变化性越小，文本的信息量相对较低，文本难度也相对较低"（赵朝永，2020：67）。

杨译《红楼梦》词长分布图

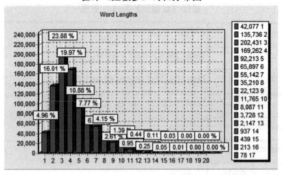

霍译《红楼梦》词长分布图

　　一般来说，词长与词汇难度称正比，平均词长可以反映译本的难易程度。词长数字越大，表明译本难度越大，词长数字越小，说明阅读难度越小，译本更倾向于通俗易懂，老少咸宜。

　　从上图词长分布对比可见，杨译和霍译偏好均是使用二字母词汇、三字母词汇和四字母词汇，其中杨译使用二字母词汇占比为 15.05％，霍译为 16.01％；杨译使用三字母词汇比率为 23.79％，霍译为 23.86；三字母词汇为二者最频繁使用类型；杨译四字母词汇在词汇长度分布中所占比例为 20.53％，霍译比例为 19.97％。

杨译高频词 1—30

THE	26198
TO	21575
AND	17771
A	11204
OF	10702
"	10091
HER	8658
YOU	8262
IN	7949
SHE	7755
HE	6218
THAT	5917
WAS	5757
FOR	5577
'	5528
IT	5254
WITH	5122
I	4707
THIS	4660
HAD	4447
ON	4360
AS	4178
HIS	4051
BUT	3534
THEY	3246
BE	3172
SO	3077
HIM	3062
LADY	2951
NOT	2949

霍译高频词 1—30

THE	36272
TO	28706
AND	24836
OF	19556
A	16627
'	15992
HER	11628
IN	11554
YOU	11312
THAT	9702
SHE	9495
WAS	9446
IT	8840
I	7807
FOR	7625
HE	7223
WITH	6799
HAD	6104
ON	5994
SAID	5803
BE	5377
HIS	5257
AS	4916
HAVE	4713
THIS	4472
AT	4443
JIA	4303
IS	4288
ALL	4040
THEY	3925
BUT	3878
HIM	3793

　　高频词的定义可以从以下几个方面来理解：一是指该词语出现频率高：在文本中出现的次数远高于其他词汇，通常占据文本总词汇量的较大比例；二是指常见性和实用性：高频词通常是日常生活中使用频繁的词汇，涵盖了基本需求和常见场景。语料库翻译学范畴的高频词主要是指第一种情形。对同一原著的不同译

本进行高频词考察和对比，能够反映出不同译者的用词偏好。

从上表对照可见，杨译和霍译的前三十位高频词有重合之处：the，to，and，a，of，her，you，in，she，I，was，it，for，he，had，on，as，they，be，with 等，也有明显的差异，例如杨译前三十位高频词中出现了 lady，not，so 等词语，而霍译的前三十位高频词中却没有出现。同时，霍译本中的高频词 jia，动词过去式 said 也是杨译本前三十位中没有出现的词语。

杨译《红楼梦》主要高频词 so 使用情况索引

	so	
he account you have copied out is quite correct. I'll tell you someone who will circulate it,	so	that this extraordinary case can be concluded.
s. We still have to return him to his original place and record his experiences in the world,	so	that he won't have descended there for nothing.
laughed, "I get it! One of the sons of their house called Lan4 has passed the examination;	so	that prediction of yours has come true.
In these two mansions now, the good are laying up virtue, the bad repenting their crimes;	so	naturally their houses will prosper again with the on
r. But why, with such a spiritual origin, was Baoyu so enamoured of girls before he became so	so	enlightened?
he way it was! I was too ignorant to know. But why, with such a spiritual origin, was Baoyu	so	enamoured of girls before he became so enlightened
use in Renqing Lane." "How could that be?" exclaimed Yucun in surprise. "With the capital	so	far from your honourable district!
ny own inveterate folly, I've now been reduced to this." "Last time you were a high official,	so	how could a poor priest claim acquaintance with you
erself. Deeply impressed by her loyalty, Jiang Yuhan showed her even more consideration	so	that Xiren felt she had really nowhere to die.
entered the house she was addressed by the maid-servants as "Mistress." All treated her	so	well that,
at a loss for words. After a couple of days at home she thought, "My brother's done things	so	handsomely,
telling her which items had been given by Lady Wang, which they had bought themselves,	so	that Xiren was even more at a loss for words.
died here that would be a poor return for Her Ladyship's kindness. I'd better die at home."	So	suppressing her grief she bade them all farewell,
rawn to Baochai, finding her so submissive. Baochai also spoke of a woman's duties in life,	so	they found themselves in complete accord.
ever dream of disobeying the mistress." Aunt Xue felt even more drawn to her, finding her	so	submissive.
aoyu had been someone quite unique and this had been fated to happen.When she spoke	so	reasonably her mother.
has happened to her. It seems that everyone's lot in life is predestined? Though she wept	so	bitterly,
ir such a blood-curdling oath?" she scolded. "Now I've a proposal to make. Xiangling's had	so	much to put up with since becoming your concubine.
they came to explain the miraculous nature of the jade; the second time, when Baoyu was	so	ill and the monk took the jade in his hand and inton
Baoyu and Jia Lan had passed the examination delighted him; but Baoyu's disappearance	so	perturbed him that he felt constrained to hurry back
and not the least feeling for the other girls either, as if he'd awoken to the Truth. But even	so	
id Sister Xiren fall so ill?" Qinojie asked. Baochai explained. '~The other evening she wept	so	bitterly that she fainted away.
of boiled water, then laid her down again and sent for a doctor. ~ 'How did Sister Xiren fall	so	ill?
finger he shed tears of gratitude, although he could not express his feelings in public. And	so	much had she.
this, had two carts prepared for them and urged Qiaojie to mount one. But by now she felt	so	at home here that she was reluctant to leave.
at a lot we owe you, granny! If not for the way you fixed things, our young lady wouldn't be	so	happily placed today.
Jia Lan went to offer his thanks at court, he learned that Zhen Baoyu had also passed and	so	they ranked as classmates.
en have given up rank and wealth to achieve Buddhahood and become immortals." "If he's	so	unfilial as to abandon his parents,
d a fair idea of the truth of the matter, while Xiren was sobbing as if she would never stop.	so	Jia Qiang without waiting for orders went out with o
while I took some men with me to search all the cells. But he wasn't there. That's why I'm	so	late back.
ame place," he told them. "And in the examination grounds our cells weren't too far apart.	so	we kept in close touch.
his to Lady Wang, they sent round to other relatives to ask, but in each case drew a blank.	So	Lady Xing inside and Jia Huan and the others outside
ool about with young actors, and even bring women from outside into the house. Isn't that	so	
. was willing, and told me to write out the horoscope. But that family has turned her down,	so	how did we hound her to death?

由上图可见，杨译使用 so 主要集中在以下三种情形中：1. 做副词用：so＋形容词，so＋副词，如 so late，so ill，so unfilial，so suppressing，so submissive，so handsomely，so bitterly，so far

等；2. 做连词，so＋句子，表示"于是"，例如 so we kept in close touch，so Lady Xing inside and Jia Huan and others outside；3. 引导目的状语从句和结果状语从句，如 so that this extraordinary case can be concluded，so that Xiren felt she had really nowhere to die，all treated her so well that，so that prediction of yours has come true 等等。

杨译《红楼梦》主要高频词 lady 使用情况索引

	lady	
d someone outside talking with a child. He jumped to his feet in haste and, peeping, saw a young	lady	
ped in consternation. Did this mean fresh calamity? To find out, read the next chapter. Chapter 2	Lady	Jia Dies in the City of Yangzhou Lenq Zixing Describes the Ronq M
he had two sons, Jia She and Jia Zheng. Jia Daishan has been dead for many years but his wife,	Lady	Dowager Shi,
ffairs in one of the ministries. He has now risen to the rank of Under-Secretary. "Jia Zheng's wife,	Lady	Wang,
ter by a concubine. The fourth, Xichun, is the younger sister of Jia Zhen of the Ning Mansion. The	Lady	Dowager is so attached to these grand-daughters that she makes
, the elder, is over twenty now. He married a relative, the niece of Jia Zheng's wife,	Lady	Wang,
d the chapter which follows. Chapter 3 Lin Ruhai Recommends a Tutor to His Brother-in-Law The	lady	Dowager Sends for Her Motherless Grand-Daughter To continue.
s dressed in red and green rose from the terrace and hurried to greet them with smiles. "The old	lady	was just talking about you.
, and a voice could be heard announcing, "Miss Lin is here." A silver-haired old	lady	supported by two maids advanced to meet her.
d to meet her. She knew that this must be her grandmother, but before she could kowtow the old	lady	threw both arms around her.
st the others prevailed on her to stop, Daiyu made her kowtow to her grandmother. This was the	Lady	Dowager from the Shi family mentioned by Lenq Zixing,
tors prescribed? How had the funeral and mourning ceremonies been conducted? Inevitably, the	Lady	Dowager was most painfully affected.
tion, of course, to such crazy talk. Now I'm still taking qinsenq pills." "That's good," approved the	Lady	Dowager.
lips parted, her laughter rang out. Daiyu rose quickly to greet her. "You don't know her yet." The	Lady	Dowager chuckled.
knew from her mother that Jia Lian, the son of her first uncle Jia She, had married the niece of	Lady	Wang,
took her hand and carefully inspected her from head to foot, then led her back to her seat by the	Lady	Dowager.
a handkerchief. "I've only just dried my tears. Do you want to start me off again?" said the old	lady	playfully.
Meanwhile refreshments had been served. And as Xifeng handed round the tea and sweetmeats,	Lady	Wang asked whether she had distributed the monthly allowance.
Could your memory have played you a trick?" "It doesn't matter if there's none of that sort," said	Lady	Wang.
e material's waiting in your place for your inspection. If you pass it, madam, it can be set over."	Lady	Wang smiled and nodded her approval.
" Lady Wang smiled and nodded her approval. Now the refreshments were cleared away and	Lady	Dowager ordered two nurses to take Daiyu to see her two uncles.
he Lady Dowager ordered two nurses to see her two uncles, only Jia She's wife,	Lady	Xinq.
to her feet and suggested, "Won't it be simpler if I take my niece?" "Very well," agreed the	Lady	Dowager,
?" "Very well," agreed the Lady Dowager, "And there's no need for you to come back afterwards."	Lady	Xinq assented and then told Daiyu to take her leave of Lady Wanq,
ed for you to come back afterwards." Lady Xinq assented and then told Daiyu to take her leave of	Lady	Wang.
te pages were waiting beside a blue lacquered carriage with kingfisher-blue curtains, into which	Lady	Xinq and her niece entered.
w up in front of a ceremonial gate. When the pages had withdrawn, the sedan chair was carried	lady	led Daiyu into the courtyard.
hall they were greeted by a crowd of heavily made-up and richly dressed concubines and maids.	Lady	Xinq invited Daiyu to be seated while she sent a servant to the libr
eport, "The master says he hasn't been feeling too well the last few days, and meeting the younq	lady	would only upset them both.
it for the time being. Miss Lin mustn't mope or be homesick here but feel at home with the old	lady	and her aunts.
had risen to her feet to listen to this message. Shortly after this she rose again to take her leave.	Lady	Xinq insisted that she stay for the evening meal.
q on my second uncle. Please excuse me and let me stay another time." "You're quite right," said	Lady	Dowager's quarters.
ts and wings on either side. This was the hub of the whole estate, more imposing by far than the	Lady	Wang seldom sat in this main hall but used three rooms on the ea
n, who signed his name Mu Shi and styled himself a fellow provincial and old family friend. Since		

由上图索引可见，杨译中高频次出现的 lady 一词，主要是直译了《红楼梦》中的"夫人"一称谓。

汉代以后王公大臣之妻称夫人，唐、宋、明、清各朝还对高官的母亲或妻子加封，称诰命夫人。同时，该词指在中国封建社会，王朝对官员之母及正妻之一种封号。有封号者，称为"命妇"，因此贾母译作 Lady Dowager 是符合当时的语境和贾母本人的社会地位的。邢夫人、王夫人在译文中也以 Lady 为称谓，因其是官员或富贵人家的正妻，故此均称为"夫人"。此外，林黛玉之母出身名门世家，又系高官正房夫人，因此贾敏被译为 Lady Jia。据统计，高频词 lady 在杨译本中出现总计 2 951 次。这一高频词的使用，体现出杨译的异化翻译特点，也从一定程度上体现出译者为了传播中华文化，尽量保持异域文化特色的翻译目的和倾向。

杨译《红楼梦》主要高频词 not 使用情况索引

	not	
ver his basket, he complained: "These gentlemen are hardly reasonable. The ice has	not	melted yet 乙 where can we find peaches
e officials, who passed it from hand to hand unable to tell whether it was genuine or	not	.
wine would run out. But Wang was surprised to see that the amount of the wine did	not	diminish even after several rounds.
ank you for giving us the moonlight, but it's rather dull drinking quietly like this. Why	not	invite the moon goddess to join us?
ther month passed. Wang could stand the life no longer, especially as the priest had	not	taught him any magic.
ere for some time. Please teach me just one small trick so that my coming here may	not	have been in vain.
commanded Wang, who was facing a wall, to walk through it. Wang, however, dared	not	
The recorder of these marvels comments: "Hearing this, who can help laughing? But	not	everyone realizes that there are quite a
tive at first. Then they think they can act in this way wherever they please. They will	not	stop until they bump their heads against
rrived, however, the magistrate had just died. This put Kong in difficulties, for he had	not	enough money to make his way home.
im in. Kong admired the young man and gladly followed him inside. The rooms were	not	large,
that since the young man was living in the mansion he must be the owner, Kong did	not	inquire about his family status.
n't reject me for my lack of ability, I'd like to be your pupil." Kong was overjoyed, but	not	presuming to be the young man's tutor,
e're putting up here temporarily." Only then did Kong learn that the young man was	not	a Shan.
hen the young man ordered her to serve them wine in huge goblets. Their revels did	not	stop until midnight.
the gate locked from the outside. The young man explained to him, "My father does	not	wish to have visitors,
her does not wish to have visitors, for fear they would disturb my studies." Kong did	not	press the matter further.
f a bowl. He lay groaning in pain, while the young man waited on him day and night,	not	eating or sleeping.
I gushed forth, staining the mat on the bed. But Kong, glad to be near such a beauty,	not	only felt no pain but,
er, and she is too young. My aunt has a daughter named Asong. She is eighteen and	not	at all bad-looking.
ng of was now suddenly in his own room, and he wondered if the Moon Palace might	not	be on earth after all.
tion and was appointed Judge of Yan'an. He took his family there but his mother did	not	go on the grounds that it was too far.
worried. He said to Kong, "We're threatened by disaster. Can you help us?" Kong did	not	know what he meant,
ly in to kowtow to Kong in the hall. Greatly alarmed, Kong asked why. "We are foxes,	not	human beings,
are life and death with them, Kong was told to take a sword and guard the gate and	not	move even when a thunderbolt struck hir
most concerned and advised him to empty his purse and beg for help, but he would	not	hear of it.
to her. The old woman was delighted, and thanked him for his goodness. "The pin is	not	worth much,
g your grandfather's lifetime, I could have had all the silver I wanted; but since I was	not	of this world I had no need for money,
ed, the price dropped further; and Wang, unable to make a satisfactory profit, would	not	sell.
urse only to find all his money gone! In consternation he told the innkeeper, who did	not	know what to do.
good the loss, the young man said with a sigh: "This is my bad luck. The manager is	not	to blame.
is quails he found that they were dying off. He was filled with consternation, but did	not	know what to do.
od man pitied him with all his heart. Now that all his money was spent and he could	not	return home.
possible that this quail killed the others. Since you have nothing to do anyway, why	not	train this quail?"

高频词 not 在杨译中出现的频率为 2949 次，出现在前三十位高频次词中，而在霍译中，not 一词在前三十位高频词以外，且

杨译搭配多为 dared not，could not，why not，did not，but not，will not，might not，也可从中看出作者的用词偏好和惯用搭配。

　　否定句和含否定意义的句子的翻译特点体现出译者不同的处理方式，由此可见译本的语言特点和表述方式的差异，这些差异最终能够体现出译者风格的个性化特征。

杨译《红楼梦》主要高频词 when 使用情况索引

not dwell on the transports of their love. The next morning	when	Xifeng had gone to pay her respects to the senior ladies, Pin
y heard Xifeng's voice. Pinger had barely regained her feet	when	Xifeng came in and told her: "Get the patterns out of that bo:
one to suffer." "Don't be afraid of her. One of these days	when	I really lose my temper, I'm going to give that vinegary whore
Jia girls and Li Wan, and their choices were put on in turn.	When	the feast was ready the Lady Dowager told Baochai to sele
closer inspection found them even sweeter. All marvelled	when	it was disclosed that the heroine was only eleven, the clow
"What's the hurry?" asked the maid. "We can start packing	when	it's time to leave. "We're leaving tomorrow morning. Why sho
son with him just then. So he was standing there like a fool	when	Daiyu opened the door, thinking him gone. When she saw hi
like a fool when Daiyu opened the door, thinking him gone.	When	she saw him still standing there, she hadn't the heart to shu
u mean?" asked Xiren. "This is the beginning of a new year	when	all the ladies and girls are enjoying themselves. Why carry o
emained no more to test, That test would be of all the best.	When	nothing can be called a test, My feet will find a place to
s were. Told that he was asleep she was turning to leave	when	Xiren said with a smile: "Just a minute, miss! He wrote some
what way are you precious? In what way are you solid?"	When	Baoyu could not answer, the girls clapped their hands and l
ntinued, "The last two lines of your verse are all very well	When	nothing can be called a test My feet can find a place to
to me they still lack a little something. Let me add two more:	When	there's no place for feet to rest, That is the purest state and
shows real understanding," put in Baochai. "In the old days	when	the Sixth Patriarch Huineng of the Southern Sect went to Sh
tendance. Li Wan and Xifeng had a table in the inner room.	When	Jia Zheng commented on Jia Lan's absence, a nurse went i
ays he won't come because the master hasn't invited him."	When	this was reported to Jia Zheng the others laughed and rema
oday, in his father's presence, he simply answered briefly	when	spoken to; and Xiangyun, although a great chatterbox for a
y thunderous crash Strikes dread into the hearts of all, Yet	when	they look around I've turned to ash. "Isn't this a firecracker'
e turned to ash. "Isn't this a firecracker?" asked Jia Zheng.	When	Baoyu said that was right, his father read on: No end to the
e steps look up: Spring surely has no fitter decoration. But	when	the silk cord breaks it drifts away, Blame not the east wind
or this separation. "That sounds like a kite," said Jia Zheng.	When	Tanchun had confirmed this he looked at another riddle: A f
a Lian. Jia Lian and Xifeng were having their meal together	When	this summons arrived. Not knowing what he was wanted fo
Garden, as well as more flowers at the foot of the Garden.	When	that job comes up, I promise to let Yun have it." "All
e chuckled. "But why were you so uncooperative last night	when	all I wanted was to try something different?" Xifeng snorted
I and went on with her meal. Grinning broadly, Jia Lian left.	When	he found that his uncle had indeed sent for him about the no
erence to her, so that nobody could go there. The more so	when	the girls of the family had a taste for poetizing, why sho
it with his grandmother, demanding this, that and the other,	when	a maid announced that his father wanted him. At this bolt fr
ay your father only wants to warn you to behave yourself	when	you're there. Just say 'Yes' to whatever he tells you and yo
ant to taste it?" Caiyun pushed her away. "Don't tease him	when	he's feeling low," she scolded. "Go in quickly, while the mas
yu rose to confess: "I remembered that line of an old poem:	When	the fragrance of flowers assails men we know the day is v
e is Hua (Flower), I called her Xiren. " "You must change it	when	you go back," put in Lady Wang quickly. Then she turned to
leaning in the doorway of the entrance hall. Her face lit up	when	she saw that he was back safely, and she asked what his
Nothing much. Just to warn me to be on my best behaviour	when	I move into the Garden." Having by now reached the Lady D
lake good tea And gathers up fresh fallen snow to brew it.	When	some toadies learned that these poems were the work of a
these in, keeping them on the canopy over his bed to read	when	he was alone. The cruder and more indecent he kept hidder
ch-tree. He had just reached the line Red petals fall in drifts	when	a gust of wind blew down such a shower of petals that he
ith blossoms and was wondering how to dispose of them	when	a voice behind him asked: "What are you doing here?" He tu
swallow me, so that I change into a big turtle myself. Then	when	you become a lady of the first rank and go at last to
t Daiyu's heart was touched, her thoughts were in a whirl,	when	someone came up from behind and shoved her in the back a
before Xiangling took her leave. But let us return to Baoyu.	When	Xiren fetched him back he discovered Yuanyang leaning ov

　　考察发现，杨译在使用 when 一词时，大多数作为时间状语从句的连词用于连接主从句，因此译文整体看来，句子结构严谨，同时也增加了句长。在杨译前 30 位高频词中，除了 and 和

but 具有同等句法效果外，就只有 when 一词频次较高。而作为对比，霍译本前 30 位的高频词中，连接并列句和主从句的连词只有 and 一词，when 和 but 均出现在前 30 位高频词以外。可见，高频连词的考察可以展示译者在句子构成上采取的不同处理方式，从而可见译者的语言风格差异。

霍译《红楼梦》主要高频词 said 使用情况索引

	said	
cannot see that it would make a very remarkable book.' 'Come, your reverence,'	said	the stone (for Vanitas had been correct in assu
The Story of the Stone has now been made clear. The same cannot, however, be	said	of the characters and events which it recorded
II, so another lot of these amorous wretches is about to enter the vale of tears,'	said	the Taoist.
s begin? And where are the souls to be reborn?' 'You will laugh when I tell you,'	said	the monk.
down to earth with the rest of these romantic creatures.' 'How very amusing 1'	said	the Taoist.
e a few souls? It would be a work of merit.' 'That is exactly what I was thinking,'	said	the monk.
wait this last batch to make up the number.' 'Very good, I will go with you then,'	said	the Taoist Shi-yin heard all this conversation q
ne operations of karma such as the one I have just been privileged to overhear,'	said	Shi-yin.
talking about? Is it possible that I might be allowed to see it?' 'Oh, as for that,'	said	the monk:
him standing there holding Ying-lian, the monk burst into loud sobs. 'Patron,' he	said	.
s again there. we can go together to the Land of illusion to sign off.' 'Excellent!'	said	the other.
standing there gazing, sir. Has anything been happening in the street?' 'No, no,'	said	Shi-yin.
of some old poet. But what brings you here, sir?' 'Tonight is Mid Autumn night,'	said	Shi-yin.
made no polite pretence of declining. 'Your kindness is more than I deserve,' he	said	.
arts on its starry ways. On earth ten thousand heads look up and gaze.' 'Bravo!'	said	Shi-yin loudly.
can earn from my copying is not enough-' 'Why ever didn't you say this before?'	said	Shi-yin interrupting him.
at five o'clock this morning, sir. He says he left a message to pass on to you. He	said	to tell you,
ncern himself with almanacs, but should act as the situation demands," and he	said	there wasn't time to say good-bye.
ou can make out "won" and "done",' replied the Taoist with a smile, 'you may be	said	to have understood;
you like me to provide your "Won-Done Song" with a commentary? 'Please do!'	said	the Taoist;
r ago. Could he be the one you want?' '"Feng" or "Zhen", it's all the same to us,'	said	the runners;
d to Shi-yin, and he seemed very upset. Then he asked me about Ying-lian, and I	said	she was lost while out watching the lanterns.
g-lian, and I said she was lost while out watching the lanterns. 'Never mind,' he	said	.
dence!' 'I went home at the end of last year to spend New Year with the family,'	said	Zi-xing.
cently in the capital. 'I can't think of anything particularly deserving of mention,'	said	Yu-cun,
usual event that took place in your own clan there.' 'What makes you say that?'	said	Yu-cun,
Yu-cun, 'I have no family connections in the capital.' 'Well, it's the same name,'	said	Zi-xing.
wn the Jias of the Rong-quo mansion as unworthy of you.' 'Oh, you mean them,'	said	Yu-cun.
es in the family get more degenerate from one generation to the next.' 'Surely,'	said	Yu-cun with surprise,
d that there was something very unusual in the heredity of that child.' 'Humph,'	said	Zi-xing.
l in the heredity of that child.' 'Humph,' said Zi-xing. 'A great many people have	said	that.
like-completely ignoring all the other objects. Sir Zheng was very displeased. He	said	he would grow up to be a rake.
osed, 'Zhang victorious is a hero, Zhang beaten is a lousy knave?' 'Precisely so,'	said	Yu-cun.
neral of the Nanking Secretariat. Perhaps you know who I mean?' 'Who doesn't?	said	Zi-xing.

霍译前 30 位高频词中出现了引导动词 said，作为小说类文本转述语的主要标志，该词语频次的不同能体现出译者风格和文本叙事风格的差异。杨译中前 30 位高频词中没有出现 said，而霍译共计出现 5 803 次，在文本中占据显要位置。

　　原著中 700 个人物形象纷纷登场，主要人物 60 余人，这些人物的会话与独白文本占全文文本的 35.35％（冯庆华，2012）。各类会话和独白的引导语包括"道""说""问""问道""笑道"等，每一千字里就有 13 个作为引导语的"道"字，因此这一引导语的翻译能体现出作者的用词特点，也就是说，霍克斯更偏好使用 said 来引导对话和独白，但会根据序号在其后面加上解释性词语，或添加原文中不存在的词语的译文进行补充翻译，明显属于交际翻译范畴。在统计中，可见霍译多处使用了 said＋主语＋状语结构，如 said Baoyu with a smile，said with a sigh，said angrily，said bitterly，said coldly，said merrily，said scornfully 等词语对会话和会话发起者进行了描述和补充，语言风格明显异于杨译。

霍译《红楼梦》主要高频词 jia 使用情况索引

	Jia	
him the Story of the Stone to read. This Mr Cao smiled and said: 'Rustic fiction indeed (	Jia	Yu Cun Yan Ji
ing academic distinction and leaving behind a creditable heir? Is his posthumous son a	Jia	Gui (Cassia) destined for glory?
nore than an undistinguished end", as you put it?' As he listened to the hermit's words,	Jia	Yu-cun found himself stroking his beard meditatively and heaving a long sigh.
s it that of all the ladies in these noble families, none, including Her Grace the Imperial	Jia	Concubine.
lodge and I would be delighted if you could stop by and pass the time of day with me.'	Jia	Yu-cun consented with pleasure and the two men walked hand in hand.
ecognized him at once as Zhen Shi-yin and promptly bowed in response. 'Esteemed Mr	Jia	Yu-cun.
y?') Aroma's married life is the first chapter of another history. Our narrative returns to	Jia	Lian sent someone to invite Grannie Liu over.
y obligations to the throne do not permit us.' Jia Zheng went in to see Lady Wang, while	Jia	Zheng went into to see Lady Wang,
enough,' commented Jia Zheng. 'But alas my obligations to the throne do not permit it.'	Jia	Zheng.
nds, Uncle.' 'A quiet retirement in the country would suit me well enough,' commented	Jia	Lian replied appropriately and continued:
and make his way in the world. Not every official at court is from a city family, after all.'	Jia	Zheng had heard the full details of Qiao-jie's story the previous evening,
th Mother and Father are wifing that Qiao-jie should be married to this Master Zhou.'	Jia	Lian took the opportunity of raising the issue of his daughter's marriage:
g gave them a long homily on their debt of gratitude to the throne for all these favours.	Jia	Zheng gave them a long homily on their debt of gratitude to the throne for all these favours.
arden has been set aside for my sister Xi-chun's devotions.' After a pause for reflection	Jia	Lian and Cousin Zhen.
thanks for this great honour, and took his leave. On his return home he was received by	Jia	Zheng kowtowed again to express his thanks for this great honour.
fer upon him the religious title Ma~ster Verbi Profundi - Master of the Profound Word.	Jia	Zheng told him the full story of Bao-yu's disappearance.
ral Imperial instructions and enquired after his son, the successful Provincial Graduate.	Jia	Zheng a special audience.
ffered to present a memorial on his behalf. The Emperor most magnanimously granted	Jia	Zheng nodded in silence.
med him that Bao-chai was with child, and that all Bao-yu's maids would be dismissed.	Jia	Zheng tried to dispel as best he could.
see the womenfolk. Bao-yu's absence cast a shadow of gloom over the gathering, which	Jia	Zheng went in to see the womenfolk.
now, and they spent some time with Jia Zheng, catching up on each other's news. Then	Jia	Zheng.
Cousin Zhen had also returned from their exile by now, and they spent some time with	Jia	She and Cousin Zhen had also returned from their exile by now.
A few days later Jia Zheng came home and was greeted on his arrival by all the family.	Jia	Zheng came home and was greeted on his arrival by all the family.
Xue parted from Aroma their minds were considerably more at ease. * A few days later	Jia	Zheng's words of advice.
y Wang, Bao-chai and Aroma most bitterly of all. Then they listened as Jia Lan read out	Jia	Lan read out Jia Zheng's words of advice.
wept bitterly, Lady Wang, Bao-chai and Aroma most bitterly of all. Then they listened as	Jia	Zheng described his encounter with Bao-yu.
y Wang told Jia Lan to read the letter Out aloud. When he reached the passage where	Jia	Lan to read the letter Out aloud.
the boat. 'The Master will be arriving in a matter of days,' he reported. Lady Wang told	Jia	Zheng had written on the boat.
and they were still chatting when a messenger arrived and presented the letter which	Jia	Zheng completed and sealed his letter.
conversation to Jia Lan's success in the exams and the revival of the family fortunes. Then	Jia	Lan's success in the exams and the revival of the family fortunes.
tainly unique.' In an effort to restore his spirits, the servants turned the conversation to	Jia	Zheng with a sigh.
ms before disappearinq?' 'How can you ever hope to understand these things?' replied	Jia	Zheng dismissed the idea.
had happened. They sought his authority to mount a search for Bao-yu in the area, but	Jia	Zheng sat down to regain his breath and told them what had happened.
n the distance hurried forward to meet him, and then all returned to the boat together.	Jia	

　　杨译本中 Jia 一词出现在高频词 30 位之外，共计出现频次 2538 次，而霍译中该词则在前 30 位以内，共计 4303 次，产生

如此巨大差异的原因，查看具体搭配可见，霍译将"贾母"译为"grandmother Jia"，从而导致译文中 Jia 一词出现频次明显高于将"贾母"译为"Lady Dowager"的杨译。

霍译《红楼梦》主要高频词 jia 搭配 Grandmother 使用情况索引

aged streak in her nature which had made her utterly devoted to Grandmother Jia as long as she was	Grandmother	Jia's servant,
er talking a little longer, they all settled down and went to sleep.' Rising early next day, they visited	Grandmother	Jia to wish her a good morning and then went over to Lady Wang's.
After an exchange of information about the years of separation, and after they had been taken to see	Grandmother	Jia and made their reverence to her,
ir children to move in there?' Lady Wang had wanted all along to ask her sister to stay.	Grandmother	Jia had sent someone round to tell her that she should 'ask Mrs Xue to stay with us here,
is passage-way Aunt Xue would now daily repair, either after dinner or in the evening, to gossip with	Grandmother	Jia or reminisce with her sister.
tment performs the 'Dream of Golden Days' From the moment Lin Dai-yu entered the Rong mansion,	Grandmother	Jia's solicitude for her had manifested itself in a hundred different ways.
the gardens and came over in person, bringing her son Jia Rong and his young wife with her, to invite	Grandmother	Jia.
is young wife with her, to invite Grandmother Jia, Lady Xing and Lady Wang to a flower-viewing party.	Grandmother	Jia and the rest went round as soon as they had finished their breakfast.
ao-yu was overcome with tired-ness and heaviness and expressed a desire to take an afternoon nap.	Grandmother	Jia ordered some of the servants to go back to the house with him and get him comfortably
and maidservants who were in attendance on Bao-yu. 'Come, my dears! Tell Uncle Bao to follow me.'	Grandmother	Jia had always had a high opinion of Qin-shi's trustworthiness-she was just a charming,
ks suffused by a crimson blush of embarrassment. When he was properly dressed, they went to rejoin	Grandmother	Jia and the rest.
ly, anxious to share with her the lesson he had learned from Disenchantment, Aroma knew that when	Grandmother	Jia gave her to Bao-yu she had intended her to belong to him in the fullest possible sense,
box of flowers. Zhou Rui's wife presently came to the part of the house behind Lady Wang's quarters.	Grandmother	Jia had recently decided that her granddaughters were becoming too numerous and declar
ife she asked her to convey Xi-feng's thanks to the donor. Zhou Rui's wife now made her way towards	Grandmother	Jia's apartments.
Xi-feng had completed her toilet, she first reported to Lady Wang and then went to take her leave of	Grandmother	Jia.

t back into their carriage and continued their journey into the city. Rome once more, they first called on	Grandmother	Jia and Lady Wang and then Went off to their several rooms.
and rode away. Still no wiser, Jia Zheng hurried into his court dress and hastened to the Palace, leaving	Grandmother	Jia and the rest in an extreme state of alarm which they endeavoured (un
to His Majesty for the great favour he has shown us!' Unable in her agitated state to remain indoors,	Grandmother	Jia had been waiting outside in the loggia.
Wang, You-shi, Li Wan, Xi-feng, Aunt Xue and the girls - had also congregated to await news of Jia Zheng.	Grandmother	Jia called Lai Da inside to explain his cryptic message in somewhat great
dyships to come to the Palace and give thanks."' Lai's Da information at once dispelled the anxiety that	Grandmother	Jia and the others had all this time been feeling.
costume appropriate to her rank. Then off they went to the Palace in four sedans one behind the other.	Grandmother	Jia's at the head.
s Cousin Zhen also changed into court dress, and taking Jia Rong and Jia Qiang with them, accompanied	Grandmother	Jia to the Palace as her male escort.
holy-a melancholy which the news of his sister Yuan-chun's dazzling promotion was powerless to dispel.	Grandmother	Jia's visit to the Palace to give thanks.
ning else. One morning, just as he had finished washing and dressing and was thinking of going round to	Grandmother	Jia to ask if he might pay Qin Zhong another visit.
that's what the old gaffer said just now who came round to tell me.' Bao-yu hurried back and told	Grandmother	Jia.
e before Li Gui and the rest could calm him. Then at last Bao-yu, having him continued tearful and distressed.	Grandmother	Jia contributed thirty or forty taels towards Qin Zhong's funeral expenses
they were coming. As Bao-yu was in very low spirits these days because of his grief for Qin Zhong,	Grandmother	Jia had hit on the idea of sending him into the newly made garden to play
suitable. Jia Zheng, who was secretly beginning to be apprehensive about the possible consequences of	Grandmother	Jia's anxiety for her darling grandson.

hand in hand together. As soon as they had eaten, it was time to talk about chousing the plays and	Grandmother	Jia called on Bao-chai to begin.
thday, and in the end she gave in and selected a piece about Monkey from The Journey to the West.	Grandmother	Jia was pleased.
ased. Aunt Xue was now invited to pick a play, but as her own daughter had just chosen, she refused.	Grandmother	Jia did not press her and passed on to Xi-feng.
nally have refused to take precedence over her aunt and mother-in-law, who were both present, but	Grandmother	Jia had been waiting and must be obeyed.
order to make sure that this element was not lacking from the programme. As she had anticipated,	Grandmother	Jia was even more delighted by this second choice.
this second choice. Next Dai-yu was asked to choose. She deferred to Aunt Xing and Aunt Wang; but	Grandmother	Jia was insistent.
rder in which they had been selected. When the time came to bring in the wine and begin the feast,	Grandmother	Jia invited Bao-chai to choose again.
Acts the Madman I Xiang-yun found this very fanny. They continued to watch plays until the evening.	Grandmother	Jia had taken a particular fancy to the little player who had acted the heroine's parts
e clown only nine There were murmurs and exclamations from all present when they heard this, and	Grandmother	Jia told someone to save them delicacies from the table and a present of money each,
try it on me: it makes me thick!' With these words she walked off into the inner room of	Grandmother	Jia's apartment and lay down on the kang in a rage.
it back to her. As soon as they heard this, the four of them hurried to the reception room in	Grandmother	Jia's apartment,
st back from Court and came along himself in the evening to join in the fun. There were three tables.	Grandmother	Jia made him squeeze up beside her on her side of the table and gave him a handful c
for that. Jia Zheng quickly sent Jia Huan with two of the old women to fetch him. When he arrived,	Grandmother	Jia knew as well as everyone else that this state of affairs was entirely owing to Jia Zh
quence, what should have been a jolly, intimate family party was painfully unnatural and restrained.	Grandmother	Jia laughed.
have so much affection for your grandchildren, Mama. Can you not spare just a tiny bit for your son?'	Grandmother	Jia.
Zheng eagerly. 'And if I guess right, I shall expect to be given a prize.' 'Of course,' said	Grandmother	Jia.
wer to Bao-yu, who, readily understanding what was expected of him, surreptitiously passed it on to	Grandmother	Jia.
ne forward bearing trays and boxes of various shapes and sizes which they handed up onto the kang,	Grandmother	Jia examined them one by one.
and Ying-chun handed it ceremoniously to her uncle. 'Have a look at the riddles on the screen,' said	Grandmother	Jia when Jia Zheng,
said Jia Zheng. 'There is no name on it.' 'I expect that one is Bao-yu,' said	Grandmother	Jia.
ed him was evident in the melancholy expression on his face and in his bowed and dejected stance.	Grandmother	Jia noticed it but attributed it to fatigue.

o begin a systematic tour of the premises. The pagos in the outer courtyard, who had a moment before witnessed	Grandmother	Jia and her train trooping through the gateway
aware that, though Abbot Zhang had started life a poor boy and entered the Taoist church as 'proxy novice for	Grandmother	Jia's late husband,
and give it a good pull. Come on, follow me!' Abbot Zhang followed him inside, laughing delightedly. Having found	Grandmother	Jia;
Zhen ducked and smiled deferentially. 'Papa Zhang has come to pay his respects, Grannie.' 'Help him, then!' said	Grandmother	Jia.
Old Ladyship, but I thought you look more blooming than ever!' 'And how are you, Holy One?'	Grandmother	Jia asked him with a pleased smile.
when I sent round to invite him, they told me he was out. 'He really was out,'	Grandmother	Jia was insistent.
old Taoist embraced him affectionately and returned his greeting. 'He's beginning to fill out,'	Grandmother	Jia, addressing
'He's beginning to fill out,' he said, addressing Grandmother Jia. 'He looks well enough on the outside,' said	Grandmother	Jia herself showed a disposition to be tearful.
moves, to me he's the spit and image of Old Sir Jia.' The old man's eyes grew moist, and	Grandmother	Jia herself showed a disposition to be tearful.
family.' 'A monk once told the boy's fortune said that he was not to marry young,' said	Grandmother	Jia;
laughter from the assembled company. Even Cousin Zhen was unable to restrain himself. 'Monkey! Monkey!' said	Grandmother	Jia.
in that case let the boy go with it round his neck and show it to them himself!' said	Grandmother	Jia told Bao-yu to take off the Magic Jade and
is certainly not used to it. We shouldn't want him to be overcome by the-ah-effluvia, should we?' Hearing this,	Grandmother	Jia and the others now continued their sightse
and, holding it like a sacred relic at eye level in front of him, conveyed it reverently from the courtyard.	Grandmother	Jia looked at the tray.
like our young friend to keep them, either to amuse himself with or to give away to his friends.'	Grandmother	Jia could no longer decline She told one of the
I cannot really have the connection with our honoured family that I have always claimed to have.' After this	Grandmother	Jia.
outside for me and I'll distribute it to the poor?' 'I think that's a very good idea,' said	Grandmother	Jia and her party went up to the galleries.
o the servant, 'and this evening you will distribute a largesse.' This being now settled, Abbot Zhang withdrew, and	Grandmother	Jia and her party went up to the galleries.
esse.' This being now settled, Abbot Zhang withdrew, and Grandmother Jia and her party went up to the galleries.	Grandmother	Jia sat with Bao-yu and the girls in the gallery
will of the gods could be known. The first play selected was The White Serpent. 'What's the story?' said	Grandmother	Jia.
his reception-hall piled high with their insignia. 'It seems a bit conceited to have this second one played,' said	Grandmother	Jia.

对比可见，霍译的"grandmother Jia"使用频率高，而杨译侧重贾母的身份高贵，因此使用 lady Dowager，旨在保持原文中的社会等级文化，将其原汁原味传递给目的语读者。

根据柯林斯词典，dowager 用来指"the wife of a dead duke, emperor, or other man of high rank.（已故公爵、君主等上层人士的）遗孀"，贾母又称史老太君，贾府上下尊称她为"老太太""老祖宗"，为保龄侯史公的长女，荣国公贾代善之妻，贾代善死后作为荣国公这样显赫门第的掌权人，其地位和影响力之大，在小说中处处可见。因此，杨译将其与 dowager 一词等同，归化结合异化的翻译策略之下，贾母 the Lady Dowager 与霍译的 Grandmother Jia 形成了鲜明对照。

杨译《红楼梦》lady 搭配 dowager 使用情况索引

l although Baoyu was most upset he could hardly come between her and her father. The Lady	Dowager	decided that Jia Lian should accompany her granddaughte
d up to help him back to bed, asking anxiously what was the matter. Should they get the Lady	Dowager	to send for a doctor?
nsion. Anxious though Xiren was, she dared not stop him when he was in this mood. The Lady	Dowager	however protested.
s not see can only be surmised, and far be it from us to speculate. The next morning the Lady	Dowager	and Lady Wang sent to urge Baoyu to dress more warmly
atisfy Jia Zhen; in the second, she could attend to the abbess's business; in the third, the Lady	Dowager	would be pleased to know that Baoyu was enjoying himse
his court robes and going to the Palace, leaving the whole family in dire suspense. The Lady	Dowager	sent one mounted messenger after another in search of n
old lady to go at once to the Palace with the other ladies to thank His Majesty." The Lady	Dowager	had been waiting anxiously in the corridor outside the gre
failed to raise his spirits. He alone remained silent throughout the trip made by the Lady	Dowager	and the rest to offer thanks for the Imperial favour.
ow. That's what an old fellow from his home just told me. At once Baoyu went to tell the Lady	Dowager	
uld prevail on him to leave off. Even after his return he could not overcome his grief. The Lady	Dowager	gave the Qin family several dozen taels of silver in additic
arrived in the garden. For he was still grieving so much over Qin Zhong's death that the Lady	Dowager	had been asking where Baoyu was.
u leant over her begging, "Dear cousin, dear kind cousin, do forgive me!" Meanwhile the Lady	Dowager	
sutras and incantations. Then Jia Zheng, able at last to breathe more freely, invited the Lady	Dowager	to make a final inspection of the Garden and see that all v
v, slept a wink that night. Before dawn the next day all those with official ranks from the Lady	Dowager	downwards put on full ceremonial dress.
lemn silence. Jia She and the other men waited outside in the west street entrance, the Lady	Dowager	and the women outside the main gate.
ened off. They were growing tired of waiting when a eunuch rode up on a big horse. The Lady	Dowager	welcomed him in and asked for news.
eror. She can hardly set out until seven." This being the case, Xifeng suggested that the Lady	Dowager	and Lady Wang should go inside to rest and come back lat
the Lady Dowager and Lady Wang should go inside to rest and come back later. So the Lady	Dowager	and others retired.
silence, Jia She and the young men of the family by the entrance of the west street, the Lady	Dowager	and the women in front of the main gate.

day after lunch or in the evening, Aunt Xue would walk over to chat with the Lady	Dowager	or to talk over the old days with her sister.
n, but now let us return to Daiyu. Since her coming to the Rong Mansion, the Lady	Dowager	had been lavishing affection on her.
bloom in the Ning Mansion's garden, Jia Zhen's wife Madam You invited the Lady	Dowager	
Jia Rong and his wife with her to deliver the invitations in person, and so the Lady	Dowager	and the rest went over after breakfast.
ecial interest to record. Soon Baoyu was tired and wanted to have a nap. The Lady	Dowager	ordered his attendants to take good care of him and bring
ne." She told his nurses and maids to follow her with their young master. The Lady	Dowager	had every confidence in this lovely slender young woman \
o tidy his clothes without any further questions. They went then to where the Lady	Dowager	was and after a hasty meal returned to his room.
he urged her to carry out the instructions with him; and as she knew that the Lady	Dowager	had given her to Baoyu she felt this would not be an undu
ook the flowers to the back of Lady Wang's principal apartment. Recently the Lady	Dowager	had found it inconvenient to have all her grand-daughters
l her toilet she went to tell Lady Wang that she was off. She then went to the Lady	Dowager	
Xifeng and Baoyu reached home and had paid their greetings, Baoyu told the Lady	Dowager	of Qin Zhong's eagerness to attend their clan school.
this news to invite her to the opera in two days' time. In spite of her age, the Lady	Dowager	looked forward to any excitement.
ted Nanny Li. "Just one cup, dear nanny," begged Baoyu. "No, you don't! If the Lady	Dowager	or Lady Wang were here I wouldn't mind your drinking a w
anked their hostess and made their way to the Lady Dowager's quarters. The Lady	Dowager	had not yet dined but was very pleased when she learned

is the younger sister of Jia Zhen of the Ning Mansion. The Lady	Dowager	is so attached to these grand-daughters that she makes th
Lin Ruhai Recommends a Tutor to His Brother-in-Law The Lady	Dowager	Sends for Her Motherless Grand-Daughter To continue.
Daiyu made her kowtow to her grandmother. This was the Lady	Dowager	from the Shi family mentioned by Leng Zixing,
and mourning ceremonies been conducted? Inevitably, the Lady	Dowager	was most painfully affected.
y I'm still taking ginseng pills." "That's good," approved the Lady	Dowager	.
iyu rose quickly to greet her. "You don't know her yet." The Lady	Dowager	chuckled.
her from head to foot, then led her back to her seat by the Lady	Dowager	.
pproval. Now the refreshments were cleared away and the Lady	Dowager	ordered two nurses to take Daiyu to see her two uncles.
n't it be simpler if I take my niece?" "Very well," agreed the Lady	Dowager	was seated alone on a couch at the head of the table with
ut out the chopsticks and Lady Wang served the soup. The Lady	Dowager	told Lady Wang to sit down;
e that seat." With a murmured apology, Daiyu obeyed. The Lady	Dowager	now.
more, this time for drinking. "You others may go," said the Lady	Dowager	and upon her instructions went to see his mother.
efore. He looks so familiar." Baoyu paid his respects to the Lady	Dowager	scolded,
imitate this youth's perversity! With a smile at Baoyu, the Lady	Dowager	laughed.
g again after a long separation." "So much the better." The Lady	Dowager	in desperation took Baoyu in her arms.
all the maids rushed forward to pick up the jade while the Lady	Dowager	agreed to this.
ove over and disturb you?" After a moment's reflection the Lady	Dowager	considered Xueyan too young and childish and Nanny Wan
who had also attended her since she was a child. Since the Lady	Dowager	she thought of no one but the Lady Dowager,
Xiren. Xiren's strong point was devotion. Looking after the Lady	Dowager	so forth...
king after the Lady Dowager she thought of no one but the Lady	Dowager	.
to bed. The next morning, after paying her respects to the Lady	Dowager	,
ences. Lady Wang took them in to pay their respects to the Lady	Dowager	also sent to urge,
there." Before Lady Wang could extend this invitation, the Lady	Dowager	or to talk over the old days with her sister.
in the evening, Aunt Xue would walk over to chat with the Lady	Dowager	had been lavishing affection on her,
eturn to Daiyu. Since her coming to the Rong Mansion, the Lady	Dowager	.
Mansion's garden, Jia Zhen's wife Madam You invited the Lady	Dowager	.
ife with her to deliver the invitations in person, and so the Lady	Dowager	and the rest went over after breakfast.
cord. Soon Baoyu was tired and wanted to have a nap. The Lady	Dowager	ordered his attendants to take good care of him and bring
urses and maids to follow her with their young master. The Lady	Dowager	had every confidence in this lovely slender young woman w
ithout any further questions. They went then to where the Lady	Dowager	was and after a hasty meal returned to his room.
rry out the instructions with him; and as she knew that the Lady	Dowager	had given her to Baoyu she felt this would not be an undue
the back of Lady Wang's principal apartment. Recently the Lady	Dowager	had found it inconvenient to have all her grand-daughters
nt to tell Lady Wang that she was off. She then went to the Lady	Dowager	;

霍译《红楼梦》主要高频词 and 使用情况索引

When grief for fiction's idle words More real than human life appears. Reflect that life itself's a dream	And	do not mock the reader's tears.
breezily on his way. As he went he said to himself: 'So it was really all utter nonsense! Author, copyist	and	reader were alike in the dark!
ning-pegs glued fast.' Vanitas lifted his head and guffawed at this, dropped the manuscript to the ground	and	went breezily on his way.
his boat; you are like a man playing a zither with the tuning-pegs glued fast.' Vanitas lifted his head	and	guffawed at this.
it. You in your insistence on ferreting out facts are like the man who dropped his sword in the water	and	thought to find it again by making a mark on the side of his
structed: he repeated Yu-cun's words and handed him the Story of the Stone to read. This Mr Cao smiled	and	said:
erusing the histories of bygone days. Vanitas did as he had been instructed: he repeated Yu-cun's words	and	handed him the Story of the Stone to read.
gh, after an incalculable number of generations, an infinity of aeons, there was indeed a Nostalgia Studio	and	in it a Mr Cao Xue-qin.
tell him: 'Jia Yu-cun says...' and ask him to do such-and-such and so forth...' Yu-cun dozed off again,	and	Vanitas made a careful note of his instructions.
will find a certain Mr Cao Xue-qin. Just tell him: 'Jia Yu-cun says...' and ask him to do such-and-such	and	so forth...
a certain Nostalgia Studio, where you will find a certain Mr Cao Xue-qin. Just tell him: 'Jia Yu-cun says...'	and	ask him to do such-and-such and so forth...
errors. Allow me to tell you of a man who can transmit this story to the world on your behalf,	and	by so doing bring this strange affair to a proper conclusion.
him up and gave him a good shake, and the man slowly opened his eyes. He skimmed through the book	and	let it fall from his hand;
out, he could not rouse him from his slumber. Eventually he heaved him up and gave him a good shake,	and	the man slowly opened his eyes.
owever many times he called out, he could not rouse him from his slumber. Eventually he heaved him up	and	gave him a good shake.
by Rushford Hythe; there he found a man asleep (from which he deduced him to be a man of leisure)	and	thought he would give him this Story of the Stone to read.
of the Magic Mountain, a reflected light to quicken their own aspirations.' So Vanitas copied it all down	and	slipping this new version into his sleeve took it off with him
nd transmit its message: that things are not as they seem, that the extraordinary and the ordinary, truth	and	fiction,
its hard to publish it and transmit its message: that things are not as they seem, that the extraordinary	and	the ordinary,
down again in this complete form and find someone in the world with leisure on his hands to publish it	and	transmit its message;
of the inscription may wear away and be misread. I had better copy it down again in this complete form	and	find someone in the world with leisure on his hands to publi
et. But with the passing of the years the characters of this new version of the inscription may wear away	and	be misread.
ler can indeed see that Brother Stone's experience of life sharpened the edge of his spiritual perception.	and	brought them to a more complete awareness of the Tao.
riginal story. 'When I first saw this strange tale of Brother Stone's I thought it worth publishing as a novel	and	copied it down for that purpose.
the o了and the with which the earlier version concluded. This new material provided several dénouements	and	tied up various loose ends in the plot,
lying there still, with characters inscribed on it as before. He read the inscription through carefully again	and	noticed that a whole new section had been appended to the
he become once more a single whole. 5 One day Vanitas the Taoist passed again by Greensickness Peak	and	saw the Stone 'that had been found unfit to repair the heav
heir burden and each drifted off on its way. An otherworldly tome recounts an otherworldly tale. As Man	and	Stone become once more a single whole.
had once smelted their fiery amalgam to repair the vault of Heaven, they carefully deposited their burden	and	each drifted off on his way.
Taoist continued on their way bearing the jade, until finally they came to the foot of Greensickness Peak	and	there.
ll not have been in vain.' Shi-yin clasped both hands together in salutation and took his leave. The monk	and	the Taoist continued on their way bearing the jade,
its little trip into the world will not have been in vain.' Shi-yin clasped both hands together in salutation	and	took his leave.
'But that senseless Block has already returned. Now all that remains is to restore it to its place of origin	and	to record the last instalment of its story.
Illuminate! My felicitations! Is the love karma fulfilled? Have all those souls involved been duly returned	and	entered in the registers?

霍译《红楼梦》主要高频词 but 使用情况索引

(be a man of leisure) and thought he would give him this Story of the Stone to read.	But	however many times he called out,
rious, opulent world of men, to seek out a suitable mortal for the task of publication.	But	all the men he encountered were either too busy establishing th
e complete awareness of the Tao. At the end he had no cause for remorse or regret.	But	with the passing of the years the characters of this new version o
Stone's I thought it worth publishing as a novel and copied it down for that purpose.	but	at the time it was unfinished;
eal, Yu-cun was still curious, this time wanting to know the secrets of his own future;	but	his luck had run out.
e wrong to make predictions about this now. Yu-cun had still more questions to ask,	but	Shi-yin was clearly unwilling to provide any further replies.
He nodded his head and sighed: 'So that is the truth of the matter. And I never knew.	but	if Bao-yu is a person of such a remarkable spiritual pedigree,
one of these are coincidental. Nor is our meeting again like this today a coincidence,	but	rather a meaningful and marvellous event.
e (as Aroma concluded) that life is predestined and that 'there's naught to be done'.	but	unfortunately this argument is too often adduced by sons and sta
q and a sincere respect, never venturing to steer her forcibly into any new direction,	but	showing her an ever more gentle affection and regard.
ght she wept without ceasing and would not at first yield to her husband's embrace,	but	gradually he won her over with gentle affection.
bridal sedan. At her new home, she trusted to herself, she would make plans afresh.	but	once she arrived at the Jiang household,
and set off for home. When she saw her brother and his wife, there were more tears,	but	she could not bring herself to say what was on her mind.
insist on remaining single and faithful to his memory, people will call me shameless.	But	if I do go,
to Aroma. Poor Aroma was inconsolable at the prospect of leaving Rong-quo House,	but	she could not offer any resistance.
and land and a pawnshop business of his own. He was a few years older than Aroma	but	had never married and was exceptionally good-looking.
other plane. Such a person could have excelled at court if such had been his destiny;	but	since he had not deigned to earn honours of a worldly nature,
d she won't want to go, and may even try to take her own life. We could keep her on,	but	I am afraid Sir Zheng would not approve.
a true husband he no longer. And a chamber-wife may do the same if she wishes.	but	Aroma was never formally declared to be Ba~yu's chamber-wife,
go home that night but stayed to comfort Bao-chai, afraid she might weep to excess.	but	in the end,
en she could discuss it privately with her sister. Aunt Xue did not go home that night	But	stayed to comfort Bao-chai,
he older ones can be married off, the younger ones can continue to wait on Bao-chai.	But	what am I to do with Aroma?
listened as Jia Lan read out Jia Zheng's words of advice, that they were not to grieve	but	to understand that this was Bao-yu's destiny,
your mind up to mend your ways! There's no need for all these blood-curdling oaths!	but	what are you going to do about Caltrop?
was a great deal of news for him to catch 'p on, some of it sad, some more cheerful.	But	this we can safely leave to the reader's imagination.
ants to deliver it to Rong-quo House while he himself continued his journey by boat.	But	of this no more.
-yu was in some way blessed and that these two holy men had come to protect him.	but	the truth of the matter must be that he himself is a being from a
his jade, and there was always something strange about it. I knew it for an ill omen.	because	his grandmother doted on him so,
t had happened. They sought his authority to mount a search for Bao-yu in the area,	but	Jia Zheng dismissed the idea.
en they disappeared and I could see no one but you.' Jia Zheng wanted to continue,	but	all he could see before him was a vast expanse of white,
aw you following them, so I came too. Then they disappeared and I could see no one	but	you.
strode off into the snow. Jia Zheng went chasing after them along the slippery track,	But	although he could spy them ahead of him,
o arrange for the payment of Xue Pan's commutation fine, by no means an easy task.	But	of this no more.

　　赵朝永（2020）指出：当 and 是连接词，出现频次异于其他译本时，表明译者处理文本词语搭配、句法结构和语篇连贯的方式有所不同，是衡量译者风格差异的一个重要指标。霍译的高频词 and 共使用 24 836 次，明显高于杨译的 17 771 次，而霍译高频词第三十位的 but 出现频率为 3 878 次，也高于杨译 but 出现频率的 3 534 次。对比可发现，杨译与霍译在用词上的偏好也导致了平均句长和句式的差异。杨译平均句长为 13.68 个词语，霍译平均句长为 15.46 个词语，这与高频词使用总频次是密切相关的。"不同的句长有不同的高频字或高频词，这充分显示了句长与语体的关系。而两个译文中高频词的差异反映了不同译者之间思维模式与翻译风格上的差异"（冯庆华，2014：4）。

　　除了对《红楼梦》两个全译本的高频词进行对比分析外，本文也研究了霍译和杨译的独特词。

霍译与杨译独特词比较

独特词	霍译（出现频次＞15）	杨译（出现频次＞15）
独特名词	mamma 76；kotow 66；coz 46；hermitage 40；preceptor 30；area 27； Penny 27；interview 27；priory 23；chamber-wife 23；drams 22；kylin 21； solution 19；bond；viceroy18；winecup；trunk；intendant；lycoperdon；posting 16；humiliation；ditto；granule；bushes 15	operas 49；hamper 22；corridor 21；park 19；aunty 17；pachyma 16；unicorn 16；tiara 14； annex 12；deaconess 12；priestess 12；translator 12；brigands 11；hostel 11；numskull 11
独特形容词	numerous；cupful 20； Peculiar 19； preliminary；discreet 17； insistent；dark-red 16； feigned；surprising 15； Patterned 13； Aristocratic 12； deliberate；enthusiastic 11； well-bred；relaxed；carmine；desultory10	Illusory 17
独特词	霍译（出现频次＞10）	杨译（出现频次＞10）
独特动词	enquired；posting15； encountered，leaped 14； deemed；maintain 13； sniffed 12； retreated 11；anticipate 11； consisting 10	fumed 36； chortled 17； assign 15； consternated 10； flare 10

霍译《红楼梦》主要独特词 kotow 搭配使用情况

	kotow	
se present succeeded in calming them both down and Dai-yu was at last able to make her	kotow	.
everently before Jia Dai-ru when he took Qin Zhong to the old teacher's house to make his	kotow	.
d hands and made Qin Zhong a bow. But Bao-yu said this was not enough. He insisted on a	kotow	.
puzzling disease Outnumbered, and hard pressed by Jia Rui to apologize, Jokey Jin made a	kotow	to Qin Zhong,
" he said, "and don't come yourself! If it will set your mind at zest you can give me a	kotow	now and get it over with.
was to observe carefully whether or not his grandfather was pleased, and having made his	kotow	
grandmother Jia. 'Rong's wife asked me to give you her regards, Grandma. She sends you a	kotow	and she says she feels somewhat better
when she's made a bit more progress she's going to come over to see you and make you a	kotow	in person.
e period of mourning is over,' he said, 'I shall bring the young fellow round to your house to	kotow	his thanks.
take turns by the spirit tablet, making offerings of rice and tea, kotowing when the visitors	kotow	
er Jia's apartment Yuan-chun became a grandchild once more and knelt down to make her	kotow	
the women servants and maids, who were allowed to come inside the room to make their	kotow	
, and presently he was brought in by one of the little eunuchs. When he had completed his	kotow	she called him over,
and taking the salver from the eunuch, made Mademoiselle Charmante come forward and	kotow	her thanks.
your brother's birthday; so apart from not giving him a present, I couldn't even make him a	kotow	this year.
id Bao-yu. 'No,' said Aroma. 'They said it was for me personally; but I'm not to go over and	kotow	for it.
been made for her by Lady Wang. She was told that she should go over to Lady Wang's to	kotow	her thanks,
ny don't you go first thing in the morning, when it's still cool? All you need do is make your	kotow	and drink a cup of tea.
ped it on the burning charcoal; then, with tears in his eyes, he knelt down and made, not a	kotow	
and his mother, it really was as if a phoenix had appeared. Hurriedly he made his birthday	kotow	to Xi-feng.
e her back home with you. Otherwise you can just take yourself off, for I shan't accept your	kotow	!
ncern myself with their affairs. I just let them get on with it. When he came round to me to	kotow	the other day,
en his visiting-card at New Years and birthdays. He did come in the other day, however, to	kotow	to Her Old Ladyship and Lady Wang.
ld see that done. After that Zhou Rui's wife kotowed to Xi-feng in gratitude. She wanted to	kotow	to Mrs Lai as well,
write poetry? It would be such a piece of luck for me if you would.' 'You can make your	kotow	and become my pupil if you like;
n. After all the time she's been here, your daughter could at least make the young ladies a	kotow	before she goes.
set much store by it if she had-but she might at least have the decency to make - them a	kotow	to the two inside.
- them a kotow. You can't both just up and go.' Trinket was obliged to come in again and	kotow	in earnest.
was their senior, they were in the same generation as her and too elderly to be allowed to	kotow	
Jia She came forward with all the menfolk in the family in rows behind them to make their	kotow	?
do so much for me during the year,' Grandmother Jia protested. 'Can't we forget about the	kotow	
e recovers, I promise you a handsome reward, and Bao-yu himself shall bring it to you and	kotow	to you when he brings it.
hands up in front of him. He called in at the main apartment on his way out and made his	kotow	to You-shi,
y senior to Bao-yu but not enough to warrant an obeisance and whose efforts to prevent a	kotow	

霍译《红楼梦》主要独特词 numerous 搭配使用情况

	numerous	
Vang's quarters. Grandmother Jia had recently decided that her granddaughters were becoming too	numerous	and declared that she would retain only Bao
ao-yu would not be gainsaid, so she gave instructions for a carriage to be made ready for him and a	numerous	retinue of servants to attend him there.
ght, Xi-feng in an inner room and Bao-yu and Qin Zhong in an outer room adjoining it. As there were	numerous	old women on night duty lying about everywl
and deep once and distorted by many anfractuosities. The fallen blossoms seemed to be even more	numerous	and the waters on whose surface they floate
ther-o'-pearl and semi-precious stones. In addition to being panelled, the partitions were pierced by	numerous	apertures,
twelve-year-old acolyte, who had been going round with a pair of snuffers trimming the wicks of the	numerous	candles that were burning everywhere and v
though there were plenty of young ladies of outstanding beauty and breeding among the Jia family's	numerous	acquaintance,
ade she was standing, she presently observed Li Wan, Ying-chun, Tan-chun and Xi-chun, attended by	numerous	maids,
scernible glimpses of brightly-coloured dresses and golden hair-ornaments betrayed the presence of	numerous	younger women behind the green muslin cur
en it comes to sites which are famous because of people who never even existed, they are still more	numerous	.
o company and incapacitated by shyness that they dared not come-in short, although the clan was a	numerous	one,
tion that she was still, in her sixteenth year, without employment. Recently, however, observing how	numerous	the maids in Bao-yu's apartment and h
s not well enough to go over daily, but on days when there were sutra-readings and the callers were	numerous	
face. 'Don't let Skybright get me! She's trying to hit me.' Inside the room there was a clatter of	numerous	tiny objects striking the floor and a moment
our pairs of silver ingots twelve lengths of tribute satin four jade cups And there were presents too	numerous	to mention from princes and princesses and
d there have been deficits in the accounts that I have simply been unable to make good, despite the	numerous	unsecured debts I have had to negotiate.
ponsibilities. But your case is totally different. Ours is a golden age, and we ourselves have received	numerous	favours from the throne,

霍译《红楼梦》主要独特词 enquired 搭配使用情况

Yu-cun sensed something very mysterious about the old man. Making a deep bow, he	enquired	:
..factor's face had not changed. He dismissed his attendants. 'Tell me the truth, sir,' he	enquired	confidentially,
..ne, and was welcomed at the main gate by a full turn-out of the younger male Jias. He	enquired	first after Grandmother Jia,
..an for them.' 'I'm growing old and senile,' said Grandmother Jia. 'It's years since I last	enquired	about the family's finances.
..r affections lay. They came into the room looking a picture of misery. Grandmother Jia	enquired	after Xiu-yan,
..m studies, and felt certain it must be to do with Dai-yu again, though she still had not	enquired	whether his dream had been fruit
..ther Jia's room. The ladies all welcomed Adamantina, and she went up to the bedside,	enquired	after the old lady's health and cha
..-chun, and with her Xi-feng, who had dragged herself there despite her illness. Jia Yun	enquired	after Xi-feng's health,
..i-chun's apartment when Adamantina's old women arrived on their search. Landscape	enquired	what their mission was and was s
..ne had seen on the previous occasion. 'From which holy establishment do you hail?' he	enquired	.
..Drink up! This gossip will get us nowhere!' 'How old is the young lady you mentioned?'	enquired	the two Singsong girls.
..it you both. You'd better hurry and take the letter for Bao-yu to read.' 'Please tell me.'	enquired	old Mrs Li,
..ied unsurprised was Xi-chun. She did not feel free to express her thoughts, but instead	enquired	of Bao-chai.
..nd Jia Lian hurried to the main hall to make his kowtow to the Imperial emissary, who	enquired	after Jia She's health and said:
..to his formal expression of thanks favoured him with several Imperial instructions and	enquired	after his son,

杨译《红楼梦》主要独特词 operas 搭配使用情况

..en and geese to be reared in appropriate places; Jia Qiang had twenty	operas	ready;
..ne from Jia Zhen inviting him over to the Ning Mansion to watch some	operas	and see their New Year lanterns.
..the other mansion. He was rather taken aback to find them performing	operas	like Master Ding Finds His Father,
..sked thoughtful. Mingyan asked, "Why aren't you watching those grand	operas	.
..you were going?" "No, I changed to go to Cousin Zhen's to watch some	operas	.
..urged her to wait until after Baochai's birthday and the performance of	operas	.
..ger and then gone on to chat, she asked Baochai to name her favourite	operas	and dishes.
..esses had been hired who were able to perform both Kunqu and Yiyang	operas	.
..ways choose something rowdy," objected Baoyu. "You've been watching	operas	all these years for nothing if you don't know how good this is,
..al Feigns Madness. This set Xiangyun giggling. They went on watching	operas	until dusk.
..e heard sweet fluting and singing over the wall. Normally the words of	operas	made little appeal to her,
..the spring? Daiyu nodded and sighed. "So there are fine lines in these	operas	.
..ly Wang wanted a detailed account of the party—the other guests, the	operas	and the feast.
..f the next month, she urged the young people to go there to watch the	operas	.
..peras. "It's too hot for me," objected Baochai. "Besides, there aren't any	operas	I haven't seen.
..Zhen came to report that lots had been drawn before the shrine for the	operas	.
..iger had hoped they would stop sulking and make it up while watching	operas	together.
..stand and will overlook it." He added, "But why aren't you watching the	operas	.
..fan. She decided, as it was, to change the subject. "What were the two	operas	you saw,
..ght to live in stables! You've all heard those descriptions in ballads and	operas	of the elegance of young ladies' boudoirs.
..en knew that Madam You had arranged for a grand party with not only	operas	but acrobatics and blind story-tellers too,

杨译《红楼梦》主要独特词 illusory 搭配使用情况

..ith the Taoist through a large stone archway on which was inscribed:	Illusory	Land of Great Void.
..of Emanating Fragrance on the Mountain of Expanding Spring in the	Illusory	Land of Great Void.
..his delight, Baoyu followed the goddess to a stone archway inscribed:	Illusory	Land of Great Void.
..s is simply to let you know that after you have proved for yourself the	Illusory	nature of pleasures in fairyland you should realize the vanity of love in your dusty world.
..s men, the aroma of wine. As he raptly recalled his dream here of the	Illusory	Land of Great Void.
..e inscription: Precious Mirror of Love. "This comes from the Hall of the	Illusory	Spirit in the Land of Great Void,
..lay, at the order of the goddess of Disenchantment, I am going to the	Illusory	Land of the Great Void to register all the amorous spirits in this case.
..g death unjustifiably. The more so, as she has already returned to the	Illusory	Land of Great Void.
..to heaven, there is no one in charge of the Board of Infatuation in the	Illusory	Land of Great Void.
..n." His thoughts wandering, he recalled Zhuang Zi's saying about the	illusory	nature of life and felt that men were born to drift with the wind and scatter like clouds.
..116 Baoyu, His Divine Jade Recovered, Attains Understanding in the	Illusory	Realm Jia Zheng Escorts His Mother' S Coffin Home to Fulfil His Filial Duty At Sheyue's re
..n to wait while my mother gets it ready. May I ask if you are from the	Illusory	Land of Great Void?
..opened, read the next chapter. Chapter 120 Zhen Shiyin Expounds the	Illusory	Realm Jia Yucun Concludes the Dream of Red Mansions On hearing from Qiuwen that Xir
..uld you explain that? "This may be for you to grasp fully, sir. The	Illusory	Land of Great Void is the Blessed Land of Truth.
..ream of Rapid Reversal, while Shiyin went to conduct Xiangling to the	Illusory	Land of Great Void to enter her name in the record of the Goddess of Disenchantment.
..it again and find someone with the leisure to circulate it, to show the	illusory	nature of marvels.

杨译《红楼梦》主要独特词 fumed 搭配使用情况

n both the living and the dead will be everlastingly grateful!" "This is a scandal!"	fumed	Yucun.
s included. "Let me go to the Ancestral Temple and weep for my old master," he	fumed	.
ong is only ha Rong's brother-in-law, not a son or grandson of the Jia family," he	fumed	.
e Zhao. "Why don't you teach that spiteful brat of yours to behave himself?" she	fumed	.
s slippers for Baoyu." Tanchun frowned. "Did you ever hear such nonsense?" she	fumed	.
it. But I'll dash out my brains sooner than leave this house." "That's strange!" he	fumed	.
and swear he must clear himself. "Who's been shifting the blame on to me?" he	fumed	.
nding for him. And his old wife is deaf.' Jia She swore. 'You scurvy scoundrel!' he	fumed	.
to Jia She. Jia She flew into a rage. 'Tell your wife to tell her this from me,' he	fumed	.
all the fault of that upstart Jia Yucun ' the bastard deserves to starve to death!'	fumed	Pinger,
they are ' their affairs are none of my business.' 'Who asked you to help others?'	fumed	the concubine.
ianqyun grew most indignant. 'Wait till I go and take this up with Yingchun,' she	fumed	.
, pounded the sill with his cane. 'How can these old women be so heartless?' he	fumed	.
nt would not let her get a word in. Pointing to the flower basket on the rock she	fumed	:
ng the rage she was in asked where she was going. 'Just look at this household!'	fumed	the concubine.
ind mistresses. But when Concubine Zhao heard of this, she flew into a rage and	fumed	that I was getting too many perks.
olved, dared not bring such a charge. When Lai Wang reported this to Xifeng she	fumed	.
You'll have to ask Xiren or Sheyue, madam.' 'You deserve a slap on your mouth,'	fumed	Lady Wang.
eaking ' slap! Tanchun boxed Mrs. Wang's ears. 'Who do you think you are?' she	fumed	.
l man now and will soon have a son of your own, yet you're still such a fool!" she	fumed	.
loss, she could do nothing except berate Xue Pan. "You degenerate wretch!" she	fumed	.
were other wounds. How are there none today?" "You are talking nonsense," he	fumed	.
who came, knowing he was in for it. "Tie them all up!" Jia Zhen ordered. Jia Lian	fumed	at Zhou Rui,

　　本文从两个译本中选取了名词、动词和形容词的独特词部分进行对比，经过数据分析，搭配考察和句子分析，可见两位译者在词汇运用方面的差异：霍译词汇运用的广度与深度远远高于杨译；霍译的独特词体现出译者的语言更为书面化，而杨译语言相对而言倾向于口语化；霍译词汇丰富，译文翔实，而杨译词汇量较之于霍译略低，行文偏于简洁；霍译句长高于杨译；杨译偏好直译和异化手段，霍译意译之处较多，翻译策略多采取归化。

　　综上所述，基于语料库翻译软件，通过对类符/形符比、高频词、独特词、平均句长、篇幅等方面的数据收集和对比，本文描述了不同译者在总体风格上的异同，分析结果从一定层面上可反映译者的语言风格和翻译风格。

　　误译，尤其是涉及原著中文化因素的有意误译，如果在译本或译文中出现的比重较大，误译频率较高，就可以认为有意的文化误译也是译者风格的一部分。

"有意误译是指译者在翻译过程中为了达到某种目的或满足一定需要，故意使原文和译文不完全对等的翻译行为。有意误译是译者故意为之产生的结果，有可能是为了迎合目的语读者的文化心态，引入外来文化，或者是由于文化空缺必须适当加工等等"（张叉，2022：316）。可见，有意的文化误译包括归化和异化手段以及增译、减译、改译、改写、注释等翻译方法，是译者"受制于主观因素，出于某种翻译目的而对译文的一种操控，是一种译者主体权力的运用，是一种创造性的行为"（江滨，王立松等，2014：68）。这种创造性的翻译活动，既可以顺应原文的风格产生相应的对等的译文，也可以是对原文的叛逆性的改造和改写。

刘军平（2009）认为：由于语言和文化差异的存在，译文不可能在各个方面都和原文达到一致，要么有所保留，要么有所变动。误译是不可避免的，也是译文文本中能体现作者翻译观和翻译策略的抉择的重要指征之一。

4.2　译者的文化身份与译者风格

译者的文化身份主要指翻译者所处的文化背景和身份认同，包括译者本人所属的国家、民族和所使用的语言等方面。

张裕禾认为文化身份的内容包括：1）价值观念或价值体系，包括宗教信仰、伦理原则、世界观和人生观、集体和个人的社会理想；2）语言，包括书面语、口语、方言、行话和表达语言的符号；3）家庭体制，包括家庭形式、婚姻关系和家庭内部人与人之间的关系；4）生活方式，主要指衣食住行；5）精神世界，指的是一个民族在历史发展过程中集体记忆里所储存的各种形象（张裕禾、钱林森，2002：73）。

　　文化身份不仅受到个人经历、教育背景、语言能力等因素的影响，还受到所在国家的社会、历史、宗教等方面的综合影响。译者的文化身份在翻译过程中起着至关重要的作用，因其会影响译者对原文的理解和解释，进而影响翻译过程中翻译策略和方法的选择，影响译者的整体风格。

　　"由于生活经历、艺术素养、思想气质的不同，作家、艺术家们在处理题材、结构的布局、熔铸主题、驾驭体裁、描绘形象、运用表现手法和语言等艺术手段方面都各有特色，这就形成作品的个人风格。"（《辞海》，2002：459）

　　方梦之（2004）认为"译者的风格是由其世界观、创作天赋、艺术偏好、审美观念决定的，并在翻译实践中形成和发展起来。"

　　由此可见，译者风格的形成涉及诸多因素，译者在世界观、价值观、道德取向、思维模式、语言习惯、艺术素养等方面的差异都会使译文在语言、内容、风格上显现出个性化特征。

4.2.1　赛珍珠的文化身份探析

　　赛珍珠的文化身份非单一的美国女作家。百度百科对其定义为"以中文为母语的美国女作家、人权和女权活动家"。

　　赛珍珠（Pearl Sydenstricker Buck）于1892年6月26日出生在西弗吉尼亚州的希尔斯伯勒。她的父母阿布索伦和卡洛琳·赛登斯特里克是美南长老会的传教士，派驻在中国。赛珍珠在七个孩子中排行第四（且是仅有的三个活到成年的孩子之一）。她出生时，父母在美国的休假已接近尾声；赛珍珠即被身为传教士的双亲带到中国，在镇江度过了童年、少年，进入到青年时代，前后长达 18 年之久。赛珍珠在中国生活了近 40 年，她把中文称为"第一语言"，把镇江称为"中国故乡"。

赛登斯特里克一家住在江苏省的镇江（当时叫"京口"）。赛珍珠的父亲常常离家数月，在中国乡村四处游历，寻找愿意皈依基督教的人；赛珍珠的母亲则在自己开设的一个小诊所里为中国妇女提供服务。

从儿时起，赛珍珠首先学会了汉语和中国风俗，然后她母亲才教她英语。1900 年因中国北方发生义和团运动，赛珍珠首次回到美国故乡。1910 年，赛珍珠进入弗吉尼亚州林奇堡的伦道夫-梅肯女子学院学习，并于 1914 年毕业。尽管她原本打算留在美国，但毕业不久后，她得知母亲病重的消息，便返回了中国。1917 年赛珍珠结婚后立即搬到了安徽省农村的南宿州（今南徐州）。在这个贫困的地方，赛珍珠积累了后来用于创作《大地》及其他中国题材故事的大量重要的素材。

赛珍珠于 1922 年在庐山牯岭开始尝试写作。1923 年赛珍珠的处女作《也在中国》发表。1925 年，赛珍珠写了短篇小说《一个中国女子的话》，影射她与徐志摩之间的恋情。1931 年春，经出版商建议，赛珍珠将《王龙》一书改名为《大地》（*The Good Earth*），出版后好评如潮，成了 1931 年和 1932 年全美最畅销的书。并且，很快就有了德文、法文、荷兰文、瑞典文、丹麦文、挪威文等译本。赛珍珠于 1935 年荣获普利策奖和豪威尔斯奖章，《大地》在 1937 年被米高梅公司改编成一部重要影片。此后，她的其他小说和其他类书籍也相继问世。1938 年，在她首部作品问世不到十年后，赛珍珠荣获诺贝尔文学奖，成为首位获此殊荣的美国女性。到 1973 年她去世时，赛珍珠已经出版了七十多部作品，涵盖小说、故事集、传记与自传、诗歌、戏剧、儿童文学以及中文翻译作品等诸多类别。

从移居美国那天起，赛珍珠就积极投身于美国的民权和女权运动。她致力于亚洲和西方之间的文化交流，反对种族歧视，为美亚混血儿童提供支持，还创立了赛珍珠基金会，该基金会为亚洲六个国家的数千名儿童提供资助资金。

由此可见，赛珍珠的文化身份具有复杂性和多元性。她首先是出生在美国的美国公民，先后毕业于美国伦道夫-梅肯女子学院和康奈尔大学，接受了系统的西方教育，这为她的文学创作奠定了坚实的西方文化基础，使她在写作技巧、文学理念等方面深受西方文化的熏陶；第二，赛珍珠因为长期生活和工作在中国，深受中国文化影响，对中国社会有着深入的了解和深刻的体验，中国的风土人情、社会百态成为她创作的重要素材。正因如此，赛珍珠的"对中国农民生活丰富而真实的史诗般描述以及她的传记杰作"荣获诺奖；第三，赛珍珠是一位熟练掌握中文语言和文学素养较高的西方作家。她不仅能够阅读和欣赏中国的古典文学作品，还深入研究中国文化典籍，并且习惯按中国姓先名后的顺序使用中国人名，并不采用名前姓后的西方习惯，这体现了她对中国文化传统的尊重和认同（摘自《新京报》）。

唐艳芳（2009）认为，赛珍珠的文化身份实际上已经超越了纯粹的"中国人"或"美国人"范畴，而呈现出典型的杂糅性和"混血"特征，并称其为"文化混血儿"。赛珍珠在《我的中国世界》中称自己"在一个双重世界长大",因此这种特殊的文化身份,双语、双文化的特征使其具有了独特的超越两种文化的视角与洞察力,从而可以在两种文化之间自由切换,去探索两种文化的互补性。

这一特殊的文化身份首先影响的是她的创作。赛珍珠的作品多以中国为背景,以独特的视角和传神的文笔描绘了中国农民的生活,展示了中国传统文化以及社会变革,体现了她对中国人民的同情和对中国文化的热爱。这些作品在向西方读者介绍中国方面发挥了重要作用,改变了西方国家对中国的固有的偏见和误解,尤其是对西方世界对中国的妖魔化的形象产生了巨大冲击和挑战,极大地促进了中西方文化的交流。

其次,也是不容忽视的一点,就是赛珍珠文化混血儿的糅合身份对其翻译产生了显著影响。赛译的异化策略和直译手段一度颇受争议和诟病,例如人尽皆知的"放屁"均译为"pass the wind","青春多少"译为"how many green springs have you passed","面如土色"译作"face turned the color of clay","眼见得"译为"the eye can see", "高姓大名"为"what is your noble surname and your high name"等,这种直译甚至达到了令人瞠目无语的境地,然而一些翻译批评家开始为赛珍珠的误译正名,探讨其直译的初衷和对翻译过程操纵的根本原因及其误译的合理性。

《水浒传》译文正是在复杂的文化身份作用之下,赛珍珠做出的自主选择的集合体。"作为译者的赛珍珠的真正价值在于,她在一个'西学东渐'的时代却自觉选择了一个'东学西渐'的翻译立场;在一个要求译者'隐身'的时代却选择了一个反抗强势文化的角色定位，即'在场'"（唐艳芳，2009：97）。

4.2.2　芮效卫的文化身份探析

百度百科对芮效卫的介绍比较简略：芮效卫原名戴维·托德·罗伊，美国学者，芝加哥大学研究中国文学的荣誉退休教授。1933 年，芮效卫出生于中国南京，抗日战争期间，跟随在金陵大学哲学系教书的父亲芮陶庵，搬到成都华西大学，并在四川待了 7 年。抗日战争胜利后，芮效卫随全家返回美国，1948 年又和全家一起回到南京。1950 年，时年 17 岁的芮效卫在南京秦淮河边一家二手书店找到期待已久的"淫秽之书"——《金瓶梅》，从此与《金瓶梅》结下不解之缘。60 年代，芮效卫开始教授中国文学。1982 年，芮效卫在 20 余年潜心研究的基础上，以万历本为源本，发愿为英语读者提供《金瓶梅词话》真正的全译本。1993 年，译本第一册出版，受到了广泛好评。2001 年，在漫长的八年之后，第二册出版。2013 年译完最后一卷（第 5 卷），从而成为美国汉学界的盛事，11 月 19 日《纽约时报》艺文版以半版篇幅专访芮效卫。

必应国际版词条的介绍较为详细，主要突出了芮效卫作为翻译家的伟大成就，从同事和家人的视角展示了芮效卫翻译《金瓶梅》的所做出的努力和取得的令人瞩目的成就，对于芮效卫的人生经历，也有大篇幅的记述。芮效卫于 1933 年出生在南京，父母都是长老会传教士。他的父亲安德鲁·托德·罗伊（Andrew Tod Roy）曾是南京（金陵）大学的哲学教授，至 1972 年里的大部分时间一直在中国内地和香港等地度过。芮效卫后来被送回美国，完成高中学业。他在哈佛大学获得了学士、硕士和博士学位，此后他从事中国文学课程的教学工作。20 世纪 80 年代，他开始翻译《金瓶梅》，芮效卫本人曾称这部作品是"对一个道德沦丧、腐败不堪的社会极为详尽的描述"。他还在课堂上讲授这部小说，激励了一代又一代的学生投身中国文学研究。

从可获得的资料可见，芮效卫的文化身份首先是研究中国文学的西方学者、专家。他自幼在中国长大，17 岁以后回到美国接受高等教育，1958 年获哈佛大学历史学学士学位，1960 年获哈佛大学历史与东方语言学硕士，5 年后获哈佛大学远东语言文学系博士学位。1963—1967 年，任普林斯顿大学中国文学教授，1967 年起任教于芝加哥大学。芮效卫在哈佛大学历史系时期，师从费正清、海陶玮、史华慈、杨联陞、柯立夫和大卫·霍克斯等知名学者。从 20 世纪 60 年代起，芮效卫先后在普林斯顿大学、芝加哥大学讲授《三国演义》《水浒传》《金瓶梅》《红楼梦》等明清小说和中国历史。因此，芮效卫是西方高等教育体系培养出来的研究中国文学和历史的西方学者，集教学、研究于一身，有着深厚的中国文学功底。

据张义宏（2017）考证，芮效卫早期著述有论文《曹植诗中的弃妇主题》（*The Theme of the Neglected wife in the Poetry of Ts'ao Chih*）、专著《郭沫若的早年生活》（*Kuo Mo-jo：The Early Years*）。芮效卫是英语世界较早开展《金瓶梅》研究的西方学者之一。代表性学术论文有：《张竹坡对〈金瓶梅〉的评论》（*Chang Chu-po's Commentary on the Jin Ping Mei*）、《对〈金瓶梅〉的儒学阐释》（*A Confucian Interpretation of the Jin Ping Mei*）、《汤显祖创作〈金瓶梅〉考》（*The Case for Tang Hsien-Tsu's Authorship of the Jin Ping Mei*）、《论〈金瓶梅〉中歌曲

在自我表达和自我性格塑造的运用》（*The Use of Songs as a Means of Self-expression and Self-characterization in the Jin Ping Mei*）等，著述颇丰，成就斐然。

芮效卫的第二重文化身份是专业型的汉学家。自从未满 17 岁的少年芮效卫在南京的一家二手书店中，意外发现了《金瓶梅》后，他便沉浸在这部作品的丰富内涵中，为文中丰富的俚语表达和浓郁的民俗文化深深打动。芝加哥大学 Tableau 刊物的编辑 Elizabeth Station 曾用"终生迷恋"（a life fascination）一词来形容芮效卫对《金瓶梅》的钟爱。在接受潘佳宁（2024）访谈时，芮效卫讲述了自己如何与中国古典文学，尤其《金瓶梅》结缘的历程。"童年大部分时间随父母在南京、成都、上海多地辗转，所以和弟弟芮效俭（J. Stapleton Roy）从小就接触中文，并且对中国传统文化有种天然的亲切感……父母从南京各高校聘请教授到家里给我俩上课，父亲本人也利用闲暇给我俩介绍中国古诗词……我却对中文书写表现出极大兴趣……我的中文进步明显，很快就能读中文报纸和文学作品"。

出于对中国文学作品和文化的热爱，以及将其展示给英语世界的满腔热情，在芮效卫的译文里，他努力使英文读者感受到原文复杂的结构，领会到繁复精彩的修辞。他将译文中的诗词、谚语、散文、骈文都做了注释。这也是芮译的显著特点和风格之一。

然而，始于少年时期偶发的爱好，后期却能将其转变为自己的研究对象和事业的重心，却不是普通的中文爱好者能做到的。年幼时就开始接受中国文学和文化熏陶的芮效卫走上了教授和研究中国文学的道路，从爱好者到专业人士，他跨越山海，一路走来终成大家。在潘佳宁（同上）访谈录中，芮效卫教授对《金瓶梅》原著的研究深度和广度可略见一斑。

"我始终认为《金瓶梅》是中国文学史乃至世界文学史上里程碑式的作品。首先，与中国同时代问世的几部长篇小说相比，《金瓶梅》是首部由文人独立创作完成的长篇小说。《三国演义》《水浒传》和《西游记》则经历了漫长复杂的成熟过程，即在小说问世之前，相同题材的说唱、戏曲、图像等艺术形式早已在民间流传，形成了相对稳定的故事体系。其次，《金瓶梅》在故事情节上突破了之前几部作品的主题，一改以往长篇小说只关注帝王将相、绿林好汉和神魔鬼怪的叙事传统，转而聚焦世俗男女的日常起居，细致入微地刻画明末社会的众生百态。此外《金瓶梅》的百回篇幅也充分体现了明代章回体小说的结构特征。论结构布局，《金瓶梅》的结构之精巧，中国古典小说中能与之媲美的只有《红楼梦》"。

在接受张义宏（2017）访谈时，芮效卫指出了《金瓶梅》这部小说在文学史上的重要地位，是一部百科全书式的巨著，并为其正名，认为将其认作是一部色情小说是误读，同时指出《金瓶梅》中的观点内容包含文学、经济、政治、历史等多方面，内涵深刻。

芮效卫的第三重身份是学术型的翻译家，作为从事《金瓶梅》等中国文学作品研究的专家，转而成为百万字巨著的译者，这一身份的转变与霍克斯有相同之处，但与其他翻译中国文学作品的译者有着明显的区别。芮效卫的特殊之处在于他的翻译家身份是基于长期从事中国文学的教学和研究。

在接受张义宏（同上）访谈时，芮效卫对《金瓶梅》在西方国家的译介史如数家珍，侃侃而谈，他指出，西方世界《金瓶梅》的译介和传播始于19世纪中叶，至今已有160多年之久。芮效卫从最早的欧洲译本谈起，历数在西方世界经历的"节译片段""节译本""全译本"等阶段和后期出现的不同语言和篇幅长度的欧洲语译本，其专业程度已经超出了译者的范畴。从其访谈中可见，芮效卫不仅是杰出的翻译家，也是一名优秀的翻译研究专家和翻译批评家。正如温秀颖、李兰（2010）的评价："芮译本之所以获得西方读者，特别是美国读者的青睐，主要可归结为三个原因：一是内容全，'是世界文学宝库中第一个最完整的英语译本'；二是质量优，'充分把握了原作的精神实质和文学价值'，运用了恰当的翻译策略和版式体例，满足西方读者的阅读期待；三是价值高，拥有'富于哲理和学术价值的导言'和'极富见地的注释'"。这段文字高度概括了芮译本的成就，也凸显了芮效卫作为专业型的翻译家和学术性的译者的特殊身份。

4.2.3　《聊斋志异》译者文化身份探析

译者的文化身份对译者风格的形成有着不可忽视的影响。

《聊斋志异》的众多译者中，有一位身份特殊、不容忽视的人物，他就是以传教士身份出现的翻译家和汉学家郭实腊（Karl Friedrich August Gützlaff，1803—1851）。

在1842年4月的《中国丛报》（*Chinese Repository*）第十一卷第4期上，郭实腊向英语读者介绍了《聊斋志异》，翻译了其中九则故事，包括《宫梦弼》《武孝廉》《祝翁》《章阿端》《张诚》《曾友于》《续黄粱》《瞳人语》及《云萝公主》。译文虽然简单粗略，且经译者大量删改，但却是目前已知的《聊斋志异》在西方的最早译介。

本文在分析《聊斋志异》的文化误译过程中没有详细提及此译者及其译例，原因在于郭译《聊斋志异》从篇幅上来讲不能算作译本，充其量是几篇介绍性质的译文，其间被郭实腊大量篡改、删减，其改写程度远远超过了误译范畴，因此并没有选取郭译的案例进行文化误译分析和解读，但郭实腊的文化身份最为复杂和特殊，在研究中明显异于其他译者。

郭实腊的身份一直备受争议和诟病。他披着传教士外衣在中国进行搜集情报等间谍活动，借牧师身份在中国上海等地贩卖鸦片，身为翻译家、汉学家的同时却又是帝国主义文化侵略和武力入侵中国的帮凶。

维基百科对其身份的定义是"普鲁士来华新教传教士，曾任香港英治时期的高级官员抚华道"；而百度百科对其身份的概括则是"德国基督教路德会牧师、汉学家、传教士、鸦片贩、间谍"。郭实腊于1831年来华，受英国东印度公司派遣，在上海等地贩卖鸦片的同时，从事间谍活动。1832年曾乘"阿美士德"号在中国沿海航行，以传教和经商为掩护，专门搜集情报。第一次鸦片战争期间，任英国侵略军在舟山的"行政长官"。1842年8月，郭实腊参与签订《南京条约》。之后担任过香港英国当局中文秘书，并参加《圣经》的翻译工作。1851年病故于香港。其外文著述约有70余种，包括英文61篇（部）、德文7篇、荷兰文5篇、日文2篇、逻罗文1篇。其中较著名的包括：《中国史略》《三次航行中国沿海记》《开放的中国——中华帝国概述》《道光皇帝传》等书。郭实腊披着宗教的外衣从事鸦片贸易、进行间谍活动，充当帝国主义文化侵略和武力入侵中国的帮凶，长期以来备受争议。

郭实腊的语言能力和个人智慧毋庸置疑。除了德语外，他精通中文、荷兰文、日文，对中国官话和福建、广东方言也有相当的了解，还了解马来语、暹罗语。郭实腊平生著述多达 80 几种，涉及英语、荷兰语、日语等多语种，所涉及的领域包括历史、地理、经济、科技、金融等方面。尽管郭实腊成就显著，他归根结底是基督教的信徒，他从基督教的中心地位出发，带有强烈的种族优越论，以文化扩张为目的进行文化渗透和文化侵略，"把东方的传统文化视为推行基督教的主要阻力，因而他们致力于从根本上攻击东方的传统文化"（章开沅主编，唐文权著，1991：80）。因此，他的生活经历和求学过程、研习的宗教文化内容决定了其在艺术素养和文化鉴赏力、审美等方面存在欠缺，因此在其译介《聊斋志异》时，并没有像翟理斯等人一样将《聊斋志异》作为文学作品介绍给目的语读者，而是将其列为"异教信仰"类，通过多个故事中的中国人的风俗习惯、宗教文化、行为模式等介绍性文字试图论证中国民众所信仰的道教与佛教思想其本质上是一种迷信思想，持此信仰者是愚昧无知的人群，进而证明道教、佛教与正统的基督教的教义和核心价值观相左，是异教徒的信仰。

郭实腊（1842）对《聊斋志异》的介绍和译文总长 9 页，分作两部分。第一部分可以认为是郭译文的译序，以较长篇幅阐述中国民众的意识形态和宗教信仰，认为"大多数中国人承认精灵鬼怪的存在"，因其"没有受到基督教的有益的影响"从而走入对外部世界的理解和知识启蒙的误区。"中国民众认为自身与另外一个世界（神鬼世界）有着不可割舍的联系，对这一未知的世界的本质无法理解和把握，因此想象宇宙间充斥了无数的精灵鬼怪，妖仙神魔，并对此深信不疑"（郭实腊，1842：202—210）。

对于佛教的和尚和道教的道士的传教活动，郭实腊也持有强烈的质疑并进行了贬低。他认为，与基督教的传教士相比，"中国的和尚、道士之活动未能在政府的政策法规严格制约管理之下进行，因而这些传播迷信的所谓宗教人士无法从政府那里得到资助，"郭还认为中国民众信奉的宗教充满欺骗性，道士的本质无非是骗取无知民众的钱财。对于中国人普遍的信仰，郭实腊予以了蔑视："中国许多信奉佛教和道教的民众并无真正意义上的宗教信仰，其目的无非是在饥寒交迫之时到寺院中寻求救助和庇护而已。"

带着这样的目的和偏见，在《祝翁》译文中，蒲松龄原文中的"济阳祝村"的普通村民祝翁被郭实腊篡改为能够控制自己和妻子生死的"老道"（an old priest of Tau）。此类被肆意篡改、离题万里的译文令人瞠目。郭实腊《祝翁》译文全文通过描绘死而复生的异状仅突出了一个"异"字，而原文中老翁死后对相濡以沫的老妻命运的担忧和二人生死相依的难舍之情只字不提。例如原文中祝翁死而复生后劝导其妻："我适去，拚不复还。行数里，转思抛汝一副老皮骨，在儿辈手，寒热仰人，亦无复生趣，不如从我去。故复归，欲偕尔同行也。"这样的描述世情、人情和亲情的段落多被郭实腊大刀阔斧地删除后加以改写，目的是与序言部分郭实腊的断言"佛道皆为骗术"前后保持一致，因此郭实腊编造了祝翁"老道士"的身份，借以揭示中国民众的信仰实为愚昧荒谬。郭实腊在序言中对道教进行了尖刻的评述，认为"道教在借各种骗术愚民方面落后于佛教。尽管道教也充斥了神鬼之传说，然而普及程度略逊。"

因此，郭实腊进行文化交流和传播的本意是：只有接受基督教的教义，改信基督教才能将中国人从愚昧和迷信中拯救出来。郭实腊对《聊斋志异》的译介目的很明显，就是为在中国传播自己的信仰、进行文化侵略以及以后进行武力入侵做铺垫。

以《聊斋志异》之《瞳人语》为例，小说原文共计 920 字，郭实腊的译文则为简单概述，仅 155 字；《云萝公主》篇，郭实腊删除了近一半的原文内容，因其大量的删减和篡改，严重影响了译文质量，降低了文学作品传播效果。

总之，郭实腊的文化身份对其翻译风格有着显著影响，无论是叙事方式、独特词的用法、对篇章的选择，对内容的肆意的歪曲和大刀阔斧的删减，均带有产生于郭实腊文化身份和历史背景的强烈的偏见。郭实腊在从事翻译活动时，没能够正确理解自身所处的特定历史文化语境从而去克服自身理解的局限性，而是深受其理解的历史性的局限，使其翻译的《聊斋志异》译文成为抬高本民族宗教与文化、贬低并打压东方异质文化的工具。郭译没能够起到向英语世界传播中国优秀文学作品的应有作用，而是被其偏见所左右，使其翻译作品沦为其传播基督教文化、进行文化侵略的工具之一。

出身于英国文化世家的翟理斯与郭实腊有着不同的教育背景。其父约翰·艾伦·贾尔斯（John Allen Giles，1804—1884）是一位有名的牧师，也是一位知名作家。翟理斯很早就学习古希腊罗马神话，研读历史书籍，有着深厚的文学功底。翟理斯虽然没有子承父业成为一名传教者，但是却在文学、文化和翻译领域做出了杰出贡献。

　　1867 年，翟理斯通过了英国外交部的选拔考试来到中国。此后长达 20 多年在中国生活。翟理斯曾在上海、天津等多地担任翻译和领馆的领事。他精通汉语，甚至还熟悉汕头方言。翟理斯在华期间对中国文化的深入体会、潜心学习和研究使其在中国语言和文化方面有着较深的造诣。从中国回到英国后，翟理斯任剑桥大学的汉学教授。在教学之余，他继续潜心研究汉学，向西方世界译介中国文学作品，编著语言教材。

　　翟理斯是一位出色的语言学家。他对汉语学习的主要贡献是他所编著的两部重要教材和一部词典。1872 年时，翟理斯出版了第一本汉学著作：《汉言无师自明》(*Chinese without a Teacher*：*Being a Collection of East and Use Sentences in the Mandarin Dialect*，*with a Vocabulary*)，这是一部专门为初学汉语的外国人编写的汉语语言教材。1874 年，翟理斯又出版了名为《字学举隅》的汉语学习教材。翟理斯负责编著的《华英字典》于 1892 年出版，内容极其丰富，词条众多，释义详细，侧重介绍中国文化。翟理斯还将威妥玛 (Thomas Francis Wade，1818—1895) 的拼音法进行修订，成为后来著名的威氏拼音法 (Wade-Giles System)。该拼音法应用广泛，影响较大，直至今日，仍然在一些代表中国文化的词语中看到威氏拼音的使用。

　　此外，翟理斯撰写了大量的工具书和杂论。然而，翟理斯最重要的身份是文学家和翻译家，他最杰出的贡献是他所翻译的大量中国文学作品，如《闺训千字文》《洗冤录》《聊斋志异》。这些译作与他所编译的《古今诗选》《古文选珍》《中国文学史》等作品一道，展现了中国文学发展的概貌，将中国文学作品译介给英语世界的普通读者和文学研究人员，在中西文化交流史上发挥了重要的作用。

　　翟理斯的文化身份的主要特征是文人，是在西方文学中浸淫的学者，翟理斯在介绍中国文学时同样不可避免地站在西方人的立场上来评价和选译中国文学，在翻译文学作品时，也深受英国小说的主流叙事模式的影响，因此，他摒弃了故事的叙述者在文本之前、之中和文末进行的插入式点评的模式，参照了西方文学作品的叙事模式。翟译从自身的文化身份出发，既顾及于原作者的视域，也充分考虑到读者的期待视域，因而调整了自己的翻译策略，在篇章上舍弃了"异史氏曰"部分，以期符合当时英国文学界的普遍的叙事方式，将自己的视域与读者的视域融合，从而使译本为更多的读者所接受。

　　翟译《聊斋志异》中最明显的特色是其归化的翻译策略。例如人名翻译的归化策略。在《陈云栖》中，原文中女道士说："便道潘郎待妙常已久"，翟译文为"tell the fair Eloisa that her Abelard is awaiting her"。此处潘姓书生被比作 Abelard，陈云栖被称作 Eloisa，两个人名来自 18 世纪英国著名诗人亚历山大·蒲柏（Alexander Pope）的名诗 *Eloisa to Abelard*（艾洛伊斯致亚伯拉德）；又如《孙必振》中主人公的名字被译作 *A Chinese Jonah*（中国的约拿，约拿为《圣经》故事中的先知，曾经在渡海之时为大鱼所吞）；《折狱》被译为 *A Chinese Solomon*（中国的所罗门王，所罗门是以色列最有智慧的国王，传说中以其过人的智慧判冤决狱）；在《夜叉国》中，翟理斯选择以 Cannibals（食人族）代替"夜叉"；在《阎罗宴》中，以西方宗教文化中的炼狱 purgatory 代替中国的"地府"，阎罗成了"the Ruler of Purgatory"（炼狱的统治者）；《贾奉雉》被译成 Rip Van Winkle

（美国小说家华盛顿·欧文小说中的传奇人物，因酒后在山坡上沉睡，醒来时已经是多年之后）等，都采用了本国文化中的固有形象和特有词汇来代替原文中的异国文化负载词语。

从对翟译的语言风格的统计数据中可以看出，翟译类符形符比最高，用词准确，词汇丰富，语言优美，表现力强。因此，从问世至今，翟理斯的译作 *Strange Stories from a Chinese Studio* 一直被认为是翻译的佳作，是译介和传播中华文化过程中的一座里程碑，对《聊斋志异》这部名著在英语世界的经典化做出了贡献。

出版于 20 世纪 80 年代末期的梅译《聊斋志异》的译者之一的梅维恒的文化身份既是汉学家、语言学家，也是涉猎广泛的在中国文化、中外关系史和考古学、文字改革等领域均卓有成就的学者，同时，梅维恒也是一位优秀的翻译家，通过翻译《道德经》《庄子》和《孙子兵法》及与梅丹理合译《聊斋志异》，对中国典籍在西方世界的传播和促进中西文化交流做出了贡献。梅维恒的同胞兄弟梅丹理的文化身份首先是一名诗人，然后是翻译家和汉学家。他的中文造诣较高，能自如地翻译中国古典小说和哲学以及宗教类书籍。梅丹理曾经在台湾、南京、北京都工作生活过，是个有名的"中国通"，他还能用汉语写作诗歌。

因此，梅译《聊斋志异》是汉学家、语言学家、诗人和翻译家携手奉献给世界的一部优秀的译著。

从梅译的词汇层面的统计数据可见，梅译对中国文化中的特殊词汇的处理得当，用词准确，例如其独特词 underworld 一词（对应于原文中的"冥界"一词）中体现出：译者不仅是熟练掌握两种语言的译者，同时也是底蕴深厚的双文化人的身份。因此，两位译者的汉学家、语言学家、诗人、翻译家的综合型的文化身份决定了梅译《聊斋志异》在遣词造句上既有语言学家的严谨、汉学家的精心考证，也有诗歌语言的优美、灵动和精雕细琢，在保持了原作风格的基础之上，尊重原语文化的同时也尊重译语读者，多种翻译策略灵活运用，使梅译成为最成功的译本之一。

可见，梅译的风格与梅丹理、梅维恒兄弟二人的文化身份关系紧密。梅译综合考虑到原语文化传播的重要性，也重视目的语读者的接受程度，因此，译者采取的翻译策略和方法的目的都是使译文最终达到与原文的视域融合，与目的语国家的读者的接受视域融合。

原文：一夕翁赴饮，久不归，生吟益苦。有人徘徊窗外，月映甚悉。怪之，遽出窥觇，则十五六倾城之姝。望见生，急避去。(《聊斋志异》《白秋练》)

在翻译过程中，梅译首先从语言层面忠实地传递原语信息，还原了慕生与白秋练初见时的情景，如"生吟益苦"译作"chanted with a fervor"，"徘徊窗外"译为"walking back and forth outside the window"，"月映甚悉"译作"plainly visible in the moonlight"等，将"拂墙花影动，疑是玉人来"的神秘而浪漫的月夜初见的情景描摹得如诗如画，如在眼前。其次，梅译并没有如多数目的语国家的译者一样，对原文中的文化意象进行归化，从而丧失了原语文化的独特魅力。在此，梅译并没有将"倾城之姝"这一特殊的中国文化意象归化为"Helen of Troy"（特洛伊战争中的绝代佳人海伦，源于荷马史诗），而是保留了原语文化中的独特的文化意象，将此词直译为"the soft of beauty that can bring a city tumbling down"，既可使读者感受到中国文化对美女的独特赞誉方式，也容易使西方读者联想到引起了十年争战最终导致特洛伊城陷落的绝代佳人海伦，从而使读者体会到两种文化的魅力交织，更好地理解原著及译文中传递的丰富的文化信息。

梅译在翻译《聊斋志异》中的文化负载词语时，考虑到了原文与读者之间的时间距离和空间距离可能产生的理解的障碍，梅译时而对原文中的特殊文化意象进行直译加注释，时而采取归化的策略。从而使对于西方读者而言的"陌生的、遥远的、时空中分离出来的东西变成熟悉的、现刻的、跨越时空的东西"（章启群，1998：129），克服了理解的历史性所造成的误读和误解，进行了积极的、建设性的阐释，从而使译本能够为英语读者接受和欣赏，促进了中华文化在西方世界的传播。

《聊斋志异》的重要译者杨宪益夫妇的文化身份，本文将在下一节的《红楼梦》译者的文化身份部分重点探讨。

4.2.4 《红楼梦》译者文化身份探析

提及杨译，无论是《聊斋志异选》的翻译，还是《红楼梦》全译本，都是指杨宪益戴乃迭夫妇共同完成的作品。

杨宪益被奉为"中国最后一位集士大夫、洋博士和革命者于一身的知识分子"、知名翻译家、文化史学者、诗人，作为文化输出国的杰出译者，其文化身份反映了 20 世纪初西学东渐、中西文化交流之初的中国文人的身份的重大变迁。

出身世家的杨宪益有着祖父是前清翰林、父亲是天津中国银行行长的世家、豪门背景，幼年即接受旧学启蒙教育，国学根底厚实。杨宪益幼时所研习的四书五经、文学经典、诗词曲赋等中国文化中的精华，为其打下了深厚的中国语言和文化基础，也使之产生了对中国文化的强烈认同感和自豪感。1928 年杨宪益就读于英国基督教教会开办的天津新学书院，在此期间掌握了英语语言知识，为进一步学习西方语言和文化奠定了基础。1936 年，杨宪益进入牛津大学学习，在牛津大学默顿学院学习古希腊、罗马文学和英国文学。这样的人生经历使杨宪益在打下了深厚的中文基础后又得到了西方文化的熏陶，博采众长、熟练掌握两种语言的同时又具备了较高的跨文化素养，这些都为杨宪益从事文学翻译事业奠定了基础并产生了深远影响。

杨宪益的文化身份注定他将成为中西方文化交流的使者，成为一名笔耕不辍的优秀译者。幼年时对中文典籍的学习使杨宪益对传播中国优秀文学作品产生了浓厚兴趣，在英国的学习更加使杨宪益萌发了促进东西方文化交流、译介中国优秀文学作品、填补西方对中国文学了解的空白的强烈愿望。

在提及杨宪益时，不容忽视的是"杨宪益背后的女人"，他的英国籍妻子戴乃迭。戴乃迭对杨宪益的支持和帮助、向英语世界译介中国文学作品的贡献同样是同样重要的。戴乃迭具有东西交融的双重民族文化身份，这一属性"使她既能充分理解原作的精神，在翻译时尽力传递原作的风味，同时又能关注泽入语读者的阅读习惯，避免生硬拗口的译文，使读者能够充分享受到阅读的乐趣"（王惠萍，2014：180）。

戴乃迭凭借其对母语英语的自如运用和对中国文化的热爱与深入了解，与杨宪益珠联璧合、中西互融，携手笔耕数十载，进行了大量的中译英工作，合译的中国名著和作品集几乎涵盖了整个中华历史时期，几乎涉及了所有的文学种类，将上百万字的中国文学作品译成了英文，为弘扬中华文化做出了巨大贡献。

由于杨译是杨宪益与戴乃迭共同完成，因此杨译的作品集中西文化于一身，二人的跨文化身份和多元文化观也在翻译中国文学作品中体现出文化的平等和中西文化的共融。在词汇的使用上、对篇章的选取、对"异史氏曰"部分的处理上，杨译都尽力忠实地向目的语读者展示原文中的文化历史知识，用词讲究精确，行文造句最大限度地接近原文；同时尽可能准确地传达原作的意蕴和风格。

杨宪益与戴乃迭特殊的文化身份决定了二人在翻译时的用词风格和行文特点，以及对所译内容的取舍、对翻译策略的选择。由于理解的历史性而产生的偏见，郭实腊的《聊斋》翻译中出现大量删除和篡改，在翟译中也有部分删节和改写，而在杨宪益夫妇的《聊斋志异》译介中则体现为忠实的特征。

原文：曰："阿甥已十七矣，得非庚午属马者耶?"（选自《聊斋志异》《婴宁》）

杨译："So you're seventeen already," remarked the old woman. "Were you born in the year of the horse* ? （译者脚注：Chinese chronology was computed in cycles of twelve years, and each year was marked by a symbolical animal. ）

在这一译例中，对原文中的"属马"，杨译不仅忠实于原文，译为 born in the year of the horse，为了有效传播原语文化，杨译还通过注释手段进行补充说明，解释了属相由来：中国的年表是以十二年为一个周期计算的，每年都用一种象征性的动物来标记，因此其译文忠实准确，没有对原文中特有的文化现象采取回避和删改的手段，旨在向外国读者展示中国特有的属相文化。再看《红楼梦》的其他译文：

原文：他父亲给他娶了个媳妇，今年才二十岁，也有几分人材，又兼生性轻薄，最喜沾花惹草。（《红楼梦》第二十一回）

杨译：While he was young his parents had found him a wife who was now just about twenty, and whose good looks were the admiration of all. But she was a flighty creature who loved nothing better than to have affairs.

原著中贾府的厨子多浑虫嗜酒如命却娶了美貌妖娆，轻狂无比的老婆，众人都叫她"多姑娘儿"。杨译将"有几分人材"译为 whose good looks were the admiration of all，"生性轻薄"译为 she was a flighty creature，"最喜沾花惹草"译为 who loved nothing better than to have affairs，一字不漏地描绘了外表美貌，为众多男子所爱慕追求，本质上轻浮易变，又常与他人有婚外不伦恋的风流女子多姑娘的形象。其中的 flighty，creature，have affairs 准确生动地勾勒了人物形象，将其鲜活生动地呈现在读者面前。成语"拈花惹草"出自元·杨立斋《哨遍》："三国志无过说些战伐，也不希咤，终少些团香弄玉，惹草沾花"，意为"挑逗、勾引异性，到处留情"，杨译采取了意译方法，符合成语的比喻意义。

杨氏夫妇的译介活动植根于中国文化，出于对中国文化的热爱和促进中西文化交流的目的，正如戴乃迭曾经说过："我来中国不是为了革命，也不是为了学习中国的经验，而是出于我对杨宪益的爱，我儿时在北京的美好记忆，以及我对中国文化的仰慕之情。"因此二人携手同行，译海泛舟，将忠实、优雅的文风贯穿二人的译介生涯。因此，杨译的翻译风格与两位译者的文化身份、人生经历紧密相关。二人各自的文化身份合二为一后，在传播中华文化过程中无往不利，笔耕不辍，高质量的译著不断问世。杨氏夫妇的中西合璧的特殊文化身份具有全球化的特征，在全球多元文化语境下，有效地传播了中华文化，在中国翻译史上书写了一页页璀璨的篇章。

作为杨译的对照组的霍克斯译本，其译者的文化身份并非复杂，但霍克斯的人生经历却涉及多元文化，因此也注定其译介人生的不平凡。

1923 年 7 月 6 日，霍克斯出生在英国伦敦东部。他在公立中学就读时便展露出语言学习上的天赋，在法语和德语之外，又被老师选中学习拉丁语。1942 年，霍克斯获得牛津大学"开放奖学金"，进入基督教会学院古典学专业学习。一年后他应召入伍，在情报部门工作。二战结束后，霍克斯再次进入牛津大学学习，改学中文专业，师从传教士 ER Hughes（修中诚）。然而当时的汉学科课程设置局限于四书五经，霍克斯开始读的是《大学》，然后读《论语》《诗经》《易经》《礼记》，再后来是《道德经》《庄子》。对于中文几乎零基础的英国学生，研读这些典籍的困难可想而知，但霍克斯并没有退缩，坚持苦读了两年半时间。在此期间，霍克斯对自己中文功底不满意，尤其认为自己的中文听说能力差，于是 1948 年，26 岁的霍克斯在英国政府奖学金的资助下，由海路辗转，历时一个月来北京大学中文系就读。读书期间，他尝试翻译了《红楼梦》片段，但并没有继续下去。就读不久后他即见证了新中国成立，参加了开国大典，这是一段颇具传奇色彩的经历。三年留学生活，给霍克斯留下了终生的美好回忆。这个城市的语言、文化和氛围，对他产生了不可磨灭的影响。北京话也正是《红楼梦》人物所说的语言，北京这座城市极大地激发了他的想象力，为他日后翻译《红楼梦》提供了动力。

1951年，霍克斯学成归国，继续在牛津攻读研究生，1953年受聘为汉学科讲师，与著名红学家吴世昌成为同事。他们一道开设了现代的中文课，收入了鲁迅和明清小说，1955年霍克斯获得该校博士学位。毕业后，霍克斯留校任教，教授汉语和中国文学课程，1959年被牛津大学聘为教授，这一年，36岁的霍克斯发表了《楚辞》英文版。在接下来的任职期间，霍克斯推动牛津专业汉学的确立与完善，培养汉学专业人才，为牛津大学出版社主编牛津东亚文学丛书，先后组织出版多部中国古代诗文的译研著述，影响波及西方汉学界。1970年，霍克斯抓住了和企鹅出版社合作的机会，启动了《红楼梦》120回的全本翻译工作，为了全身心投入到翻译工作中，他辞去了牛津大学中文系主任的教职，潜心译介，耗费10年的时间，翻译了《红楼梦》前80回，最后四十回由霍克斯的女婿汉学家约翰·闵福德完成。霍克斯的《红楼梦》英文版在西方世界独领风骚，是经久不衰的经典之作。

霍克斯的译作包括：《楚辞：南方之歌——中国古代诗歌选》(The Songs of the South：An Anthology of Ancient Chinese Poems by Qu Yuan and Other Poets)，《杜诗初阶》(A Little Primer of Tu Fu)，此外，霍克斯对中国的戏剧也进行了深入研究，尤其是元代杂剧，代表译作有《柳毅与龙公主》，又名《元杂剧（洞庭湖柳毅传书）》(Liu Yi and the Dragon Princess) 等。霍克斯还著有《中国的传统、现代与人文》《中国诗歌与英国读者》《象征主义小说〈红楼梦〉》《石头记英译笔记》等著作（王丽耘，2013：161)。

霍克斯的文化身份包括：第一，著名汉学大师，对中国文化有着极其深刻的造诣，是英国汉学家中的佼佼者。霍克斯借鉴历史分析等传统中西学术研究方法，综合自如地运用西方新史学理论、接受传播学理论、文本发生学理论、文本细读理论、跨文化研究理论、文化诗学及文化传递中的误读、误释理论等汉学领域、翻译领域、社会历史领域和比较文学领域的最新理论成果，在六十余年的汉学生涯成为英国专业汉学的奠基人与中坚力量。霍克斯的汉学研究坚持人文主义原则，广涉楚辞、汉赋、杜诗、宋词、元曲、明清小说及现代文学等领域（王丽耘，2013：8）。

第二重身份：红学大师，在红学研究领域，研究颇为深入。霍克斯热爱中国文化，更是为《红楼梦》的魅力所征服。在 2002 年霍克斯写给刘士聪先生的信中，他说："我认为，所有翻译红楼梦的人都是首先被它的魅力所感染，然后才着手翻译的，期望能把他们所感受到的小说的魅力传达一些给别人。译者的方法可能有所不同，成就也有高低，但所有译者都感到一种很大的冲动；因为我也是其中的一员"（转引自王鹏飞，2014：73）。

霍克斯与杨宪益不同，后者说他并不喜欢看《红楼梦》，小时候读一半就读不下去了；霍克斯是基于对这部文学巨著的热爱才投身于翻译当中，且其本人对《红楼梦》原著的谙熟程度、研究深度完全可以跻身红学家之列。在商务印书馆 2023 年出版的霍克斯翻译红楼梦的《英译笔记》一书中，霍克斯留下的文字和图例无一不昭示了他对《红楼梦》原著的深入钻研和所获取的红学研究的宝贵的第一手资料。

第三重身份：翻译家。霍克斯曾说过："我开始翻译这部小说后，感到了无穷的乐趣，我想好吧，我从来不觉得自己是个很好的教授；这才是我真正擅长的事情，我应该成为一名翻译家而不是一位教授"。霍译《红楼梦》因其译笔传神、流畅，被学界公认为汉译英的经典，也实现了他 1961 年在牛津汉学教授的就职演说中曾经立下的豪言壮志："我们须得使中国文学成为整个人类文化遗产的一部分"。

霍克斯作为通晓多门外语的翻译家加上母语优势，使其译笔堪与第一流的英语文学作品媲美。针对《红楼梦》中的神通广大又来无踪、去无影的神仙、道士、和尚、尼姑等人物时，霍克斯为了突出其神秘色彩和神奇力量，还特意用拉丁语来翻译这些神仙的名字。例如空空道人译为 Vanitas，茫茫大士译为 Impervioso，渺渺真人译为 Mysterioso，妙玉译为 Adainantina，智能译为 Sapientia。

霍克斯的翻译从来都是一丝不苟，反复考证研究。为了翻译一个人名、一句诗句，为了厘清众多场景的方位或繁复的人物关系而犹豫反复、字斟句酌。在 2023 年出版的《英译笔记》就通过霍克斯翻译全过程中留下的笔记文字详细展现了译者高度负责的专业精神和为翻译事业付出的每一滴辛勤汗水。在这部笔记中，读者可以看到霍克斯手绘的《红楼梦》各种人物关系图和地理方位图，其细致和精准程度令人叹服。

霍克斯为何用了十年时间才翻译完成《红楼梦》？其间为了翻译所参考、阅读的深度与广度，都足以解释这漫长十年里译者付出的艰苦和繁重的劳动。《英译笔记》出版当年，新京报（2023）介绍：为了理解"星宿不利"到底是什么意思，霍克斯参考了《大正藏》的七种佛典。语言方面，《佩文韵府》《国语辞典》《北京话语汇》《小说词语汇释》是他常用的参考书。而史部要籍，他参考过并且留下记录的有《汉书》《后汉书》《新唐书》《唐书·乐志》《宋书》《南史》《明史》等。还有其他常用书如《诸子集成》《六十种曲》《曲海》《中国戏曲史》《古今小说》《唐宋传奇集》，专书如《中国医学大辞典》《中国药学大辞典》《中国植物图鉴》《清代货币金融史稿》。

霍克斯在翻译《红楼梦》时，努力做到逐字逐句地翻译，从不偷懒取巧，连双关语、诗词的不同格式都要表现出来。正如他在译序中所写："我自始至终恪守一个原则，把所有一切甚至双关语都译出来"。

原文：富贵又何为？襁褓之间父母违；展眼吊斜晖，湘江水逝楚云飞。（《红楼梦》第五回）

霍译：

What shall avail you rank and riches,

Orphaned while yet in swaddling bands you lay?

Soon you must mourn your bright sun's early setting.

The Xiang flows and the Chu clouds sail away.

这首判词原文中藏"湘云"两字，是史湘云的判词。然而，诗中蕴含的深层文化信息是"湘江"和"楚云"两个典故。湘江是娥皇、女英二妃哭舜之处，象征着悲伤和离别，此处喻其夫妻生活的短暂；而"楚云"则来源于宋玉的《高唐赋》，讲述了楚怀王梦见巫山神女的故事，象征着短暂而美丽的爱情或梦境。霍译文准确达意，诗歌韵律优美，画面唯美生动，对双关语的翻译采取了直译，完整译出了湘江和楚云两个意象。诗中 bright sun's early setting, the Xiang flows and the Chu clouds sail away 为落日余晖、湘江水逝、楚云易散，这三个意象形成了一幅如诗的画面：云聚云散，欢乐从来无法挽留；白日将尽，斜阳余晖空惹人愁；江水东流，悲伤如斯平添烦忧。译者不仅在抒写史湘云的悲剧命运，也在感慨人生的落寞、事与愿违和命运的难以捉摸。同时，霍克斯译诗中的意象与原文判词的配图完全一致：几缕飞云，一湾逝水，便是如花少女凄凉一生的预示和写照。因此霍译的《红楼梦》诗词之优美完全可以与英语诗歌媲美，译者的巧妙构图和再创造体现得淋漓尽致。

王丽耘（2013）认为："霍译本的最大突破点在于完整翻译了原文中大量诗词，不仅完整传达了诗词的内容，还兼顾了诗歌形式，将原文的阅读效果最大限度地展示给西方读者。霍克斯根据诗词意象翻译方法中体现的文化差异，选取多种频率高、译法多样、具有代表性的意象，归纳基本含义并进行比较。他的译法体现的中西文化差异主要在于同一意象在不同文化语境下信息量和含义的差异，其诗词意象充分理解了意象在诗词乃至中国文化语境中的意蕴和作用，为后人提供了成功经验"。

由此可见，霍克斯的《红楼梦》英译本，不仅推动了中国文学在世界范围内的传播，其译本本身也是一部供译者和学者进行翻译研究的宝典。

泰勒（1998）认为，身份问题与意义和价值相关，因此，在"身份"与"取向"之间存在基本的联系。译作的成功离不开翻译家的呕心沥血和十年一译的执着精神，而究其根源，译者的文化身份也对译文质量和翻译风格起到深刻影响甚至定位和定向的作用。译者对原著的选取，对翻译过程的操控，翻译方法的选取，语言风格的把握，均植根于译者的文化身份当中，反过来个人的文化身份不可避免会对其翻译行为造成影响。

4.3　历史文化语境与译者风格

胡开宝（2011）认为："尽管译者自身因素是译者风格形成的关键原因，然而译者并非生活在真空之中，译者对原语文本的选择，以及译者翻译策略和方法的应用都会受到具体历史时期的社会意识形态、审美观和翻译规范等因素的制约"。

因此，译者受其所处的历史文化语境的制约，在翻译过程中，对词汇的选择、对翻译策略的偏好、对篇章的选择和对内容的增删都与译者在翻译该作品时所处的历史和文化的整体背景有着密切关联。

4.3.1　赛珍珠译《水浒传》的历史文化语境

赛珍珠翻译《水浒传》所处的历史文化语境具有多方面特点：首先是当时的中国处于社会动荡与变革之中。20世纪初的中国内忧外患，面临着诸多问题和挑战，如帝国主义列强的侵略、封建统治的腐朽等，社会矛盾激化，启蒙思想抬头，有识之士渴望变革与进步，《水浒传》中所蕴含的原始民主思想及对社会现实的反映，与当时中国社会对民主、民权思想的探索相呼应。赛珍珠在中国期间经历了新文化运动，这一运动倡导民主与科学，反封建礼教和旧传统，对中国社会的思想观念、文化教育等方面产生了深刻影响。赛珍珠受到其熏陶，关注中国社会的变革与发展，也促使她更深入地思考中国文化与西方文化的差异与融合。

　　另外尤为重要的一点是，当时的中国正处于西学东渐的潮流中，中国也希望将自身的优秀文化传播到西方，以消除西方世界对中国的误解，增进西方对中国的了解，减少文化隔阂。赛珍珠鉴于这种文化交流的需求，翻译《水浒传》顺应了时代趋势。

　　作为双文化人的赛珍珠，研究其翻译的历史文化语境自然要研究当时西方社会的背景。19 世纪以来，多数西方人心目中的中国和中国人形象偏于刻板甚至扭曲，中国文化被神秘化、离奇化。为了满足西方民众对真实的中国的好奇和探究，赛珍珠试图通过文学创作和翻译中文作品以打破西方对中国的误解，向西方读者展现一个真实的中国。

　　赛珍珠翻译《水浒传》符合 20 世纪的西方文学呈现出的多元化的发展趋势。西方读者对不同文化背景下的文学作品的阅读有了新的需求。《水浒传》作为一部具有独特魅力和深刻思想内涵的中国古典名著，因其鲜活的人物形象和丰富的情节、所呈现的多彩的社会文化，迎合了西方读者的阅读需求，译文能够满足他们的期待视域。

　　从更广阔的视角看，赛珍珠翻译《水浒传》符合文化交流与融合的趋势。赛珍珠的时代处于全球化的初期阶段，不同文化之间的交流与融合开始加强。赛珍珠的跨文化身份和她对中西方文化的深入了解，使她能够自如地游走于两种文化之间，通过文学作品的译介促进东西方的文化交流。

4.3.2　芮效卫译《金瓶梅》的历史文化语境

　　芮效卫译《金瓶梅》的时代是 20 世纪后期，这一时期到 21

世纪初，西方对中国文化的探究转为深入，西方世界对中国文学经典的关注度持续上升。《金瓶梅》作为中国古代世情小说的杰出代表作品，其丰富的社会文化内涵引起了西方学者和一般读者的浓厚兴趣，期望通过《金瓶梅》这一类的世情文学来了解中国古代社会的人际关系、道德伦理、世情人情和丰富的社会文化。

这一时期，文化多元主义在西方社会盛行，强调不同文化之间的平等和相互尊重。这一思潮促使西方读者以更开放和包容的心态去接受异质文化和其他民族的文艺创作成果。芮效卫在翻译《金瓶梅》过程中充分考虑到了文化多元主义，他努力在传递中国文化和满足西方读者的期待视域、符合其阅读习惯之间实现平衡，运用多种翻译方法，尽力避免引起误解和文化冲突。

芮效卫译《金瓶梅》是在中国文化"走出去"战略的历史文化语境中开展和完成的。中国政府和文化机构积极推动中国文化"走出去"，在这一大背景下，《金瓶梅》这一类的经典文学作品的翻译备受瞩目，也得到了多方支持。当时西方汉学研究的发展也取得了较大成果，基础较为坚实，为芮效卫的翻译提供了学术支持，使其能借鉴前人的研究成果，更好地完成翻译工作。同时，在东西方文化交流不断加强的语境下，芮效卫有更多机会与中国学者、文学家、文化界人士交流，获取关于《金瓶梅》的最新研究成果和更准确的文化解读，从而使他的《金瓶梅》译本翻译质量得到提升。他的译本为西方读者了解丰富的中国文化提供了窗口，有助于促进东西方文化交流。

4.3.3　《聊斋志异》译者所处的历史文化语境

郭实腊的译文的产生背景是在 19 世纪 40 年代，正是西方列强虎视眈眈东方诸国、迅速开始殖民主义者侵略扩张的历史时期。郭实腊与其同时代的绝大多数的文化输入国的译者一样，深受西方文化中心主义意识和种族优越论的影响，在西方文化和宗教与中国文化相碰撞、交流的过程中存在着强烈的偏见，和同时期的很多西方译者一样，"流露出强烈的'西方文化中心主义'意识，在翻译过程中用西方的诗学观念和意识形态指导着自己的翻译过程，翻译策略上多选取一种迁就译入语文化的归化策略。此外，为了其特定的翻译目的，他们在翻译过程中经常有意识地采取删减、增添、改写等方式操纵原文，结果导致中国文化和中国形象在翻译过程中的扭曲和变形"（李海军，2011：79）。

在郭实腊译介《聊斋志异》的案例中，译者在 19 世纪特殊的殖民文化语境中，没有从主观上去克服自身理解的局限性，形成全球化的视野，从多元文化的视角去传播异质文化，平等对待异国文化，反而是利用这种理解上的固有的偏见，使其译介成为抬高本民族文化、贬低并打压异质文化的工具。

《聊斋志异》的另一位译者翟理斯译介《聊斋志异》的时代特点是：维多利亚时代是英国的鼎盛时期，工业飞速发展，英国本土的文学创作繁荣、各种文艺流派和众多世界级的作家不断涌现。同时，随着第二次鸦片战争的结束，帝国主义列强用枪炮彻底打开了闭锁多年的东方古国的大门后，东西方经济贸易、文化交流逐渐增多、古老的东方帝国神秘的面纱慢慢揭开。在这一特定历史条件下，翟理斯来到中国工作，接触了中国文化，对中国文学产生了浓厚的兴趣，编著了学习汉语的语言教材、翻译了大量中国文学作品，并编写工具书等。翟理斯作为文化交流中的先驱者，作为外交人员首先意识到了在中西交流中学习中文的重要意义，同时在这样一个西学东渐的时代，翟理斯也敏锐地感觉到：反其道而行之，能够满足英语读者对神秘东方的好奇心和求知欲。

在翻译过程中，翟理斯针对原语和目的语文化之间的差异，大量采用归化策略，使目的语文本易为本国读者所接受。同时，作为维多利亚时代的学者和文学家，翟理斯由于自身理解的历史性的制约和对读者接受能力的时代性考虑，自创作之初就带着一种强调道德教化的偏见，对原作中的性爱描写进行了彻底的删除或含蓄的改写，以期达到使文本纯洁的目的，这样的方法符合当时的主流诗学观。同样，翟译删除了"异史氏曰"部分，也是为了使译文符合翟理斯所处的时代英国小说的主流叙事模式。

梅译《聊斋志异》的时代背景是 20 世纪后期，时值中国对外开放进一步加强，文化界逐步从文化大革命的冰冻期快速回暖，翻译出版的目的是增强西方世界对中国文化的了解，加强中西文化交流和融合，因此对中国经典文学作品的翻译提出的要求是"力求全面而准确地反映中国文学及中国文化的基本面貌和灿烂成就"。在这一大背景之下，梅氏兄弟不可避免地将自己的翻译行为与时代紧密结合起来，在特定的文化语境中深入思考译者与读者的关系、译者与出版赞助方的关系、译者与时代的关系、读者与时代的关系、译者与原作者的历史间距、译者对原著的解读方式等因素并最终确定翻译目的、翻译内容和相应的翻译策略。表现在翻译策略上，梅译主要运用了异化手段，对中国文化特有的负载词语采取直译加注释的方法。梅译的词汇量也较丰富，语言优美富有表现力，在篇章层面也保持了原文的完整，忠实地再现了原文的故事情节和思想内涵，对"异史氏曰"也进行了准确的翻译，领会并体现了原著精髓。

4.3.4 《红楼梦》译者所处的历史文化语境

在 20 世纪中叶杨宪益着手翻译《红楼梦》时，世界处于冷战的大环境中。一方面，东西方之间存在意识形态的分歧和对立；另一方面，各国之间也有相互了解的潜在需求。中国作为一个有着悠久历史文化的国家，希望打破西方对中国国家形象和中国文化的误解和偏见。通过翻译《红楼梦》等经典文学作品，可以向西方展示中国文化的深度和广度，这是一种文化外交的策略。鉴于冷战格局下的文化交流的需要，中国希望通过优秀文学作品的翻译和对外传播，向世界展示自身文化魅力，提升国际形象，增强文化软实力。

杨宪益夫妇接受翻译《红楼梦》的任务时，中国国内正经历社会变革与文化转型，对传统文化的研究与传承受到重视，《红楼梦》作为中国古典文学的巅峰之作，其翻译对于对外传播中国传统文化、增强民族自豪感具有重要意义。从翟理斯等汉学家翻译中国文学作品开始，即使到了 20 世纪中后期，西方对中国文化的了解仍相对有限。《红楼梦》中丰富的文化内涵对于西方读者来说较为陌生，翻译难度较大，对译者准确忠实地传递中国文化提出了挑战。

20 世纪中期以来，红学研究在国内蓬勃发展，众多学者对《红楼梦》的研究取得了大量成果，为翻译工作提供了丰富的学术资源和理论支持。因此杨宪益夫妇在翻译过程中，充分吸收了当时的学术研究成果，注重对原著文化内涵的准确传达，使译本具有较高的学术价值。

　　以上历史文化语境推动了杨译《红楼梦》高质量完成，同时，杨译《红楼梦》顺应了加强对外宣传、推广文学经典、传播中华文化的历史潮流。

　　因此杨宪益夫妇在翻译工作中，在进行语言转换的同时高度重视中华文化的有效输出。杨译尽可能地保持原文本中丰富的文化内容，通过异化手段将文化意象和历史典故原汁原味地呈现给西方读者，同时杨译也考虑到目的语读者的接受程度，因此多以直译加注的方法来帮助读者理解原语文化，从而在阅读的过程中接受译文所承载的历史文化信息。杨译的翻译策略和具体翻译方法的选择是杨氏夫妇所处的时代的历史性所决定的，同时时代也赋予了他们特有的翻译目的：通过译介中国优秀文学作品，向西方读者展示中国文化的真实面貌，提升中国文化的国际地位，同时推动东西方文化的交流与融合。

　　霍克斯翻译《红楼梦》所处的语境首先是西方世界对东方文化的浓厚兴趣时期。20 世纪后半叶，西方对东方文化的探求日益增强。随着全球化进程的加快，跨文化交流更加频繁。西方读者渴望了解中国这个古老国家的文化、社会和价值观。《红楼梦》作为中国古典文学的杰出代表和巅峰之作，自然成为西方文化界关注的对象。霍克斯的翻译工作顺应了这一文化潮流，满足了西方读者想要深入了解中国文化的需求。

　　同时，西方汉学蓬勃发展，许多西方学者致力于研究中国的语言、文学、历史等诸多领域。这为霍克斯翻译《红楼梦》提供了一个良好的学术环境，他可以参考众多西方汉学家对中国文化和《红楼梦》的前期研究成果。例如，西方汉学家对中国古典诗词格律、中国古代社会制度等方面的研究成果，都有助于霍克斯理解和翻译《红楼梦》中复杂的内容。

　　霍克斯翻译《红楼梦》的另一背景是文化相对主义的兴起。人们开始认识到不同文化各自的价值和特点。这种观念促使霍克斯以更加尊重和理解的态度去解读《红楼梦》原著，去翻译《红楼梦》中的各种文化信息。他试图在翻译中保留中国文化的原汁原味，而不是简单地将中国文化元素西方化。例如，在翻译书中的中国传统礼仪、风俗习惯等内容时，他会尽力通过注释等方式向西方读者解释清楚这些文化现象的内涵。

　　霍克斯翻译《红楼梦》的理论背景是文学翻译理论稳步发展的阶段。当时的翻译理论更加注重功能对等和文化传递。尤金·奈达的功能对等理论对霍克斯产生了一定的影响。霍克斯在翻译《红楼梦》时，不仅关注语言层面的转换，更注重在目标语文化中再现原语文化的特质。同时，动态对等理论也引导他在翻译时考虑西方读者的接受能力。例如，对于《红楼梦》中的诗词翻译，霍克斯既要保留诗词的意境和美感，又要让西方读者能够理解诗词所表达的情感色彩，因此霍译本采用了灵活的翻译策略，如调整句式结构、意象转换等。

　　此外，霍克斯的翻译风格体现了英国文学传统对其翻译再创造的影响。英国文学注重叙事的连贯性和逻辑性，他在翻译过程中可能会对《红楼梦》的叙事结构进行适当的调整，以便更好地符合西方读者的阅读习惯。霍克斯在译文中，涉及人物描写和心理刻画时也遵循英国文学的传统。他将人物的内心独白、情感变化等内容细致而准确地翻译成目的语，更加注重挖掘和传达人物的心理深度，使西方读者能够更好地理解《红楼梦》中复杂的人物关系和情感世界，从而体会到这部中文经典名著的恒久魅力。

4.4　小结

基于语料库翻译研究所常用的软件对明清小说的代表作品进行分析，对语言层面所涉及的词汇、句子特征进行量化分析和比较，通过对词长、平均句长、高频词、独特词等进行分析比较，本文对所涉及的诸位译者的翻译风格进行了探讨，通过量化呈现，科学地展示了译者风格上的差异与特色。

译者风格差异产生的根源首先是由于译者文化身份的特殊性。译者的文化身份对其翻译风格有着深远的影响。文化身份不仅包括译者的民族背景、语言能力、教育程度和社会经历，还涉及其个人的价值观、信念和审美取向。译者语言水平与表达习惯、译者的价值观与审美取向、译者的文化敏感度、译者身份认同与自我定位、译者对读者期待与市场需求的了解程度、译者在跨文化交流中的自我认知均会影响他们如何在翻译中传达文化信息，进而影响翻译风格的形成。

译者的文化身份在多个层面上影响其翻译风格。这种影响是复杂而多样的，既包括语言的风格和翻译策略的选择，也涉及对文化差异的理解和处理方式。

如果说译者的文化身份是影响译者风格的内在因素，那么历史文化语境对译者的影响则是来自外部的力量。"翻译不是在真空中进行的，总是要受到译者所处历史文化语境的影响。翻译活动总是发生在某一特定社会的某一特定时期中，因此，译者的翻译行为便不可避免地打上了译者所处历史文化语境的烙印"（李海军，2014：131）。历史文化语境是一个复杂而深刻的主题，涉及语言、文化、社会和历史等多个层面。译者翻译某部作品所处的历史时期对译者的翻译风格和策略有重要影响。例如，在某些历史时期，特定的意识形态或政治环境可能会影响译者的选择，导致某些内容被强调或被淡化。此外，不同历史时期的译者的伦理观念也会影响其翻译策略，出版商和赞助机构的倾向性也同样影响译者的译作风格。

第五章　结论

5.1　研究的主要发现与结论

本文梳理了明清小说中极具代表性的《水浒传》《金瓶梅》《红楼梦》和《聊斋志异》四部作品的英译本在英语世界的传播，来分析其翻译研究现状，对明清小说误译的研究进行了概述，对四部经典文学作品的多个英译本中的误译现象进行分析，同时对误译成因进行研究探索，研究从误读到误译的整个认知过程，探讨译本中无意误译、有意误译和文化误译问题，并从诠释学、误读理论进行解读和分析，探究有意的文化误译本身的积极因素，研究误译在文化传播中的价值，力图从误译研究中得出有益于文化传播的翻译策略，研究误译与译介效果的关联，译者的文化身份、历史文化语境导致的风格特征和差异与译介效果的关联等，以期利用误译研究推动中文经典作品向英语世界的有效译介和高质量传播。

研究后有如下发现：

首先，本文通过对《水浒传》赛珍珠译本和沙博理译本的对比分析、《金瓶梅》芮效卫译本的误译梳理、《聊斋志异》的郭实腊译文、翟理斯、杨宪益夫妇、梅氏兄弟译本的翻译差异研究、对《红楼梦》的霍克斯译本和杨译本的比较分析，运用大量误译案例，对物质文化、社会文化、宗教文化、语言文化、生态文化五大类文化负载词进行了深入的研究，发现在跨文化交流中，译者往往基于自己所处的历史文化语境，从自身的文化身份和偏好出发，选择翻译策略和方法，因而导致各具特色的文化误译和翻译风格的差异。然而，译者必须克服历史文化语境和各自的前见，综合运用多种翻译方法，才能达到译者、原作者和读者之间的视域融合，使文化输出的策略最优化，最大程度上有利于文化的传播。

在 19 世纪中西方文化交流的初始阶段，归化翻译有其积极的一面，但是随着经济文化全球化的不断发展，语言和文化的不断交流、融合，在跨文化翻译中一概采取归化的翻译策略已不利于世界范围内的语言文化的多样化发展。本文研究发现，任何一位译者都没有单一地采取归化或者异化策略，或全文仅进行了直译或者意译，分析后发现译者均对翻译策略进行了最优化和有机整合，虽然在个人特征上，某些译者直译所占比重较高，某些译者归化策略是主要的翻译手段，某些译者异化特征显著，但通观全文，研究的译本中均出现了归异并存、直意交替的情形。

第二个发现是：采用语料库翻译学的研究模式和技术手段分析译本后发现，译者的文化身份、译者所处的历史文化语境等因素对译者翻译风格的形成也有着不容忽视的影响。译者的有意误译也是译者翻译风格的重要特色之一。有意误译的表现形式即包含了大量使用直译或者异化策略，或者译本体现出鲜明的归化倾向，从而产生了译者总体风格的差异。译者对不同词语的偏好，句长的差异、高频词和特色词的使用差异，都在相当大的程度上反映了译者的翻译观和文化观。因此在中华文化典籍外译过程中，译者务必要克服理解的历史性的局限性，发挥译者的自身文化身份的积极作用，优化翻译策略，正确处理文化差异，在译介活动中有效地弘扬原语文化，推动中文经典作品向英语世界的传播。

第三个发现：文化输出国和文化输入国译者采取的翻译策略迥异，归化和异化策略泾渭分明；而进入 21 世纪后，在中国文学作品外译过程中，归化和异化亟待重新思考。

随着历史文化语境的变迁，21 世纪的东西方文化交流已经不复郭实腊、翟理斯时代西强中弱的面貌，尤其是 20 世纪末开始，世界范围内的多元文化趋势使文化输出国与文化输入国之间地位渐趋平等，对话与合作成为主流，在我国的译者和研究人员中也展开了归化和异化的重新思考。译者必须认识到，如果依旧大量进行归化势必会弱化原语文化的影响力，模糊自身的民族文化身份。在新的历史文化语境下，作为文化输出国的译者，应该有意识地增加异化翻译在典籍英译中的比重，还原中国文化的真实面目，从而通过翻译作品中的文化输出保持本民族的文化身份，扩大对外文化交流，加强国际传播能力和对外话语体系建设，推动中华文化走向世界。在翻译策略的选择和具体翻译方法的运用上，应该"在可能的情况下，应尽量争取异化；在难以异化的情况下，则应退而求其次，进行必要的归化。简而言之，可能时尽量异化，必要时尽管归化"，在涉及文化传播时，异化策略是首选，因为"归化主要表现在'纯语言层面'，在'文化层面'上则应力求最大限度的异化"（孙致礼，2002：42）。

此外，通过本研究获得的启示：研究文化误译和译者身份过程中，笔者发现，在中国文学作品外译过程中，合作模式有利于提升翻译质量，扩大受众群体，从而有助于文化交流和文学经典的对外传播。

杨宪益、戴乃迭二人的翻译生涯是著名的珠联璧合，中西合璧，具有得天独厚的语言和文化的整体优势。杨宪益有着深厚的中国文化和文学功底，戴乃迭虽然七岁之前生活在中国，但她的母语是英语，所以二人的翻译合作模式主要有以下特点：

明确分工协作：杨宪益负责把握文学作品的内涵，戴乃迭则侧重于语言文字的处理，将其转化为符合英语表达习惯的文字，发挥各自母语优势，使译文既忠实反映原著精神内涵，又流畅自然、易于理解。

口译笔译配合：通常由杨宪益先将中文原著口译成英文，戴乃迭再根据口译内容进行整理、润色和修改，形成准确、流畅的书面译文。

共同攻克难题：遇到文化背景、历史典故等复杂问题时，二人会共同查阅资料、深入探讨，确保翻译准确传达原文意义与文化内涵。在翻译《红楼梦》时，杨氏夫妇对众多文化元素的翻译进行反复斟酌，引经据典，最终才确定译文。

全程紧密合作：从作品选择、翻译过程到最终校对审核，两位译者全程紧密合作、相互支持。在翻译《鲁迅选集》时，杨氏夫妇共同确定篇目、完成翻译，并在译后进行细致校对和修订，保证译文质量。（AI提供资料）

而霍克斯出于对中国文学的热爱，在中国同事、红学家吴世昌的鼓励下，开始《红楼梦》的翻译工作。在翻译过程中得到了多位汉学家的帮助，具体如下：

修中诚：他是霍克斯在牛津大学汉学系的老师，曾在中国福建传教，并说服牛津设立汉学荣誉学位。其课程设置让霍克斯打下了坚实的中国古典文学基础，使其能够更好地理解《红楼梦》中的文化内涵和历史背景。

吴世昌：作为著名红学专家，吴世昌与霍克斯成为同事后，在研究和翻译《红楼梦》的过程中，与霍克斯共同开设中文课，向学生展现中国文学的魅力，这一过程也加深了霍克斯对《红楼梦》的理解。此外，他还在具体的文本解读、人物分析、诗词理解等方面为霍克斯提供了专业意见和建议，并指出文化误译部分，帮助霍克斯更准确地把握原著从而进行高质量的翻译。

燕卜荪：当时正在北大执教，帮助霍克斯顺利进入北大中文系成为一名研究生。霍克斯初到北平时语言不通，燕卜荪夫妇为其提供了住所，并介绍他跟一位老先生学习《红楼梦》，使他有机会深入了解这部作品，为之后的翻译工作奠定了基础。（AI 提供资料）

而梅氏兄弟在翻译《聊斋志异》时候，出版方外文出版社对中国古代经典作品的翻译提出的要求是"力求全面而准确地反映中国文学及中国文化的基本面貌和灿烂成就"，因此出版社设定的目标也决定了在翻译过程中译者如何采取有效手段去准确传递原语文化，促进东西方的文化交流。

因此，在文学作品译介、出版和发行这一系列的对外传播的过程中，建立中外译者合作＋出版方监督设定导向＋读者、专家预读的多方合作译介模式，符合当前"中国文化走出去"的国家战略和文学翻译的趋势，有助于向西方读者展现中国文化的魅力和中国文学的成就。

5.2 研究的局限性和研究展望

本研究对四部明清小说的英译本进行了深入的研究，分析有意文化误译现象，研究译者翻译风格及其成因和制约机制，译例丰富，信息量大，内容雅俗共赏。但是笔者也始终意识到由于自身科研能力、研究视野等主观因素，同时受到研究条件、时间、技术手段等客观条件的制约，本文难免有疏漏，尚有一定的局限性。

首先是研究目标选取的局限性：一方面，现有研究仅局限在《水浒传》《金瓶梅》《红楼梦》和《聊斋志异》四部作品的英译本上，原著固然具有极高的文学价值与代表性，但大量其他优秀明清小说未能纳入研究范围，因此资料覆盖面窄，难以呈现明清小说英译全貌，导致误译研究样本缺乏多样性，无法归纳出普适性更强的翻译规律。另一方面，研究资料多源于已出版的正式译本，对于民间自发翻译、网络翻译等新兴翻译形态下的误译关注甚少，而这些"非正统"翻译在当下文化交流中也有一定影响力，其误译现象同样值得探究。

其次为文化考量的不足：明清小说蕴含着深厚独特的中国传统文化内涵，物质文化、社会文化、语言文化、宗教文化和生态文化内容丰富庞杂，为翻译带来了众多实际困难和挑战。本研究对误译研究多侧重于词汇、语法层面的转换错误，对文化因素剖析不够深入，文化分析部分偏重介绍性和信息类呈现，文化维度考量欠缺使误译研究不够深入。

第三点是理论应用的片面性：在误译分析中，部分研究局限于单一翻译理论，译者误译产生的根源来自译者身份和历史文化语境以及由此产生的理解上的偏见，这种诠释哲学理论视角无法应对明清小说翻译的高度复杂性，需综合多理论视角。单一理论框架无法全面解读误译成因，限制了研究深度与解释力。

第四点是语料库研究方法和研究内容不足：可以通过最新的软件和语料库翻译学方面的研究成果和研究模式，更加深入地研究译者的风格和译者风格形成的制约机制。在对多个译本翻译特征的宏观对比研究中，可以增加词块特征分析、句对类型统计分析、主题词分析等更多研究项目。在多译本翻译风格的微观研究中，应更多地分析语料，对典型动词、高频文化负载词进行分析和深入研究，从而增强研究样本的可信度，以足量的语料数据阐明译者风格上的差异。

值得一提的是，笔者在创作本文的过程中，借助了 AI 的文本生成功能，使用 ChatGPT、豆包和 Kimi 等工具来收集资料和生成统计，例如对个别译者所处的文化历史语境、当前明清小说误译研究的局限性等问题提问，根据 AI 生成的文字指导本文写作，有效利用了新工具，进行了一定程度的尝试。

未来的翻译研究可以将语料库研究方法和 AI 结合，以提升翻译质量与效率。AI 能够快速处理大规模语料库数据，通过深度学习等技术，更精准地分析译文的语法、语义和语用信息，从而提高翻译的准确性和流畅性。除此之外，二者结合将进一步拓展翻译研究的领域和深度。一方面，能够对不同领域、不同文体的翻译进行更全面、更细致的分析，如法律、医学、科技等专业领域的语料库翻译研究，有助于深入了解各领域的术语、句式和语篇特点。另一方面，还可以从认知、社会文化等多维度探讨翻译现象，揭示翻译过程中的认知机制和社会文化因素的影响。

语料库翻译研究与 AI 的结合涉及语言学、计算机科学、认知科学、数学等多个学科领域，这种跨学科的研究模式将促进不同学科之间的交流与合作，为翻译研究带来新的理论和方法，推动翻译学科的发展与创新。

相信在今后的翻译研究中，AI 会逐渐凸显其大模型的优势，融合多学科研究成果，从而提升翻译质量，大幅度提高研究效率。

参 考 文 献

Bassnett, S. *Translation Studies* [M]. Shanghai: Shanghai Foreign Language Education Press, 2004.

Bloom, H. *A Map of Misreading* [M]. London: Oxford University Press. 1975.

Buck, Pearl S., trans. *All Men Are Brothers (Shui Hu Chuan)*. New York: The Heritage Press, 1948.

Cao Xueqin. *A Dream of Red Mansions* [M]. trans by Yang Xianyi and Gladys Yang. Beijing : Foreign Language Press, 1978.

Cao Xueqin. *The Story of the Stone* [M]. trans by David Hawkes and John Minford. Penguin Books Ltd, 1979.

Gadamer, Hans. G *Truth and Method* [M]. New York: Crossroad, 1989.

Giles, Herbert A. (trans.) *Strange Stories from a Chinese Studio* [M]. Hong Kong: Kelly &.Walsh, ltd., 1968.

Giles, Herbert A. *A History of Chinese Literature*. New York: D. Appleton-Century Company, 1937.

Lefevere, A. *Translation, Rewriting and the Manipulation of*

Literary Fame[M]. London: Routledge, 1992.

Mair, Denis C & Victor H. *Strange Tales from Make-do Studio* [M]. Beijing: Foreign Languages Press, 2000.

Munday, J. *Introducing Translation Studies Theories and Applications* [M]. London and New York: Routeledge, 2001.

Nida. Eugene A. *Language in Culture and Society* [M]. Dell Hymes. Allied Publilshers pvt, . Ltd. 1964.

Nord, C. *Translating as a Purposeful Activity: Functional Approaches Explained* [M]. Shanghai: Shanghai Foreign Language Education Press, 2001.

Steiner, G. *After Babel: Aspects of Language and Translation* [M]. Shanghai: Shanghai Foreign language Education Press, 2001.

Taylor, C. *Sources of the Self . The Making of the Modern Identity*[M]. Cambridge: Harvard University Press. 1989.

Taylor, E. B. *Primitive Culture* [M]. Brighton (US): Lighting Source Inc. 2006.

Venuti, L. *The Translator's Invisibility* [M]. London: Routledge, 1995.

Venuti, L. *The Translation Studies Reader(ed.)* [M]. London/ New York: Routledge, 2000.

Wimmer, G., Kohler, R., Grotjahn, R. and Altmann, G. *Toward a Theory of Word Length Distributions* [J], Journal of QuantitativeLinguistics, 1994, (1).

包惠南,包昂. 中国文化与汉英翻译[M]. 北京:外语出版社,2004.

曹雪芹. 红楼梦[M]. 北京：人民文学出版社，1983.

陈宏薇，江帆. 难忘的历程——《红楼梦》英译事业的描写性研究[J]. 中国翻译，2003，(05).

陈竞春，马佳瑛，中华传统文化的传播及英译研究[M]. 陕西人民出版社，2023.

陈可培. 误读 误译 再创造——读霍克斯译《红楼梦》札记[J]. 湛江师范学院学报，2011，(4).

邓婕. 文学翻译中的"有意误译"[J]. 宁波教育学院学报，2006，(12).

董琇. 译者风格形成的立体多元辩证观——赛珍珠翻译风格探源[D]. 上海：上海外国语大学，2009.

樊登·樊登读书团队著，樊登漫画《论语》成才篇，江苏凤凰文艺出版社[D]. 2023.

方梦之主编. 译学辞典. 上海：上海外语教育出版社，2004.

范祥涛，刘全福. 论翻译选择的目的性[J]. 中国翻译，2002，(6).

冯庆华，王昱. 从文化交流的宏观角度研究翻译——《飘》的译本研究[J]. 外国语，1998，(3).

冯庆华. 文体翻译论[M]. 上海：上海外语教育出版社，2002.

冯庆华. 母语文化下的译者风格[M]. 上海：上海外语教育出版社，2008.

冯庆华. 思维模式下的译文词汇[M]. 上海：上海外语教育出版社，2012.

冯庆华. 思维模式下的译文句式初探——以《红楼梦》的霍译与杨译为例[J]. 外语电化教学，2014，(6).

冯全功. 霍译《红楼梦》艺术胜境探微：《译者的风月宝鉴》[J]. 燕山

大学学报(哲学社会科学版),2023,(3).

付岩志.20世纪以来《聊斋志异》海外研究综述[J].山东大学学报
　(哲学社会科学版),2012,(2).

葛锐(美),李晶(译).道阻且长:《红楼梦》英译史的几点思考[J].
　红楼梦学刊,2012,(2).

龚贤.中国文化导论[M].北京:九州出版社,2018.

郭安.对现代西方哲学释义学的几点思考[J].苏州大学学报,
　1999,(3).

郭建中.文化与翻译[M].北京:中国对外翻译出版公司,2000.

哈罗德·布鲁姆.误读之图[M].朱立元、陈克明译.天津人民出版
　社,2005.

何敏.英语世界《聊斋志异》译介述评[J].外语教学与研究,2009,
　(9).

洪畅.杨柳青木版年画的戏曲文物价值与戏曲传播价值研究[M].
　天津人民出版社,2021.

洪汉鼎.理解的真理——解读伽达默尔《真理与方法》[M].济南:
　山东人民出版社,2001.

洪志凡主编.平江记忆[M].湖南人民出版社,2019.

胡庚申.翻译适应选择论的哲学理据[J].上海科技翻译,2004,(4).

胡开宝.语料库翻译学概论[M].上海:上海交大出版社,2011.

胡令毅.高山仰止:《金瓶梅词话》危言[J].洛阳师范学院学报,
　2014(9).

胡文仲.跨文化交际学概论[M].北京:外语教学与研究出版
　社.1999.

胡玥.大学英语能力突破系列数字教材汉英翻译精讲第2版[M].

上海外语教育出版社,2023.

黄东琳.论提高古诗词英译的可译度[J].西安外国语学院学报,
　2001,(3).

黄立波.翻译学核心话题系列丛书 语料库翻译学理论研究[M].外
　语教学与研究出版社,2021.

伽达默尔.真理与方法[M].洪汉鼎译.上海:上海译文出版
　社,2004.

江滨,王立松,刘蕾主编.语言运用与文化传播[M].天津大学出版
　社,2014.

姜智芹.当东方与西方相遇:比较文学专题研究[M].齐鲁书
　社,2008.

金辉.中国古代官职名称翻译策略探析——以《世说新语》英译为
　例[J].中国科技翻译,2023,(5).

兰陵笑笑生.金瓶梅词话.北京:人民文学出版社,1992.

李海军.追随蒲松龄的足迹——《聊斋志异》英译概述[J].外国语
　文,2009,(5).

李海军,劲松.翟理斯与《聊斋志异》在英语世界的经典化[J].广西
　师范大学学报:哲学社会科学版,2010,(6).

李海军.传教目的下的跨文化操纵——论《聊斋志异》在英语世界
　的最早译介[J].上海翻译,2011,(2).

李海军.从跨文化操纵到文化和合《聊斋志异》英译研究[M],上海
　交通大学出版社,2014.

李晓静.生态翻译学视角下《红楼梦》回目中的文化负载词英译研
　究[J],华东理工大学学报,2022,(4).

梁佳英.多元系统论视角下赛珍珠《水浒传》英译本的研究[D].河

北农业大学,2011.

梁扬,谢仁敏.《红楼梦》语言艺术研究[M].人民文学出版社,2006.

廖七一.当代西方翻译理论探索[M].南京:译林出版社,2004.

林木阳,陈移瑜.大学人文素养[M].厦门大学出版社,2018.

刘桂兰.论重译的世俗化[M],武汉大学出版社,2015.

刘克强.《水浒传》四英译本翻译特征多维度对比研究[D].上海外国语大学,2013.

刘绍棠.刘绍棠文集[M].北京:十月文艺出版社,2003.

卢红梅编著.华夏文化与汉英翻译(第二部)[M].武汉:武汉大学出版社,2008.

卢静.语料库辅助译者风格研究,上海交通大学出版社,2021.

鲁迅.中国小说史略[M].北京:中国和平出版社,2014.

马海燕.陈义华总主编,天涯论丛——黎族经典民间文学英译研究[M].中山大学出版社,2022.

马红军.为赛珍珠的“误译”正名[J].四川外语学院学报,2003,(3).

孟天伦.霍克斯译《红楼梦》的误译现象及成因[J].长春师范大学学报,2024,(5).

苗怀明.乡关何处觅英魂——清代民间艺人石玉昆生平著述考论[J].南京大学学报,2003,(6).

闵家胤.系统科学和系统哲学[M].中国民主法制出版社,2023.

宁宗一.中国古典小说名作十五讲[M].北京:北京出版社,2023.

潘群辉,贾德江.《水浒传》两译本的粗俗语英译评析——以“屁”的翻译为例[J].南华大学学报(社会科学版),2009,(6).

蒲松龄.聊斋志异[M].上海:上海古籍出版社,2008.

齐林涛.赞助人的隐身:《金瓶梅》首部英文全译本的副文本研究

[J].翻泽界,2018,(2).

莎士比亚著.朱生豪译.麦克白(英汉对照)[M].北京:中国对外经济贸易出版社,2000.

石麟.明代四大奇书的历史地位[J].广西师范大学学报,2006,(4).

施耐庵.水浒传[M].北京:人民日报出版社,2007.

孙雪瑛,周睿.诠释学视角下的误译[J].黑龙江教育学院学报,2010,(10).

孙雪瑛.诠释学视阈下的《聊斋志异》翻译研究[M].上海:上海三联书店,2016.

孙致礼编.新编英汉翻译教程[M].上海:上海外语教育出版社,2011.

孙致礼.中国的文学翻译:从归化趋向异化[J].中国翻译,2002,(1).

田建鑫.文化过滤视角下《碧奴》英译本中的有意误译探析[J].文化传播,2023,(34).

唐艳芳.赛珍珠《水浒传》翻译研究——后殖民理论的视角[D].华东师范大学,2009.

王德春.汉语国俗词典[M].南京:河海大学出版社,1990.

王恒展.浅论《聊斋志异》与话本小说的关系[J].蒲松龄研究,1997,(2).

王惠萍.后殖民视域下的戴乃迭文化身份与译介活动研究[D].上海外国语大学,2014.

王珺.跨文化视域下的英汉翻译策略探究[M].吉林大学出版社,2020.

王克非.语料库翻译学探索[M].上海:上海交通大学出版社,2012.

王丽娜.《金瓶梅》在国外[J].《河北大学学报》,1980,(2).

王丽耘. 文学交流中的大卫·霍克斯[M]. 燕山大学出版社,2013.

王鹏飞. 英语世界的红楼梦译介与研究[M]. 陕西师范大学出版总社,2014.

王松亭. 俄语语言与文化研究新视野.[M]. 黑龙江人民出版社,2011.

王燕. 试论《聊斋志异》在西方的最早译介[J]. 明清小说研究,2008,(2).

王燕. 文化转向视角下的英汉翻译问题再审视[M]. 吉林大学出版社,2020.

文军,冯丹丹. 国内聊斋志异英译研究:评述与建议[J]. 蒲松龄研究,2011,(3).

温秀颖,李兰. 论芮效卫《金瓶梅》英译本的体制与策略[J]. 中国外语,2010,(1).

吴冰,跨文化的翻译研究[M],中国科学技术大学出版社,2021.

无名氏. 科举制度、酷刑、人物介绍、古诗词等百科知识[OL]. 见于2024年10月11日⟨http://baike. baidu. com⟩.

无名氏. 翻译家百科知识[OL]. 见于2024年9月12日⟨http://zh. wikipedia. org/wiki⟩.

吴永昇,郑锦怀.《水浒传》百年英译的描述研究及其修辞启示[J]. 宁夏大学学报,2017,(7).

习斌. 中国绣像小说经眼录[M]. 上海:远东出版社,2016.

许翠敏,刘泽权.《红楼梦》中的文化负载词及其在三个英译本中的翻译[J]. 外语艺术教育研究,2008,(3).

杨宪益,戴乃迭译. 聊斋故事选[M]. 北京:中国文学杂志社,1981.

杨宪益. 杨宪益自传[M]. 北京：人民日报出版社，2010.

叶丽娅. 中国历代鞋饰[M]. 北京：中国美术学院出版社，2011.

余建忠. 大学国文精读[M]. 昆明：云南大学出版社，2007.

余苏凌. 翟理斯英译《聊斋志异》的道德和诗学取向[J]. 天津大学学报，2011，(9).

袁荻涌. 林纾的文学翻译思想[J]. 中国翻译，1994，(3).

张叉. 外国语文论丛[J]. 四川文艺出版社，2022.

张德让. 伽达默尔哲学解释学与翻译研究[J]. 中国翻译，2001，(4).

张慧琴，武俊敏. 服饰礼仪文化翻译"评头"之后的"论足"[J]. 上海翻译，2016，(6).

张静. 译者的文化身份及其翻译行为——赛珍珠个案研究[J]. 当代外语研究，2011，(2).

张文珍. 中国古代通俗小说发展研究[M]. 济南：山东教育出版社. 2016.

张义宏. 从译者主体性看《金瓶梅》书名的英译[J]. 跨语言文化研究，2016，(2).

张义宏. 《金瓶梅》英译比较研究[D]. 北京外国语大学，2017.

张裕禾，钱林森. 关于文化身份的对话[C]. 上海：上海文化出版社，2002.

张玉蕾主编. 快乐心灵的语文故事[M]. 江苏凤凰美术出版社，2018.

张玉梅. 语言学视角下《金瓶梅》的海外传播[J]. 社会科学家，2015. (11).

赵朝永. 基于语料库的《金瓶梅》英文全译本语域变异多维分析[J]. 外语教学与研究，2020，(2).

赵朝永.基于语料库的《红楼梦》译者风格描写[M].上海:华东师
范大学出版社,2020.

赵祥云.赛珍珠英译《水浒传》的译者惯习与翻译策略探究[J].郑
州轻工业大学学报(社会科学版),2021,(6).

郑振铎.插图本中国文学史[M].上海:上海世纪出版集团,2005.

钟再强.论赛珍珠英译《水浒传》的译者主体选择[J].山东外语教
学,2018(6).

周蓉.近十年《水浒传》英译研究综述[J].名作欣赏,2023,(24).

周晓寒.从文化误译看译者的再创造——解读霍克斯译《红楼梦》
[J].湘潭师范学院学报(社会科学版),2009,(5).

朱彤.朱彤红学论集[M].安徽师范大学出版社,2022.

朱振武,洪晓丹.《金瓶梅》芮效卫译本的"入俗"与"脱俗"[J].复旦
外国语言文学论丛,2017,(2).

朱振武.归异平衡 英语世界汉学家的中国故事书写[M].上海交通
大学出版社,2023.

文献综述部分参考资料

1.《红楼梦》英译研究文献

［1］蔡魏立.文化过滤视角下的有意误译研究[D].江西财经大学,2016.

［2］陈功,陈颖.《红楼梦》翻译研究的热点、问题及思考[J].北京科技大学学报(社会科学版),2019,35(04):104—111.

［3］陈银春,刘泽权.汉语主动句英译的语篇功能探索——以《红楼梦》第一回及其英译的被动句为例[J].大学英语(学术版),2007,(02):94—101.

［4］郭挺.基于语境理论的《红楼梦》四个英译本中称谓语误译的比较研究[D].西南交通大学,2014.

［5］黄敏,王慧娟.基于关联理论的《红楼梦》判词英译对比评析[J].中国矿业大学学报(社会科学版),2016,(03):140—144.

［6］蒋亦文,张政.英译《红楼梦》副文本推介模式与接受度研究——基于英语世界的读者访谈[J].外语与翻译,2020,27(02):25—31.

［7］李美.从《红楼梦》的误译看译者母语在文化传递中的角色[J].南京理工大学学报(社会科学版),2012,25(04):81—86.

［8］李晓静,杨铠瑷.生态翻译学视角下《红楼梦》回目中的文化

负载词英译研究[J].华北理工大学学报(社会科学版),
2022,22(04):125—130.

[9] 刘佳,周琦玥.近十年《红楼梦》英译研究述评[J].红楼梦学
刊,2021,(03):282—299.

[10] 刘晓天,孙瑜.《红楼梦》霍克斯译本中习语英译的跨文化阐
释[J].红楼梦学刊,2018,(05):236—253.

[11] 刘晓天,孙瑜.《红楼梦》霍克斯译本中的比喻添加研究[J].
红楼梦学刊,2019,(06):260—273.

[12] 卢晓敏,常青,郭陶等.霍克斯《红楼梦》误译原因剖析[J].语
文学刊(外语教育教学),2016,(09):86—87.

[13] 宋鹏.从误译现象考证邦斯尔神父英译《红楼梦》之底本[J].
文化学刊,2017,(01):182—185.

[14] 王坤.从文化角度看《红楼梦》中称谓语的误译[J].戏剧之
家,2016,(06):239—240.

[15] 王燕.马礼逊英译《红楼梦》手稿研究[J].文学遗产,2021,
(03):148—160.

[16] 肖家燕.优先概念化与隐喻的翻译研究——《红楼梦》"上—
下"空间隐喻的英译策略及差额翻译[J].四川外语学院学
报,2016,(04):105—109.

[17] 许丹.认知视域下《红楼梦》中的植物隐喻英译研究——以霍
克斯译本为例[J].现代语文,2018,(04):117—122.

[18] 张冰.《红楼梦》中"小人物"粗鄙语英译对比研究[J].外国语
言文学,2020,37(02):199—211.

[19] 赵朝永.《红楼梦》邦斯尔译本误译考辨[J].红楼梦学刊,
2015,(03):274—302.

[20] 周晓寒. 从文化误译看译者的再创造——解读霍克斯译《红楼梦》[J]. 湘潭师范学院学报(社会科学版),2009,31(05):130—131.

2.《聊斋志异》英译研究文献

[1] 陈吉荣,都媛. 顺应理论视域下的对话翻译语用失误——以《聊斋志异》对话英译为例[J]. 天津外国语大学学报,2014,21(05):29—34.

[2] 程怡雯.《聊斋志异》英译本注释研究[D]. 上海师范大学,2023.

[3] 迟庆立. 文化翻译策略的多样性与多译本互补研究[D]. 上海外国语大学,2008.

[4] 付岩志.《聊斋志异》海外诠释及其文化融合功能[J]. 明清小说研究,2013(02):101—111.

[5] 李海军. 论早期《聊斋志异》英译中的伪翻译现象——以乔治·苏利埃·德·莫朗的译本为例[J]. 上海翻译,2014(01):49—52.

[6] 卢慧慧. 从阐释学的角度分析《聊斋志异》中文化负载词的翻译[D]. 中南大学,2010.

[7] 卢静. 基于语料库的译者风格综合研究模式探索——以《聊斋志异》译本为例[J]. 外语电化教学,2013(02):53—58.

[8] 牟晋蕾. 形象学视角下《聊斋志异》英译狐妖形象研究[D]. 北京外国语大学,2023.

[9] 潘向雪. 符号学视角下《聊斋志异》官职相关词语英译[D]. 北京外国语大学,2014.

[10] 彭劲松,李海军.早期西方汉学家英译《聊斋志异》时的误读[J].社会科学家,2010(08):156—158.

[11] 任增强."媒、讹、化"与翟理斯《聊斋志异》英译[J].山东社会科学,2012(06):172—176.

[12] 舒瀚萱.《聊斋志异》两个英译本中的典故翻译对比研究[D].广东外语外贸大学,2017.

[13] 王春强.《聊斋志异》闵福德英译本研究[D].北京外国语大学,2014.

[14] 王树槐.翟理斯译《聊斋志异》的古代中国形象建构及其在西方世界的影响[J].外国语文,2023,39(04):23—31.

[15] 王文君.认知识解视角下《聊斋志异》闵福德译本中的显化现象研究[D].暨南大学,2022.

[16] 余欢.从动态顺应角度研究文学翻译[D].西南交通大学,2009.

[17] 张强.中国志怪小说的叙事重构:以卫三畏英译《聊斋志异》为例[J].中国比较文学,2018(03):52—65.

[18] 钟迪.布迪厄理论视角下闵福德《聊斋志异》英译行为解读[D].上海外国语大学,2019.

[19] 周志莹.翻译伦理视域下的《聊斋志异》重译研究[D].吉林大学,2018.

[20] 朱瑞君.从斯坦纳翻译四步骤理论看译者主体性——以翟理斯《聊斋志异》译本为例[J].合肥工业大学学报(社会科学版),2009,23(06):92—96.

3.《金瓶梅》英译研究文献

［1］房宇华.回顾与展望:1980—2018 年间中国《金瓶梅》翻译研究述评［A］厦门大学外文学院第十二届研究生学术研讨会、第二届外国语言文学博士论坛论文集［C］.厦门大学外文学院,厦门大学外文学院,2019:18.

［2］冯全功,赵瑞.《金瓶梅》中的隐喻型性话语及其翻译研究——以芮效卫的英译本为例［J］.燕山大学学报(哲学社会科学版),2020,21(05):17—23.

［3］胡桑.《金瓶梅》感官叙事英译研究［D］.上海外国语大学,2021.

［4］黄粉保.《金瓶梅》英译本误译解析［J］.韩山师范学院学报,2009,30(01):74—78.

［5］金学勤.芮效卫英译《金瓶梅》的文化战略启示［J］.外国语文,2017,33(06):103—107.

［6］李燕,李思龙.《金瓶梅》服饰文化英译策略研究［J］.汉字文化,2022,(21):193—195.

［7］李志华,姬生雷,傅之敏.文学翻译与文化缺失——以《金瓶梅》英译本中“哭”的翻译为例［J］.石家庄学院学报,2010,12(04):106—108.

［8］聂影影.《金瓶梅》的服饰文化与翻译——以埃杰顿和芮效卫两个英译本为例［J］.河北工业大学学报(社会科学版),2012,4(04):82—87.

［9］潘佳宁.芮效卫的《金瓶梅》研究及其“深度翻译”模式阐释［J］.沈阳师范大学学报(社会科学版),2021,45(04):115—121.

[10] 齐林涛.原作之死:《金瓶梅》英译的去经典化研究[J].燕山大学学报(哲学社会科学版),2020,21(03):39—48.

[11] 施红梅.功能对等理论视角下《金瓶梅》双关语英译策略研究——以厄杰顿和芮效卫的两个英译本为例[J].唐山师范学院学报,2021,43(04):34—38.

[12] 孙会军.《金瓶梅》英语译本研究的新成果——评齐林涛新著《〈金瓶梅〉的英语译本:文本、副文本和语境》[J].燕山大学学报(哲学社会科学版),2019,20(04):39—43.

[13] 汤孟孟.操控理论视角下《金瓶梅》中大运河文化的英译研究[D].江苏科技大学,2019.

[14] 唐军,鲍欣蕊.女性主义视域下《金瓶梅》卜龟章节的英译[J].滁州学院学报,2018,20(06):56—61.

[15] 王振平,陈家骅.从译者主体性看《金瓶梅》两英译本中动物隐喻的翻译[J].华北理工大学学报(社会科学版),2022,22(06):121—127.

[16] 王振平,陈家骅.从译者的创造性叛逆看《金瓶梅》中"天"的翻译[J].绍兴文理学院学报,2022,42(05):106—113.

[17] 温秀颖,李兰.论芮效卫《金瓶梅》英译本的体制与策略[J].中国外语,2010,7(01):101—105.

[18] 温秀颖,聂影影.叙事学视角下人物话语表达方式翻译研究——以《金瓶梅》两个英译本为例[J].天津外国语大学学报,2015,22(05):23—27.

[19] 温秀颖,孙建成.《金瓶梅》英译中的中西文化互动与关联[J].中国翻译,2014,35(06):78—81.

[20] 温秀颖,王颖.呈现"他者":文学翻译者的核心责任——以埃

杰顿英译《金瓶梅》为例[J].山东外语教学,2013,34(06):91—95.

[21] 温秀颖,张雁.概念隐喻框架下《金瓶梅》两个英译本比较研究[J].河北旅游职业学院学报,2012,17(01):76—79.

[22] 张慧芳.社会翻译学视角下《金瓶梅》宗教文化英译对比分析[D].华东师范大学,2023.

[23] 张慧琴,武俊敏.服饰礼仪文化翻译"评头"之后的"论足"——基于《金瓶梅》两个全译本中的"足衣"文化[J].上海翻译,2016,(06):53—59.

[24] 张义宏.《金瓶梅》两个英译本茶饮名称英译策略探究[J].牡丹江师范学院学报(哲学社会科学版),2018,(05):93—98.

[25] 张玉梅.语言学视角下《金瓶梅》的海外传播——兼谈中国文科的"复兴"[J].社会科学家,2015,(11):141—146.

4.《水浒传》英译研究文献

[1] 陈新月.文学作品的可译限度——论《水浒传》的再创造性翻译[D].广东外语外贸大学,2004.

[2] 成矫林.习语,文化空缺与翻译[D].湖南大学,2002.

[3] 黄靖雯.古典诗学视域中《水浒传》好汉形象及情节异质语境的翻译改写[D].四川外国语大学,2019.

[4] 李雅静.跨文化视角下的《水浒传》俗语翻译及其在对外汉语教学中的运用[D].广西大学,2020.

[5] 刘婷.概念隐喻理论框架下的动物隐喻翻译[D].兰州大学,2011.

[6] 刘幼玲.《水浒传》中男性服饰的英译研究[D].安徽大

学,2016.

［7］卢艳春.语用学与翻译——《水浒传》中粗俗俚语的翻译之管见[J].内蒙古农业大学学报（社会科学版）,2005,（03）：132—135.

［8］路东平.试谈《水浒传》中称谓的使用及其翻译[J].社科纵横,2003,（01）:79—81

［9］马菁悦.析《水浒传》赛珍珠译本中的创造性叛逆[D].西南交通大学,2013.

［10］潘莹,禹一奇.从目的论角度看《水浒传》中女性人物形象的翻译[J].安徽文学（下半月）,2015,（08）:6—7.

［11］宋颖.论《水浒》沙译本的文化意象缺失问题[J].芒种,2014,（14）:175—176.

［12］温秀颖.翻译目的与登译《水浒传》语言文化知识误译[J].中国翻译,2012,33(05):67—72.

［13］徐剑平,梁金花.从接受理论视角看赛珍珠的《水浒传》翻译[J].时代文学（双月上半月）,2009,（05）:170—172.

［14］徐松健.文化概念化视角下中国酒形象在翻译中的传播[D].上海外国语大学,2018.

［15］闫玉涛.翻译中的归化和异化:沙译《水浒传》分析[J].山东外语教学,2010,31(02):95—98.

［16］杨阳.女性主义翻译理论视角下的译者主体性[D].中南大学,2007.

［17］袁滔.《水浒传》英译本文体学研究[D].四川大学,2006.

［18］赵觅.认知隐喻视角下《水浒传》英译本翻译策略对比研究——以成语英译为例[J].海外英语,2021,（24）:68—

69＋79.

[19] 周莉芬.文学作品翻译中文化信息的处理[D].上海外国语大学,2008.

[20] 周梁勋,耿智.翻译伦理与经典英译——以《水浒传》英译为例[J].上海翻译,2017,(04):27—30.

图书在版编目（CIP）数据

明清小说误译与译者研究/孙雪瑛著．—上海：
上海三联书店，2025.6.—ISBN 978-7-5426-8941-2

Ⅰ.I046；I207.41

中国国家版本馆 CIP 数据核字第 2025Y9E559 号

明清小说误译与译者研究

著　　者／孙雪瑛

责任编辑／宋寅悦　徐心童
装帧设计／徐　徐
监　　制／姚　军
责任校对／王凌霄

出版发行／上海三联书店

　　　　　（200041）中国上海市静安区威海路 755 号 30 楼
邮　　箱／sdxsanlian@sina.com
联系电话／编辑部：021-22895517
　　　　　发行部：021-22895559
印　　刷／上海盛通时代印刷有限公司

版　　次／2025 年 6 月第 1 版
印　　次／2025 年 6 月第 1 次印刷
开　　本／890 mm×1240 mm　1/32
字　　数／220 千字
印　　张／9.625
书　　号／ISBN 978-7-5426-8941-2/I·1940
定　　价／78.00 元

敬启读者，如发现本书有印装质量问题，请与印刷厂联系 021-37910000